21 XII/07 ~ 12/08

MAY 2 0 2004

Nowhere in Africa

Nowhere in Africa

An Autobiographical Novel

Stefanie Zweig

With a new preface

Translated by MARLIES COMJEAN

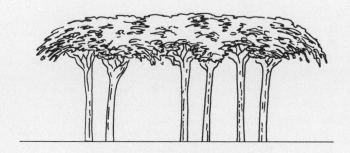

THE UNIVERSITY OF WISCONSIN PRESS
TERRACE BOOKS

The publication of this work was supported by a grant from the Goethe-Institut

The University of Wisconsin Press
1930 Monroe Street
Madison, Wisconsin 53711

www.wisc.edu/wisconsinpress/

Originally published as *Nirgendwo in Afrika*

1   3   5   4   2

Printed in the United States of America

Library of Congress Cataloging-in-Publication Data
Zweig, Stefanie.
[Nirgendwo in Afrika. English]
Nowhere in Africa : an autobiographical novel / Stefanie Zweig;
translated by Marlies Comjean ; with a preface.
      p.   cm.
ISBN 0-299-19960-6 (alk. paper)
   1. Zweig, Stefanie—Fiction.   I. Comjean, Marlies.   II. Title.
PT2688.W45N57   2004
833´.914—dc22   2003021169

Terrace Books, a division of the University of Wisconsin Press, takes its name from
the Memorial Union Terrace, located at the University of Wisconsin–Madison.
Since its inception in 1907, the Wisconsin Union has provided a venue for students,
faculty, staff, and alumni to debate art, music, politics, and the issues of the day.
It is a place where theater, music, drama, dance, outdoor activities, and
major speakers are made available to the campus and the community.
To learn more about the Union, visit www.union.wisc.edu.

In memory of
my father

Preface

In my childhood my father and I, who loved each other so dearly that I thought love was happiness for a lifetime, had one mutual grief. We had neither a common mother tongue nor a common fatherland. Hitler had seen to that. He first drove the Jews out of Germany, burned down their synagogues and then murdered them in concentration camps. We escaped in time. In 1938 we landed in Kenya, my parents bewildered, helpless, and having not learned to live without roots, with the constant insecurity of the homeless. I, nearing my sixth birthday, fell in love at first sight with Owuor, our "houseboy," after a week with Africa's splendor. Forever. For the three of us the first big safari of our lives ended on a farm in a place called Rongai. There my father was to look after the cattle and poultry. He received his wages in milk, butter, and eggs, and tried to pull out his own tooth because he could not afford a dentist. From then on he claimed that he had had two lives. In his first he had been a renowned attorney in a small German town, a man of property, pride, self-esteem, and with a promising future. In his second life as a so-called farm manager he only looked backward, and even after years in the country he barely earned enough money to send his daughter to school. He dreaded losing his first job and then his courage to carry on with life. To my utter amazement this loveable, gentle, admired father could not see the beauty in a cow's eye, had no ear for the cock's call at sunrise and had never heard of my favorite poet Wordsworth. He had learned only Latin and Greek at school—and in Rongai, Swahili. When we had no paraffin for the lamps he lit the African darkness with Caesar's wars and Plato's wisdom. Even as a sergeant of the British Army his German tongue rolled the English R's like mountain thunder.

He always remained a "Papa," which was most embarrassing for a daughter who secretly dreamed of a "Daddy." Thanks to her father's hard-earned money she had been turned into an English snob at an English boarding school.

Each morning Papa gazed at Mount Kenya and yearned for the delights of a German winter. When he said "zuhause," he meant Sohrau, a tiny town in Upper Silesia. There he had been born and had been led to believe that it was a man's duty to love Germany and that Germany loved the Jews. His daughter pronounced the word "zuhause" with an English Oxford accent. Home for her was Ol' Joro Orok in Kenya's White Highlands. There the flax bloomed the most beautiful blue I have ever seen, the evening sun dropped out of the sky like a ball of fire, and the people spoke neither German nor English. They spoke Swahili with the gentle sounds and whispering syllables of folks who think living and laughing are synonyms. Up to this very day Ol' Joro Orok, on the equator, never forgotten and ever loved, is the home of my heart. There my novel *Nowhere in Africa* is mainly located.

When I started writing the story of my life I had only one ambition—to honor the father who had lost everything that makes a man a man, his hope, dignity and future, his fatherland and his family. But he never gave up his faith, neither in God nor in humanity. Both my parents had seen friends turning to foes, their dreams shattered, their lives falling to shambles, and they knew, long before the end of World War II, that their families had been killed in Germany's concentration camps. Yet, my father taught me, when I could barely read and write, not to give in to hatred, not to generalize people, history, and emotion, to despise prejudices, and despite all that had happened, to believe, as he did, in God.

It was in memory of this remarkable father that I wrote my life-story. When I started remembering and writing I never fathomed that *Nowhere in Africa* would be the bestseller that it immediately was. Did I reap what I had sowed? Not without the sigh of those who have not done their task in time. It saddened me to think that my parents, who both died young, could not read it. And it distressed me even more that people were all too eager to feed their minds with the alleged romanticism of colonial Africa. To most German readers Owuor, the man with the mighty hands and witty tongue, was of far greater interest than the refugees who had to leave their home country to escape death. Wherever and whenever I read my book in public I was asked whether I was still in touch with Owuor. The questioners with the childish longing for fairy tales were sorely disappointed when I explained that by now Owuor would most probably be over one hundred, and that it was rather difficult to keep in touch with a man who could neither read nor write. Whoever had seen the film had an even greater urge to talk about Owuor. The day that the news came out that *Nowhere in Africa* had won the Oscar for the best foreign film, one fax reached me saying "well done, Owuor!" and another one asking "does Owuor know?"

A short time later *Nowhere in Africa* opened in the United States and in Great Britain. Heaps of letters lay in my mailbox; there were calls from the United States, England, South America, South Africa, and Israel. Owuor was not mentioned once by the people who contacted me. A large number of them had been refugees themselves, many had lived in Kenya. Some had known my family, others wanted to know if I knew them. And they all wanted to read the book. Immediately and word for word.

Since my novel *Nowhere in Africa* appeared on the German market I, to whom English had once been mother tongue and is still the language dearest to my heart, had been hoping fervently for a translation into English. The book has been translated into French, Spanish, Hungarian, Dutch, Czech, and Japanese. Each translation nourishes my pride. The English version—the only one I can read—is pure happiness.

My gratitude to The University of Wisconsin Press for having the courage to give a German author a chance is immense. My thanks also go to Marlies Comjean who has translated my work with an admirable respect for the original. Finally, I must thank my copyeditor, Jeri Famighetti, whose guiding and interpreting hand I felt on every page I read.

STEFANIE ZWEIG
September 2003

Nowhere in Africa

1

Rongai, February 4, 1938

My dear Jettel,
First of all, get out your handkerchief and sit down quietly. You will
need strong nerves now. God willing, we will see each other again very
soon. At any rate, much earlier than we ever dared expect. Since my last
letter from Mombasa, which I wrote the day I arrived, so much has
happened that my head is still spinning. I was in Nairobi less than a
week and was already feeling quite dejected, because everybody there
told me that it would be no use at all looking for work in the city without knowing any English. Also, I did not see any possibility of finding
work on a farm, which almost everyone here does at first just to get a
roof over their heads. And then, a week ago, I was invited with Walter
Süßkind (he is from Pomerania) to visit a rich Jewish family here.

I did not give it much thought at first, just assumed they would not
be much different from my mother, who, in Sohrau, always had some
poor souls at her table. In the meantime, however, I have found out
what a miracle is. The Rubens family has been living in Kenya for a
good fifty years. Rubens Senior is president of the Jewish community in
Nairobi, and they, for their part, take care of the "refugees" (that is what
we are) when they first arrive in the country.

At the Rubenses' (five adult sons), everyone was beside themselves
when they found out that you and Regina are still in Germany. They
look at things very differently here from the way I did at home. You and
Father were quite right when you did not want me to emigrate alone, and
I am ashamed that I did not listen to you. As I found out later, Rubens

3

called me all kinds of terrible names, but I was unable to understand him. You cannot imagine how long it took me to comprehend that the community was willing to advance a hundred pounds to the Immigration Office for you and Regina. I was instantly dispatched to a farm so that the three of us will initially have a place to stay and I can at least earn something.

This means that you will have to leave as quickly as possible. This sentence is the most important one in the whole letter. Even though I acted like a sheep, you will have to trust me now. Every additional day you stay in Breslau with the child is lost. So go see Karl Silbermann immediately. He has more experience than anyone else with emigration issues and will introduce you to the man who treated me so decently at the German Travel Agency. He will tell you how to get tickets for a steamer as soon as possible, and it does not matter what kind of ship it is and how long the journey takes. If possible, take a cabin with three beds. I know that might not be pleasant, but it is a lot cheaper than traveling second class, and we will need every penny once you get here. The main thing, though, is that you will finally be on board and at sea. Then, at last, we all will be able to sleep again.

Also, do contact the Danzig Company immediately about our containers. You know, we left one empty for things that we might remember later. An icebox is very important for the tropics. We also definitely need a Petromax lamp. Make sure to get some extra mantles. Otherwise, we might have a lamp, but we will still be in the dark. There is no electric light at the farm where I am. Also, buy two mosquito nets. Three, if there is enough money. Rongai is not really a malaria site, but you never know where we still might end up. If there is not enough room for an icebox, have the Rosenthal china unpacked. Most likely, we will not need it anymore in this life, and we have had to say goodbye to more important things than plates with pretty floral patterns.

Regina will need rubber boots and Manchester pants (you, too, by the way). If anyone wants to give her a farewell present, ask for shoes that will still fit her two years from now. I cannot imagine, today at any rate, that we will ever be rich enough here to buy shoes.

Finally, make a detailed list of all pieces only after you have gotten everything together. It is important that each item that is supposed to go be listed. Otherwise, you will have tremendous problems. And, above all, do not let anyone persuade you to take anything along for someone else. Just remember poor B. He has only his good heart to blame for the trouble he got himself into with the customs officials in Hamburg. Who knows if he will ever get to England, and how long he will have to walk under the beech trees?* It is best if you talk as little as possible about your plans. You never know where a conversation might turn up and how people we have known all our lives may have changed these days.

I will give you only a little bit of news about myself; otherwise, your head will start spinning, too. Rongai is about three thousand feet above sea level, but very hot. The evenings are quite cold (so bring some woolens along). The main crop on the farm is maize, but I have not found out yet what I am supposed to do with it. Other than that, we have five hundred cows and any number of chickens. So there is a good supply of milk, butter, and eggs. Make sure to bring a recipe for baking bread.

What the houseboy bakes looks like matzos but tastes even worse. He can prepare coddled eggs beautifully, scrambled eggs not at all. And he sings a certain song for soft-boiled eggs. Unfortunately, the song is too long, and the eggs always come out hard-boiled.

As you can see, we already have our own houseboy. He is tall, black, of course (you will have to explain to Regina that not all people are white), and his name is Owuor. He laughs a lot, which in my current restlessness is good for me. Houseboys are servants here, but it does not mean anything to have a houseboy. You can have as many servants on a farm as you want. You can, therefore, forget your worries about a maid right away. There are many people living here. I envy them because they are unaware of what is happening in the world and have all they need.

In my next letter I will tell you more about Süßkind. He is an angel; he is going to Nairobi today and will take my mail along. That saves at least a week, and a fast exchange of letters is very important for us now. Number your letters when you answer, and write exactly to which one of mine you are responding. Otherwise, our lives will be even more confused than they already are. Write to Father and Liesel as soon as you can, and tell them not to worry about us.

*Translator's note: This is an allusion to the concentration camp Buchenwald ("Buchen" are beech trees).

My heart is bursting when I think that maybe I will be able to embrace you and Regina very soon now. But it gets heavy when I think how much this letter is going hurt your mother. She will now have only one of her two girls left, and who knows for how long? But your mother has always been a wonderful woman, and I know that she would rather see you and her granddaughter in Africa than in Breslau. Give Regina a big kiss from me and do not pamper her. Poor people can't afford doctors.

I can imagine how much anxiety this letter will cause you, but you have to be strong now. For all of us. I embrace you with all my love,

Your old Walter

P.S. You would have liked Mr. Rubens's sons, quite dashing fellows. Just like the ones at dance school in our days. I thought they were all single but discovered later that their wives always meet to play bridge when we refugees are around. They are sick and tired of the topic.

Rongai, February 15, 1938

My dear father,
I hope you will have heard from Jettel by now and, therefore, know that your son has become a farmer. Mother would probably have said, "nice, but hard," but a disbarred attorney and notary cannot ask for anything better. This morning, I already pulled a newborn calf from the belly of a cow and christened it Sohrau. I would have preferred to play midwife when a foal was born because you already taught me how to ride before you put on the Kaiser's uniform.

Please do not think that it was a mistake to have me study at a university. It only seems that way at the moment. How long can this last? My boss, who lives in Nairobi, not on the farm, has a lot of books in his bookcase, among them the Encyclopedia Britannica and a Latin dictionary. As I see it, I would not be able to learn English out here in the wilderness if I had not studied Latin. This way, I can already talk about tables, rivers, legions, and wars and can even say, "I am a man without a country." Unfortunately, that works only in theory, because there are only black people here on the farm, and they speak Swahili and find it terribly funny that I cannot understand them.

I was just reading about Prussia in the general lexicon. Since I do not know the language, I have to look for topics I am familiar with. You cannot imagine how long the days on this farm can be, but I am not complaining. I am grateful to Fate, especially since I now can hope that Regina and Jettel will be here soon.

I am very worried about the two of you. What will happen if the Germans march into Poland? They are not going to be interested that you and Liesel have remained Germans and did not opt for Poland. To them, you are Jews, and do not think that your military decorations will make any difference. We already discovered that after 1933. On the other hand, especially since you did not choose Poland, you may not be part of the Polish quota that makes emigration so difficult everywhere. If you sold the hotel, you could consider emigration, too. You should do this above all for Liesel's sake. After all, she is only thirty-two and has not been able to enjoy life so far.

I told a former banker from Berlin (he is now counting sacks of coffee on a farm) about Liesel, and that she is still in Sohrau. He thinks that the immigration offices here are not at all adverse to single women. They are sought after as nannies by rich English farming families. If I had the hundred pounds to sponsor the two of you, I would urge you even more strongly to emigrate. But I am already more than unbelievably lucky that I can bring Jettel and the child over.

Maybe you could contact attorney Kammer in Leobschütz. He was extremely decent to me to the very end. When I was disbarred, he agreed to take the client fees that were still outstanding into safekeeping for me. I am sure he would help you if you explained to him that you still own a hotel but have no money. In Leobschütz, they know how the Germans have been treated in Poland all these years.

Only here, where I am quite alone with my thoughts, have I truly come to the realization that I did not do enough for Liesel. With her kindness and willingness to make sacrifices, she does deserve a better brother. And you a son who would have thanked you in time for all you have done for him.

You really do not need to send anything to me here. Food is free on the farm, it provides me with everything I need to live, and I hope very much that one of these days I will find a position that will pay me enough so that I can send Regina to school (enormously expensive here, and school is not compulsory, either).

I would be very happy, however, with some rose seeds. Then, the same flowers would bloom on this god-forsaken piece of earth as in front of my father's house. Maybe Liesel can also send me a recipe for sauerkraut. I have heard that cabbage does grow here.

Embracing both of you with love,

Your Walter

Rongai, February 27, 1938

My dear Jettel,

Today your letter of January 17 arrived. It had to be forwarded to me from Nairobi. That this worked at all is a miracle. You cannot begin to imagine what distances mean in this country. It is about thirty-five miles from here to the next farm, and it takes Walter Süßkind three hours to get here over bad, partly mud-covered roads. Despite this, he has come every week up to now to observe the Sabbath with me. He is from a religious family. He is also lucky in that his boss has given him the use of a car. My boss, Mr. Morrison, unfortunately believes that since wandering in the desert, all the Children of Israel like walking. I have not gotten away from the farm since Süßkind brought me here.

Unfortunately, there are no horses here. The only donkey on the farm threw me off so often that I turned black and blue. Süßkind laughed terribly and said that it was impossible to ride African donkeys. They were not as stupid as the ones at German seaside resorts. When you come, you will also have to get used to the fact that it rains directly into our bedroom. One simply puts down a pail and is happy about the water. For water is precious. Last week there was fire everywhere. I was terribly upset. Luckily, Süßkind was visiting at the time and taught me about bushfires. They happen here all the time.

I feel good about the fact that your letter for the most part is already outdated. In the meantime, you will have found out that your days in Breslau are numbered. The thought of having the two of you here makes my heart jump as it did in the old days, when we dreamt about our great future together. Today we both know that only one thing is important—to escape.

You should definitely continue your English lessons, and it really does not matter that you do not like the teacher. You can give up Spanish right away. Anyway, that had been planned only in case we should get visas for Montevideo. In order to talk to the people on the farm, you will have to learn Swahili. And the good God has been kind to us there. Swahili is an easy language. I did not know a word of it when I arrived in Rongai, and now I am already able to converse moderately well with Owuor. He thinks it is wonderful if I point to things and he then can tell me their names. He calls me *bwana*. That is the way white men are addressed here. You will be the *memsahib* (the term is only used for white women) and Regina will be the *toto*. That means "child."

Maybe I will have learned enough Swahili before I write again so that I can tell Owuor that I do not like to eat my soup after the pudding. Pudding, by the way, is his specialty. The first time he made it, I kept on smacking my lips. He smacked his lips, too, and from that day on he has been cooking the same pudding every day. I really should laugh more often, but it is not easy to laugh alone. Especially not at night, when one is defenseless against all the memories.

If I only already had news from you and knew if you have tickets for the boat. Who would have thought that it would become so important to get away from one's homeland? I have to go milk the cows now. That is, I am looking on while the boys do the milking, and I memorize the names of the cows. It does distract me.

Please write instantly when you get my letters. And try not to get too upset. You can be sure that my thoughts are with you day and night.

A big kiss for both of you, your mother and sister,

Your old Walter

Rongai, March 15, 1938

My dear Jettel,
Today your letter of January 31 arrived. It made me very sad because I am so completely unable to help you with your fears. I can well imagine

that you hear a lot of sad things now, but it should also show you that Fate has not touched only us alone. By the way, it is not true that I am the only one who emigrated alone. There are many men here who wanted to try to get established first before bringing their families, and they are now dealing with the same situation as I—only without the good fortune that an angel like Rubens came to the rescue. You have to believe firmly that we will see each other again soon. We owe that to God. Also, there is no point in brooding now if it would have been better to go to Holland or France. We did not have any choice in the end, and who knows what it is good for?

It is not important anymore that they do not want to accept Regina in kindergarten. And it does not matter for our future happiness that people whom we have known for years all of a sudden do not give you the time of day. You really have to learn now to differentiate what is important and what is not. Life does not take into account anymore that you grew up as a spoiled daughter of an upper-class family. For emigrants, it is no longer important what they used to be, but only that a husband and a wife will pull together. I am sure that we are going to succeed. If you were only here already and we could get started.

A very big kiss for the two of you,

Your old Walter

Rongai, March 17, 1938

Dear Süßkind,
I do not know how long it will take the boy to deliver this letter. I have a temperature of 103 and my head is not clear at all times. If anything should happen to me, you will find my wife's address in the little case on the box next to my bed.

Walter

Rongai, April 4, 1938

My dearest Jettel,
Today, your letter arrived with the good news that I had longed for so much. Süßkind brought it from the train station and was, of course,

quite shocked when I burst into tears. Just imagine, this giant of a man then cried with me. That is the advantage of being a refugee and not a German man anymore. You do not have to be ashamed to cry.

The time until June, until you are on board, is going to be endless for me. If I remember correctly, the *Adolf Woermann* is a luxury liner and goes all around Africa. That means that you will frequently stop at different ports for extended stays and will be on your way for a longer time than I was on the *Ussukuma*. Try to enjoy the time as much as possible, but it will be best for you if you associate with people who celebrate the new year in September. Otherwise, you will have unnecessary problems. I hid too much in my cabin on the way over, and it was my last chance to talk to people.

It is too bad that you did not follow my advice to take a three-bed cabin. It would have saved us a lot of money, which we will need over here, and sharing the cabin with another sleeping companion would not have done any harm to the child. She will have to learn that even though her name is Regina, she is not a queen.

But I do not want to reproach you at a moment when I am so grateful and happy. It is more important now for you to keep your wits about you and see to it that the boxes can travel with you. Not because we need our things so badly, but I have heard of people who decided to have their belongings sent after them and are still waiting for them. I am afraid you did not understand how important an icebox is for us. In the tropics, it is as important as your daily bread. You should really try again to find one. Süßkind could bring me meat from Nakuru, but without an icebox it spoils in just a day. And Mr. Morrison is a very detail-minded boss. Only when he visits the farm can one of his chickens be slaughtered. I am glad that he at least lets me eat the eggs.

Congratulations on the Petromax lamp. Now we will not have to go to bed with Mr. Morrison's precious chickens. You should not have bought the evening gown. You will have no opportunity to wear it here. You are sadly mistaken if you think that people like the Rubenses will invite us to their parties. First, there is already a huge gap between the old, well-established, rich Jews and us poor refugees, and second, the Rubens family lives in Nairobi and that is further from Rongai than Breslau from Sohrau.

I cannot blame you, though, for your illusions about Africa. I did not have any idea what to expect either and am still constantly amazed about things that Süßkind considers completely normal. I am already quite good at speaking Swahili and realize more and more how movingly Owuor cares for me.

As a matter of fact, I was ill. One day I was running a high fever, and Owuor insisted that I send for Süßkind. He arrived late that same night and realized immediately what was wrong with me: malaria. Luckily, he had brought some quinine, and I recovered quickly. But you must not be shocked when you see me. I have lost a lot of weight, and my face is rather yellow. You see, the little mirror your sister gave me as a farewell present, and which I considered quite superfluous at the time, is very useful after all. Unfortunately, it mostly tells me unhappy stories.

My illness made me realize how important medical supplies are in a country where you cannot call a doctor, let alone pay for one. Above all, we need iodine and quinine. I am sure your mother must know a physician who is willing to help people like us and will get us these things. Let him also explain to you how much quinine you can give to a child. I do not want to scare you, but in this country you have to learn to help yourself. Without Süßkind, I would have been in very bad shape. And, of course, without Owuor, who did not leave my side and fed me like a child. By the way, he cannot believe that I have only one child. He has seven, but, if I understood him correctly, he also has three wives. Just imagine if he had to sponsor all of them! But he has his native country. I really envy him because of that. Also because he cannot read and does not know what is going on in the world. Strangely enough, though, he seems to know that I am a different kind of European from Mr. Morrison.

Tell Regina about me. I wonder if she will still recognize her Papa. How much does she understand about things? It is best if you wait to talk to her till you are on board. It will not matter then if she blurts out something. Do not make too many farewell visits. Those are just heartbreaking. My father will understand if you do not go to Sohrau again. I believe he will even think it is better. And give your mother and Käthe a kiss from me. The day of your departure will be terrible for the two of them. There are some thoughts one cannot even finish.

Embracing you with love,

Your old Walter

Rongai, April 4, 1938

My dear Regina,
Today you are getting your own letter because your Papa is so very happy that he will be able to see you soon. You will have to be especially good now, pray every night, and help Mama wherever you can. I am sure you will like the farm where the three of us are going to live. There are a lot of children here. You will have only to learn their language before you can play with them. The sun shines every day here. Cute little chickens hatch from eggs. Two calves have also been born since I came here. But you have to know one thing: Only children who are not afraid of dogs can come to Africa. Practice, therefore, to be courageous. Courage is a lot more important in life than chocolate.

I am sending you as many kisses as have room on your face. Give some of them to Mama, Oma, and Tante Käthe.

Love, Papa

Rongai, May 1, 1938

My dear father, my dear Liesel,
Yesterday your letter arrived with the rose seeds, the recipe for sauerkraut, and the latest news from Sohrau. If only I could find the words to tell you how much a letter like that means to me. I feel like the little boy again, to whom you, Father, wrote from the front. In each of your letters, you talked about courage and loyalty to the fatherland. Only that none of us were thinking at the time that one needs the most courage when one does not have a fatherland anymore.

I am more worried about you than ever before now that the Austrians have been welcomed home into the Reich. Who knows if the Germans are not planning a similar stroke of luck for the Czechs? And what is going to happen to Poland?

I always thought I would be able to do something for you when I finally got to Africa. But, of course, I had no way of knowing that it was possible to hire people in the twentieth century by offering them only room and board. Until Jettel and Regina arrive, I cannot think of changing my position. And, even after that, it will be difficult to find a job that pays a salary in addition to eggs, butter, and milk.

At the very least, you should contact a Jewish agency that gives advice to emigrants. That is certainly worth a trip to Breslau. You would also be able to see Jettel and Regina there. I did not want the two of them to come to Sohrau before their departure. I can tell from Jettel's letters how nervous she is.

Above all, dear Father, do not have any more illusions. Our Germany is dead. It has trampled our love into the ground. I am tearing it out of my heart every day anew. Only our Silesia will not budge.

You probably ask yourselves how living out here I know so much about what is going on in the world. The radio, which Stattlers gave me as a farewell present, is a real miracle. I can receive German broadcasts here as clearly as at home. Except for my friend Süßkind (he lives on the neighboring farm and already was a farmer in his first life), the radio is the only one speaking German to me. I wonder how Mr. Goebbels would like the fact that the Jew of Rongai quenches the thirst for his mother tongue by listening to his speeches?

I allow myself this pleasure only at night, though. During the day, I talk with the black people, which is becoming easier, and tell the cows about my lawsuits. Those animals with their soft eyes understand everything. Only this morning, an ox was telling me that I was right not to leave my copy of the Civil Code behind. Still, I cannot shake the feeling that it is less useful to a farmer than to an attorney.

Süßkind keeps on telling me that I have just the kind of humor that is needed to survive in this country. I am afraid he is confused about certain things. Wilhelm Kulas, by the way, would have a great career here. Mechanics call themselves engineers and find work quickly. On the other hand, if I were to maintain that I had been minister of justice at home, it would not advance me an inch. Instead, I have taught my houseboy to sing "Ich hab' mein Herz in Heidelberg verloren." If somebody has as much trouble with every word as he does, the song takes exactly four and a half minutes and is perfectly suited as an egg timer. My soft-boiled eggs now taste just the way they used to at home. So you see, I do have my little triumphs. What a shame that the bigger ones take so long.

In the hope that something will work out for you after all, I embrace you longingly,

Your Walter

Rongai, May 25, 1938

My dear Ina, my dear Käthe,
When you get this letter, Jettel and Regina, God willing, will already be on their way. I can imagine how you must feel, but I cannot put into words the emotions that move me when I think about you in Breslau. You helped Jettel to bear the time of our separation, and if I know my pampered Jettel, she did not make it easy for you.

Do not worry about Jettel. I have high hopes that she will adjust well to life here. I am certain that the events of the last years and especially the last months have made her understand that only one thing counts now, namely that we are together and safe. I know, dear Ina, that you often worry because I am a hothead and Jettel is a stubborn child who quickly loses her temper when things do not go her way, but that does not affect our marriage. Jettel has been and will always remain the great love of my life, even though she sometimes makes it very hard for me.

You see, the eternal African sun opens one's heart and mouth, but I also think that certain things need to be said in time. And since I am at it: There is no better mother-in-law than you, my dearest Ina. And I am not talking about your home fries, either, but about all my years as a student. I was nineteen when I came into your home and you made me feel like a son. How long ago that seems to have been now, and how little have I been able to repay you.

You will need all your strength now for yourselves. I have great hopes about your correspondence with America. Use every possibility. I know that you do not think much of praying, Ina, but I cannot stop asking God for His help. I hope that He will give me the opportunity to thank Him one of these days.

Jettel and Regina will be received like royalty. I had a wonderful bed made of cedar for Regina with a crown at the headboard. (I do not have anything to live on here, but can cut down as many trees as I want to.) I drew the crown on paper, and Owuor, my loyal houseboy and companion, brought in a nearly naked giant with a knife who carved our crown. I am certain there is nothing as beautiful as this in Breslau. For Jettel, we paved the way between our living quarters and the "long drop" loo with boards so that she does not sink into the mud when she has to go during the rainy season. I hope that she does not get too shocked when she finds out that you do have to calculate even the smallest matters in detail here. The distance between the house and the loo is three minutes. Less when you have diarrhea.

Give my regards to the town hall and everyone who has helped my family. And take good care of yourselves. How stupid I feel writing this, but how can I express what I feel?

With much love,

Yours, Walter

Rongai, July 20, 1938

My dearest Jettel,

Today your letter from Southampton arrived. Can a single human being be this grateful, happy, and relieved? At last, at last, at last! We finally can write to each other again without fear. I admire you very much for writing about the ports where the *Adolf Woermann* will pick up mail. I did not think about that when I went. This letter will go to Tangiers. If the mail follows my calculations, it should reach you there in plenty of time. There was not enough time to write to you in Nice. I hope you were not too disappointed. I have found out only too well in the meantime what it is like to wait for mail.

Regina will see the first black people in Tangiers. I hope our little frightened bunny will not be too afraid. I am very happy that she survived the excitement of the departure so well. Maybe we always assumed that she was more delicate than she is. I can imagine how you must have felt. I was very touched that your mother accompanied you to Hamburg. That a heart without hope can still think about others!

Do not lose any sleep over not having bought an icebox after all. We will just wrap the meat and butter in your new evening gown and hang the whole thing in the full sun, into the wind. This is really the way food is kept cool here, even though not in silk, but we can try it. At least, that will give you the feeling that such an evening dress has a purpose here. Yesterday, I bought bananas. Not a pound or two, but a whole bunch of about fifty. Regina will be amazed when she sees something like that. Every once in a while women come by here with huge bunches of bananas and offer them to the farmers. The first time, all the black people came running and almost died laughing because I wanted to buy only three. Bananas are very cheap (even for a nebbish) and completely green, but they are delicious. I wish everything here tasted that good.

I believe Owuor is happy that you are coming. He was angry with me for three days. After I had learned enough Swahili to form whole sentences, I gave away the secret that I did not want the same pudding every day. This took him completely by surprise. He kept reminding me that I had praised his pudding on the very first day. He imitated the smacking noises from our first pudding encounter and looked at me disdainfully. I stood there crestfallen and, of course, did not know the word for "variety" in Swahili if, indeed, there is such a word.

It does take a very long time before one does understand the mentality of the people here, but they are lovable and certainly also smart. Above all, they would never conceive the idea of imprisoning people or chasing them out of the country. They do not care that we are Jews or refugees or, unhappily, both. On a good day I sometimes believe that I could get used to this country. Maybe black people have some medicine (called *dawa* here) against memories.

Well, I still have to tell you something terribly exciting. A week ago, Heini Weyl all of a sudden stood in front of me. The very one with the big linen and drapery store at the Tauentzienplatz whom I went to see on Father's advice when I was disbarred and did not know where we should emigrate. Heini was the one who suggested Kenya at the time because one needed only fifty pounds per person.

He has been here for eleven months and has tried to find work in a hotel but has not succeeded so far. To be a waiter is not considered appropriate for whites, and for the better positions you need to know English. He has now found a job as a manager (that is what everyone is here, even I) at a gold mine in Kisumu. He has retained his optimism, even though Kisumu is supposed to have a terribly hot climate and also has a bad reputation as a malaria site. Since Rongai is on the way from Nairobi to Kisumu, Heini stopped by with the car he bought with his last money and his wife, Ruth, to see me. We stayed up the whole night gossiping and talking about Breslau.

Owuor forgot his anger about the pudding and arrived with a chicken, even though those are supposed to be killed only for Mr.

Morrison. He explained that the chicken had run directly in front of his feet and had fallen over dead.

You cannot imagine what visitors mean on the farm. You feel like a dead man who has been called back to life.

Unfortunately, the Weyls told me that Fritz Feuerstein and the two Hirsch brothers had been arrested. As I know from a letter from Schlesingers in Leobschütz, they also took away Hans Wohlgemut and his brother-in-law, Siegfried. I have known this for a long time, but I was afraid to write to you about the arrests as long as you were still in Breslau. I did not tell you either that our good, loyal Greschek, who insisted on going to a Jewish lawyer to the very end, accompanied me by train to Genoa. He also wrote a letter to me here. I hope he understands that I did not answer for his sake.

How lucky we are that we can write to each other without fear. What does it matter that on the *Adolf Woermann* you have to hear about how the Nazis at your table adore Hitler's picture? You really have to learn not to consider insults important anymore. Only rich people can afford that. The only thing that counts is that you are on the *Adolf Woermann,* not who your fellow passengers are.

A month from now, you will never again have to see these people who make you sick to your stomach at the moment. Owuor does not even know how to insult people.

Süßkind has high hopes that his boss will let him drive his car to Mombasa. The two of us can then pick you up and bring you here directly. Directly, by the way, means a journey of at least two days on unpaved roads, but we can stay a night in Nairobi with the Gordon family. The Gordons have been living there for four years and are always willing to help newcomers. If Süßkind's boss cannot bring himself to acknowledge that a refugee, after months of being frightened to death, has the desire to embrace his wife and child, do not be sad. Someone from the Jewish community will put you on the train to Nairobi in Mombasa and then will make sure that you continue on to Rongai. The communities here are wonderful. Too bad that this applies only to the arrival.

I no longer count the weeks but the days and hours till we see each other and I feel like the bridegroom before the wedding night.

A loving hug from

Your old Walter

2

"*Toto*," Owuor laughed as he lifted Regina out of the car. He threw her a little way up into the air, caught her again, and pressed her close to his body. His arms were soft and warm, his teeth were very white. The big pupils in his round eyes lit up his face, and he wore a high, dark-red hat that looked like one of those upside-down pails that, before the big journey, Regina used to take outside for baking cakes in the sandbox. A black tassel with fine fringes was swinging from the hat; very small black curls crept out from under the rim. Owuor was wearing a long, white shirt over his trousers, just like the cheerful angels in the picture books for good children. Owuor had a flat nose and thick lips, and his head looked like a black moon. As soon as the sun shone on the droplets of sweat on his forehead, the droplets changed into multicolored beads. Regina had never seen such tiny beads before.

Owuor's skin smelled delightful like honey, chased away any fear, and made a big person out of a little girl. Regina opened her mouth wide so that she would be able to swallow the magic that drove all the pains and tiredness from her body. First, she felt herself getting strong in Owuor's arms, and then she realized that her tongue had learned to fly.

"*Toto*," she repeated the beautiful, strange word.

The giant with the mighty hands and smooth skin put her gently down on the ground. He released laughter from his throat that tickled her ears. The high trees swirled, the clouds began to dance, and black shadows were chasing each other in the white sun.

"*Toto*," Owuor laughed again. His voice was loud and good, quite different from that of the weeping and whispering people in the big gray city of which Regina dreamed at night.

"*Toto,*" Regina cheered back and waited eagerly for Owuor's exuberant joy.

She opened her eyes so wide that she saw shimmering points that turned into balls of fire in the bright light before they disappeared. Papa had put his small white hand on Mama's shoulder. The awareness of having both Papa and Mama again reminded Regina of chocolate. With a start, she shook her head and immediately felt a chill on her skin. Would the black man in the moon never laugh again if she thought of chocolate? There was no chocolate for poor children, and Regina knew that she was poor because her father was not allowed to be a lawyer anymore. Mama had explained it to her on the boat and told her she was a very good girl because she had understood everything so well and had not asked any stupid questions, but now in the new air, which was hot and humid at the same time, Regina could no longer remember the end of the story.

She saw only that the blue and red flowers on her mother's white dress flew about like birds. On Papa's forehead, too, tiny beads were shining, not as beautiful and colorful as the ones on Owuor's face, but funny enough to make her laugh.

"Come on, child," Regina heard her mother say, "we have to get you out of the sun right away," and she felt that her father reached for her hand, but her fingers were not her own anymore. They were glued to Owuor's shirt.

Owuor clapped his hands together and gave her back her fingers.

The big black birds that had been squatting on the small tree in front of the house flew toward the clouds shrieking, and then Owuor's naked feet flew across the red ground. The wind turned the angel's tunic into a bullet. To see Owuor run away was bad.

Regina felt the sharp pain in her chest that always came before some great sorrow, but she remembered in time that her mother had said she was not allowed to cry anymore in her new life. So she pressed her eyes together to hold back her tears. When she was able to see again, Owuor was coming through the high yellow grass. He had a small deer in his arms.

"This is Suara. Suara is a *toto* like you," he said, and, even though Regina was not able to understand him, she opened up her arms. Owuor handed the trembling animal to her. It was lying on its back and had thin legs and ears as small as those of the doll Annie, which had not been allowed to come on the trip because there was no more room in the boxes. Regina had never touched an animal before. But she did not feel any fear. She let her hair fall across the eyes of the little deer and touched its head with her lips as if she had waited a long time already, not to call for help anymore, but to give protection.

"It is hungry," her mouth whispered. "Me, too."

"Good God, you have never said that in all your life."

"My deer said that. I didn't."

"You will get far here, timid little princess. You already talk like an African," Süßkind said. His laughter was different from Owuor's, but also good to hear.

Regina pressed the deer close and no longer heard anything but the regular heartbeat coming from its warm body. She closed her eyes. Her father took the sleeping animal out of her arms and gave it to Owuor. Then he lifted Regina up as if she were a small child and carried her into the house.

"How nice," Regina exclaimed, "we have holes in the roof. I have never seen anything like this before."

"Neither had I before I came here. Just wait, everything is different in our second life."

"Our second life is so beautiful."

The deer was named Suara because Owuor had called it that on the first day. Suara lived in a big shed behind the small house, licked Regina's fingers with its warm tongue, drank milk from a small tin bowl, and after only a few days was already able to chew tender ears of maize. Each morning Regina would open the shed door. Suara leapt through the high grass and, on returning, rubbed its head against Regina's brown pants. She had been wearing those pants ever since the day the big magic had begun. When the sun fell from the sky at night and covered the farm with a black cloak, Regina had her mother tell her the fairy tale of Little Brother and Sister. She knew that one day her deer, too, would turn into a boy.

When Suara's legs had become longer than the grass behind the trees with the big thorns and Regina already knew the names of so many cows that she could tell her father their names while milking, Owuor brought a dog with white fur and black spots to the farm. His eyes were the color of bright stars. His nose was long and moist. Regina slung her arms around his neck, which was as round and warm like Owuor's arms. Mama came running out of the house and shouted, "But you are afraid of dogs."

"Not here."

"We will call him Rummler," Papa said in such a deep voice that Regina swallowed the wrong way when she laughed back at him. "Rummler," she giggled, "is a pretty word. Just like Suara."

"But Rummler is German. Don't you only like Swahili now?"

"I like Rummler, too."

"What made you come up with Rummler?" Mama asked. "Wasn't that the District Commander in Leobschütz?"

"Agh, Jettel, we need our games. Now we can shout, 'Rummler, you dirty bastard' all day long and be happy that no one will come and arrest us."

Regina sighed and stroked the big head of her dog, which flicked away the flies with his short ears. His body was steaming in the heat and smelled like rain. Papa too often said things she did not understand, and when he laughed it was only with a short high note, which did not bounce back from the mountain like Owuor's laughter. She told the story of the transformed deer in a low voice to the dog, and he looked in the direction of Suara's shed and immediately understood how much Regina was longing for a brother.

The wind was caressing her ears and she heard her parents mention Rummler's name over and over again, but she was not able to understand all they said, even though their voices were very clear. Every word seemed like a soap bubble that burst immediately once you reached for it.

"Rummler, you dirty bastard!" Regina finally said, but only when she saw her parents' faces light up like a lamp with a new wick did she realize that those four words held a magic spell.

Regina also loved her Aya, who had come to the farm shortly after Rummler. She stood in front of the house one morning after the last bit of red had disappeared from the sky and the black vultures on the thorn-trees moved their heads out from under their wings. *Aya* was the word for a nanny and much more beautiful than others because you could say it forward and backward. Aya, just like Suara and Rummler, was a present from Owuor.

All rich families on a big farm with a deep well on the lawn in front of a huge white stone house had an *aya*. Before Owuor had come to Rongai, he had worked on such a farm for a *bwana,* who kept a car and many horses and, of course, an *aya* for his children.

"A house without an *aya* is no good," he had said the day he brought the young woman from the huts near the bank of the river. The new *memsahib,* whom he had taught to say "*asante sana*" when she wanted to thank someone, had praised him with her eyes.

Aya's eyes were gentle, coffee-brown, and large like Suara's. Her hands were delicate and as white on the inside as Rummler's fur. She moved as quickly as young trees in the wind and had lighter skin than Owuor, even though both belonged to the Jaluo tribe. When the wind tore at the yellow wrap that was fastened with a big knot on Aya's right shoulder, her firm, small breasts moved like small spheres on a string. Aya never was angry or impatient. She did not talk much, but the short sounds she released from her throat sounded like songs.

Regina learned to talk so well and so quickly from Owuor that everyone soon understood her better than her parents, but Aya brought silence into her new life. Every day after the midday meal, the two of them would sit in the round patch of shadow under the thorn-tree that grew between the house and the kitchen building. Here, the nose was more able than anywhere else on the farm to hunt for the sweet smell of warm milk and fried eggs. As soon as the nose was satisfied and the throat moist, Regina lightly rubbed her face on Aya's wrap. Then she heard two hearts beating before she fell asleep. She woke up only when the shadows grew long and Rummler was licking her face.

Hours followed, in which Aya wove small baskets out of long blades of grass. Her fingers tore small animals with minute wings from their sleep, and only Regina knew that those were air-horses that flew to heaven with her wishes. Aya made small clicking sounds with her tongue while she worked, but she never moved her lips while doing so.

The night, too, had its constantly recurring noises. As soon as it turned dark, the hyenas howled, and snatches of songs made their way from the huts. Regina's ears found nourishment even in bed. Since the walls of the house were so low that they did not reach the ceiling, she heard every word her parents said in their bedroom.

Even when they whispered, the sounds were as clear as their voices during the daytime. On good nights, they sounded sleepy like the humming of bees and Rummler's snoring after he had emptied his bowl with only a few movements of his tongue. But there also were very long and angry nights, with words that attacked each other along with the first howls of the hyenas, which created fear and were smothered by silence only when the sun awoke the roosters.

After those nights with the big noises, Walter was in the shed in the morning earlier than the herdsmen who were milking the cows, and Jettel stood in the kitchen red-eyed, stirring her anger into the pot of milk on the smoking stove. After the ordeal of the night, neither of the two found a way to the other before the cool evening air of Rongai erased the heat of the day and took pity on their bewildered heads.

In such moments of reconciliation, full of shame and embarrassment, Walter and Jettel were left with only the strange miracle that the farm had worked on Regina. Gratefully, they shared their amazement and relief. The timid child who at home had crossed her arms behind her back and had lowered her head if strangers only smiled at her had become a chameleon. Regina had recovered her health in the uniformity of the days at Rongai. She rarely cried, and laughed as soon as Owuor was near. Her voice was no longer childlike then, and she showed a determination that made Walter envious.

"Children adjust quickly," Jettel said on the day that Regina reported that she had learned Jaluo so that she could talk to Owuor and Aya in their own language. "My mother always said so."

"Well, then, there is hope for you."

"I don't think that is funny."

"Neither do I."

Walter immediately regretted his small outburst. He missed his former knack for harmless jokes. Since his irony had become biting and Jettel's dissatisfaction had made her unpredictable, their nerves had made them both unable to tolerate the minor taunts that in better times had been a matter of course for them.

Walter and Jettel were able to experience the happiness of finding each other again for only too short a time before the low spirits that plagued them returned. Without daring to admit it, both suffered more from the forced togetherness that the loneliness of the farm brought about than from the isolation itself.

They were not used to adapting to each other completely, and yet they had to spend every hour of the day together without the stimulation and diversion of the outside world. The small-town gossip, which they had ridiculed during the first years of their marriage and even found tiresome, now seemed funny and exciting in retrospect. There were no longer any short separations and, therefore, also not the happiness of seeing each other again that had taken the sting out of their fights, which in retrospect now appeared to have been harmless skirmishes.

Walter and Jettel had been fighting since the day they met. His explosive temper did not tolerate any contradiction; she had the self-assurance of a woman who had been a strikingly beautiful child, adored by a mother who had been widowed at an early age. During their long engagement, their arguments over virtually nothing and their mutual inability to give in had already bothered them without their ever knowing how to find a way out. Only during their marriage had they come to accept the now familiar interplay between their small fights and their animated reconciliations as part of their love.

When Regina had been born and Hitler came to power six months later, Walter and Jettel found more support in each other than before, without realizing that they had already become outsiders in their supposed paradise. Only in the monotonous pace of life in Rongai were they becoming aware of what had really happened. They had used the strength of their youth for five years to hold on to the illusion of a homeland that had already expelled them long ago. Now both were embarrassed by their nearsightedness and by the knowledge that they had not been willing to see what many had already been able to recognize early on.

Time had easily beaten down their dreams. The boycott of Jewish stores on April 1, 1933, in the western part of Germany had already pointed toward a future without hope. Jewish judges were chased out of their offices, professors from universities; attorneys and physicians lost their livelihoods, merchants their stores, and all Jews their original confidence that the terror would not last long. For a time, though, the Jews in Upper Silesia were protected from a fate they were unable to comprehend by the Geneva Minority Protection Agreement.

Walter did not understand that he would not be able to escape the destiny of the other outlaws when he started his law practice in

Leobschütz and even became a notary. In his recollection, the people of Leobschütz were friendly and tolerant, of course with some exceptions, whom he could list by name and did so over and over again in Rongai. Despite the propaganda against the Jews that was starting in Upper Silesia, some, and their number became larger and larger in his memory, did not let themselves be prevented from consulting a Jewish lawyer. With a pride that in retrospect seemed as degrading as presumptuous, he had considered himself to be one of the exceptions among those condemned by fate.

The day the Geneva Minority Protection Agreement expired, Walter was discharged as a lawyer. It was his first direct confrontation with a Germany he had not wanted to acknowledge. The blow was devastating. He perceived it as his own irreparable failure that his instincts had failed him just as much as his sense of responsibility for his family.

Jettel, with her zest for living, had felt even less threatened. For her, it had been enough to be the idolized center of a small circle of friends and acquaintances. As a child she had had, more by chance than intentionally, only Jewish girlfriends; after school she worked in the office of a Jewish attorney; and then, through Walter's student fraternity, the K.C., she again had contact only with Jews. She did not mind that, after 1933, she was able to socialize only with Jews in Leobschütz. Most were her mother's age and considered Jettel's youth, her charm, and her friendliness revitalizing. In addition, Jettel was pregnant and touching in her naiveté. Soon she was spoiled in the same way by the women in Leobschütz that she had been by her mother, and, despite her earlier fears, she enjoyed life in a small town. And, anytime she got bored, she took a trip to Breslau.

On Sundays, they often went to Troppau. It was only a short walk to the Czech border. There, in addition to a tasty schnitzel and a great selection of pastries, Jettel could always have the illusion that the emigration, of which one had to talk occasionally, because so many of one's acquaintances did, would not be much different from the delightful outings to the hospitable neighboring country.

It would never have occurred to Jettel that her needs, like daily shopping, invitations to friends, trips to Breslau, visits to the movies, and a sympathetic doctor who made house calls as soon as the patient had the slightest temperature, might not be met. Only the move to

Breslau, the first step toward emigration, the desperate search for a country that was willing to take in Jews, the separation from Walter, and finally the fear of not ever seeing him again and having to stay in Germany alone with Regina caused Jettel to wake up. She now realized what had happened during those years when she had enjoyed a present that for quite a while already had no longer promised a future. So Jettel, too, who had considered herself worldly-wise and who believed that she was a good judge of character, was afterward ashamed of her heedlessness and gullibility.

In Rongai, her feelings of self-reproach and dissatisfaction grew rampant like wild grass. During the three months on the farm, Jettel had seen nothing else but the house, cowshed, and forest. Her aversion to the drought, which upon her arrival had exhausted her body and drained all willpower from her head, was as intense as that against the great rains, which started soon afterward. The rains reduced life to a losing battle against mud and the futile endeavor to keep the wood dry for the kitchen stove.

At all times there was the fear of malaria and that Regina might get fatally ill. Above all, Jettel was in a constant panic that Walter might lose his job and all three of them would have to leave Rongai and have no place to live. With her heightened sense of reality, Jettel realized that Mr. Morrison, who was unfriendly even to Regina, held her husband responsible for everything that happened on the farm.

It had been too dry for maize in the beginning, and then too wet. The wheat had not germinated. The chickens developed some kind of eye disease, and at least five were dying each day. The cows did not give enough milk. The last four newborn calves had lived less than two weeks. The well, which Walter had dug at Mr. Morrison's request, did not produce any water. The only things that grew bigger were the holes in the roof.

The day of the first bushfire after the great rains turned the Menengai into a red wall was especially hot. Despite that, Owuor placed chairs for Walter and Jettel in front of the house. "One has to look at a fire after it has slept for a long time," he said.

"Why are you not staying here then?"

"My legs need to go."

The wind was too strong for the hour before sunset, and the sky was gray with the heavy smoke, which rolled in thick clouds over the farm. The vultures rose from the trees. The monkeys shrieked in the forest, and even the hyenas howled too early. The air stung. It made talking difficult, but suddenly Jettel said very loudly, "I cannot take it anymore."

"Don't be afraid. The first time I thought the house would burn down, too. I wanted to call the fire department."

"I am not talking about the fire. I cannot stand it here anymore."

"You will have to, Jettel. We are not being asked anymore."

"But what is going to become of us? You don't earn a cent, and our last money will be gone soon. How are we supposed to send Regina to school? This is no life for a child, just sitting under a tree with Aya."

"Don't you think I know that? Children here have to go to boarding school because of the long distances. The nearest one is in Nakuru, and it is five pounds a month. Süßkind got some information on it. And, unless there is a miracle, we will not even be able to afford that for years."

"We are constantly waiting for miracles."

"Jettel, God has already provided us with a few. Otherwise, you would not be here to complain. We are alive, and that is the main thing."

Jettel choked, "I cannot even listen to that anymore. We are alive. What for? To get excited about dead calves and croaking chickens? I already feel dead myself. Sometimes I even wish I were."

"Jettel, do not ever say that again. For heaven's sake, this is fighting God."

Walter rose and pulled Jettel from her chair. He was motionless in his despair and allowed the rage in himself to burn justice, kindness, and reason. But then he saw Jettel crying without being able to sob. Her pale face and her helplessness touched him. Finally, he managed to find enough compassion to swallow his reproaches and anger. With a gentleness that bewildered him as much as his earlier vehemence had done, Walter pulled his wife close to him. For a short moment, the excitement of having her body close to his gave him warmth, but then his head took away that consolation, too.

"We have escaped. It is our duty to carry on."

"Now, what is that supposed to mean?"

"Jettel," Walter said quietly, and he realized that he would not be able to hold back the tears much longer that had weighed on him since daybreak, "yesterday the synagogues burned in Germany. They shattered the windows of Jewish stores and dragged people out of their apartments and almost beat them to death. I have wanted to tell you all day but I did not know how."

"How do you know? How can you say such a thing? How could you find out such a thing on this damned farm?"

"I got the Swiss channel this morning."

"They can't just burn down synagogues. Nobody can do such a thing."

"Yes, they can. These devils can. We are no longer human beings to them. Burning the synagogues is only the beginning. The Nazis cannot be stopped anymore. Do you understand now that it is not important when and whether Regina learns how to read?"

Walter was afraid to look at Jettel, but when he finally did he realized that she had not grasped what he had been trying to tell her. There was no longer any hope for her mother and Käthe, his father and Liesel to escape from hell. Ever since he had turned off the radio in the morning, Walter had been ready to carry out his duty and tell her the truth, but when the moment came, speechlessness had paralyzed his tongue. It was his inability to speak that shattered him, not the pain.

Only when he was able to avert his eyes from Jettel's trembling body did he feel his limbs come alive. His ears were able to take in sounds again. He heard the dog barking, the vultures screeching, voices coming from the huts, and the muffled sound of drums in the forest.

Owuor ran through the parched grass towards the house. His white shirt shone in the last light of the day. He looked so much like the birds that try to make themselves look big, that Walter could not suppress a smile.

"*Bwana,*" Owuor panted, "*Nzige na kuja.*"

It was good to see the perplexity in the *bwana*'s eyes. Owuor loved this expression because it made his *bwana* as dumb as a donkey that is still drinking its mother's milk and himself as clever as a snake that has gone hungry for a long time and, by using its head, finds its prey just in time. The great feeling of knowing more than the *bwana* tasted as sweet as tobacco, which will not be completely chewed for quite some time, in one's mouth.

It took a lot of time before Owour could let go of his triumph, but then he started to long for the excitement that his words would produce.

He was about to repeat them when he realized that the *bwana* had not understood him at all.

So Owuor simply repeated *"nzige"* and slowly removed a locust from his pants pocket. It had not been easy to keep it alive while he ran, but it was still beating its wings.

"This," Owuor explained in the voice of a mother who has a slow child, "is a *nzige*. This was one of the first. I caught it for you. When the others are here, they will gobble up everything."

"What are we going to do?"

"A lot of noise is good, but one mouth is not big enough. It is no use if you scream alone, *bwana*."

"Owuor, help me. I don't know what to do."

"It is possible to chase the *nzige* away," Owuor explained, now talking exactly like Aya when she brought Regina back from her sleep into the heat. "We need pots and spoons and have to bang them. Like drums. It is even better if glass breaks. Every animal is afraid when glass dies. Did you not know that, *bwana*?"

3

WHEN THE SUN ROSE the day after the locusts, everyone on the
shambas and in the huts, as well as the drums in the forests of the distant
neighboring farms, knew that Owuor was more than just a houseboy
who stirred the pots and made raging holes from soft little bubbles. In
the fight against the *nzige* he had been faster than the arrows of the
Masai. Owuor had made them all into warriors, the men and the
women and even all the children who were able to run without holding
on to the *kangas* around their mothers' waists.

Their cries and the mighty clamor of pots, the sound of heavy iron
bars banging against each other, and, most of all, the shrill lightning
storm of splintering shards of glass on big stones had chased away the
locusts before they alighted on the *shambas* where maize and wheat were
growing. They had flown on like lost birds that are too weak to know
their destination.

On that day, on which the *bwana* cried like a child burned by its own
rage and Owuor became the avenging savior, he had pushed even the
round *krais* in which the *posho* was cooked at night into the hands of his
fighters. After the grand victory, Owuor had neither wasted the night
sleeping nor opened his ears to the loud jokes of his friends. The knowledge that he could work magic was too powerful, the taste in his mouth
when he let his tongue say the word *"nzige"* was too sweet.

On the day after this glorious long night, the *bwana* returned from
milking before the pail had caught the last milk. He called Owuor into
the house just when he was ready to start his song for the eggs. The
memsahib sat on the chair with the red blanket, which looked like a
piece of the setting sun, and smiled. Regina squatted on the floor with

Rummler's head between her knees. She shook the dog from his sleep when Owuor entered the room.

The *bwana* had a big black ball in his hand. He unfolded it, made a coat from it, and pulled Owuor's hand toward it so that he could feel the cloth. The coat was like the earth after the long rains. On both sides and at the collar shone some material that was even softer than the cloth on the back; the *bwana*'s voice was just as smooth when he put the coat over Owuor's shoulders and said, "This is for you."

"You are giving me your coat, *bwana*?"

"This is not a coat, it is a robe. A man like you has to wear a robe."

Owuor immediately tried out the new word. Since it came from neither the Jaluo language nor from Swahili, it caused a lot of trouble in his mouth and his throat. The *memsahib* and the child laughed. Even Rummler opened his mouth, but the *bwana*, who had sent his eyes on safari, just stood there like a tree that has not yet grown tall enough to have its crown steeped in the coolness of the wind.

"Robe," the *bwana* said, "you have to repeat it often. Then you will be able to say it as well as I."

For seven nights when he went home to the men in the huts after work, Owuor, behind a bush, would put on the black coat that billowed so mightily in the wind that children, dogs, and even the old men who could not see too well anymore would screech. As soon as the material, which emitted a black light in the sunshine and even in the moonlight was darker than the night, touched his neck and shoulders, Owuor's teeth tried out the strange word. The coat and the word were magic for Owuor, and he knew that it was related to the locusts. When the sun rose on the eighth day, the word finally had become as soft in his mouth as a small bite of *posho*. It was good that he now could follow his urge to find out more about the coat.

Until it was time to wake up the fire in the kitchen, Owuor had stilled his hunger with the knowledge that his *bwana*, the *memsahib*, and the *toto* had been able to understand him for some time now just as well as the people who were not afraid of locusts and big ants. For a while he still allowed the question that had disturbed his head for a long time to grow, but the curiosity ate away at his patience, and he went to look for the *bwana*.

Walter was standing next to the metal tank and was tapping the grooves to hear how long the drinking water would last when Owuor asked, "When did you wear the robe?"

"Owuor, this was my robe when I was not yet a *bwana*. I wore this robe to work."

"Robe," Owuor repeated and was happy because the *bwana* had finally understood that good words had to be said three times. "Can a man work in this robe?"

"Yes, Owuor, yes. But I cannot work in my robe in Rongai."

"Did you work with your arms before you were a *bwana*?"

"No, with my mouth. One has to be clever for the robe. In Rongai you are clever. Not I."

Only afterward, in the kitchen, did Owuor realize why the *bwana* was so different from the other white men for whom he had worked so far. His new *bwana* used words that during the magic of repetition made one's mouth dry but that stayed in one's ear and head.

It took exactly eight days until the news of the defeated locusts arrived in Sabbatia and brought Süßkind to Rongai, even though the first cases of East Coast fever had started to affect the cows on his farm.

"Man," he shouted already from the car, "you are going to be a farmer after all. How did you ever manage this? I have never in a life-time been able to do that. After the last rainy season, those creatures ate half the farm."

The evening turned out to be a harmonious and cheerful one. Jettel surrendered her last potatoes, which she had kept for a special occasion, and taught Owuor to prepare the most typical Silesian dish and told him about the dried pears that she had always gotten for her mother in a small store on Goethestraße. Wistful, yet happy, she put on the white skirt with the red and white striped blouse, which she had not worn since Breslau, and was soon able to bask in Süßkind's admiration.

"Without you," he said, "I would not be able to remember how beautiful a woman can be. All the men in Breslau must have been after you."

"Yes, that's the way it was," Walter confirmed, and Jettel enjoyed the fact that his jealousy had not lost any of its previous sting.

Regina did not have to go to bed. She was allowed to sleep in front of the fire, and, whenever the voices woke her, she imagined the fire-place to be the Menengai and the black ash chocolate after a bushfire.

She learned a few new words for the secret box in her head. She liked the expression "German Reich refugee tax" best, even though it was the hardest to remember.

Walter told Süßkind about his first trial in Leobschütz and how he had toasted the unexpected success afterward with Greschek at a feast in Hennerwitz. Süßkind tried to remember Pomerania but was already getting confused about the years, places, and people he tried to retrieve from his memory.

"Just wait," he said, "this will happen to you soon, too. The best thing about Africa is the big memory loss."

The day after, Mr. Morrison came to the farm. There was no doubt that the news about saving of the crops had even reached Nairobi, because he extended his hand to Walter, which he had never done before. Even more striking was the fact that, in contrast to earlier visits, he now also understood Jettel's hints that she had prepared tea for him. He drank tea from a Rosenthal cup with multicolored flowers and shook his head every time he used the silver tongs to take a piece of sugar out of the porcelain bowl.

When Mr. Morrison came back from the cows and chickens and returned to the house, he took off his hat. His face seemed younger; he had light blond hair and bushy eyebrows. He asked for a third cup of tea. He played with the sugar tongs for a while and shook his head again. Then he suddenly got up and went to the cabinet with the Latin dictionary and the Encyclopedia Britannica, took an ivory napkin ring out of one of the drawers, and pushed it into Regina's hand.

The ring seemed so beautiful that she could hear her heart beat. But it had been such a long time since she had to thank anyone for a present that she could not think of anything to say but "*asante sana,*" even though she knew that a child was not allowed to speak Swahili to such a powerful man as Mr. Morrison.

It could not have been completely wrong, though, because Mr. Morrison displayed two gold teeth while he laughed. Regina ran out of the house full of suspense. It was true she had seen Mr. Morrison often before, but he had never once laughed and had hardly ever noticed her. If he had changed that much, maybe he was her deer after all that had been changed back into a human being.

Suara lay asleep under a thorn-tree. The realization that the white ring did not have any special powers took away some of its beauty. So Regina only whispered "next time" into Suara's ear, waited till the deer moved its head, and slowly went back to the house.

Mr. Morrison had put on his hat and looked the same as always. He made a fist with his right hand and looked out of the window. For a moment he seemed a little like Owuor on the day the locusts came, but he did not pull a wing-beating little devil from his pants; instead, he took out six bank notes, which he put on the table one by one.

"Every month," Mr. Morrison said in English and went to his car. First the starter howled, then Rummler, and then there was a cloud of dust in which the car disappeared.

"My God, what did he say? Did you understand him, Jettel?"

"Yes. Almost, that is. 'Monat' means month. I know that for sure. We learned that word in our course. I was the only one who could pronounce it correctly, but do you think that ogre of a teacher would ever praise me or even acknowledge it?"

"But that is not at all important now. What was the other word?"

"You don't have to shout at me. We learned that, too, but I can't remember it just now."

"You will have to. There are six pounds here. They must mean something."

"'Monat' means month," Jettel repeated.

Both were so excited that for a while they pushed the notes back and forth between them, leafed through them, and shrugged their shoulders.

"Well, we do have a lexicon," Jettel finally remembered. Excited, she pulled a book with a yellow and red cover out of a box. "Here: *A Thousand English Words*," she laughed. "We also have *A Thousand Spanish Words*."

"Those are not doing us any good now. Spanish was for Montevideo. Shall I tell you something, Jettel? We'll have to give up. We do not even know what word we are trying to look up."

Excited from the expectation that burned her skin, Regina sat down on the floor. She realized that her parents, who were continually fetching a single word from their throats and in the process smelled like Rummler when he was hungry, had invented a new game. In order to enjoy the pleasure for a while, it was best for her not to join in. Regina also suppressed the desire to get Owuor and Aya. She nibbled on

Rummler's ear until he made small, low noises of joy. Then she heard her father say, "Maybe you know what Morrison said?"

Regina wanted to savor the happiness that she was finally allowed to join the game of the cycle foreign words, head shaking, and shoulder shrugging a little longer. Her parents still smelled like Rummler when he had to wait too long for his food. So she already opened her mouth, slipped the napkin ring over her hand, and pushed it inch by inch up to her elbow. It was good that Owuor had taught her to catch sounds that she did not understand. One had only to lock them up in one's head and take them out from time to time without opening one's mouth.

"Every month," she remembered, but she let her parents' amazement stroke her for too long and so missed the right moment to repeat the magic. Despite that, her ears were rewarded when her father praised her: "You are a clever child," he said. He looked like the white cock with the blood-red comb when he said that. But he quickly changed back into her father, with his red eyes full of impatience, who took the book from the table, put it down immediately again, rubbed his hands together, and sighed, "I am a real blockhead. A real nebbish of a blockhead."

"Why?"

"One has to be able to spell the words one wants to look up in a lexicon, Regina."

"Your father does not have enough spunk; he thinks and I act," Jettel said. "Aver," she read, "means to hold one's own, stand one's ground. Aviary is a birdhouse. That is even more stupid. Then there is 'avid,' which means eager."

"Jettel, that is pure nonsense. We will never find out this way."

"What good is a lexicon if you can't find anything in it?"

"Okay, just give it to me. I am going to look under E. 'Evergreen,'" Walter read, "means always green."

Regina noticed for the first time that her father could spit even better than Owuor. She let go of Rummler's head and clapped her hands.

"Be quiet, Regina. Damn it, this is not child's play. It must be evergreen. Of course, Morrison talked about his maize fields that are always green. Funny, I would never have thought that of him."

"No," Jettel said and her voice had become very soft, "I know. Really, I know. 'Every' stands for each and all. Walter, listen, every month must mean 'jeden Monat.' That is definitely it. Do you think that is supposed to mean that he is going to give us six pounds every month?"

"I do not know. We have to wait and see if this miracle is going to be repeated."

"You always talk of miracles." Regina lay in waiting to see if her father would recognize that she had imitated her mother's voice, but neither her eyes nor ears captured any prey.

"This time he is right," Jettel whispered, "he simply must be right." She got up, pulled Regina close to her body, and gave her kiss that tasted like salt.

The miracle became reality. At the beginning of each month, Mr. Morrison came to the farm, had two cups of tea first, went to see his cows and chickens, walked to the maize fields, returned for a third cup of tea, and, without saying anything, put six pound notes on the table.

Jettel could puff up her pride like Owuor when the fateful day was mentioned that had changed life in Rongai. "See," she would say, and Regina repeated the well-known sentence with her without moving her lips, "what good is all your wonderful education if you haven't even learned English yet?"

"No good, Jettel, no good at all. Just like my robe. That is no good either."

When Walter said this, his eyes were not as tired as in previous months. On good days, they looked the way they had at the time before his malaria, and then he even laughed when Jettel relished her triumph, called her "my little Owuor," and, during the night, he enjoyed the tenderness that both had thought lost forever.

"They made me a brother last night," Regina said under the thorn-tree.

"That is good," Aya replied. "Suara is not going to turn into a child."

One night, Walter suggested, "We are going to send Regina to school. When Süßkind goes to Nakuru next time, he will have to find out how to go about it."

"No," Jettel objected, "not yet."

"But you were always so intent on it. And I want it to happen, too."

Jettel felt that her skin started to burn, but she was not ashamed of her embarrassment. "I have not forgotten," she said, "what happened the day before the locusts came. You thought at the time that I did not understand what you were telling me, but I am not as stupid as you think. Regina will still be able to learn to read when she is seven. We need the money for mother and Käthe now."

"How do you think that is going to work?"

"We have enough to get by here. Why can't we leave it at that for a while? I figured it out exactly. If we do not touch the money, it will take us seventeen months to get the hundred pounds we need to bring mother and Käthe here. And we will even have two pounds to spare. You will see, we are going to make it."

"If nothing happens."

"What is supposed to happen? Nothing ever happens here."

"But in the rest of the world, Jettel. Things do not look good at home."

Jettel's eagerness and her willingness to sacrifice, the joy with which she put the six pounds into a little box every month and counted them again and again, the confidence that she would succeed in accumulating the sum for the rescue in time, were harder to bear for Walter than the news that he heard every hour of the day and often also during the night.

The intervals between the letters from Breslau and Sohrau, too, had become longer; the letters themselves, despite all efforts not to express fear, were so worrisome that Walter often asked himself if his wife really did not understand that hope was a crime. Sometimes, when he thought that she was indeed unsuspecting, he was touched and envious. When his depression, however, tortured him to such a degree that he was even unable to feel gratitude for his own rescue, his despair turned into hatred for Jettel's illusions.

His father had written that he had been unsuccessful in his attempts to sell the hotel, that he hardly was going out anymore, that there were only three Jewish families still living in Sohrau, that he was, however, well under the circumstances and did not want to complain. The day after the burning of the synagogues, he wrote, "Liesel might be able to emigrate to Palestine. If I could only persuade her to leave this old donkey behind." After November 9, 1938, his father had eliminated the confident incantation "Until we see each other again" from his letters.

In the letters from Breslau, the fear of censorship was evident in every line. Käthe wrote of restrictions "that are very hard on us" and, in every letter, mentioned friends "who suddenly had to go on a trip and had not been heard from since." Ina reported that she was unable to rent out rooms any longer and wrote, "I leave the house only at certain times." The present for Regina's birthday in September had been sent in February. Walter shuddered when he grasped the hidden meaning. His mother- and sister-in-law no longer dared to count on longer periods of time and had given up all hope that they still might escape from Germany.

He suffered because it was his duty to confront Jettel with the truth, and he knew that it was a sin not to do so. But when she counted her money and while doing so looked like a child who has exactly calculated when her wishes are going to come true, he let every opportunity for a discussion go by. His silence struck him as a defeat; he was disgusted with his own weakness. He went to bed after Jettel and got up before she did.

Time seemed to stand still. Mid-August, Süßkind's boy brought a letter with the message: "We now definitely have the damned East Coast fever in Sabbatia. For the time being, there is no more Sabbath. I have to pray for my cows and make an attempt to save at least some. If your cows start running around in circles, it is too late. That means that the disease is already in Rongai."

Jettel was upset when Walter showed her the letter. "But why can't he come? After all, he is not sick."

"He has to at least be on the farm when his cows are dying. Süßkind, too, fears for his job. There are more and more refugees coming into the country who want to be on a farm. That makes each of us easier to replace."

Süßkind's visits on Fridays had been the high point of the week, remembrance of a life full of discussions, diversion, a mutual give and take, a spark of normality. Now the anticipation and the pleasure itself were gone. The more monotonous life became, the more Jettel longed for Süßkind's reports about Nairobi and Nakuru. He always knew who had just arrived in the country and where they had ended up. Even more, she missed his good spirits, his jokes and compliments, and his optimism, which always made him look ahead and confirmed her belief in the future.

Walter suffered even more. Since he had been on the farm, and especially after his malaria, he had looked on Süßkind as the one who had saved his life. He needed his friend's self-confident nature to counteract his depression and his longing for Germany, which made him doubt his sanity. Süßkind was proof to him that a man could reconcile himself to the fate of being homeless. Even more, he was his only contact with life.

Even Owuor lamented that the *bwana* Sabbatia no longer came to the farm. Nobody jiggled his mouth as well as he did when the pudding was brought in. Nobody could laugh as loud as the *bwana* Sabbatia when Owuor wore the robe and sang "Ich hab' mein Herz in Heidelberg verloren." "*Bwana* Sabbatia," Owuor complained when another day turned into night without a visit, "is like a drum. I beat it in Rongai, and it calls back from the Menengai."

"Even our radio misses Süßkind," Walter said on the night of September 1. "The battery is dead, and without his car we cannot recharge it."

"Do you not listen to the news anymore now?"

"No, Regina. The world has died for us."

"Is the radio dead, too?"

"Dead as a doornail. Now only your ears will know what is new. So lie down on the ground and tell me something nice."

Regina was dizzy with joy and pride. After the short rains, Owuor had taught her to lie down flat and motionless to coax the sounds out of the earth. After that, she often heard Süßkind's car before it could be seen, but her father had never believed in her ears, had always said angrily, "Nonsense," and had not even been ashamed when Süßkind actually arrived after she had announced him. Now that he was no longer able to hear voices from the dead radio, he finally understood that without Regina's ears he was as deaf as old Cheroni, who led the cows to be milked. She felt strong and clever. Still, she took her time when hunting for those sounds, which had to go on safari across the Menengai before they could be heard in Rongai. After the death of the radio, Regina first lay down at night on the stony path that led to the house, but the earth did not release any sounds other than the trees talking in the wind. The next morning, too, she received only silence, but at midday her ears became awake.

When the first sound reached her, Regina did not dare to disturb it even with her breath. The next one should have taken as little time as a bird that flies from one tree to the next. But she had to wait so long for the sound that Regina was afraid that she might have held her ear too high and had heard only the drums in the wood. She wanted to get up before disappointment made her throat dry, but a knocking in the earth jumped at her so violently that she had to hurry. This time, her father should not think that she had seen the car and not heard it beforehand.

She cupped her hands in front of her mouth to make her voice heavy and shouted, "Quick, Papa, somebody is coming to visit us. But it is not Süßkind's car."

The truck that labored up the steep slope to the farm was bigger than all others that had ever come to Rongai. The children ran from the huts to the house and pushed their naked bodies together. They were followed by the women with infants on their backs, young girls with calabashes full of water, and goats guided by barking dogs. The *shamba* boys threw down their hoes and left the fields, the herdsmen abandoned their cows.

They held their arms above their heads, screamed as if the locust had returned, and sang songs that otherwise only wafted over from the huts at night. The laughter of the curious and excited people again and again pushed against the Menengai and returned as a clear echo. It stopped as suddenly as it had started, and in the silence the truck came to a halt.

First, there was nothing to see but a cloud of red dust, which simultaneously rose and fell from the sky. When it dissolved, eyes became big and limbs stiff. Even the oldest men in Rongai, who no longer counted the rainy seasons they had lived through, first had to conquer their eyes before they were ready to see. The truck was as green as the woods, which never get dry, and in the back on the platform for animals were no oxen or cows on their first safari but men with light skin and big hats.

Next to Aya and Owuor, Walter, Jettel, and Regina stood motionless near the water barrel in front of the house and were afraid to lift their heads, but still they all saw the man next to the driver push the truck door open and climb down slowly.

He wore short khaki pants and had very red legs and black shiny boots, which chased the flies out of the grass with every step he took. In one hand, the man held a piece of paper that was brighter than the sun. With the other, he touched his cap, which lay like a flat, dark-green plate on his head. When the stranger finally opened his mouth, Rummler barked too.

"Mr. Redlich," the big voice commanded, "come along. I have to arrest you. We are at war."

Nobody had moved yet. Then a familiar sound came from the truck. It was Süßkind who exclaimed, "Walter, old chap, don't tell me you didn't know. The war has started. We are all being interned. Come on, climb in. And do not worry about Jettel and Regina. The women and children will be picked up later today and brought to Nairobi."

4

THE YOUNG MEN with memories still fresh of school in England and happy nights at Oxford considered the outbreak of the war as not too unwelcome a diversion, as much as they regretted it for the endangered mother country. The same was true for the veterans with their withered illusions, who were fulfilling their duties in the police force in Nairobi and the military forces within the country with a certain discontent brought on by the monotonous routine of colonial life. For them, all of a sudden, instead of stolen cattle, occasional tribal wars between the natives, and dramas of jealousy within the proper British society, the fate of the crown colony itself was at stake.

Within the past five years, the colony had accepted more and more people from the continent, and it was just those people who were now leading the government agencies into uncharted waters. During times of peace, these penniless refugees with names that were as hard to pronounce as to spell had already been considered a nuisance because of their horrible accents and their ambitions, which the British, with their tendency for moderation, did not consider sportsman-like. Still, they were generally regarded as disciplined and easy to control. For a long time, it had been the main goal of the government agencies not to shake up the established life and economic structure of Nairobi, thus to protect the city from emigrants, and to settle the newcomers on farms. This always had happened very quickly, thanks to the Jewish community, whose long-standing members felt the same way, and to the great satisfaction of the farmers.

The war brought new challenges. The only important thing now was to protect the country from people who by birth, language, education, tradition, and loyalty might be linked more closely to the enemy than to the host country. The authorities knew that they had to act quickly and efficiently and were at first not at all dissatisfied with the way they had handled this unusual task. Within three days, all enemy nationals from the towns and even those from the remote farms had been handed over to the military forces in Nairobi and informed that their status had been changed from "refugee" to "enemy alien."

Circumstances had been similar during the World War, which at this point had become the First, and there were enough veteran officers who knew what had to be done. All men from the age of sixteen on were to be interned; men who were sick and in need of care were sent to hospitals with adequate facilities to guard them. The barracks of the second regiment of the King's African Rifles in the Ngong, twenty miles from Nairobi, were immediately evacuated.

The soldiers who had been ordered to pick up the men from the farms had proceeded unexpectedly fast and had been very thorough. "A little too thorough," as Colonel Whidett, who was in charge of Operation Enemy Aliens, stated in his first address after its successful conclusion.

The young soldiers had not even given the "bloody refugees," as they called them in their recently revived patriotism, any time to pack a suitcase and through their overzealous actions had promptly created totally avoidable difficulties for their superiors. The men, who were delivered to Ngong dressed only in pants, shirt, and hat, and occasionally even in pajamas, had to be dressed. In the mother country, putting them into jail outfits would immediately have solved this problem.

In Kenya, however, it was as immoral as it was tasteless to put whites into the same clothes as black inmates. There was not a single European in any of the country's jails, and consequently there were not even such matter-of-fact items for daily use as toothbrushes, underwear, or wash-cloths. In order not to burden the budget during the first days of the war and to avoid unpleasant questions from the Ministry of War in London, the surprised citizens were asked for appropriate donations. This resulted in a number of painfully ironic letters to the *East African Standard*.

Even worse was the fact that the interned men were now wearing the same kind of khaki uniforms as their guards. In military circles, especially, the unwanted but necessary similarity in appearance between the defenders of the homeland and their potential aggressors created a lot of annoyance. It was impossible to silence rumors that the men from the continent were abusing the seriousness of the situation. There were already reports that they saluted each other grinning and, if they spoke English, asked the guards quite unabashedly for the way to the front. The Sunday *Post* suggested to its readers, "If you meet a man in a British uniform, for your own safety, have him first sing 'God Save the King.'" The *Standard* limited itself to a simple commentary, which, however, ran under the headline "Scandal."

Even under the strictest interpretation of the safety rules, women and children did not have to be interned right away. The military forces thought it quite sufficient just to confiscate radios and cameras to prevent their misuse during potential contacts with the enemy on the European battlegrounds. On the other hand, they remembered that, even in 1914, and also during the Boer War, it had been customary to bring women and children into camps. Even stronger was the argument that it was contrary to the British tradition of honor and a sense of responsibility to leave defenseless people without male protection on the farms. Once again, the reaction was fast and unofficial. As soon as the war began, no woman had to stay more than three hours alone on a farm.

Women and especially children could not be interned in the military barracks, but here, too, Colonel Whidett found a satisfactory solution. Without regard for the weekend pleasures of farmers from the highlands, the Norfolk Hotel, with its rich traditions, and the luxurious New Stanley were requisitioned as housing for the families of enemy aliens. This solution offered itself particularly because only Nairobi had enough competent officials to deal with a situation that could not remain long unchanged.

The interned women were stunned when they arrived in Nairobi after long and arduous journeys from the farms. They were greeted enthusiastically by the hotel personnel, who up to then always had been instructed to greet guests cheerfully and who had not had enough time to become familiar with the changes the war had brought about. Physicians, nurses, childcare personnel, and teachers had also been ordered to the two hotels. Because of the urgency of the calls, these workers expected to find circumstances that could only have been caused by the war. Instead, they found out rather quickly that they were dealing not with an outbreak of contagious diseases or psychological problems but rather with language difficulties. Those could have been solved best with Swahili, which self-confident colonial officials, however, knew only half as well as the people who had been in the country only for a short time and who did not correspond at all to the usual notions of enemy agents.

The transport from Nakuru, Gilgil, Sabbatia, and Rongai was the last to arrive at the Norfolk Hotel. Jettel, consoled and reassured by her companions in misfortune, had, during the journey, overcome her fear of an uncertain future and the shock of the sudden separation from Walter, and she considered the unexpected release from the loneliness and monotony of the farm a blessing. She was so fascinated by the elegance and animated atmosphere of the hotel that, just like the other women, she at first lost sight of the reason for the abrupt change in her life.

Regina was blinded, as well. She had refused to get onto the truck at Rongai and had had to be pulled up by force. During the journey, she had cried and called for Owuor, Aya, Suara, Rummler, and her father, but the radiance of the many lights, the blue velvet curtains on the high windows, the pictures in gilt frames, and the red roses in silver goblets immediately distracted her from her sorrow. She stood with her mouth open, held onto her mother's dress, and stared at the nurses with their starched white bonnets.

Dinner had just started. It was one of those carefully composed menus for which the Norfolk was famous not only in Kenya but all over East Africa. The chef, a man from South Africa with previous experience on two luxury liners, had no intention of breaking with the tradition of the house just because somewhere in Europe a war had broken out and there were only women and children in the dining room.

The day before, lobster had been delivered from Mombasa, lamb from the highlands, and green beans, celery, and potatoes from Naivasha. The meat was accompanied by a mint sauce, which was considered a legendary specialty of the Norfolk, a gratin in the French manner, tropical fruits in delicate sweet pastry, and a selection of cheeses, which, with Stilton, Cheshire, and Cheddar from England, still matched peacetime offerings. The cook attributed the fact that many portions of lobster and lamb were returned to the kitchen untouched the first night to the fatigue of the guests. When the distaste for shellfish and meat remained, however, a representative from the Jewish community in Nairobi was asked for advice. He was able to shed light on Jewish dietary laws but did not know why the children had poured the mint sauce over their desserts. The cook cursed first the "bloody war" and very soon afterward the "bloody refugees."

Even a spacious hotel like the Norfolk did not have enough room for such an unusual rush of guests. Thus, two women and their children had to share a room. There was some hesitation about using the rooms intended for personnel. Those were empty because the women and children, contrary to the usual custom in the Norfolk, had arrived without their personal houseboys and *ayas,* but it went against the hotel manager's sense of good taste to have Europeans live in rooms intended for black people.

Regina shared a couch with a girl who was a few months older than she. This created difficulties during the first night because both of them, as only children, were not used to close contact, but it helped them all the sooner to overcome their fear and shyness. Inge Sadler was a robust child who wore Bavarian dresses and slept in flannel night-gowns with blue and white checks. She was very independent, amiable, and obviously happy about the prospect of having a girlfriend. Regina mistook her Bavarian dialect initially for English, but she soon got used to her new friend's pronunciation and admired her because she was able to read and write.

Inge had gone to school in Germany for a year and was ready to pass on her knowledge to Regina. When Inge woke up at night, she cried with fear and had to be calmed down by her mother, who, despite the energy and strictness she displayed during the day, could console her as softly as Aya and who won Regina's heart as quickly as Owuor had done in their old life. When Regina told Mrs. Sadler about Suara, she took some blue wool out of her sewing basket and crocheted a deer for her.

The Sadlers were from Weiden, in the Upper Palatinate, and had arrived in Kenya only half a year before the war broke out. There were two brothers who had owned a clothing store; the third had been a farmer. Their three wives were too determined to bemoan the splendor of their past. They knitted sweaters and sewed blouses for a well-known store in Nairobi and had encouraged their husbands to lease a farm in Londiani, which after only six months had already turned its first profit.

Inge had witnessed the November 9 pogrom in Weiden and had watched as the storefront windows of her parents' business were shattered, fabric and clothes were thrown into the street, and their apartment plundered. Her father and both uncles had been dragged from the house, beaten, and deported to Dachau. When they returned four months later, Inge was hardly able to recognize them. During the second week in the Norfolk, because she was embarrassed about her nightly crying, she told Regina about her experiences, which she had never discussed with her parents.

"My Papa," Regina said when Inge had finished, "did not get beaten by anyone."

"He is not Jewish, then."

"You're lying."

"You do not even come from Germany."

"We come from the homeland," Regina explained, "from Leobschütz, Sohrau, and Breslau."

"In Germany, all Jewish people get beaten up. I know that for sure. I hate the Germans."

"Me, too," Regina agreed. "I hate the Germans."

She intended to tell her father as soon as possible about her new hatred, about Inge, about the clothes on the street and Dachau. Even though she mentioned her father far less frequently than Owuor, Aya, Suara, and Rummler, she did miss him and felt the separation even more because her conscience bothered her. She had been lying on the ground and had been the first to hear the truck that had driven all of them away from Rongai.

At the small pond with the white water lilies, which in the midday heat were covered by yellow clouds of butterflies, she told Inge her secret: "I started the war."

"Nonsense, the Germans started the war. Everyone here knows that."

"I have to tell my Papa that."

"He already knows."

Only after this conversation did Regina notice that all the women were talking about the war. They were no longer as happy as in the first days after the internment. More and more they were saying, "When we are going to be back at the farm," and none of the women wanted to be reminded of the high spirits with which they had arrived in Nairobi.

The change of tone at the Norfolk increased their longing for life on the farm.

The hotel manager, a gaunt and not very amiable man by the name of Applewaithe, had long ago ceased all endeavors to hide his revulsion for people who were unable to pronounce his name. He loathed children, with whom up till then he had not been forced to interact privately or professionally, and did not allow the young mothers to warm up the milk for their babies in the kitchen, to hang diapers to dry on the balconies, or to put prams under the trees. He made it increasingly more obvious to the women that to him they were unwelcome guests and, even worse, enemy aliens.

After the first confused euphoria, which had been created by the happiness of being together, the women returned to reality with consternation and guilt. Almost all of them still had relatives in Germany, and they understood now that there was no escape anymore for their parents, siblings, and friends. The knowledge of this finality and the additional realization of the uncertainty of their own future paralyzed them. They longed for their husbands, who had previously made all decisions alone and who had been responsible for the family and whose whereabouts they did not even know. The knowledge of their powerlessness perplexed them and led first to small conflicts and then to apathy, which made them seek refuge in the past. The women tried to outdo each other with descriptions of how wonderfully they had fared in a life that with every day of enforced idleness shone more brightly in their memories. They were embarrassed about their tears and even more when they said "home" or "at home" and did not know anymore if they were talking about the farms or about Germany.

Jettel suffered very much from her unfulfilled longing for protection and consolation. She yearned for the life in Rongai, with Owuor's good mood and the familiar rhythm of the days, which seemed not lonely to her anymore but full of confidence and future. She even missed her fights with Walter, which in retrospect had become a series of tender banter, and she started crying if she only mentioned his name. After each outbreak, she would say, "If my husband knew how I am suffering here, he would immediately come and get me."

Most of the time, the women retired to their rooms when Jettel indulged in her despair, but one night when her grief was even louder than usual, Elsa Conrad snapped at her rather unexpectedly and quite loudly: "Just stop whining and do something. Do you think I would sit here and wail if they had taken my husband away? You young women are disgusting."

Jettel was so taken aback that she immediately stopped sobbing. "What am I to do?" she asked in a voice that had lost all its weepiness.

From the first day in the Norfolk on, Elsa Conrad had been an authority who was respected by everyone and who did not tolerate any contradictions. She was not afraid of confrontations and people, was the only Berliner in the group, and was the only one who was not Jewish. Her outward appearance was immediately imposing. Elsa, so heavy that she was nearly immobile, wrapped her body in long flowery garments during the day and in low-cut, festive ones at night. She wore fire-engine-red turbans, which frightened the babies so much that they started screaming the moment they saw her.

Elsa never got up before ten in the morning, had succeeded in persuading Mr. Applewaithe to have her breakfast served in her room, and constantly admonished children and, with the same impatience, women who buried themselves in their grief or complained about trifles. She was feared only during the first days. Her ready wit made her provocations tolerable, and her sense of humor made up for her temperament. When she told her story, she became a heroine.

Elsa had owned a bar in Berlin and had never made it a habit to put up with guests whom she disliked. A few days after the burning of the synagogues, a woman had come into Elsa's bar with two companions, and, even before taking off her coat, she had started giving an inflammatory speech against the Jews. Elsa had taken her by the collar of her coat, put her outside, and shouted, "Where do you think your expensive fur came from? You stole it from the Jews, you whore."

This had gotten her six months in prison and then an immediate deportation from Germany. Elsa had arrived penniless in Kenya, and already during the first week she had been hired as a nanny by a Scottish couple in Nanyuki. She did not get along well with the children; all the better, though, with the parents despite the fact that she only knew a few bits of English, which she had learned on the boat. She taught the parents German card games and the cook how to pickle eggs and fry hamburgers. At the start of the war, the Scots, with a heavy heart, had to let Elsa go, but they had not allowed her to be taken by truck. They had brought her to the Norfolk in their car, bade her farewell, embraced her, and cursed the English and Chamberlain.

Elsa knew only victory. "What am I to do?" she imitated Jettel's voice on the evening when she set the tracks for the future. "Do you want to sit here throughout the entire war and twiddle your thumbs while your husbands are being detained? Why do you look at me so stupidly? Can't you forget for once that you were placed on a pedestal? Sit down on your spoiled behinds and write to the government agencies. It can't be that hard to make them understand that the Jews are not for Hitler. One of the fine ladies here I am sure will have gone to school and will know enough English to write a letter."

The suggestion, even though it promised little success, was accepted for the sole reason that they all were more afraid of Elsa's fury than of the British army. She was as good at organizing as talking and ordered four women with sufficient knowledge of English and Jettel because of her good handwriting to formulate letters that documented their experiences and explained their point of view. It took surprisingly little time to convince Mr. Applewaithe that it was his duty to forward the mail for people who were not allowed to leave the hotel premises.

Even Elsa had not anticipated the quick success the action would have. The military agencies were swayed not by the tone or content of the letters but by the fact that they themselves had developed misgivings. After the first reaction from London, there had been doubts in Nairobi about whether all of the refugees really needed to be interned and whether it would not have been more rational to examine their political attitudes first.

Another factor was that many farmers anticipated being called up for military duty and wanted to be assured that their farms would be taken care of by the inexpensive and pleasantly reliable refugees. The letters in the *East African Standard* almost exclusively concerned the question why on earth prisoners of war had to live in luxury hotels in Nairobi. The owners of the Norfolk and the New Stanley, too, urged their release. Colonel Whidett considered it wise to show some flexibility for a start. As a first measure, he allowed contacts between couples with children and promised further considerations. Exactly ten days after Mr. Applewaithe had delivered the letters to the military agencies, the army trucks arrived again. Their mission was to bring mothers and children to the men's camp in Ngong.

The men's experiences had been similar to those of the women. The internment had brought them out of their loneliness and speechlessness back to life. The exultation brought on by the release from their isolation had been tremendous. Old acquaintances and friends who had seen each other last in Germany met again; fellow sufferers from the boats embraced each other; strangers found out that they had mutual friends. Through days and nights, experiences, hopes, and views were exchanged. The escapees found out about others' anguish that made their own appear small. They learned to be part of something again and were allowed to talk. It seemed as if a dam had broken.

After the time on the farms, alone with wife and children and the obligation to keep a stiff upper lip and to deny fear, or even after years alone on a farm, they all were glad to live with a group of men. Temporarily at least, all were without financial worries and without the tormenting certainty that a dismissal meant the immediate loss of a place to live. This breathing spell alone tricked the spirit into believing in a healing sense of security. It was Walter who came up with words that were quoted again and again afterward: "Now the Jews finally have a king again who takes care of them."

During the first days at the camp, it seemed to him as if, after a long journey, he had met distant relatives with whom he immediately felt a bond. The former attorney Oscar Hahn, from Frankfurt, for more than six years a farmer in Gilgil, Kurt Piakowsky, a physician from Berlin and now the supervisor of laundry services in the Nairobi hospital, and the dentist Leo Hirsch, who had found a place as a manager of a goldmine in Kisumu, had been Walter's fraternity brothers, and they were always ready to exchange reminiscences about mutual friends and the pleasures of student life.

Heini Weyl, the friend from Breslau, had retained his courage to face life and his sense of humor despite yellow fever and amoeba-induced dysentery. Henry Guttman, with his enviable optimism, was also from Breslau. He had been too young to lose a profession and livelihood in Germany and was one of a small circle of chosen ones who had more of a future than a past. Max Bilawasky, who had ruined himself within a year on his own farm, was from Kattowitz and knew Leobschütz.

Siegfried Cohn, a bicycle dealer from Gleiwitz, was a well-paid engineer in Nakuru now and had even succeeded in finding a linguistic connection to his new life by mixing his hard Upper Silesian accent with a nasal English intonation. Walter was ecstatically happy about Jakob Oschinsky. He had owned a shoe store in Ratibor, had found shelter at a coffee farm at Thika, and on a journey once had stayed overnight at Redlich's hotel in Sohrau. He remembered Walter's father well and raved about Liesel's beauty, kindness, and spice cake.

All the interned men had had similar experiences. They retrieved long-buried pictures from their subconscious, which worked like a fountain of youth on their confused souls. Still, the euphoria among the men did not last as long as that among the women. They realized only too soon that a common mother tongue and memories are insufficient substitutes for a homeland, stolen possessions, the loss of pride and honor, and the erosion of self-confidence. When the hastily scarred wounds opened up again, they were more painful than before.

The war had extinguished any spark of hope that they could establish new roots in Kenya quickly and for the simple reason that they no longer wanted to be outsiders or outcasts. Also, the illusion, long held against all common sense, that they might yet be able to help their loved ones back in Germany and to bring them to Kenya had died in each of them. Even though he tried to fight it, Walter gave up his father and his sister as just as irretrievably lost as his mother- and sister-in-law.

"They cannot expect any help from the Poles," he told Oscar Hahn, "and the Germans regard them as Polish Jews. Fate has confirmed once and for all for me that I have failed."

"We have all failed. Not now. In 1933. We believed in Germany for too long and closed our eyes. We must not lose our courage, though. You are not only a son; you are also a father."

"A great father, who does not even earn enough money for the rope to hang himself with."

"You should not even think that way," Hahn responded angrily. "So many of us are going to die who wanted to live that the ones who have been saved have no other choice but to carry on for their children's sake. Getting away with life is not only luck but also an obligation. Faith in life, too. Tear Germany out of your heart for good. Then you will be able to live again."

"I have tried. It does not work."

"That's what I thought, too, before, and now when I think of the splendid Frankfurt attorney and notary Oscar Hahn, who had a huge office and more honorary positions than hair on his head, he seems like a stranger to me whom I might have known a long time ago. Walter, old boy, use the time here to come to peace with yourself. Then you will be able to start anew once we get out of here."

"That is just what is driving me crazy. What is going to happen to me and my family once King George is no longer taking care of us?"

"You still have your position in Rongai."

"You pointed out the 'still' beautifully."

"How about calling me Oha?" Hahn smiled. "My wife invented that name for the emigration. She thought it sounded less German than Oscar. My Lilly is a splendid woman. Without her, I would never have dared to buy the farm in Gilgil."

"Does she know that much about agriculture?"

"She was a concert singer. She knows a lot about life. The houseboys adore her when she sings Schubert. And the cows immediately give more milk. I hope you will meet her soon."

"So you subscribe to Süßkind's theory?"

"Yes."

"People like the Rubenses," Süßkind used to expound when they had discussions about the future and the attitude of the military agencies, "cannot afford to have all Jews classified as enemy aliens and left to simmer here for the entire war. I bet old Rubens and his sons are already busy explaining to the British that we were against Hitler a long time before they ever caught on."

Colonel Whidett, indeed, had to deal with problems for which he was quite insufficiently prepared. Almost every day, he asked himself if even more serious differences with the War Ministry in London could have been any more unpleasant than the regular visits of the five Rubens brothers in his office, not to mention the temperamental father. The colonel unashamedly admitted to himself that, until the outbreak of the war, the events in Europe had not interested him much more than the tribal conflicts between the Jaluo and the Lumbwa around Eldoret. However, it irritated him that the Rubens family was so well informed about truly shocking details and that he felt like an ignoramus whenever they came to visit him.

Whidett did not know any Jews with the exception of the brothers Dave and Bennie, whom he had met in his first year at boarding school at Epsom and whom he remembered as horribly ambitious students and miserable cricket players. He thus felt absolutely justified in the beginning when, during those unpleasant conversations to which he had been subjected by the times, he pointed to the country of origin of the interned men and to the resulting difficulties for his mother country, which could not be underestimated. Regrettably, however, his objections did not seem as irrefutable as he had originally thought—especially when he was forced to present them to these unwelcome discussion partners who had the persuasiveness of Arab rug dealers and the hypersensitivity of artists.

Like it or not, the Rubens family, who had deeper roots in Kenya than he himself and who spoke the same refined English as the "old boys" at Oxford, set Whidett thinking. Reluctantly, he began to consider the fate of people "who apparently had been wronged." Still, he used this careful expression only in private circles, and even then only grudgingly. After all, it was in keeping with neither his education nor his principles to know more than others about the events in that damned Europe.

Without much confidence in his own judgment, Whidett finally agreed to consider the suggestion that at least those people who worked on farms and most likely had no opportunity to establish contacts with the enemy might be released from camp. To his surprise, the suggestion was welcomed in military circles as quite perspicacious. Very soon, it also became evident that it was even necessary. Because of the situation in Abyssinia, London announced that it would dispatch an infantry regiment from Wales for which the colonel needed the barracks in the Ngong.

The trucks from the Norfolk and the New Stanley arrived at the camp one Sunday after lunch. When the men appeared in their khaki uniforms at the barbed-wire fence, the children waved full of embarrassment and their mothers seemed just as tense. Most of the women were dressed as if they had been invited to a high-society garden party.

Some were wearing low-cut dresses that they had last worn in Germany; some held small withered flowers in their hands, which the children had picked in the hotel gardens.

Walter saw Jettel in her red blouse and the white gloves she had bought for the emigration. He remembered the evening gown and found it difficult to swallow his anger. At the same time, though, it hit him how beautiful his wife was and that, even in their most intimate and fulfilled moments, he had deceived her with his broken heart, which was able to feel only the pulse of the past. He felt old, worn out, and insecure.

For a frightening few seconds, which seemed unmercifully long, even Regina was a stranger to him. She seemed to have grown during the four weeks of separation, and her eyes were different from the days at Rongai when she used to sit under the tree with Aya. Walter tried to remember the name of the deer in order to find the common bond he was longing for, but he could not think of the word anymore. At that moment, he saw Regina run up to him.

While she jumped up at him like a puppy, and even before she put her thin arms around his neck, he realized, paralyzed with alarm, that he loved his daughter more than his wife. Guiltily, and yet with an excitement that he considered revitalizing, he swore that neither of them would ever know this truth.

"Papa, Papa," Regina shouted in Walter's ear and brought him back to the present, which all of a sudden was a lot easier to bear than before, "I have a friend. Her name is Inge. She can even read. And Mama wrote a letter."

"What kind of a letter?"

"A real letter so that we could come and visit you."

"Yes," Jettel said, after having pushed Regina aside far enough to find a place at Walter's breast, "I wrote a petition to have you released."

"Since when does my Jettel know what a petition is?"

"But I had to do something for you. I could not just sit there and twiddle my thumbs. Maybe we can soon return to our Rongai now."

"Jettel, Jettel, whatever happened to you? After all, you were so miserably unhappy at Rongai."

"But the women all want to return to the farms."

Walter was touched by the pride in Jettel's voice, even more by the fact that she did not have the courage to look at him while she was lying. He longed to make her happy, but he could remember flatteries just as little as he could recall the name of the deer. He was glad when he heard Regina speak.

"I hate the Germans, Papa. I hate the Germans."

"Who taught you that?"

"Inge. They beat up her father and broke the windows in Dachau and threw all the clothing into the street. Inge cries during the night because she hates the Germans."

"Not the Germans, Regina, the Nazis."

"Are there Nazis, too?"

"Yes."

"I'll have to tell Inge. Then she will hate the Nazis, too. Are the Nazis as bad as the Germans?"

"Only the Nazis are bad. They drove us out of Germany."

"Inge never told me that."

"Well, go and find her and tell her what your father said."

"You will drive the child crazy," Jettel scolded after Regina had left, but she did not give Walter any time to answer. "Do you know," she whispered, "that there is no longer any hope for Mother and Käthe now that the war has started?"

Walter sighed but he felt nothing but relief about the fact that he finally was able to speak freely.

"Yes, I know. Father and Liesel are now trapped, as well. And just don't ask me how we can cope with this. I do not know."

When Walter saw that Jettel was crying, he hugged her and felt consoled that the tears, which he himself had not been able to summon for a long time now, could still give her relief. Despite its cause, this short moment of common emotions seemed too precious to him not to extend it and let it alleviate his despondency for a few heartbeats. But then he forced himself not to give in once again to that fear that had seduced him before into silence.

"Jettel, we are not returning to Rongai."

"Why? How do you know that?"

"I got a letter from Morrison this morning."

Walter took the letter from his pocket and held it out to Jettel. He knew that she was not able to read it, but he needed the reprieve that her confusion provided to pull himself together. He allowed himself to be humiliated by watching helplessly as Jettel's eyes were glued to the lines that Süßkind had translated for him a few hours earlier.

"Dear Mr. Redlich," Morrison had written, "I regret to inform you that there is at present no possibility of employing an enemy alien on my farm. I am sure you will understand my decision and wish you all the best for the future. Yours faithfully, William P. Morrison."

"Jettel, look at me, not at the letter. Morrison has given me his notice."

"But where are we going to go when you are released from here? What are we going to tell Regina? She is asking for Owuor and Aya every day."

"We had best leave it to Inge." Walter sounded tired. "I, too, will miss Owuor. Our lives consist only of farewells now."

"Did the others get the same type of letter?"

"Some of us. Most did not."

"Why us? Why always us?"

"Because you chose a nebbish for a husband, Jettel. You should have listened to your Uncle Bandmann. He told you so before we got engaged. Come on now, don't cry. There is my friend Oha. He was lucky; the Nazis already disbarred him in 1933. He now has his own farm in Gilgil. You have to meet him, and you do not have to be embarrassed. He already knows. He has even promised to help us. I do not know how he is going to be able to do that, but it makes me feel better that he said so."

5

On October 15, 1939, the notice board at Camp Ngong had two announcements that elicited widely different responses among the refugees. The news that the British battleship *Royal Oak* had been sunk by a German submarine was written in short British military terms and caused more confusion than sympathy for the simple reason that it was unclear to most of the readers who had started the attack at Scapa Flow Bay and who had won. The announcement, in flawless German, however, that any enemy alien with a steady position on a farm could count on an impending release created much excitement. The rumor, which had been making the rounds for several days, that the military agencies in Nairobi were planning the deportation of male internees to South Africa gained new life.

"Now I will have to take a manager for my farm after all," Oha declared when he found Walter behind the bathroom barracks after looking all over the place for him.

"Why? You will be out of here soon."

"But you won't."

"No, I have won the big prize. And Jettel and Regina, too. Do they send women and children to South Africa, too?"

"Good God, don't you ever get anything? You are going to manage my farm. At least, till you find a job. I am sure there is no provision against one enemy alien employing another. Süßkind is already translating the employment contract I have set up for you."

Even though Süßkind's knowledge of legal terms was imprecise and awkward, Colonel Whidett was satisfied. He was not inclined to spend the rest of the war dealing with people who upset his life, and his main goal was to release as many of them as possible. Not only did he order that Oscar Hahn and Walter should be among the first permitted to leave the camp; he also made arrangements for Lilly to be picked up from the New Stanley and for Jettel and Regina to be collected from the Norfolk and for all of them to be transported to Gilgil with the two men.

"Why are you doing all of this for us?" Walter had asked the last night at Ngong.

"I really should be telling you that it is my duty to help a fraternity brother," Hahn had replied, "but I will make it easier. I have gotten used to you, and Lilly needs an audience."

The Hahns' farm, with cows and sheep on gentle green hills and chickens that scratched in a sanded area next to the vegetable garden, with precisely laid-out maize fields and a white stone house with a freshly cut lawn behind it, surrounded by roses, carnations, and hibiscus, was called Arcadia and was reminiscent of a large German farm. The paths around the house were covered with stone, the outer walls of the kitchen building were painted in a blue and white diamond pattern, the outhouse was green, and the light-colored doors of the main house had a lacquer finish.

Under a tall cedar stood a pagoda covered with purple bougainvillea and with white chairs surrounding a round table. Manjala, the houseboy, sported a silver belt, which Lilly had worn at the last ball of her life, over his white *kanzu*, in which he served the meals. The poodle with the black curls, which glistened in the sun like tiny pieces of coal, was called Bajazzo.

Walter and Jettel felt like lost children in Arcadia who have been dropped home by their rescuers with the admonition never to run away by themselves again. It was not only the warmth and the serenity of their hosts that gave them new strength but also the safety of the house itself. Everything reminded them of a homeland that they had never experienced in such abundance.

The round tables covered with green leather, the heavy wardrobe from Frankfurt in front of the eggshell-colored curtains, chairs upholstered in gray velvet, easy chairs covered with flowered English linen, and a mahogany chest of drawers with gold mountings came from Oha's parents; the heavy sterling silver knives, forks, and spoons, the crystal glasses, and the bone china were part of Lilly's dowry. There were cabinets full of books, copies of Frans Hals and Vermeer on the light-colored walls, and in the living room a picture of an emperor's coronation in the Frankfurt Römer under which Regina sat every night and had Oha tell her stories. In front of the fireplace stood a piano with a white bust of Mozart on a red velvet cloth.

Immediately after sundown, Manjala carried in drinks in colorful glasses and, soon afterward, such familiar dishes as if Lilly were able to shop daily at a German butcher, bakery, and grocery store. Her voice, which seemed to sing even when she just called for the houseboys or fed the chickens, and Oha's Frankfurt accent seemed to Walter like messages from a foreign world. At night, Lilly sang the repertoire of her past.

The houseboys squatted in front of the door; the women with infants on their backs stood at the open windows and, during the intermissions, the poodle sat on its hind legs and barked quietly and melodically into the night. Even though Walter and Jettel had never been exposed to such musical events, they forgot all their depression during the nightly concerts and let romantic feelings sweep over them and restore their hopes and youth.

Oha enjoyed his guests as much as they did his hospitality, because neither he nor the people on the farm were able to sustain Lilly's need for a new audience long enough, but he knew that this state of happy giving and grateful receiving could not last.

"A man has to be able to support his family," he told Lilly.

"You talk like in the old days, Oha. You are and will always remain a German."

"Unfortunately. Without you we would be in the same hopeless situation as Walter. We lawyers just have not learned anything useful."

"A singer is more fortunate."

"Only if she is like you. By the way, I have written to Gibson."

"You wrote a letter in English?"

"It is only going to be in English once you have translated it. I would imagine that Gibson could use Walter. But don't tell him yet. He might get too disappointed otherwise."

Oha knew Gibson, who had sold him pyrethrum a few times, only casually. But he knew that he had been looking for a while for a man who was willing to work for six pounds on his farm in Ol' Joro Orok. Geoffrey Gibson owned a vinegar factory in Nairobi and had no intention of visiting his farm, on which he grew exclusively pyrethrum and flax more than four times a year. He reacted quickly.

"Exactly the right thing for you," Oha rejoiced when Gibson's answer arrived. "You will be killing neither cows nor hens there, and you do not have to be afraid of him, either. You will only have to build a house for yourself."

Ten days after the small truck had sputtered up the muddy road into the mountains of Ol' Joro Orok, the little house between the cedars was getting its roof. The Indian carpenter Daji Jiwan and thirty workers from the *shambas* built the house for the new *bwana* out of rough, gray stones. Before the roof was covered with grass, mud, and dung, Regina was allowed to sit one last time on the wooden planks, which, unlike those in the native huts, did not form a point but ran together diagonally.

Regina was lifted up by Daji Jiwan with his black shiny hair, light-brown skin, and gentle eyes, and climbed exactly to the middle of the roof. She sat there for a long time quietly just as she had lain with Aya under the trees at Rongai when she was a child and did not know what life was about.

She let her eyes travel to the high mountain with its white cover, which her father had told her was made of snow, and waited till they were satisfied. Then she turned her head quickly to the dark woods from where the drums at night told about the *shauris* of the day and the shrieks of the monkeys came at sunrise. After her body had gathered heat, she called down to her parents on the ground, "There is nothing more beautiful than Ol' Joro Orok." The echo came back more quickly, louder and clearer than in the days, which no longer existed, when the Menengai had answered. "There is nothing more beautiful than Ol' Joro Orok," Regina shouted again.

"She has forgotten Rongai quickly."

"So have I," Jettel said. "Maybe we will have better luck here."

"Oh, one farm is like the other. What is important is that we are together."

"Did you miss me at the camp?"

"Very much," Walter answered, wondering how long the new feeling of togetherness would be able to survive at Ol' Joro Orok. "What a pity about Owuor," he sighed. "He was a friend of the first hour."

"We were not enemy aliens then."

"Jettel, since when have you become cynical?"

"Cynicism is a weapon. That is what Elsa Conrad said."

"I think you should stick to your own weapons."

"I somehow have the feeling that this place is going to be even lonelier than Rongai."

"I am almost afraid so. Without Süßkind."

"On the other hand, we are not too far from Gilgil, from Oha and Lilly," Jettel said consolingly.

"Only three hours if you have a car."

"And without?"

"Then Gilgil is as far away as Leobschütz."

"Just wait, we will get there," Jettel insisted, "and, besides, Lilly has promised to visit us here."

"I hope she does not find out beforehand what people are saying here."

"What are they saying?"

"That even the hyenas do not last more than a year at Ol' Joro Orok."

Ol' Joro Orok consisted only of a few sounds, which Regina loved, and a *duka,* a tiny shop built of corrugated tin. Patel, the Indian who owned the shop, was a rich and dreaded man. He sold flour, rice, sugar, salt, lard in cans, pudding mix, jam, and spices. When dealers came to him from Nakuru, he offered them mangoes, papayas, cabbages, and leeks. He stocked gasoline in canisters, paraffin for lamps in bottles, and alcohol for the farmers in the area and thin wool blankets, khaki shorts, and rough shirts for his black customers.

The unfriendly Patel had to be kept in good humor, not only because of his merchandise but also because, three times a week, a car came from the railroad station at Thomson's Falls and delivered the mail to him. Whoever fell out of favor with Patel, and that could happen if one hesitated too long about a purchase, was punished by not getting his mail and thus being cut off from the world. The Indian had discovered very quickly that people from Europe were as avid about their letters and newspapers as his compatriots were about their rice, of which he never had a sufficient supply anyway.

In his surly way, Patel actually felt some sympathy for the refugees. Even though, for his taste, they were excessively careful with their

money, they had been declared "enemy aliens," and that was a clear in-
dication that the British did not like them. For his part, Patel despised
the British, who made him feel that he was on the same low level as the
blacks for them.

Gibson's farm was six miles from Patel's *duka;* it was situated nine
thousand feet high at the equator and was bigger than any other farm in
the area. Even Kimani, who had lived there before the first flax had
been planted, had to think for a long time about which way to go when
he wanted to reach a certain destination. Kimani, a Kikuyu about forty-
five years of age, was small, clever, and known to have a tongue that was
faster than the legs of a fleeing gazelle. He told the *shamba* boys what
they needed to do in the fields, and, as long as the farm was without a
bwana, he had determined their salaries.

As soon as the shadow reached the fourth groove on the water tank
late in the afternoon, Kimani banged against the metal to let everyone
know that the day's work had ended. Everyone on the farm respected
Kimani as the master of time and because he distributed the daily ration
of maize for the *posho* meal at night. Even the Nandis, who neither
worked in the fields nor received any maize but lived across the river
and tended their own herds, respected him.

Kimani had longed for a *bwana* on the farm for a long time. Most of
the farms at Gilgil, Thomson's Fall, and even Ol' Kalao had a *bwana.*
What use were all the respect and recognition if the land he was in
charge of was not good enough for a white man? The new house nourished his pride. When the work was finished at night and cold settled
on his skin, the stones remained warm enough to rub one's back against.
He talked full of respect with Daji Jiwan, who had achieved this splendor, even though he generally had an even lower opinion of Indians
than of the people of the Lumbwa tribe.

Kimani liked the new *bwana* with the dead eyes and the *memsahib*
with the flat stomach that looked as if no other child would come out of
it. He killed his distrust of strangers faster than usual and chased away
his reticence. He led Walter to the fields at the edge of the forest and to
the river that was filled with water only during the rainy season. He
touched the flowers of the pyrethrum and the bright blue flowers of the
flax, pointed to the color of the earth and again and again to the distance that the plants needed from each other in order to thrive. Kimani

had realized quickly that the new *bwana* had a long safari behind him and did not know anything about the things a man needed to know.

After the house was finished, Daji Jiwan constructed a kitchen building in the round shape of the native huts, and, after that, very reluctantly, a wooden shed over a deep pit with a bench with three holes in different sizes cut out of it. The toilet was Walter's invention, and he was as proud of it as Kimani was of his fields. He had the wooden door decorated with a cut-out heart, which soon became such an attraction on the farm that even Daji Jiwan finally made peace with the building, for which he himself did not have any use. His religion did not allow him to purge his body twice in the same location.

When the kitchen was finished, Kimani brought along a man whom he introduced as his brother, who was called Kania and who was supposed to sweep the rooms. He brought Kinanjui from the fields to make the beds. Kamau came to clean the dishes. He spent many hours sitting in front of the house, polishing the glasses, which he made sparkle in the sun. Finally, Jogona arrived. He was still almost a child, and his legs were as thin as the branches of a young tree.

"Better than an *aya*," Kimani told Regina.

"Was he a deer once upon a time?" she asked.

"Yes."

"But he does not talk."

"He is going to talk. *Kesho*."

"What is he supposed to do?"

"Cook for the dog."

"But we have no dog."

"We do not have a dog today," Kimani said, "but *kesho* we will."

Kesho was a good word. It meant tomorrow, soon, sometime, perhaps. *Kesho* was what people said when they needed peace for their head, ears, and mouth. Only the *bwana* did not know how impatience could be cured. Every day he asked Kimani for a boy who was to help the *memsahib* in the kitchen, but Kimani would only chew the air with his teeth closed before he answered.

"But you have a boy for the kitchen, *bwana*."

"Where, Kimani, where?"

Kimani loved this daily conversation. Often, when they got it to it, he released small barking sounds from his mouth. He knew that they irritated the *bwana*, but he could not do without them. It was not easy to tame the *bwana* with silence. His safari had been too long. Kimani's stubborn refusal to clarify the situation made Walter insecure. Jettel needed some help in the kitchen. She was not able to knead the bread dough by herself and found it difficult to lift the heavy containers with drinking water and impossible to motivate Kamau, the dishwasher, to tend to the smoky oven in the kitchen or to carry the food from the kitchen to the house.

"That is not my job," Kamau said as soon as he was asked to help and continued polishing the drinking glasses.

The daily discord made Jettel bad-tempered and Walter nervous. He knew that having insufficient personnel in the house made him look ridiculous in the eyes of the people on the farm. He was even more frightened at the thought that Mr. Gibson might appear suddenly and see immediately that his new manager was not even capable of getting a houseboy for the kitchen. He felt that he did not have much time left to insist on his demand.

On his walks with Kimani, he asked men who greeted him with an especially friendly *jambo* or who even just looked as if they might not have any objections to working in the house instead of the *shambas* whether they wanted to help the *memsahib* to do her cooking. Day after day, the same thing happened. The workers he talked to turned their heads away in embarrassment and uttered the same barking sounds as Kimani, stared at the sky, and then quickly ran away.

"It is like a curse," Walter said the night they had the fireplace lit for the first time. Kania had been busy with the new fireplace all day long, had swept it, wiped it clean, and piled wood in a pyramid in front of it. Now he crouched contentedly on his legs, lit a piece of paper, blew at the flame carefully until it glowed, and coaxed some warmth into the room.

"Why in heaven's name is it so difficult to find a boy for the kitchen?"

"Jettel, if I knew that, we would have one."

"Why don't you just order one to come?"

"I have too little experience as a commander."

"Oh, you with your refinement. All the women in the Norfolk were talking about how well their husbands were able to handle the houseboys."

"Why don't we have a dog?" Regina asked.

"Because your father is too dumb to even find a kitchen-boy. Did you not hear what your mother just said?"

"But a dog is not a kitchen-boy."

"Good grief, Regina, can't you once in your life keep your mouth shut?"

"It is not the child's fault."

"It is quite enough for me when you keep mourning for the fleshpots of Rongai."

"I did not say anything about Rongai," Regina insisted.

"And you," Jettel remembered, "always used to say one farm is just like the other."

"But this damned one here is not. It does have a fireplace, but no kitchen-boy."

"Don't you like the fireplace, Papa?"

It was the wary tone of Regina's voice that sparked Walter's anger. He felt only the urge, which seemed to him as childish as grotesque, not to hear and say another word. The three lamps for the night were standing on the windowsill.

Walter took his, filled it with paraffin, lit it, and turned the wick far down so that the lamp provided only a small shimmer of light.

"Where are you going?" Jettel cried, frightened.

"To the pub," Walter shouted back, but he immediately felt regret chafing his throat. "I assume a man can go tinkle by himself at times," he said and waved as if saying good-by for a longer time, but the joke misfired.

The night was cold and very dark. Only the fires in front of the *shamba* boys' huts glowed like small, light-red dots. A jackal, which had left too late to hunt, howled at the edge of the forest. Walter felt as if even that one were mocking him and pressed his hands tightly over his ears, but the noise did not stop. It teased him so painfully that at intervals he believed that he heard a dog barking. Those were the same humiliating sounds that Kimani had uttered when he had asked him for a kitchen-boy.

Walter called out Kimani's name in a low voice, but the echo that mocked him returned loudly. He realized that the rebellion in his head had begun to attack his stomach, and he rushed away from the house so that he did not have to get sick right in front of the door. The retching did not give him any relief. The sweat on his forehead, the dead feeling of his clammy hands, and the faint haze before his eyes reminded him of his malaria and the fact that at Ol' Joro Orok he had no neighbor for whom he could send if he needed help.

He rubbed his eyes and was relieved to discover that they were dry. Despite that, he felt moisture on his face and, afterward, such a frightening pressure on his chest that he felt as if he were falling down. When the barking became ever louder in his right ear, Walter threw the lamp into the grass and made his body stiff. Warmth rose up within him. A smell, which he could not place, first blew some memory across to him and then calmed his excitement. He realized that the shaky movements did not come from his heart. Finally he felt a rough tongue licking his face.

"Rummler," Walter whispered, "Rummler, you damned filthy bastard. Where did you come from? How did you ever find me?" He alternated between repeating the name and uttering terms of endearment that he never had thought of before; he held onto the strong neck of the dog with both hands, smelled his steaming fur, feeling his strength coming back. At last he was able to see clearly.

While Walter hugged the panting, excited animal in a fit of ecstasy, which embarrassed him, and petted it in amazement, he furtively looked around as if he were afraid to be discovered in the whirl of his tenderness. Then he saw a figure coming in his direction.

Slowly, because he was able to release himself only with difficulty from the embrace of excessive happiness and embarrassment, Walter picked up the lamp from the grass and turned the wick higher. First he only saw a figure that resembled a dark cloud, but soon he was able to make out the contour of a strong man who started running faster and faster. Walter also thought he could see the outlines of a coat that fluttered with each one of the big steps, even though there had been no wind for days.

Rummler whimpered and barked before his voice turned into a big happy yowl, which for a short moment drowned out every other sound and then suddenly turned into noises that could only have been uttered by a human being. A familiar sound rang loud and clear through the stillness of the night.

"'Ich hab' mein Herz in Heidelberg verloren,'" Owuor sang and stood in the yellow light of the lamp. A piece of his white shirt shone under his black robe.

Walter closed his eyes and waited, exhausted, for the moment when he would wake up from his dream, yet his hands felt the dog's back, and Owuor's voice remained. "*Bwana,* you are sleeping on your feet."

Walter managed to part his teeth, but he was unable to move his tongue. He did not even realize that he had opened his arms until he felt Owuor's body next to his own and the silk binding of the robe on his chin. For a few precious seconds, he allowed Owuor's face with the broad nose and the smooth skin to take on his father's features. He felt a cutting pain when the image of consolation and longing disintegrated, but the happiness remained.

"Owuor, you monster, where have you come from?"

"Monster," Owour repeated the strange word and swallowed with satisfaction because he had immediately succeeded in doing so. "From Rongai," he laughed and dug in his pant trousers under the robe and retrieved a small carefully folded piece of paper. "I have brought along some seeds," he said. "Now you can plant your flowers here, too."

"Those are my father's flowers."

"Those are your father's flowers," Owuor repeated. "They have been looking for you."

"You have been looking for me, Owuor."

"The *memsahib* does not have a cook in Ol' Joro Orok."

"No. Kimani did not find one for her."

"He has been barking like a dog. Did you not hear Kimani bark, *bwana*?"

"Yes. But I did not know why he was barking."

"It was Rummler who spoke through Kimani's mouth. He told you that he was on safari with me. It was a long safari, *bwana*. But Rummler has a good nose. He knew the way."

Owuor waited, full of eager expectation, if the *bwana* would believe the joke or if he were still as dumb as a young donkey and did not know that a man needed his head on a safari and not a dog's nose.

"I went back to Rongai at some point, Owuor, to get my things, but you were not there."

"A man who has to leave his house does not have good eyes. I did not want to see your eyes."

"You are clever."

"You said that," Owuor said happily, "the day the locusts came to the farm." He looked into the far clouds while talking as if he wanted to bring back the time, and yet he felt every small movement of the night. "There is the *memsahib kidogo*," he exulted.

Regina stood in front of the door. She shouted Owuor's name several times and each time louder, jumped up on him while Rummler licked her bare legs, released her throat and clicked her tongue. Even when Owuor put her back on the ground and she bent down to the dog and made his fur wet with her eyes and mouth, she did not stop talking.

"Regina, what are you babbling all the time? I don't understand a word."

"Jaluo, Papa. I am speaking Jaluo. Just like in Rongai."

"Owuor, did you know that she can speak Jaluo?"

"Yes, *bwana*. I know. Jaluo is my language. Here in Ol' Joro Orok there are only Kikuyu and Nandi, but the *memsahib kidogo* has the same tongue as I have. That is why I could come to you. A man cannot be where he will not be understood."

Owuor sent his laughter into the woods and afterward to the mountain with the hood of snow. The echo had the power that his hungry ears needed, and yet his voice was low when he said, "Of course, you know that, *bwana*."

6

THE NAKURU SCHOOL, on the steep hill that overlooked one of the most famous lakes of the Colony, was a favorite of those farmers who were unable to afford private school tuitions, yet valued the tradition and good reputation of a school. The upper-class families in Kenya considered the Nakuru School, which was public and, therefore, could not choose its students, "somewhat common," but parents who had to make do with it for financial reasons tended to negate this regrettably awkward situation by clearly pointing to the certainly unusual personality of its headmaster. He was an Oxford man with sound views, still hailing from Queen Victoria's time and, above all, without any of the newfangled pedagogical ideas: His principles did not include allowing one to have one's way or understanding the psyche of the children entrusted to him.

Arthur Brindley, who had been a member of the Oxford rowing team in his youth and had been decorated with the Victoria Cross in World War I, exhibited a healthy sense of proportion and lived up exactly to the ideal of education of the mother country. He never bored the parents with pedagogical theories, which did not interest them and which they would not have understood anyway. He limited himself to pointing out the motto of the school, "Quisque pro omnibus," which was emblazoned in gold-colored letters on the center wall of the auditorium and embroidered into the insignia sewn on to the jackets, ties, and hatbands of the school uniform.

Mr. Brindley was content and, on good days, even a little proud when he looked out of the window of his office in the imposing main building, built of white stone with heavy, round columns at the main

entrance. The many small, light-colored wooden buildings with corrugated tin roofs that served as dormitories and were, in his opinion,
unjustly derided as personnel quarters by the overly class-conscious
followers of private schools reminded him of his childhood in a village
in County Wilshire. The precisely laid-out rosebeds behind the thick
hedges around the male teachers' houses and the dense lawn between
the hockey fields and the female teachers' apartments made the headmaster think of a well-maintained English country estate. The lake,
with its surface colored pink by flamingoes, was close enough to delight
an eye trained for English loveliness, but still far enough away to prevent the children from developing an unnecessary longing for nature or
even for a world beyond the school boundaries.

Recently, however, the low trees with their thin stems, around which
climbing pepperbushes grew rampant, had begun to annoy the headmaster. For a long time he had thought that these trees were particularly
suited to the barren landscape of the Rift Valley, but he hardly found
them enjoyable anymore since he had realized that of late some of the
children were using them as a retreat during their leisure time. Mr.
Brindley had never expressly forbidden such a disturbing flight into a
private sphere, but he also had never before had any reason for such a
restriction. He was all the more upset by the fact that certain pupils, and
above all the new girls in the school, obviously found it hard to adjust to
a life that did not approve of individualism and outsiders.

For Mr. Brindley, such deviations from the harmonious norm were
indisputably the consequences of war. The headmaster had had to accept more and more students into his school who had very little sense of
the good old English virtues of not standing out and, above all, of putting the community before one's own person. A year after the outbreak
of the war, the agencies in Kenya had made school compulsory for all
white children. Mr. Brindley considered this not only a limitation on
parental freedom but also a rather exaggerated attempt on the Colony's
part to imitate the mother country in times of need.

The Nakuru School, in the center of the country, experienced especially drastic changes because of compulsory education. The school even
had to accept Boer children and had to be happy if there were not too
many of them. Most of them were sent to the Afrikaans School in Eldoret. The ones from the surrounding areas who ended up in Nakuru

were obstinate and, despite their limited linguistic skills, made no secret of their hatred for England. They did not try to get along with their fellow students, nor did they try to hide the fact that they were homesick. Yet, dealing with the hotheaded little Boers turned out to be easier than initially expected. They did not require any attention, and the teachers had only to make sure that the stubborn little rebels did not band together and disturb the school discipline.

The children of the so-called refugees represented a much bigger problem for the headmaster. They had the air of small, miserable characters from a Dickens novel when they were dropped off at the school by their parents, who had an embarrassing tendency toward typically continental goodbyes, with handshakes, embraces, and kisses. Their school uniforms were made from inexpensive material and had certainly not been purchased at the appropriate store for school supplies in Nairobi; instead, they had been sewn by Indian tailors. Almost none of the children wore the school insignia.

This contradicted the sound tradition of erasing all distinctions by wearing a school uniform and before the introduction of compulsory education would have been sufficient reason not to accept such students. But the headmaster suspected that he would be asking for unwelcome discussions with the highest school board in Nairobi if he proceeded in the usual manner. Arthur Brindley regarded the situation as disconcerting. He certainly was not intolerant of people who he had heard had been treated unjustly and were not permitted to stay where they belonged.

The fact that the Jewish children somehow seemed to be marked by their missing insignia, however, went against his pronounced sense of fairness. This also applied to the girls on Sundays, since they did not own the prescribed white dresses for church. He was sure that this was the reason that they put up such objections against going to church.

"Those damned little refugees," as Mr. Brindley called them among his colleagues, also plagued the headmaster in other ways. They hardly ever laughed, always looked older than they really were, and were driven by excessive ambition when measured by English standards. These serious, uncomfortably precocious creatures had barely mastered the language, and that had happened surprisingly fast, when, through their curiosity and their drive, which even to devoted teachers could be annoying, they became outsiders in a community in which only success in sports counted. Mr. Brindley himself, who had studied literature and history with very satisfying results, had no prejudice against intellectual achievements. Over the years, however, he had come to accept the tranquil classroom lethargy of the farmers' children as typical for the awareness of life in the Colony. He had never had to deal with religion. He was, therefore, often curious now whether the exaggerated desire to learn might have its origin in the teachings of Judaism. He also did not rule out completely his thesis that Jews had a traditional relationship to money from early on in their lives and maybe wanted to exact the most value for their tuition. After all, Mr. Brindley had found out more than once, even though he despised such insight into their private lives, that many of the refugee parents had had a hard time scraping together the few pounds for the tuition and then were unable to give their children the prescribed allowance.

A typical case for the headmaster was the girl with the unpronounceable first name and the three excited men who had delivered her six months ago for the first time to the Nakuru School. Inge Sadler did not speak a word of English then, even though she obviously was able to read and write, which, however, had seemed to her teachers more of a hindrance than an advantage. At first, the shy child had been quiet and seemed like a country girl who has been asked to serve tea at the manor house.

When Inge started to talk, though, her English was almost completely fluent if one disregarded her disturbing way of rolling all "r" sounds. After that, her progress was as impressive as it was irritating. Miss Scriver, who had fought adamantly against accepting a child without any language skills into her class, had to suggest herself that Inge should be placed in a class two grades above her own. Such advancement in the middle of the school year was unheard of in the school and was frowned upon because less talented students might suspect favoritism. Something like this could lead to unwelcome disputes with parents.

The girl from Ol' Joro Orok, with a first name as unpronounceable as that of the overambitious little one from Londiani, had also made it impossible for Mr. Brindley to maintain his established principle of not setting any precedents. Just like Inge before her, Regina had silently observed all events at the Nakuru School during her first weeks there and had only nodded fearfully when addressed. Then, with a suddenness that even Mr. Brindley found a bit provoking, she made it known to her teachers that she not only could speak English but was also able to read and write. Regina, too, had just been placed two grades higher. This way, the two little refugees, who were already inseparable, were sitting together again and would surely soon create trouble with their conspicuous ambition.

Mr. Brindley sighed whenever he thought about such complications. From habit, he looked toward the pepperbushes. His anger about talents that exceeded the norm seemed petty to him. But he did find it characteristic that just those two girls who had caused him to disregard his principle of equal treatment for all again and again separated themselves from the community. As he had expected, the two little dark-haired foreigners were sitting under the bushes. He was annoyed by the thought that they were probably studying during their free time and were also most likely speaking German to each other, even though all conversations in a foreign language were strictly forbidden outside the classroom.

The headmaster was wrong there. Inge had always spoken German to Regina only when she did not know how else to make herself understood. The unexpected reunion with her friend from the Norfolk had been happiness enough in the beginning, and she had the sure, strongly developed instinct of an outsider not to stand out more than necessary. Inge, therefore, subconsciously and unperturbed, pushed Regina to free herself from her speechlessness with as much determination as she herself had done several months earlier.

"Now," she said when Regina was allowed to sit next to her in class for the first time, "you know English, and we never have to whisper again."

"No," Regina agreed, "now everyone can understand us." Theirs was a community of fate between two contemporaries with very different temperaments. Inge considered Regina a good fairy who had liberated her from the pain of loneliness. Regina did not even try to have any contact with her fellow students. They were fascinating, but Inge was enough for her. Both girls were aware that it was not only the language barrier from their difficult beginnings that prevented their acceptance into the community. The happy, robust children of the Colony, who enjoyed their lives together despite the relentless school regulations, knew only the present. They seldom spoke of the farms where they lived and almost always without longing about their parents. They despised the homesickness of the new students, made fun of everything they did not understand, and detested physical weakness as much as intellectual achievements in class. The cold bath at six o'clock in the morning, the running before breakfast, the burned sweet potatoes with fatty mutton for lunch, and even the harassment by older students, detentions, or thrashings were unable to shake the composure of children who had been raised by their parents to be tough.

On Sundays, they only reluctantly started the prescribed letters home, while Inge and Regina regarded the hour of writing as the high-point of the week. Still, their letter writing was not without pain, because they knew that their parents were unable to read letters written in English, but they did not have the courage to confess this to any of their teachers. Inge found a solution by drawing small pictures in the margins; Regina used Swahili. Both surmised that they violated school policies and begged for help in their prayers in church. Inge had decided on that.

"Jews," she explained every Sunday, "are allowed pray in a church. If they keep their fingers crossed."

She was practical, resolute, and not as sensitive as her friend, stronger and more skillful. She had no imagination and certainly not Regina's talent for painting pictures with words. After the friends no longer had to take refuge in their mother tongue to understand each other, Inge enjoyed Regina's descriptions like a child who is being read to by her mother.

Regina reported extensively, with a marked sense of detail, full of longing and intoxicated with her memories about life at Ol' Joro Orok, about her parents, Owuor, and Rummler. Those were stories full of yearning that she conjured up from a gentle world. They set her body on fire and put salt into her eyes, but they were a great consolation in a world of full of indifference and coercion.

Regina was also able to listen. By asking over and over about the farm in Londiani and Inge's mother, whom she remembered well from the time in the Norfolk, she was able to make Inge feel that her memories were like an early homecoming. Both children hated school, feared their fellow students, and were suspicious of their teachers. Their heaviest burden, however, were the hopes their parents had invested in them.

"Father says I cannot disgrace him and have to be the best in class."

"Papa says the same," Regina nodded. "I often wish," she added on the Sunday two weeks before the vacations, "I had a Daddy and not a Papa."

"Then your father would not be your father," Inge, who usually hesitated a while before she followed Regina on her flight of fancy, decided.

"Yes, he would be my father. I would not be Regina then. With a Daddy, I would be Janet. I would have long blond braids and a school uniform made of really good material. And I would have insignia everywhere if I were Janet. I would be good at playing hockey, and nobody would stare at me because I was better at reading than the others."

"You would not be able to read at all," Inge objected. "Janet cannot read, either. She has been here for three years already and is still in first grade."

"I am sure her Daddy does not mind," Regina insisted. "Everyone likes Janet."

"Maybe because Mr. Brindley goes hunting with her father during vacation."

"He would never go hunting with my father."

"Does your father go hunting?" Inge asked, perplexed.

"No. He has no gun."

"Neither does mine," Inge answered, reassured. "But if he had a gun, he would shoot all Germans. He hates the Germans. My uncles hate them, too."

"Nazis," Regina corrected. "I am not allowed to hate the Germans at home. Only the Nazis. But I do hate the war."

"Why?"

"The war is to blame for everything. Don't you know that? Before the war, we did not have to go to school."

"In two weeks and two days," Inge calculated, "everything is going to be over. We can go home then. I could," she laughed, because she liked the idea that had just occurred to her, "call you Janet when we are alone and nobody is listening."

"Nonsense. That is just a game. When we are by ourselves and nobody is listening, I do not want to be Janet at all."

Mr. Brindley, too, longed for the vacation. The older he got, the longer the three months of school seemed to him. He did not enjoy a life with children and with a group of colleagues who were all younger than he and did not share his views or ideals. The time before the vacations, when he had to read the semester papers and produce the report cards, were so exhausting to him that he even had to work on Sundays.

Despite depressive thoughts about his increasing lack of flexibility, he deviated even further from his principle of valuing average achievements much more highly than any kind of brilliance, which he considered unreliable. With a determination that surprised him because it was not part of his nature, he told himself that a school in the end also had an obligation to shape children intellectually and not only to drill them for high performance in sports.

A little reluctantly, Mr. Brindley noticed that he had not had such thoughts since his student days at Oxford. In a good frame of mind, he most likely would not have pursued them, but in his current state of weary vexation and inexplicable obstinacy his musings revived feelings that he had given up during his long years as headmaster.

"That little one from Ol' Joro Orok," he said out loud when he saw Regina's report card, "is really an amazing student."

In general, Mr. Brindley had an aversion toward people who had a tendency to talk to themselves. However, he smiled when he heard his own voice. Immediately afterward, he caught himself thinking that he actually did not find the name Regina as unpronounceable as he had always thought. After all, he had taken Latin for many years and enjoyed it. So he pondered only what might give Germans the idea of burdening their children with such ostentatious names. He concluded that it was probably connected to their ambition to stand out, even in small matters.

Without even trying to justify his behavior, which seemed as inappropriate as strange to him, he searched for Regina's composition in a pile of papers on the windowsill and started reading. He had never experienced such an ability to express oneself in anyone eight years old. Regina not only wrote in flawless English; she also had an enormous vocabulary and unusual imagination. The comparisons, which came from a foreign world as far as Mr. Brindley was concerned and touched him in their exaggerated way, occupied him. Miss Blandford, the homeroom teacher, had written "Well done!" at the end of the paper. Following an impulse, which he attributed to his happy anticipation of the vacation, he took Regina's report card and repeated the praise in his steeply slanting handwriting.

It had never been Mr. Brindley's way to pay more attention than necessary to any individual student. He had also done well in not allowing his emotions to lead him to any kind of sentimentality, which he found foolish in his profession, but neither Regina nor her composition gave him rest. Without enthusiasm, he started reading the other papers but had a hard time concentrating. Reluctantly, he gave in to an impulse, rare for him, to immerse himself in a past that he had thought long forgotten. It confused him with a flood of pictures, which because of their detail seemed curious and obtrusive to him.

At five o'clock, he had his tea served in his room, despite the fact that this was against his principle of doing so only when he was sick. He had to force himself to hold the nightly service in the auditorium. He was alarmed when he found himself searching for Regina's face in the crowd and almost smiled when he noticed that she moved her lips only during the Lord's Prayer and did not actually pray. In his usual uncompromising way, which normally protected him well against the dangers of soft sentiments, he called himself an old fool. Still, he did not find the proof entirely unwelcome that the everyday routine had not made him nearly as rigid as he had often thought during the past semester. The next day he had Regina called to his office.

She was standing in his room, looking pale, thin, and insultingly shy to a headmaster who stressed that even the younger children should exhibit courage and enough discipline to control their emotions. Mr. Brindley remembered with annoyance that most of the children from the continent did not look strong enough and moreover always lost weight during the school months. They were probably used to different food, he pondered. Most likely they were overprotected at home and not taught to solve any problems on their own.

He had made many such observations on a trip to Italy in his youth and had experienced there how mothers adored their children in an almost shameless way and urged them to eat. Sometimes, it still galled him that he had even envied the tyrannical little princes and overdressed princesses at the time. He realized that his thoughts had wandered. This was happening only too often lately. He was becoming like an old dog that does not know anymore where it has buried its bone.

"Are you so damned clever, or are you just not able to stand it when you are not the best in your grade?" he asked. His tone displeased him immediately. He told himself with embarrassment that it was not his job, and earlier would certainly not have been consistent with his professional ethos, to talk this way to a child who had done nothing else but given her best.

Regina did not understand Mr. Brindley's question. The individual words were clear to her, but they did not make any sense. She was frightened and intimidated by the loud beating of her heart, so she only moved her head slightly from one side to the other and waited for the dryness in her mouth to disappear.

"I asked you why you learn so well."

"Because we have no money, sir."

The headmaster remembered having read somewhere that it was a Jewish trait to take every opportunity to talk about money. Yet, he despised generalizations too much to settle for an explanation that he considered simpleminded and somewhat malicious. He felt like a hunter who accidentally has killed the mother of a young animal and became aware of an unpleasant pressure in his stomach. The slight throbbing in his temples also made him numb.

He experienced the desire for a world that was easy to understand, without complications and with traditional norms, that provided stability to an aging man like physical pain. For a short moment Mr. Brindley considered sending Regina away again, but he told himself that it would be ridiculous to end a conversation before it had even begun. Did the girl still remember what they had been talking about? Most likely, as eager as she was to understand everything.

"My father," Regina broke the silence, "earns only six pounds a month, and the school here costs five."

"You know that as a fact?"

"Oh, yes, sir. My father told me."

"Really?"

"He tells me everything, sir. Before the war he was unable to send me to school. He was very sad about it. My mother, too."

Mr. Brindley had never been in the painful position of discussing the amount of the school tuition, and that he should talk with a student, of all people, and with such a young one at that, like an Indian trader, about money seemed grotesque to him. His sense of authority and honor told him to start the conversation over if he was unable to end it, but instead he asked, "What does the damned war have to do with it?"

"When the war started," Regina reported, "we had enough money for school. We did not need it for my grandmother and my aunt anymore."

"Why?"

"They are no longer able to come from Germany to Ol' Joro Orok."

"What are they doing in Germany?"

Regina felt her face burn. It was not good to change color when you are afraid. She pondered whether she had to tell now that her mother cried every time someone talked about Germany. Maybe Mr. Brindley had never heard of mothers crying, and they certainly would annoy him. He did not even like crying children.

"Before the war," she swallowed, "my grandmother and my aunt wrote letters."

"Little Nell," Mr. Brindley said in a low voice. He was amazed, but also in a nearly absurd way relieved that he had finally found the courage to pronounce the name. Regina had already reminded him of Little Nell when she entered the room, but at that point he had still been able to fight his memory. Strange, that after all these years he had to think of just this novel by Dickens. He had always regarded it as one of his worst, too sentimental, melodramatic, and completely un-English. Now, however, it seemed to him warm-hearted and somehow even beautiful. It certainly was peculiar how things changed with age.

"Little Nell," the headmaster repeated with a seriousness that did not embarrass him at all anymore and even amused him, "are you only studying this hard because this school is so damned expensive?"

"Yes, sir," nodded Regina. "My father said we cannot throw our money out of the window. If you are poor, you always have to be better than the others."

She was satisfied. It had not been easy to translate Papa's words into Mr. Brindley's language. After all, he was not even able to remember the names of his female students, and surely he had never heard of people who had no money, but maybe he had understood her anyway.

"Your father, I mean, what did he do in Germany?" Regina grew silent again from helplessness. How was she supposed to say in English that her father was a former attorney?

"He did," she remembered, "wear a black coat when he worked, but he does not need it on the farm. He gave it to Owuor. The day the locusts came."

"Who is Owuor?"

"Our cook," Regina told him and remembered the night on which her father had cried with pleasure. Warm tears without salt. "Owour ran from Rongai to Ol' Joro Orok. With our dog. He was able to come only because I speak Jaluo."

"Jaluo? What the devil is that?"

"Owuor's language," Regina replied, surprised. "Owuor has only me on the farm. All the others are Kikuyu. Except for Daji Jiwan. He is Indian. And us, of course. We are Germans, but," she added hastily, "not Nazis. My father always says that people need their own language. And Owuor says that, too."

"You love your father very much, don't you?"

"Yes, sir. And my mother, too."

"Your parents will be happy when they see your report card and read your excellent paper."

"They will not be able to, sir. But I will read everything to them. In their language. I know that, too."

"You can go now," Mr. Brindley said and opened the window. When Regina was almost at the door, he added, "I do not think your fellow students will be interested in what we talked about here. You do not have to tell them."

"No, sir. Little Nell will not do that."

7

On Mondays, Wednesdays, and Fridays, the truck, which was too big for the narrow road and had to force its way through the trembling branches of the trees, drove from Thomson's Falls to Ol' Joro Orok and delivered to Patel's store, in addition to useful things like paraffin, salt, and nails, a big bag with letters, newspapers, and packages. Kimani used to sit in the shade of the dense mulberry bushes a long while before this decisive moment. As soon as he noticed the first traces of the red dust cloud that flew toward him like a bird, he forced the life back into his sleeping feet and tensed his body like a string in a bow that is ready to shoot. Kimani loved this recurring sequence of waiting and expectation, for, as the carrier of mail and goods, he was more valuable to the *bwana* than rain, maize, or flax. All the men on the farm envied Kimani's importance.

Owuor especially, the Jaluo with the loud songs that teased laughter from the *bwana*'s throat, tried again and again to steal Kimani's day, but he always remained the unlucky hunter for some prey he was not entitled to. In the huts of the Kikuyu, too, there were many younger men with healthier legs and more air in their chests than Kimani, who could have run without trouble to Patel's *duka* and back to the farm, but the power of Kimani's clever tongue defeated all attempted assaults on his privileges.

If he left his hut in the morning when the stars were still visible in the sky, he reached the evil dog, Patel, when the sun just started to swallow its shadows. Yet, every time, it was Kimani who had to wait for the truck and not the truck for him. The long way through the woods with the silent black monkeys, their white manes the only thing visible as they jumped from tree to tree, was cumbersome. On the hot days between the rains, Kimani could already hear his bones scream on the way to the store. By the time he returned, the fires were burning in front of the huts. His feet were as hot then as if they had trampled the embers. But happiness filled Kimani's body even though he had drunk nothing but water all day. The *memsahib* used to pour it into a beautiful green bottle the night before.

There were bad days when the hyena Patel answered the question about mail for the farm with an angry shake of his head and looked as if he had snapped away the best pieces from the vultures. The *bwana* needed his letters like a man dying of thirst needs the few drops of water that prevent him from lying down forever. If Kimani did not bring anything from Patel's smelly *duka* but flour, sugar, and the little pail with the semiliquid yellow fat for the *memsahib*, the *bwana*'s eyes became more lackluster than the fur of a dying dog. Just a single newspaper could make him glad, and he took the small rolled paper with a sigh that was sweet medicine for ears that all day long had been able to devour only the sounds coming from the mouths of animals.

The *bwana* had been on the farm for three short and two long rains now. Time enough for Kimani to understand—albeit as slowly as a mule that has been born prematurely—the many things that had made his head heavy at the beginning of his life with the new *bwana*. He knew by now that the sun during the day and the moon at night were not enough for the *bwana,* nor the rain on the parched skin or a loudly roaring fire during the cold, nor the voices from the radio that never permitted themselves to sleep, nor the bed of the *memsahib* or the eyes of his daughter when she returned to the farm from the school in faraway Nakuru.

The *bwana* needed newspapers. They fed his head and oiled his throat, which then told about *shauris,* which nobody at Ol' Joro Orok had ever heard about. On the way from the house to the flax fields and the flowering pyrethrum fields, the *bwana* talked about the war. There were exciting stories about white men who killed each other the way the Masai had done in the old days when they attacked their peaceful neighbors because they wanted their cattle and wives. Kimani's ears loved the words, which were like a strong young wind, but his breast felt that the *bwana* chewed an old sadness while talking because he had not thought of taking his heart along when he started on his long safari to Ol' Joro Orok. Once, the *bwana* pulled a blue picture with many colorful marks on it out of his pants pocket and pointed to a tiny dot with the nail of his longest finger.

"Here, my friend," he said, "is Ol' Joro Orok," and then he moved the finger a bit and continued speaking very slowly. "Here was my father's hut. I will never return to it."

Kimani laughed because his big hand could touch both points on the blue picture at the same time without any effort, and yet he realized that his head did not understand what the *bwana* was trying to tell him. The pictures in the newspapers, which Kimani brought from Patel's store, were different. He had the *bwana* show them to him over and over again and learned to interpret them.

There were houses that were higher than trees, and yet they were felled by guns from angry planes like forests by a bushfire. Ships with high chimneys sank into the water as if they were small pebbles in a river that had swollen too rapidly after the long rains. Again and again, the pictures showed dead men. Some lay on the ground as quietly as if they wanted to sleep after their work was done, others were split open like dead zebras that had been lying in the sun too long. All the dead had their guns lying next to them, but those had been of no help because in the war of the well-armed whites every man had a gun.

When the *bwana* talked about the war, he always talked about his father, too. He never looked at Kimani then; he sent his eyes to the high mountain without being able to see the top made of snow. When he talked, he had the voice of an impatient child who wants the moon during the day and the sun at night, and said, "My father is dying."

The words were as familiar to Kimani as his own name, and even though he took his time before opening his mouth, he knew what he had to say: "Does your father want to die?"

"No, he does not want to die."

"A man cannot die if he does not want to die," Kimani would say every time. In the beginning, he showed his teeth while talking, the way he always did when he was happy, but in time he got used to releasing a sigh from his breast. It made him sad that his *bwana*, who knew so much, had not become smart enough to understand that life and death are not man's business but only that of the great God Mungu.

Even more than for the newspapers with the pictures of ruined houses and dead men, the *bwana* longed for letters. Kimani knew everything about letters. When the *bwana* had arrived on the farm, Kimani was still thinking that one letter was just like another. He was not that dumb anymore. Letters were not like two brothers who had come together from their mother's belly. Letters were like human beings and never alike.

It was the postage stamp that made the difference. Without it a letter was only a piece of paper and could not even go on the smallest safari. A single stamp with the picture of a man who had light hair and the face of a woman told of a journey a man could make on foot. Kimani often brought such letters from Patel's *duka*. They came from Gilgil and were from the *bwana* who let his big belly dance when he laughed and had a *memsahib* who could sing more beautifully than a bird.

The two of them often came from Gilgil to the farm, and when the long rains turned the road to mud and the *bwana*'s friends were unable to come to Ol' Joro Orok, they sent letters. From Nakuru there were letters from the *memsahib kidogo,* who had learned how to write in school. The yellow envelopes had the same stamp as the ones from Gilgil, but Kimani knew who had written the letter before the *bwana* told him. The ones from the little *memsahib* made his eyes light up like young flax flowers, and his skin never smelled like fear.

Letters with many stamps on them had traveled far. As soon as the *bwana* saw them in Kimani's hand, he did not even take time to release the air from his breast before he tore open the envelope and started to read. And there was one stamp, which by itself alone had more power than all the others together to set the *bwana* on fire. This one, too, showed a man without arms and legs, but he was not blond. The hair that cascaded from his head was as black as that of the stinking dog Patel. The eyes were small, and between his nose and mouth grew an exactly planted very low bush of black hair.

Kimani liked to look at just these stamps for a long time.

The man looked as if he wanted to talk and as if he had a voice, which might rebound heavily from a mountain. As soon as the *bwana* saw this stamp, his eyes changed into deep holes, and he himself became as stiff as a man who is threatened by a furious thief with a freshly sharpened *panga* and who has forgotten how a man has to defend himself.

The picture of the man with the hair under his nose drove all life out of the *bwana*'s body, and he swayed like a tree that has not yet learned how to cower under the wind. Before the *bwana* tore open such a letter full of fire, he would always call, "Jettel." His voice became thin, like that of an animal that no longer has the will to run away from death.

Yet Kimani knew that the *bwana* wanted more than anything to get the letters that frightened him. He was like a child who is still too restless just to sit and let the day run through his fingers like fine soil until his head sinks on his chest and sleep arrives. Kimani's throat got salty when he considered how the *bwana* needed the big excitement, which made him sick, in order to still find strength in his limbs.

It had been a long time now since such a letter had arrived. But when Kimani asked for the mail at Patel's the day before the flax harvest, the Indian reached onto the wooden shelf on the wall and took out a letter that did not satisfy Kimani's great hunger for familiarity. He saw immediately that this letter was different from all the others, which he had carried home up to then.

The paper was thin and made a noise in Patel's hand like a dying tree in the early evening wind. The envelope was smaller than that of the other letters. The colorful stamp was missing. Instead, Kimani saw a black circle with thin short lines in the middle, which looked like tiny lizards. On the right hand side of the envelope shone a red cross. It jumped at Kimani from afar like a snake that has been hungry for too long. For a moment, he was afraid that Patel, too, might like the red cross and not give him the letter. But the Indian was busy quarreling with a Kikuyu woman who had put her finger too far into a sack full of sugar and irritably pushed the letter across the dirty table.

Kimani stood still to look at the cross, free from Patel's evil eyes, only after he had reached the forest. It shone even brighter in the shadows than in the store and was a joy to his eyes, which even during the day caught the colors of night only under the trees. The cross started to dance if Kimani squeezed one eye shut and moved his head at the same time. He laughed when he realized that he was behaving like an infant monkey that sees a flower for the first time.

Again and again, Kimani asked himself if the *bwana* would like the beautiful red cross as much as he did, or if it had the same burning magic as the man with the black hair. He was unable to decide, no matter how much he pushed his head to work. The uncertainty took away from the pleasure about the letter and made his legs heavy. Fatigue made his back crooked and clung to his eyes. The cross looked different now than in the store and during the time of the long shadows. It had allowed its color to be stolen.

Kimani was startled. He felt that he had let the night come too close. It would make use of the fact that he was on his way without a lamp. If he did not make his body strong and drive it to hurry, he would hear the hyenas before he saw the first fields. That was not good for a man of his age. He had to run the last stretch of the way, and when he reached the first fields he had more air in his mouth than in his breast.

The night had not yet reached the farm. Kamau cleaned the glasses in front of the house and captured the last red sunbeam. He wrapped it into a cloth and released it again. Owuor was sitting on a wooden box in front of the kitchen cleaning his nails with a silver fork. He sent his voice to the mountain with a song that always made Kimani's skin blister and the *bwana* laugh.

The little *memsahib* ran with the dog toward the house that had the heart in the door and jumped over the high yellow grass. She swung the lamp, which had not yet been lit, from side to side as if it were as light as a piece of paper. Kania cut round holes in the air with his broom. He chewed on a little piece of wood to polish his teeth, of which he was very proud, and to make them even whiter. As usual when he was waiting for the mail, the *bwana* stood motionless in front of the house like a warrior who has not caught sight of the enemy yet. The *memsahib* was next to him. Small white birds that lived only on her dress flew toward yellow flowers on the black cloth.

Panting from the exertion of running fast, Kimani waited for the joy he usually felt when the two ran toward him, but the satisfaction hesitated to come and disappeared as suddenly as the morning mist. Even though the cold was already licking his skin, sharp drops of sweat ran into his eyes. All of a sudden, Kimani felt like an old man who is confused about his sons and mistakes the sons of his sons for his brothers.

Kimani felt the *bwana*'s hand on his shoulder, but he was too dazed to draw any warmth from the familiar pleasure. He noticed that the *bwana*'s voice was no stronger than that of a child who does not find his mother's breast right away. He knew then that the fear that had come over him like a sudden fever had urged him on just in time.

"They have written through the Red Cross," Walter whispered. "I did not even know that that is possible."

"Who? Tell me. How long are you just going to hold the letter in your hand? Open it. I am terribly scared."

"I am, too, Jettel."

"Hurry up."

When Walter took the thin piece of paper out of the envelope, he suddenly remembered the autumn leaves in the Sohrau town forest. Even though he immediately doggedly fought the memory, he saw the outline of a leaf from a chestnut tree with painful clarity. After that, his senses grew numb. Only his nose still fooled him with a scent that tortured him.

"Father and Liesel?" Jettel asked in a low voice.

"No. Mother and Käthe. Shall I read it to you?"

The time it took Jettel to nod her head was a period of mercy. It was enough for Walter to read the two lines, unmistakably written under great duress, and to hold the letter at the same time so close to his face that he did not have to look at Jettel and she could not see him.

"Dearest ones," Walter read, "We are very excited. Tomorrow, we go to Poland to work. Don't forget us. Mother and Käthe."

"Is that all? That cannot possibly be all?"

"Yes, Jettel, yes. They were only allowed to write twenty words. They have given one away."

"Why Poland? Your father always used to say that the Poles are even worse than the Germans. How could they do that? There is a war on in Poland. They will be even worse off there than in Breslau. Or do you think they still want to try to emigrate through Poland? Why don't you say anything?"

The struggle over whether it might be a pardonable sin to expose Jettel for a last time to the mercy of a lie was short. Considering flight alone seemed to Walter like blasphemy and anathema.

"Jettel," he said, and gave up searching for words to make the truth more bearable, "you need to know. Your mother wanted you to know. Otherwise she would not have written this letter. We can no longer have any hope. Poland means death."

Regina ran slowly with Rummler from the toilet to the house. She had lit her lamp and let the dog chase the swaying shadows on the path paved with light stones between the rose bed and the kitchen. The dog tried to dig into the black spots with his paws and howled with disappointment as soon as they flew toward the sky.

Walter saw that Regina was laughing, but at the same time he heard that she cried out "Mama" as if she were in mortal danger. His first thought was that the snake, of which Owuor had warned them in the morning, had appeared, and he called out, "Don't move." But when the cries became louder and swallowed every other sound in the cascading darkness, he realized that it was not Regina who had cried out for her mother but Jettel.

Walter stretched out both arms toward his wife without reaching her, and he finally succeeded in calling her name several times into her fear. The embarrassment that he had become incapable of compassion turned into a panic that paralyzed all his limbs. He was even more humiliated by the recognition that he envied his wife the terrible certainty that fate was denying him about his father and his sister.

After a time, which seemed very long to him, he realized that Jettel had stopped shouting. She stood in front of him, her arms hanging and shoulders shaking. Finally, Walter found the strength to touch her and to reach for her hand. Without saying anything, he led his wife into the house.

Owuor, who never used to leave the kitchen before he had brewed the tea for the evening meal, stood in front of the lit fireplace and sent his eyes to the piled up wood. Regina was there, too. She had taken off her rubber boots and sat under the window with Rummler as if she had never been away. The dog licked her face, but she looked down, chewed on a strand of hair, and pressed herself again and again against the animal's massive body. Walter knew at that point that his daughter was crying. He would not have to explain anything else to her.

"Mama promised me," Jettel sobbed without any tears coming, "to be there when I have another child. She promised me for certain when Regina was born. Don't you remember?"

"Don't, Jettel, don't. Memories are only torture. Sit down."

"She promised me solemnly. And she always kept her promises."

"Don't cry, Jettel. We have no right to tears anymore. That is the price we have to pay for having escaped. That will never change. You are not only a daughter; you are a mother, too."

"Who says that?"

"God. He told me in the camp through Oha when I did not want to go on. And don't worry, Jettel, we will not have any more children until times are better for us. Owuor, get a glass of milk for the *memsahib.*"

Owuor took even more time than in the days without salt to decide which piece of wood he should throw into the fire. When he got up, he looked at Jettel even though he was talking to Walter.

"I will," he said with a tongue that took a long time to obey him, "warm up the milk, *bwana.* If the *memsahib* cries too much, you again will not have a son." He went to the door without turning around.

"Owuor," Jettel called and a great astonishment made her voice firm again, "how did you know?"

"Everyone on the farm knows that Mama is having a baby," Regina said and pulled Rummler's head into her lap, "everyone, except Papa."

8

Dr. James Charters noticed the twitching of his left eyebrow, as well as the annoying mistake when the two women, who were unknown to him, stood in front of his favorite painting with the splendid hunting dogs: They still were at least two feet away from him and already extended hands toward him. That in itself was sufficient proof that these people came from the Continent. A well-practiced, inconspicuous glance at the little yellow card next to the inkwell on his desk confirmed his suspicion. Below the foreign name, Charters found a notice saying that the Stag's Head had made the appointment for a consultation with the patient.

Since the outbreak of the war, hotel receptions could no longer be relied on. They obviously had difficulties evaluating guests, who had changed the entire life structure of the Colony. The only hotel in Nakuru had been there for farmers from the surrounding areas, who treated themselves to a few days off and the illusion of life in the city when they brought their children to school, visited the doctor, or had business in one of the district offices. During that period, which Charters already called the good old times, even though it was less than three years ago, the Stag's was occasionally also host to hunters, mostly from America. They were genial, tough fellows, who certainly had no need for a gynecologist and with whom a physician could have a good conversation, unencumbered by professional matters.

With a barely suppressed sigh, Charters, who generally made it a point not to let new patients wait any longer than necessary, took some time for further unpleasant ruminations. He no longer liked living in Nakuru. Without the war he would have indulged himself with a

practice in London after the death of his aunt and an unexpectedly generous inheritance. To be on Harley Street had always been his dream,
but he had carelessly lost sight of this goal when he entered into a second marriage with a farmer's daughter from Naivasha. His young wife
had always been able to change his mind, and now she was so panic-
stricken about the blitzkrieg that there was no way she could be persuaded to move to London. He consoled himself with an elation that he
had denied himself for years, and no longer treated any patients who
were below his stratum of society.

While Charters meticulously scraped a dead fly from the window,
he looked in the glass at the reflections of the two women, who, without
being invited, had seated themselves on the newly upholstered chairs in
front of his desk. There was no doubt that the younger one was the patient and an embarrassment that could be attributed solely to the carelessness of Miss Collins, who had been working for Charters for only
four weeks and had not yet developed an intuition in matters that were
important to him.

Until she opened her mouth, one could certainly have regarded the
older of the two as a lady from the English provinces, Charters thought
with a trace of interest, which he considered rather inappropriate in
view of the discussions that were certain to follow. She was slim and
well groomed, appeared self-assured, and had the kind of beautiful
blond hair he appreciated in women. She looked somehow Norwegian,
this graceful person, and, in any case, she looked as if she were accus-
tomed to pay well for her doctor's visits.

The patient was at least in her sixth month and, as Charters realized,
not in the state of health he appreciated in pregnant women if there
were not supposed to be any disagreeable complications. She wore a
flowered dress that seemed typical to him of the fashion of the thirties
on the Continent. The ridiculous white lace collar reminded him in an
almost grotesque way of the women of the lower bourgeoisie during
Victorian times and the fact that he had never had to deal with precisely
that class. The dress already emphasized her breasts and made her
stomach look like a sphere, the way Charters permitted it to appear only
immediately before delivery. The woman most likely already had been
eating for two during the first month of her pregnancy. Nothing could
change the deviant habits of these foreign nationals. The woman was

pale and looked stressed, intimidated, like a domestic servant who is expecting an illegitimate child, and precisely as if pregnancy were a punishment by fate. He was sure she would be a whiner. Charters cleared his throat. He did not have many, but rather long-lasting, experiences with people from the Continent. They were excessively sensitive and not cooperative enough when it came to tolerating pain.

During the first months of the war, Charters had delivered the wife of a Jewish factory owner from Manchester of twins. The couple had not been able to return to England in time because of a sudden shortage of tickets for ship passengers. Those people had behaved with absolute correctness and, without complaining, had paid the heavily inflated fee, which Charters among colleagues called the doctor's compensation for personal suffering. Still, he had bad memories of the case. It had taught him that the Jewish race in general did not have enough discipline to clench their teeth at crucial moments.

At that time, Dr. James Charters had made up his mind not to take on any more patients who did not conform to his way of thinking, and he did not intend to make an exception now, which only would be a burden for both parties. Especially not in the case of a woman who obviously was not even able to afford a proper maternity dress.

When Charters could not think of anything else to do with the window other than to pull it open and close it a few times, he turned toward his visitors. He noticed with irritation that the blond woman was already talking. It was just the way he had feared. The accent was decidedly unpleasant and did not have the agreeable Norwegian timbre of the beautiful films one had seen of late.

The blond one had just said, "My name is Hahn, and this is Mrs. Redlich. She has not been feeling well. From the fourth month on already."

Charters cleared his throat a second time. It was not an accidental little cough but a tone with precisely measured acuity that did not invite any further familiarities until the situation had been clarified.

"Do not worry about the fees, please."

"I am not worried."

"Certainly not," Lilly acknowledged and made an attempt to swallow her embarrassment without having her face betray her, "but everything is taken care of. Mrs. Williamson advised us to assure you of that."

Charters made an effort to remember if and when he had heard that name before. He was just about to point out that Mrs. Williamson certainly was not one of his patients when he remembered that a dentist by that name had settled in Nakuru two years ago. Afterward, he needed some more time to remember where else he had encountered the name outside his professional realm. The unfortunate Mr. Williamson had wanted to join the Polo Club, which, however, did not admit Jewish people. It had been a rather embarrassing affair at the time. At least as provoking as the discussion of financial matters, before the physician had even had an opportunity for a first examination.

Charters felt affronted. He forced himself, however, to consider that maybe those people from the Continent did have a tendency toward this kind of crudeness without meaning any harm. Unfortunately, they also had an exaggerated desire to talk to others, as he realized with dismay when he noticed that he had not stopped the flow of words coming from the provocatively blond woman. He was already in the process of hearing an excessively confusing story of unknown people in Germany who apparently had a close relationship to the pregnant woman.

"How did she come to live at the Stag's Head?" the doctor interrupted Lilly's account. He was immediately annoyed with his brusque tone, which did not fit in at all with the obliging manner that everyone appreciated so much about him.

"The pregnancy was difficult from the start. We do not think that my friend should have her baby alone on a farm."

Charters thought it better not to ask any further questions if he did not want to be forced into a situation in which he would have to take on the case for the sole reason that he had become medically involved at too early a time. He fought his discomfort with the carefully measured hint of a smile.

"I assume," he said, and nodded absentmindedly in Jettel's direction so that he did not have to look at her, "she does not know any English."

"Not much. Well, hardly any. That is why I'm here. I live in Gilgil."

"That is very kind of you. But you will hardly stay here until the delivery and stand next to me in the hospital to translate."

"No," Lilly stuttered. "I mean we have not thought that far ahead. Mrs. Williamson recommended you as physician who could help us."

"Mrs. Williamson," Charters replied after a pause, which seemed just right to him, not too long and especially not too short, "has been living here for only a short time. Otherwise, I am sure she would have mentioned Dr. Arnold. She is just right for you. An extraordinary doctor."

As glad and as surprised as he was that he had found an elegant solution just at this moment, he had to make quite an effort not to show his satisfaction. Good old Janet Arnold, indeed, was his salvation. Sometimes he still forgot that she lived in Nakuru now. For years, she had driven her old rickety Ford, which was a joke in itself, to the most remote areas to attend to the natives on farms and reservations there.

The old girl was a mixture of Florence Nightingale and pigheaded Irish peasant and did not care a bit about taste, convention, and tradition. In Nakuru, the eternal rebel treated a lot of Indians and Goans and, of course, also many black people, from whom she most likely never collected a penny, and, without doubt, the have-nots from the Continent, too, to whom even a broken arm presented a financial catastrophe. At any rate, Janet Arnold had exclusively patients who did not care that she was no longer very young and besides had that damned un-British way of giving her opinion without being asked.

Charters put away the calendar that he used to leaf through when he had to become regrettably clear and said, "I am not the right one for you. I am planning on a complete rest in the very near future. You will like Mrs. Arnold," he smiled. "She speaks several languages. Perhaps that of your people, as well."

It disturbed him a little that he had not formulated the last sentence at any rate with his usual tact, and so he added with a show of goodwill, which he considered quite successful, "I will be happy to provide you with a recommendation to Dr. Arnold."

"Thank you," answered Lilly, shaking her head. She waited until the rage within her had subsided and she could breathe again. Then she said, in the same low voice as the doctor—but in German—"You arrogant pig, you damned dirty bastard of a physician. We have had all of this before, doctors refusing to treat Jews."

Charter's eyebrows twitched only slightly when he asked with irritation, "I beg your pardon?" Lilly, however, had gotten up and pulled Jettel, who was breathing heavily but at the same time tried to tighten her shoulders, from the chair. Lilly and Jettel left the room in silence. They giggled like schoolgirls in the dark corridor and allowed the silliness, which they could not suppress, to take away their feeling of helplessness and trembling. Only when they stopped laughing simultaneously did they realize that they were crying.

Lilly had planned to spend at least two weeks with Jettel in Nakuru, but the next day she got a letter from her husband and had to return to Gilgil.

"I am going to be back as soon as Oha can spare me," she consoled her friend, "and next time we will bring Walter along. It is important now that you are not alone too much and don't start brooding."

"Don't worry about me. I am fine," Jettel said. "The main thing is that I never have to see Charters again."

The first day without Lilly's care and her infectious optimism was filled with the black holes of loneliness. "I need to come back right away," she wrote to Walter, but she did not have any stamps and was too embarrassed to ask for them in her broken English at the hotel reception desk. At the end of the week, however, the fact that she had not been able to send the letter seemed like fate to her.

Jettel's attitude toward herself had changed. She realized that Charters and his humiliating treatment had not really hurt her all that much but, paradoxically, had given her the courage to admit something that she had suppressed for a long time.

Neither she nor Walter had wanted a second child, but neither of them had had the courage to say so. Now that Jettel was alone with her thoughts, she no longer had to pretend that she was happy. It became clear to her that she was not strong enough to live alone on the farm with a baby and the continuous fear of being without medical assistance at the critical moment, but she was no longer ashamed of her weakness. The embarrassment that the Hahns and the small Jewish community in Nakuru had to pay for her hotel room at the Stag's Head also seemed to have become less oppressive.

Jettel learned to regard the small room with its sparse furnishings, a striking contrast to the luxurious lounges, as protection from a world that was closed to her. She was unable to talk with any of the guests, could not read any of the books in the library, and, after a single attempt, had given up participating in listening to the radio broadcasts that were played after dinner for the guests in evening gowns and tuxedos. Only two of her dresses still fit; her skin was becoming dry and gray; she had trouble washing her hair in the small washbowl and could not shake the feeling that she had to spare the other guests from looking at her. So she left her room only for meals and for a daily walk in the garden, which the doctor at each visit prescribed with an imploring voice and many gestures.

"Baby needs walks," Dr. Arnold used to giggle every time she palpated Jettel's belly.

All her life, she had relied on nature and the body's ability to help itself, and she never betrayed the fact that she was worried about Jettel. Dr. Arnold came to the Stag's Head every Wednesday, brought four postage stamps, and put an Italian-English dictionary and the latest edition of the Sunday *Post* on the wobbly table, even though she had realized from her first visit that both of these were useless.

Janet Arnold was a warmhearted woman who smelled slightly of whisky and intensely of horses and radiated even more confidence than good spirits. She hugged Jettel when she greeted her, laughed heartily during the examination, and stroked her belly when she was leaving.

Jettel felt the urge to confide her worries to the small, plump woman in the worn men's clothing and to talk to her about the progress of her pregnancy, which she did not consider normal. It was impossible to overcome the language barrier.

The communication succeeded best in Swahili, but both women knew that the vocabulary for expectant mothers there was mostly suited to women who also could deliver their children without medical assistance. So Dr. Arnold limited herself, once she thought she had conveyed everything that was essential, to words from all the foreign languages that she had encountered in her adventurous life. Again and again, she tried Afrikaans and Hindi. Equally without success, she tried the Gaelic sounds of her childhood.

As a young doctor, at the beginning of World War I, Janet Arnold had taken care of a German soldier in Tanganyika. She did not remember him anymore, but, as the last days of his life ebbed away, he had often said "damned Kaiser." She had remembered those two words well enough to try them on those of her patients who she believed might be from Germany. In many cases, this had created the laughing agreement that Dr. Arnold valued as essential for a successful cure. She was sorry that Jettel of all people, whom she would have liked to see happy just once, did not react to her mother tongue at all.

The experience of not being able to share sadness and despair was new to Jettel, and yet she no longer missed having someone to talk to. She was often surprised that she even missed Walter so little and that she was almost glad to know that he was far away in Ol' Joro Orok. She felt that his helplessness would only have increased hers. All the more, she enjoyed his letters. They were full of that tenderness that in easier times she had taken for love. Yet she wondered if their marriage would ever again become more than a community of fate.

Jettel did not believe that her pregnancy would have a good outcome. She was still paralyzed by the shock of her first month, when the letter from Breslau had taken away all her hopes for her mother and sister. She did not even begin to fight against her premonition that the letter was an omen of the misfortune that threatened her. The thought that she should bring a new life into the world seemed like a mockery and a sin to her.

Jettel could no longer rid herself of the idea that she was destined to follow her mother into death. Then, she imagined with painful detail Regina and Walter on the farm, and how both of them would try to bring up the motherless infant. Sometimes, she also saw Owuor, laughing, rocking the baby on his big knees, and, when she awoke with a start during the night, she realized that she had called for Owuor and not for Walter.

When her fear and imagination threatened to choke her, Jettel longed only for Regina, whom she knew was so near, yet so far out of reach. The Nakuru School and the Stag's Head were only four miles apart, but the school regulations did not allow Regina to visit her mother. At the same time, they also did not permit Jettel to see her daughter. At night, Jettel saw the lights of the school shine on the hill and clung to the thought that Regina was waving to her from one of the many windows. It took more and more time for her to return from such reveries to reality.

Regina, too, who had never complained about the long separation from her parents, was unhappy. Almost daily, short letters written in awkward German arrived at the hotel. The mistakes and the English expressions she was unable to understand moved Jettel even more than the printed request for stamps. "You must take care of yourself," every letter started, "so that you will not get sick." Almost always, Regina wrote, "I want to visit you, but am not allowed. We are soldiers here."

The sentence "I am looking forward to the baby" was always underlined in red, and often she wrote, "I do it like Alexander the Great. You must nicht have angst."

Jettel waited for those letters with such impatience because they gave her courage. On the farm, she had suffered from the fact that she found it hard to be close with Regina, and now the loyalty and care of her daughter were her only support in her time of need. It seemed to Jettel that she was reliving her close connection to her mother. With every letter she became more aware that Regina, who was almost ten, was no longer a child.

She never asked any questions, and yet she understood everything that concerned her parents. Had it not been Regina who knew before Walter that Jettel was pregnant? She knew about birth and death and ran to the huts when a woman was in labor, yet Jettel had never had the courage to talk with her daughter about the things she had experienced there. In general, Jettel had only rarely been able to talk to Regina without embarrassment, but now she felt the urge to confide her worries to Regina.

Jettel had less trouble with her letters to Regina than with those to her husband. She felt the need to describe her physical condition in detail, and very soon she also found it liberating to write about her emotional state. When she filled the hotel's writing paper with her large, clear handwriting and the pages piled up in front of her, she was able to be once more the contented little Jettel in Breslau who at the least sign of trouble just had to run up one flight of stairs to be consoled by her mother.

On Sundays, when she could not even expect any mail from Regina, Jettel had to fight the temptation not to get up, not to eat, and just to kill the time by sleeping. Shortly after sunrise, the humidity and the heat would become so oppressive that she would get dressed after all and sit on the edge of her bed. There she would concentrate on avoiding any unnecessary movement. For hours, she would stare at the smooth surface of the lake, which had very little water left, and wish for nothing but to become a flamingo and hatch only eggs.

In this twilight state between listless waking and restless drowsiness, Jettel was particularly sensitive to sounds. She heard the houseboys lighting the stove in the kitchen, the waiters clicking the silverware in the dining room, the little dog whining in the next room, and every car that stopped in front of the hotel entrance. Even though she hardly ever saw the guests who lived on the same floor with her, she was able to distinguish their steps, voices, and coughs. Chai, the barefoot Kikuyu, who served tea at eleven o'clock in the morning and at five in the afternoon, did not even have to touch the doorknob to Jettel's room for her to know that he was there. Only when Regina came did she not hear a thing.

It was the last Sunday in July when Regina knocked three times and then very slowly opened the door, and Jettel stared at her daughter as if she had never seen her before. During that eerie moment without sense and memory, without happiness and without reaction, dazed by her inability to understand, Jettel tried only to think which language she should speak. Finally, she recognized the white dress and remembered that the Nakuru School required white dresses for the weekly church attendance.

The Indian tailor who came in regular intervals to Ol' Joro Orok and put up his sewing machine under a tree in front of Patel's *duka* had sewn it from an old tablecloth. It had been impossible to dissuade him from adding white ruffles at the neck and sleeves, and he had charged an additional three shillings for those. All of a sudden, Jettel remembered every word of the conversation and how Walter, when he saw the dress, had said, "I liked it better when it was a tablecloth at Redlich's Hotel."

Walter's voice seemed too loud and harsh to Jettel, and, very angrily, she started to object, but the words adhered to her mouth just like the old blue apron dress to her body. The effort was so great that the pressure in her throat was released and she broke into tears.

"Mummy," Regina cried in a high strange voice. "Mama," she whispered in a familiar tone of voice.

Her breathing resembled that of a hunting dog that sees the prey and does not notice that it has already lost it. Her face had the dangerous red of a flaming forest at night. There was sweat running down from her forehead through a fine layer of reddish dust. Dark drops fell from her hair onto the white dress.

"Regina, you must have run like the devil. Where on earth are you coming from? Who brought you here? For Heaven's sake, what happened?"

"I brought myself," Regina said and chewed on the pleasure that her voice was firm enough again to stay proud. "I ran away on the way to church. And I am going to do that every Sunday from now on."

For the first time since she had been living at the Stag's Head, Jettel felt that her head and body could be light at the same time, but she still had trouble speaking. Regina's perspiration smelled sweet and increased Jettel's desire to feel nothing but her daughter's steaming body and to hear her heart beating. She opened her mouth for a kiss, but her lips were trembling.

"'Ich hab' mein Herz in Heidelberg verloren,'" Regina started, but interrupted herself embarrassed. She was unable to carry the simplest tune and knew it. "Owuor's song," she said, "but I cannot sing as well as he can. I am not as smart as Owuor. Do you remember when he came to us that night? With Rummler. Papa cried."

"You are smart and good," Jettel said.

Regina allowed herself only enough time so that her ears could remember the caress of the words forever. Then she sat down on the bed with her mother, and both were silent. They held onto each other and waited patiently for the good fortune of seeing each other again to turn into happiness.

Jettel still did not have the courage to utter the words that were within her, but she was able to listen. She had Regina tell her with what determination and longing she had planned the escape and how she had separated from the group of girls and had run toward the hotel. It was a long and confusingly complicated story, which Regina told over and over again in the same words, using the art of repetition that she had acquired from Owuor, and which Jettel despite all efforts was unable to follow. She realized that her silence was beginning to disappoint Regina and was all the more startled when she heard herself say, "Why are you so excited about the baby?"

"I need it."

"Why do you need a baby?"

"I won't be alone then when you and Papa are dead."

"But Regina, what makes you think about something like that? We are not that old yet. Why should we die? Who put that nonsense into your head?"

"But your mother is dying," Regina replied and bit on the salt in her mouth. "And Papa told me that his father will die, too. And Aunt Liesel. But he told me that I should not tell you. I am sorry."

"Your grandparents and your aunts," Jettel swallowed, "were not able to get out of Germany. We did explain that to you. But nothing can happen to us. We are here. All three of us."

"Four," Regina corrected her and closed her eyes contentedly. "Soon we are going to be four."

"Oh, Regina, you do not know how hard it is to have a baby. When you were born, everything was different. I will never forget how your father danced through the apartment. Everything is so terrible now."

"I know," Regina nodded. "I was there with Warimu. Warimu almost died. The baby came with its feet first out of her belly. I was allowed to help pull."

With a quick movement, Jettel pushed the disgust back into her stomach. "And weren't you afraid?" she asked.

"But, no," Regina remembered and wondered if her mother had tried to be funny. "Warimu screamed really loud, and that helped her. She was not afraid either. Nobody was afraid."

The need to give Regina at least a little bit of the security she had withheld from her for too long became a torture for Jettel, which was harder to bear than the recognition that she had failed. Regina seemed as defenseless to her as she herself was.

"I am not going to be afraid," she said.

"Promise."

"I do."

"You have to say it again. You have to say everything again," Regina urged.

"I promise you that I will not be afraid when the baby comes. I never knew that a baby was that important to you. I do not think that other children look forward to a baby as much you do. You know," Jettel declared, taking refuge in the never-failing consolation of her memories, "I always used to talk with my mother the way I am talking with you now."

"And you were not in boarding school."

Jettel tried not to betray her sadness when she was brought back to reality. She got up and embraced Regina. "What is going to happen," she asked, "when they realize that you ran away? Are you going to be punished?"

"Yes, but I do not care."

"You mean you do not mind?"

"Yes, I do not mind."

"But no child wants to be punished."

"I do," Regina laughed. "You know, if we get punished we have to learn poems. I love poems."

"I used to like to recite poems, too. When we are all together again on the farm, I will recite Schiller's 'Glocke' for you. I still remember it."

"I need poems."

"What for?"

"Perhaps," Regina said, without realizing that she had sent her voice on safari, "I will end up in prison one day. They will take everything from me then. My clothes, my food, and my hair will all be gone. They will also not give me any books, but they will not get the poems. Those are in my head. When I am very sad, I recite my poems. I have thought all of this out exactly, but nobody knows it. Even Inge does not know anything about my poems. If I tell, the magic will disappear."

Even though she felt sharp pains in her back while breathing, Jettel kept her tears inside until Regina was gone. Then she held her sadness as close to herself as she had held her daughter. She waited almost with yearning for the despair and the support it would give her. But amazed and with a humility that she had never felt before, she became aware that the will to face life had taken over. For the sake of Regina, who had shown her the way, Jettel was determined to fight. It was only the physical pain now that accompanied her in her sleep.

During the night, four weeks early, the contractions started, and the next morning Janet Arnold told her that the baby was dead.

9

THE LAST DAY without the *memsahib* was as sweet for Owour as the juice of young sugar cane and no longer than a night filled with bright moonlight. Shortly after sunrise, he had Kania scrub the boards between the oven, the closet, and the newly stacked woodpile with boiling water. Kamau had to submerge all the pots, glasses, plates, and even the *memsahib*'s favorite little red wagon with the tiny wheels in hot sudsy water. Jogona washed the dog for a long time until he looked like a small white pig. Just in time, Kimani gave in to Owuor's pleas to make sure, with his *shamba* boys, that the vultures would disappear from the thorn-trees in front of the house. Owuor had not talked to the *bwana* about the vultures, but his head told him that white women would not be any different in that regard from black women. Whoever had seen Death did not want to listen to the wings of the vultures.

Owuor polished the cooking spoon with a cloth that was as soft as the material on the collar of his black cloak and stopped only when his own eyes looked back at him from the gleaming metal. They were already drinking in the joy of the days that had not yet arrived. It was good that the spoon would soon be able to dance again for the *memsahib* in the thick brown sauce of flour, butter, and onions. As Owuor woke his nose with the smell of pleasures that it had been forced to miss for too long, he became content again.

It was not as easy any more, as it had been in the days long passed at Rongai, to work for the *bwana* alone. When he was alone on the farm, he let the soup get cold and the pudding turn gray. His tongue no longer knew how to wrap itself around the taste of bread that had just come out of the oven. On the evil day when the *memsahib* had been taken to

Nakuru with the child in her belly, the *bwana*'s eyes had stopped waking up his heart with a drumbeat. From that time on, he had moved like an old man who waits only for the call of his screaming bones and no longer hears Mungu's voice.

In the days between the long drought and the child's death, Owuor had thought that the *bwana* had no god who guided his head as a good herdsman leads his team of oxen, but recently Owuor had discovered that he was wrong. When the *bwana* told him about his dead child, it was he, and not Owuor, who said *"shauri ya mungu."* Owuor would have said the same thing if Death had shown its teeth to him like a hungry lion to a fleeing gazelle. Only, Owuor thought, man should not wake Mungu from His sleep for a child's sake. It was not God who was supposed to take care of children but the man who wanted them.

Even while looking forward to the day when the old life would return to house and kitchen, Owuor sighed with the realization that the *bwana* was not smart enough to dry out the salt in his throat while sleeping. Without the *memsahib* and his daughter, the *bwana* opened his ears only to the radio. During the weeks when he had wanted to help the *bwana* live and did not know how, Owuor had become tired. His back had carried too much of the foreign burden. So, he now enjoyed the day when he had to take care only of the little *memsahib* like a man who has run too long and too fast and at the finishing line does not have anything else to do than lie down under a tree and watch the clouds hunt without any prey.

"All is well," he said and drilled a hole into the sky with his left eye.

"All is well," Regina repeated and treated Owuor to the soft sounds of his mother tongue.

She, too, experienced the day before Jettel's return as different from all the days that had been and were still to come. She was sitting at the edge of a field of flax that shook its thin blanket of blue blossoms in the wind. Regina stirred the thick red mud with her feet. It made her body feel warm and sent that comfortable sleepiness to her head that she could permit herself during the dazzling daylight hours only when she was alone with Owuor. Still, Regina was awake enough to see through her half-closed eyes how her thoughts turned into small colorful circles that flew up toward the sun.

It was a good thing that her father had already driven to Nakuru with the Hahns the day before. During the long rains, the roads turned into soft beds of loam and water; a trip that lasted three hours during the months of thirst became a safari scratched by the night. Regina took off her blouse with languid movements, took a mango from her pants pocket, and bit into it, but her heart started beating fast when she realized that she was in the process of tempting fate. If she succeeded in eating the mango without spilling a drop of juice, she wanted to see this as a sign that Mungu would let a miracle happen on this or at least the next day.

Regina had enough experience to know that one could not prescribe the form of His blessing to the great unknown and yet so familiar God. She made her head humble and swallowed the longing in her body, but she did not have strength enough to take the face off her wishes. She forgot about the mango. When she felt the warm juice on her breast and saw her skin turning yellow, she knew that Mungu had decided against her. He was not ready yet to set her heart free from its captivity.

She heard a small plaintive sound that could come only from her mouth and immediately sent her eyes to the mountain so that Mungu would not be angry with her. Regina had chased the grief about the dead baby away as furiously as a dog chases the rat that is clinging to the bone he has buried. But rats could never be chased away for long. They always returned. Regina's rat sometimes let her forget during the day but never at night that she was still the only one who in the future had to feed her parents' hungry hearts with pride.

Regina knew that her mother was different from the women in the huts. When a child died there, it took less than the time between the short and the long rains for their bellies to become big again. When she thought about how long it would take before she could look forward to a baby again, Regina bit hard on the stone within the mango and waited for the crunching sound in her mouth. As soon as her teeth started to hurt, her head would no longer be able to hold on to the evil. But the sadness returned immediately when Regina thought about her parents.

Their ears did not find joy in the rain, and their feet did not know anything about the new life in the morning dew. Her father spoke of Sohrau when he painted beautiful pictures with his words, her mother of Breslau when her dreams went on safari. Of Ol' Joro Orok, which Regina called "home" at school and "zuhause" during her vacations, both saw only the dark colors of the night and never the people who raised their voices only when they were laughing.

"You will see," she said to Rummler, "they will not make a new baby."

When Regina's voice woke him, the dog shook his right ear as if a fly had bothered him. He opened his mouth for such a long time that the wind made his teeth cold, barked once, and quivered all over because the echo gave him a start.

"You are a dumb rascal, Rummler," Regina laughed. "You cannot keep anything in your head." Longingly, she rubbed her nose on his damp fur, which steamed in the sun, and finally felt herself becoming calm.

"Owuor," she declared, "you are smart. It is good to smell a damp dog when one has wet eyes."

"You got his fur wet with your eyes." Owuor said. "Now we both will sleep."

The shadows were as thin and short as a lizard when Regina heard the calls of a heavily breathing motor the next day. She had been sitting at the edge of the forest for many hours, listening to the drums, watching the dik-diks and envying a mother baboon with a baby under its belly. But when she caught the first, as yet far-away sound, she was still able to run the distance to the muddy road fast enough to be able to jump on the runningboard for the last part of the drive.

Oha was at the wheel and smelled of his self-grown tobacco; next to him was Jettel, with the scent of antiseptic hospital soap. In the back were Lilly, Walter, and Manjala, from whom the Hahns never were separated during the rainy season because he was able to handle cars that got stuck in the mud better than anyone else. The white poodle was howling even though it was not evening and Lilly's throat was not yet filled with song.

Regina needed the short ride in the upcoming wind to sharpen her senses and to get her eyes used to her mother. She seemed different to her than in the days before the great sadness had settled on the farm. Jettel appeared like the slim English mothers who hardly talked and kept their smiles between their lips when they came to pick up their children from school at the beginning of the vacation. Her face was a little rounder; her eyes had become quiet like those of well-fed cows.

Her skin once again had the iridescent suggestion of color, which Regina was unable to describe in any of the languages she knew even though she tried over and over again.

When the car stopped, Owuor and Kimani stood in front of the house. Kimani did not say anything and also did not move his face, but he smelled of fresh joy. Owuor first showed his teeth and then exclaimed, "Du Arschloch," very clearly and distinctly, the way the *bwana* had taught him to greet visitors. It was a great incantation. Even though the *bwana* from Gilgil knew him, he laughed loud enough for an echo, which made not only Owuor's ears but his whole body hot.

"You are beautiful," Regina marveled. She kissed her mother and traced the waves in her hair with her fingers. Jettel smiled, embarrassed. She rubbed her forehead, looked shyly at the house, which she had so often longed to leave, and finally asked, still self-conscious but without a tremor in her voice, "Are you very sad?"

"No. You know, we can make a new baby one of these days. Sometime," Regina said and tried to wink, but her right eye stayed open too long. "We are all still very young."

"Regina, you should not say that to Mama now. We both have to make sure that she recovers first of all. She was very sick. Damn it, I explained all of that plainly to you."

"Let her be," Jettel objected, "I know what she means. One day we will make a new baby, Regina. After all, you need a baby."

"And poems," Regina whispered.

"And poems," Jettel confirmed seriously. "You see, I have not forgotten."

The fire that night smelled of the long rain, but the wood finally had to give up its fight and became a flame full of color and fury. Oha held his hands in front of the glow, turned around suddenly even though nobody had called him, hugged Regina, and lifted her up.

"How did the two of you get such a clairvoyant child?" he asked.

Regina drank in the attention of his eyes till she felt her skin get warm and her face red. "But," she said and pointed to the window, "it is already dark."

"You are a bit of a Kikuyu, little madam," Oha recognized, "always splitting hairs. You would make a good lawyer, but fate hopefully will not do that to you."

"No, not Kikuyu," Regina contradicted him. "I am Jaluo." She looked to Owuor and caught the small clicking sound that only the two of them were able to hear.

Owuor was holding a tray in one hand and with the other stroked Rummler and the small poodle at the same time. Later he brought in the coffee in the big coffee pot, which he was allowed to fill only on good days, and served the tiny rolls for which his first *bwana* had already praised him when he had not yet been a cook and knew nothing about white people who got better jokes out of their heads than the brothers of his own tribe.

"Such small loaves," Walter exclaimed and hit his plate with the fork. "How do such big hands make such small loaves? Owuor, you are the best cook in Ol' Joro Orok. And tonight," he continued, and, to Owuor's disappointment, changed languages, "we are going to drink a bottle of wine."

"And you are running to the corner store to get it," Lilly laughed.

"My father gave me two bottles as a farewell gift. They were supposed to be for special occasions. Who knows if we will ever get to open the second? We will drink the first one today because the merciful God has spared Jettel for us. Sometimes, He has time even for bloody refugees."

Regina moved Rummler's head from her knees, ran to her father, and pressed his hand so tightly that she could feel the tips of his fingernails. She admired him very much because he was able at the same time to release laughter from his throat and tears from his eyes, and she wanted to tell him that, but her tongue was too quick and she asked instead, "Does wine make you cry?"

They drank from multicolored liquor glasses, which, on the large cedar wood table, looked like flowers that are waiting for bees for the first time after the rain. Owuor received a small blue goblet, Regina a red one. Between tiny sips, which she let glide down her throat, she held the glass against the flickering light of the Petromax lamp and turned it into a glistening palace for the fairy queen. She swallowed her sadness at the thought that she could not talk to anyone about this, yet she was almost certain that there were no fairies in Germany. There definitely were none in Sohrau, Leobschütz, or Breslau. Otherwise, her parents would at least have mentioned them in the days when she still believed in fairies.

III

"What are you thinking about, Regina?"

"A flower."

"A real wine connoisseur," Oha praised her.

Owuor only stuck his tongue into the glass so that he could taste the wine and still keep it. He had never experienced sweetness and tartness in his mouth at the same time. The ants on his tongue wanted to turn the new magic into a longer story, but Owuor did not know how to start it.

"These are," it finally occurred to him, "Mungu's tears when he is laughing."

"I like to think back about Assmannshausen," Oha remembered and turned the label on the bottle to the light. "We often went there on Sunday afternoons."

"Once too often," Lilly said. Her hand had become a tiny ball. "Maybe you will remember that it was just from our cozy wine bar that we saw the SA march for the first time. I can still hear them yelling."

"You are right," Oha replied soothingly. "One should not look back. But sometimes we just get overwhelmed. Even I."

Walter and Jettel were fighting with old gusto and renewed joy over whether the glasses were an engagement present from Aunt Emmy or Aunt Cora. They were unable to agree, and, after that, they were also, once again, incapable of clarifying whether, during the last evening in Leobschütz, with the Guttfreunds, the carp had been served with horseradish or sauce polonaise. They were busy arguing and realized only too late that they had ventured too far back and now could not avoid speaking about their thoughts. The Guttfreunds' last card had come in October 1938.

"She was so efficient and always able to find a way out," Jettel remembered.

"There is no way out any more," Walter replied softly. "There are only roads without return."

The longing for the past could not be stilled. "You probably also do not know where this green tablecloth came from?" Jettel asked triumphantly. "You cannot get me there. It is from Bilschofki's."

"No. From Weyl's store."

"Mother shopped only at Bilschofki's. And the tablecloth was part of my dowry. Maybe you are going to deny even that."

"Nonsense. This one was lying in our hotel. On the game table when it was not in use. And Liesel shopped at Weyl's only when she went to Breslau. Oh, Jettel, let it go," Walter suggested, with a sudden resolve that was noticed by all, and reached for his glass. His hand trembled.

He was afraid to look at Jettel. He was not sure anymore whether she had ever heard that Siegfried Weyl was dead. The old man, who had refused even to consider emigration, had died in jail three weeks after being arrested. Walter caught himself trying to put a face to the tragedy; he could still see the dark wood paneling in the store and the monograms Liesel had always chosen for the hotel linen there. The white letters were overly distinct at first and then turned into red snakes.

Walter had not had any alcohol since his arrival in Kenya. He realized that even the small amount of wine was making him feel dazed. He massaged his hammering temples. His eyes were unable to focus on the images that crowded in on him. When the logs in the fireplace crackled, he heard songs from his university years and kept looking at Oha to share the intoxicating sounds with him. Oha was stuffing his pipe and watched with grotesque attention the running movements the small white poodle made in his sleep.

Jettel kept on raving about Bilschofki's fine table linen. "There was no better store in Breslau for damask," she reported. "My mother had the white tablecloth for twelve with the matching napkins made to order there."

Lilly, too, was thinking of her dowry. "We bought everything in Wiesbaden. Do you remember the beautiful store in the Luisenstraße?" she asked her husband.

"No," Oha responded and looked out into the dark, "I would not even have thought that there was a Luisenstraße in Wiesbaden. If you keep on going, we might as well start singing 'Oh, beautiful German Rhine.' Or would the ladies rather retire to the drawing room to discuss their wardrobe for the next opening night at the theatre?"

"Quite right! That will leave Oha and me to recap our most important legal cases."

Oha took the pipe out of his mouth. "This is," he said with a vehemence that frightened even him, "even worse than carp with sauce polonaise. I cannot remember any of my cases. And I was supposed to have been a pretty good lawyer. That's what they said. But that was in another life."

"My first case," Walter said, "was *Greschek v. Krause*. There were fifty marks at stake, but Greschek did not care. He was truly litigious. If it had not been for him, I could have closed my practice in 1933. Can you imagine, Greschek accompanied me to Genoa. We looked at the cemetery there. Just fitting for the day."

"Stop it! Have you gone completely crazy? Not even forty yet, and living completely in the past. *Carpe diem*. Didn't they teach you that in school? And for life?"

"That was once upon a time. Hitler did not permit it."

"You," Oha said, and his voice was made soft again by compassion, "are allowing him to kill you. Here, in the middle of Kenya, he is killing you. Is that what you escaped for? Walter, do finally start calling this land your home! You owe everything to it. Forget your table linens, your stupid carp, the whole damned legal system, and who you were. Forget about your Germany, finally. Take your daughter as an example."

"She has not forgotten, either," Walter contradicted and relished the kind of expectation that alone was able to vitalize his soul.

"Regina," he called in high spirits, "can you still remember Germany?"

"Yes," Regina replied quickly. She took only the time she actually needed to accompany her fairy back into the liquor glass. The attention with which everyone looked at her, however, made her insecure, and at the same time she felt the pressure not to let her father down.

Regina got up and put her glass on the table. The fairy, which spoke only English, pulled at her ear. The soft tingling helped her go on. "I still know how the windows were shattered," she said and enjoyed the surprise in her parents' faces, "and how they threw all the cloth on the street. And how people were spitting. And there was a fire, too. A huge one."

"But Regina. You did not experience any of this. That was Inge. We were not even at home at that time any more."

"Let her be," Oha said. He pulled Regina close. "You are quite right, little one. You are the only smart one in this club. Except for Owuor and the dogs. You really do not have to remember anything about Germany but a lot of broken glass and flames. And hatred."

Regina had planned to extend the praise through a question, which she wanted to release between small, but not too short, pauses from her mouth, when she saw her father's eyes. They were as moist as those of a dog who has been barking for too long and whom only exhaustion forces to close his mouth again. Rummler cried like that when he fought the moon. Regina had gotten used to helping him before the fear caused his body to smell.

The thought that her father might not be as easily consoled as the dog put a stone into Regina's throat, but she pushed it off with all her strength. It was a good thing that she had learned to turn her sighs into a cough just in time.

"You should not hate the Germans," she said and sat on Oha's knee, "only the Nazis. You know, after Hitler loses the war we will all go back to Leobschütz."

It was Oha who was breathing too loudly now. Even though Regina did not mean to, she had to laugh because he knew absolutely nothing about the magic of turning sorrow into sounds that do not betray anything that only one's own head is allowed to know.

10

BEFORE THE *BWANA* ARRIVED on the farm four rainy seasons ago, Kimani had known very little about anything that happened beyond the huts where his two wives, six children, and old father lived. It had been enough for him to know about flax, pyrethrum, and the needs of the *shamba* boys, for whom he was responsible. All the *wazungu* with the light hair and the very white skin whom Kimani had met before this black-haired *bwana* from a foreign country had lived in Nairobi. They talked to him only about new fields that had to be planted and about wood for the huts, rain, the harvest, and money for wages. When they came to the farm, they went hunting every day and disappeared again without saying *kwaheri*.

The *bwana*, who drew pictures with words, was not like those men who knew only their own language and the few bits of Swahili that they needed to get by and uttered with a tongue that stumbled between their teeth. With the *bwana*, who now gave him many of the light hours of the day, Kimani was able to talk better than with his brothers. He was a man who often let his eyes go to sleep even when they were open. He would rather use his ears and his mouth.

He used his ears to find tracks on a road that Kimani had never traveled before and for which he longed every day anew. When the *bwana* made his *kinanda* sing, he did it with the skill of a dog that on a quiet day fetches sounds that men cannot hear. But, unlike a dog that will keep those sounds to himself like a bone he has hidden, the *bwana* shared his joy in the *shauris* he discovered with Kimani.

Over time a habit had been established that was as reliable as the sun during the day and the pot of warm *posho* at night. After the morning walk around the *shambas*, both men, without either saying anything, sat down at the edge of the largest field of flax and let the big white hat of the mountain play with their eyes. As soon as the long silence began to make Kimani sleepy, he knew that the *bwana* had started to send his head on the big safari.

It was good to sit still and to swallow the sun; it was even better when the *bwana* talked about things that made his hands tremble slightly like droplets during the last hour of the day. The talks then had the same great magic as the parched earth after the first night of the long rains. In those hours, for which Kimani longed more than food for his stomach and warmth for his aching bones, he imagined that trees, plants, and even time, which one could not touch, had chewed on pepper-berries so that a man could feel them better on his tongue.

When the *bwana* began talking, he always spoke of the war. Through this war of the mighty *wazungu* in the land of the dead, Kimani had learned more about life than all the men in his family before him. The more he learned about the greedy fire that swallowed life, the less his ears could wait for the *bwana* to talk. But each silence could be cut as easily as a freshly hunted animal with a well-sharpened *panga*. To get rid of the hunger that plagued him continually and never in his stomach, Kimani had only to say one of the beautiful words that he had heard from the *bwana* at some point.

"El Alamein," Kimani said on the day when he had just become sure that the two strongest oxen on the farm would not live to see the sun go down. He remembered how the *bwana* had said this word the first time. His eyes had been much bigger than usual. His body had moved as fast as a field of young plants when a storm blows over them, but he had kept on laughing and later on even called Kimani his *rafiki*.

Rafiki is the name for a man who has only good words for another and helps him when life kicks him down like a crazed horse. Up to then, Kimani had never even been aware that the *bwana* knew this word. It was not used often on the farm and never for him by any *bwana*.

"El Alamein," Kimani repeated. It was good that the *bwana* had finally learned that a man had to say important things twice.

"El Alamein happened a year ago," Walter said and first lifted all ten fingers and then an additional two for the twelve months.

"And Tobruk?" Kimani asked in the slightly singing tone that he always used when he had great expectations. He laughed a little when he remembered how long he had tried before he was able to pronounce these sounds. They still felt in his mouth like stones that are being thrown against corrugated tin.

"Tobruk, too, did not help much. Wars take a long time, Kimani. And people keep on dying."

"They also died in Bengasi, you said so."

"They die every day. Everywhere."

"If a man wants to die, nobody should prevent him, *bwana*. Don't you know that?"

"But they do not want to die. Nobody wants to die."

"My father," Kimani said, continuing to pull at the blade of grass he tried to get out of the ground, "wants to die."

"Is your father ill? Why did you not tell me? The *memsahib* has medicine in the house. We'll go to her."

"My father is old. He is no longer able to count his children's children. He no longer needs medicine. I will carry him outside his hut soon."

"My father is dying, too," Walter said, "but I am still searching for medicine."

"Because you are unable to carry him outside his hut," Kimani realized. "That causes the pain in your head. A son has to be with his father when he wants to die. Why is your father not here?"

"Come, I will tell you tomorrow. It is a long *shauri*. And not a good one. Today, the *memsahib* is waiting with our food."

"El Alamein," Kimani tried again. It was always right to return to the beginning of the path when a safari was interrupted. But on the day the oxen were dying, the word had lost its magic. The *bwana* closed his ears and did not open his mouth on the long way back to the house either.

Kimani felt his skin getting cold even though the midday sun had more heat for the earth and plants than they needed. It was not always good to know about life beyond the huts. It made a man weak and his eyes tired before his time had come. Yet Kimani wanted to know if the hungry white fighters would also hand a gun to such old men as the *bwana*'s father to die. But he was unable to get the words that knocked at his forehead into his throat, and he felt that his legs were giving him orders. Shortly before reaching the house, he ran away as if he had just remembered some work that he had forgotten before and still needed to finish.

Walter remained standing in the light shade of the thorn-trees until he could no longer see Kimani. The conversation had made his heart beat faster. Not only because they had been talking about the war and their fathers. He became conscious once again that he liked to share his thoughts and even his fears with Kimani or Owuor much better than with his wife.

In the early days after the stillborn child, it had been different. Full of sadness and anger against fate, Jettel and he had found each other and discovered solace in their shared helplessness. A year later, however, he realized, perplexed rather than embittered, that their loneliness and speechlessness had worn out their bond. Each day on the farm pushed a thorn a little deeper into wounds that did not heal.

When his thoughts circled around the past, the way dying oxen feverishly turn around a last familiar piece of grass, Walter felt so foolish and humiliated that shame shattered his nerves. Just like Regina, he invented nonsensical games to challenge fate. When the sick workers, women and children, on the farm came to house in the morning to ask for help and medicine, he firmly believed that it would be a good day if the fifth person in line was a mother with an infant on her back.

He considered it a good omen when a reporter on the evening news mentioned more than three German cities that had been bombed. Over time Walter developed a neverending series of superstitious rituals that either gave him courage or increased his fears. He deemed his fantasies dishonorable, but they drove him further and further into an escape from reality; he despised his tendency toward wishful thinking, which became ever stronger, and feared for his sanity. Still, he was able to escape the traps he set for himself only for short intervals of time.

Walter knew that Jettel had similar experiences. Her thoughts drove her as strongly to her mother as on the day her last letter came. He had surprised her once when she pulled out the petals of a pyrethrum plant, murmuring, "Lives, lives not, lives . . ." In his shock he had torn the plant out of Jettel's hand with a brutality that he regretted for days afterward, and she had actually said, "Now I will not know today." They stood in the field and cried together, and Walter felt like a child who is not so much afraid of punishment but fears the ultimate certainty that nobody will love him anymore.

Kimani had long disappeared behind the trees in front of the huts, but Walter was still standing in the same spot. He listened to the crackling of the branches and the monkeys in the forest and wished, as if it mattered, for a small part of the joy that Regina would feel right now. To delay his return to the house at least till his overwrought senses had calmed down, he began counting the vultures in the trees. They had tucked their heads under their wings in the midday heat and looked like large black feather-balls.

Walter was going to take an even number as a sign that the day would not bring him anything worse than the restlessness he felt now. An uneven number of less than thirty meant a visitor, the sudden flight of all the detested birds together a salary increase.

"And let us not forget," he shouted into the trees, "that there has not been a single day here without you damn rabble." The fury in his voice quieted him down a little. But he lost his overview and was unable to make out the individual birds. All of a sudden, the only important thing seemed to him to be able to think of the Latin word for someone who interprets the flight of birds. But, as hard as he tried, he was unable to remember.

"You even forget the little bit you once used to know here," he said to Rummler, who came running up to him. "Just tell me, you stupid beast, who on earth is going to visit us?"

There were more and more days without end now. Walter missed Süßkind, the optimistic herald of his early emigration years. That time in itself already seemed idyllic now. In retrospect and by comparison, Rongai seemed like paradise to him. Süßkind had protected Jettel and him from the isolation that oppressed them so much in Ol' Joro Orok that they both did not even dare talk about it.

The authorities had rationed gasoline and were becoming more and more averse to granting enemy aliens the permissions they needed to leave the farm. Süßkind's refreshing visits, the only respite for their tense nerves, had become rare. Whenever he surfaced from his healthy world with news from Nakuru and the solid, unshakable belief that the war could not last longer than a few more months now, there was a short reprieve in which the bars of the prison with its black holes disappeared. Only Süßkind was still able to change Jettel back into the woman whom Walter remembered from better times.

His thoughts about Süßkind turned so intense that he carefully imagined what he would do, say, and get to hear if Süßkind suddenly were to stand in front of him. He even believed that he was hearing voices from the kitchen building. For quite a while, he had given up fighting such illusions. If he pursued them seriously enough, they enabled him for a few blissful moments to change the present according to his needs.

Between the house and the kitchen building Walter noticed four wheels and above them an open box. Irritated, he squeezed his eyes shut to protect them from the midday sun. He had not seen any car except Hahn's for such a long time that he was not sure if this was a military vehicle or one of those mirages that lately fooled him again and again. The enticing picture gradually became clearer, and with every glance Walter became more certain that there really was a jeep between the cedar with the big trunk and the water tank.

It did not even seem unlikely to him that an official from the police station at Thomson's Falls had driven to Ol' Joro Orok and was ready to detain him again. Oddly enough, the landing of the allies in Sicily had led to some arrests—only, however, around Nairobi and Mombasa. The notion of getting away from the farm in the same way that he had when the war started was not unpleasant to Walter, but he was unable to imagine such an abrupt change in his life with all its consequences.

At that moment, he heard Jettel's excited voice. It was strange and yet familiar in a disturbing way. Jettel screamed alternately, "Martin, Martin" and "No, no, no." Rummler, who had run ahead, barked in those high, whining tones that he reserved for unfamiliar visitors.

While he was still running and stumbling several times over small roots in the high grass, Walter tried to figure out when he had heard that name the last time. He could think of only the postman in Leobschütz, who had stayed friendly to the very last when he delivered the mail.

The man had come to Walter's office with a complicated inheritance matter in June 1936, despite the steadily growing massive threats against Jews. As a hello, he had always said "Heil Hitler" and as a farewell, ashamed, "Goodbye." Walter all of a sudden saw him quite clearly. His name was Karl Martin; he had a moustache and was from Hochkretscham. He had received a few acres more than he had expected of his uncle's estate and appeared at Christmas time with a goose at Asternweg—of course, only after making sure that nobody would see him. Decency in those days needed darkness to survive.

Owuor leant out of the tiny window of the kitchen building and bathed his teeth in the sun. He clapped his hands. *"Bwana,"* he called and clicked his tongue in exactly the same way as on the day when there had been wine, "come quickly. The *memsahib* is crying and the *askari* is crying even harder."

The door to the kitchen building was open, but without the lamp, which was lit only after sundown because paraffin was too expensive, the room was almost as dark during the day as at night. It took painfully long until Walter's eyes could discern the first outlines. He saw then that Jettel and a man who was actually wearing the mailman's cap from Leobschütz were closely entwined dancing around the room. They let go of each other only to jump up into the air and to fall immediately into each other's arms again and kiss each other. As much as he tried, Walter could not figure out whether the two were laughing as he thought or whether they were crying, as Owuor had maintained.

"There is Walter," Jettel shouted. "Martin, look. Walter is here. Let me go. You are squeezing me to death. I am sure he thinks you are a ghost."

Walter finally noticed that the man was wearing a khaki uniform and a British military cap. Then he heard him call out. Even before his face, he recognized his voice. First it shouted, "Walter," and then it whispered, "I think I must be going crazy. That I live to see this."

The choking moved so quickly from his throat to his stomach that Walter did not have enough time to lean on the kitchen table before his legs gave way, but he did not fall down. Dazed from a happiness that moved him more than fear had ever done, he put his head on Martin Batschinsky's shoulder. He could not believe that the friend had grown so tall in the six long years that had passed since they had last been together.

Owuor moistened his skin with the laughter and tears of the *memsahib*, his *bwana*, and the beautiful *bwana askari*. He told Kamau to put the table and chairs under the tree with the big trunk that the *bwana* used for rubbing his back when it hurt and that made his skin white as the light of the new moon. Even though the dishes were not dirty, Kania had to bathe all the plates, knives, and forks in the big tub. Owuor himself dressed in the *kanzu* that he wore only when he liked the guests. He fastened his long white shirt, which reached to his feet, with a red sash. Its cloth was as soft as the body of a freshly hatched baby chick. Right on Owuor's stomach were the words that the *bwana* had written and to which the *memsahib* from Gilgil had given the color of the sun with a thick needle and a golden thread.

When the *bwana askari* saw Owuor with his dark red fez, from which the black tassel swayed, and the embroidered sash, his eyes became as big as a cat's at night. Then he laughed so loud that his voice rebounded three times from the mountains.

"Good God, Walter, you haven't changed a bit. How your father would have loved to see this oaf with the lid on his head and the sash with 'Redlich's Hotel' on it. I don't even know when I thought of Sohrau last."

"Well, I do. An hour ago."

"We are not going to think at all anymore today," Jettel said. "We are only going to look at Martin."

"And we are going to pinch ourselves so we know that we are alive."

They had met in Breslau. Walter had been in his first and Martin in his third semester, and both soon became so jealous of each other because of Jettel that they would have ended up lifelong enemies rather than friends had it not been for the New Year's Eve ball of 1924. Their bond was cut only by Martin's hasty departure for Prague in 1937. At the ball, which all three considered fateful later on, Jettel had decided in favor of a certain Dr. Silbermann and had given her two young admirers their marching orders without any explanations whatsoever.

The sting had been equally deep for both of them. Until Silbermann married the daughter of a wealthy jeweler from Amsterdam, Martin and Walter made the pain of the first broken hearts in their lives so tolerable for each other that their rivalries became focused on Silbermann alone. Half a year later, it was Walter who embraced Jettel to console her.

Martin was not a man to forget a slight, but his friendship with Walter had become too strong and could not exclude Jettel. He spent many semester breaks in Sohrau, and for a while it seemed as if he might become Walter's brother-in-law, but Liesel took too much time to decide, and Martin had not enough tolerance for indecision and finally gave up trying. Instead, he became Jettel's witness at their wedding. After he was forced to give up his law practice in Breslau in 1933 and became a representative for a furniture company, he came to Leobschütz quite often to enjoy the illusion that nothing had changed in his life. Most of the time he spoiled Jettel with fanciful compliments, which made Walter's old jealousy flare up again, and he was crazy about Regina.

"I think she said Martin before she said Papa," he remembered.

"I have always envied you your flawed memory. Something like that is worth its weight in gold for us today. Too bad that you will not be able to meet Regina. You would like her."

"Why on earth am I not going to meet her? That's what I came here for."

"But she is at school."

"If that is all, I am sure I can think of something to do about that."

Martin's father, a cattle dealer in a small village near Neisse, had been loyal to the Kaiser and insisted that his five sons, "just like those of William II," as he never failed to mention, had to learn a trade before pursuing their university studies, for which he had deprived himself of all his own needs. Martin had passed his final examination as a locksmith before obtaining his law degree.

As the youngest of the brothers, he learned early to stand up for himself and was proud of his strong will. Even among his best friends, he was known to be quarrelsome. His tendency to exaggerate banalities and not to back down at anything had always impressed Walter and Jettel and became now, at Ol' Joro Orok, the source of their funniest recollections.

"You can't imagine how often we have talked about you."

"Oh, yes," Martin said, "I can. If I look around here, I can see that you talk only about the past."

"We were often afraid that you might not have gotten out of Prague."

"I left Prague before it became dangerous there. I worked for a bookstore owner at the time with whom I could not get along."

"And then?"

"I went to London first. When the war started, I was interned. Most of us were shipped to the Isle of Man, but we were also able to choose South Africa, if one had learned a trade. My late father had been right after all. A trade in hand finds gold in every land. Dear God, it has been a long time since I heard this sentence last."

"And why did you go into the army?"

Martin rubbed his forehead. He always used to do that when he was embarrassed. He drummed on the table with his fingers and looked around several times as if he had to hide something. "I just had to do something," he said quietly. "It started when I found out by accident that they had dragged my father to prison shortly before his death and accused him of having an affair with one of the maids. I found out for the first time then that I was not made of the hardwood that I valued so much in myself. I somehow felt that my father would have liked to see me as a soldier. *Pro patria mori*, in case you still remember what that means. Well, the old fatherland never asked me for such a sacrifice. During the First World War, I was too young, and I would not have lived to see this one if the precious fatherland had not kicked me out just in time. The new one, thank God, thinks differently about Jews."

"I haven't noticed that so far," Walter said. "Anyway," he conceded, "not here in Kenya. Here they take only Austrians. Those have become friendly aliens in the meantime. Where will you be sent?"

"No idea. In any case, I got three weeks furlough all of a sudden. That usually means the front. I don't mind."

"How do they pronounce your name in the military?"

"Very simple, Barrett. My name is no longer Batschinsky. I was incredibly lucky with the naturalization. It usually takes years. It took a little bribery for me. I flirted a bit with a girl who retrieved my application from a pile of papers and put it on top."

"I would never have been able to do that."

"Which one of all those?"

"Give up my name. And my fatherland."

"And start an affair with strange ladies. Oh, Walter, you were always the better person of the two of us, and I am the smarter one."

"And how were you able to find us?" Jettel asked during dinner.

"I already knew in 1938 that you had ended up in Kenya. Liesel wrote to me in London," Martin said. He rubbed his forehead again with two fingers. "Maybe I could have helped her. The British still took unmarried women at the time. But Liesel did not want to leave her father alone. Have you heard anything from them?"

"No," Walter and Jettel said as one.

"I am sorry. But I had to ask sometime."

"We got a letter from my mother and Käthe. They were supposed to be brought east."

"I am sorry. Dear God, what nonsense we are talking!" Martin closed his eyes to push away the pictures, but he could not help seeing Jettel, sixteen years old, in her first ballgown. Squares of taffeta—yellow, purple, and green like the moss in the small town forest of Neisse—danced in his head while he fought against anger and helplessness. He furiously killed his sadness.

"Come," he said gently and gave Jettel a kiss, "tell me something about my best friend now. I bet Regina has become an excellent student. And tomorrow we'll drive cross-country in the jeep."

"Enemy aliens need a permit to leave the farm."

"Not when a sergeant of His Royal Majesty is driving," Martin laughed.

The first trip with Walter and Jettel next to Martin, Owuor and Rummler in the back, only went to Patel's *duka*. Thanks to Martin's unbroken talent for turning a small fight into a big battle, the trip became sweet retribution for all the small arrows that over the past four years Patel had shot from his always full quiver at people who were unable to defend themselves.

The war and the difficulties associated with getting another son into Kenya every year and sending one home to India in his stead had made Patel even more cynical than he was to begin with. The refugees from the farms who spoke Swahili so much better than English and, therefore, were unable to talk to him properly, always offered a welcome release for his bad mood.

He gave them so little of everything they needed that he developed a black market of his own. Walter and several farmhands from Ol' Kalou had to pay double for flour, canned meat, rice, pudding mix, raisins, spices, cloth, dry goods, and especially paraffin. Even though this kind of profiteering was officially not permitted, Patel could count on the forbearance of the authorities as far as the refugees were concerned.

This kind of harassment was considered harmless by the officials and coincided completely with their patriotic sentiments and chauvinism, which increased with every year of the war.

Martin learned about these privations and humiliations only on the way to Patel's. He stopped in front of the last thick mulberry bush, sent Walter and Jettel into the store, and stayed in the jeep with Owuor. Later, Patel was never able to forgive himself for misinterpreting the situation and not realizing immediately that the poor wretches from Gibson's Farm could have come to his store only because they were accompanied.

Patel first finished reading a letter before looking at Walter and Jettel. He did not ask what they wanted; instead, without saying a word, he put flour with traces of mouse feces, dented cans of meat, and damp rice in front of them and then, when he thought he noticed the usual embarrassed hesitation of his customers, he moved his hand in his habitual way.

"Take it or leave it," he scoffed.

"You bloody fuckin' Indian," Martin yelled from the door, "you damn son of a bitch." He took a few steps into the little room and simultaneously swept the canned meat and the sack of rice from the table. Then he proceeded to spit out all the profanities he had learned since his arrival in England and especially in the military. Walter and Jettel understood as little as Owuor, who stood at the store entrance. But Patel's face was enough for everybody. The grumbling, sadistic dictator turned, as Owuor related again and again in front of the huts that night, into a whining dog.

Patel did not know enough about the British military to judge the situation even remotely. He mistook Martin with his three sergeant's stripes for an officer and was smart enough not to risk a discussion. Under no circumstances was he going to spoil his relationship with the combined allied forces for a few pounds of rice and several cans of corned beef. Without being asked, he retrieved perfect groceries from the next room behind the curtain, as well as three big buckets of paraffin and two bales of cloth that had just arrived from Nairobi the previous day. Sputtering, he put four leather belts on top of the pile.

"Into the car," Martin commanded in the same tone of voice with which, as a six-year-old, he had ordered the Polish maids around, and for which he had gotten his ears boxed by his father. Patel was so intimidated that he carried the goods to the jeep himself. Owuor walked in front of him with a stick in his hand as if Patel, the rotten son of a bitch, were only a woman.

"The cloth is for Jettel, and the belts are all for you. I get mine from King George."

"But what am I supposed to do with four belts? I have only three pairs of pants, and one of them is already gone."

"Well, then we'll give one to Owuor so that he will always remember me."

Owuor smiled when he heard his name and became silent with the power of the magic as the *bwana askari* handed him the belt. He gave a salute with two fingers to his head, the way the young men, who themselves were allowed to be *askaris,* did when they came back to Ol' Joro Orok to visit their brothers.

Thus ended the first day of altogether seventeen times twenty-four hours of happiness and abundance. The next morning they went to Naivasha.

"Naivasha," Walter had said doubtfully when Martin showed him the map, "is only for the upper classes. They have not put up signs saying 'No Jews allowed,' but would like to do so. Süßkind told me. He had to accompany his boss there once and had to stay in the car when that one went into the hotel for lunch."

"Well, we'll see," Martin replied.

Naivasha consisted only of a mass of small but well-built houses. The lake, with its plants and birds, was the attraction of the colony and was surrounded by hotels that all looked like private English clubs. The Lake Naivasha Hotel was the oldest and most distinguished. There, they had lunch on a terrace overgrown with bougainvilleas, ate roast beef, and drank the first beer since Breslau. Jettel and Walter dared only whisper. They were embarrassed that they did so in German. Martin's uniform seemed to them like a mother's apron behind which children can feel secure from all danger.

Later, they were riding across the lake in a boat among the water lilies and accompanied by superb starlings. Even though the hotel manager hesitated at first, Martin's threatening tone persuaded him to furnish an extra boat for Owuor and Rummler. The Indian porter emphasized before and after that he had official orders to honor the wishes of all military personnel.

A week later, Walter insisted on taking not only Owuor but also Kimani on the ride to Naro Moru, from where one had the best view of Mount Kenya.

"You know, we stare at the mountain every day, the two of us. Kimani is my best friend. Owuor is part of the family. Just ask Kimani about El Alamein."

"You are just the man I remember," Martin laughed and pushed Kimani between Rummler and Owuor. "Your father used to complain to me that you spoiled his personnel."

"You cannot spoil Kimani. He prevents me from going crazy when fear begins to eat my soul."

"But what are you afraid of?"

"That I will first lose my job and then my mind."

"You never were a fighter. I am surprised that you were able to get Jettel."

"I was her third choice. When she did not get Silbermann, she wanted you."

"Nonsense."

"You never were a good liar."

The hotel in Naro Moru had seen better days. Before the war, mountain climbers had started their tours from here. Since the mobilization, it was no longer prepared to accommodate guests. But Martin could still be as charming as stubborn. He managed to have the cook called and to have lunch served in the garden. Owuor and Kimani were taken care of in the personnel quarters of the hotel but came back immediately after eating to see the mountain. Jettel went to sleep on the deck chair, and Rummler snored at her feet.

"Jettel still looks the same," Martin said. "You, too," he added hastily.

"I am not such a nebbish that I do not own a mirror anymore. You know, I have not made Jettel very happy."

"Nobody can make Jettel happy. Didn't you know that?"

"Well, yes. Maybe just not early enough. But I do not reproach her. She was not cautious enough in the choice of her husband. We have had hard times. We lost a child."

"You have lost yourselves," Martin said.

Owuor opened his ears wide enough for the wind that was sent off from the mountain. Never before had he heard the *bwana askari* speak in a voice that was like water that jumped over small stones. Kimani saw only the eyes of his *bwana* and coughed salt.

"Now I need only Regina," Martin declared at night after returning from Naro Moru. "I am not going to war otherwise. I had looked forward to seeing her so much."

"Her vacation starts only a week from now."

"That is exactly when I have to leave. How do you pick her up from school, anyway?"

"That is a problem we have every three months. In the meantime it chokes our throats. If we are nice, the Boer from the neighboring farm gives her a ride."

"A Boer," Martin repeated in disgust. "It had to come to that! You cannot simply say that to a man from South Africa. I am going to get her. All alone. Preferably next Thursday. We'll send her a telegram tomorrow."

"It would be easier to march to the town hall in Breslau and throw stones into the Nazis' windows. The school does not let its students out one day before their vacation. They did not even allow Regina to visit Jettel in the hospital, even though Jettel's doctor had called them. The school is a prison. Regina does not talk about it, but we have known it for a long time."

"Well, let's wait and see if they dare to say no to one of their own courageous soldiers. On Thursday, I am going to stand in front of that damn school and sing 'Rule Britannia' until they send the child out to me."

11

Mr. Brindley rustled the paper in his hand and asked, "Who is Sergeant Martin Barrett?"

Regina was about to open her mouth when she realized that the answer had not even reached her head yet. She chewed more helplessly than usual on her embarrassment, which still attacked her as a sleepless dog attacks a thief in the night when she stood in the headmaster's room. With an effort that she normally did not have to make, she forced her mind to go through all the books Mr. Brindley had given her to read during the past weeks, but the name he had just mentioned did not appear in any of them.

The feeling of being at the mercy of words was no longer familiar to Regina. She felt as if she had destroyed the best magic of her life by some kind of negligence that she could not explain to herself. Alarmed, she extended her hand to hold onto the only power that could turn the school she hated into a tiny island on which only Charles Dickens, Mr. Brindley, and she herself were allowed to live. And that for a long time now.

Regina knew more than all of the other girls at school. Even Inge did not have any idea about the biggest secret in the world. A fairy that lived in the pepperbushes of Nakuru during the horrible three months of school and in a hibiscus flower at the edge of the largest flax field in Ol' Joro Orok during the vacation had split Mr. Brindley into two halves. The scary part of him, which everyone knew, did not like children, was angry and unfair, and was made up entirely of school regulations, strictness, punishment, and a cane.

Mr. Brindley's magic half, on the other hand, was soft like the rain that in a single night gave new life to the parched roses that had grown from the seeds her grandfather had sent. This strange man, whose name oddly enough was also Arthur Brindley, loved David Copperfield and Nicholas Nickleby, Oliver Twist, and poor Bob Cratchitt and his tiny Tim. Mr. Brindley especially loved Little Nell. Regina even suspected that he was fond of the bloody refugee from Ol' Joro Orok, but she rarely indulged in this fantasy because she knew that fairies did not like conceited people.

It had been a long time since Mr. Brindley had first called Regina Little Nell. But she remembered the day on which the magic had started so well because it was something very special, after all, when an English name was lent to a Jewish girl. Over the years, the recurring but unfortunately always too short time in which Regina was allowed to keep this sweet and easily pronounceable name had turned into a game with the same beautiful unyielding rules that Owuor and Kimani required at home.

The headmaster often had Regina sent for during her only free hours of the day between homework and dinner. During the first terrible moments, his mouth was very small, and sparks burned in his eyes like in those of the miser Scrooge in *A Christmas Carol*. While Regina took the few steps from the door to the desk holding her breath, Mr. Brindley always gave the impression that he had called her for some kind of punishment.

After a time, though, that always seemed very long to Regina, he rose from his chair, let air get into his lips, extinguished the fire in his eyes, smiled, and took a book out of the cabinet with the golden key. On especially good days, the small key turned into a flute, which Pan, the God of the blue flax fields and green hills, played in the hour of the long shadows. The book was always by Dickens and had a soft cover of dark red leather. When Regina took it with an uneasiness, as if she had been caught at some infraction of the school rules, the divided headmaster invariably said, "Bring it back in three weeks and tell me what you have read."

It happened only rarely that Regina was unable to answer Mr. Brindley's questions when she returned the book. During the last four weeks before the vacation, they had often talked so long about the wonderful stories that Dickens told only to the two of them that Regina had been late for dinner, but the punishments from the teacher who supervised the dining hall and always acted as if she did not know where Regina had been were light compared to the joy of the eternal magic.

During the vacation after the baby's death, Regina had tried to tell her father about all of this for the first time, but he considered fairies "English nonsense" and, except for Oliver Twist, whom he disliked, he had not met anybody Dickens, Mr. Brindley, and she herself knew. Since Regina did not want to upset her father, she talked about Dickens after that only when her mouth was quicker than her head.

"I asked you," the headmaster repeated impatiently, "who Sergeant Martin Barrett is?"

"I do not know, sir."

"What do you mean? You do not know?"

"No," Regina said embarrassed, "there is no sergeant in any of the books you gave me. I would have noticed that, sir. I would certainly remember."

"Damn it, Little Nell. I am not talking about Dickens."

"Oh. Pardon, sir. I did not know that. I mean, I could not have guessed."

"I am talking about Mr. Barrett here. He sent you a telegram."

"Me, sir? He sent me a telegram? I have never seen a telegram."

"Here," the headmaster said and held up the paper, "read it out loud."

"Picking you up Thursday. Inform headmaster," Regina read and realized too late that her voice was much too loud for Mr. Brindley's sensitive ears. "Have to be at the front in one week," she whispered.

"Do you by chance have an uncle by that name?" Mr. Brindley asked and for a terrible moment turned into Scrooge the night before Christmas.

"No, sir. I have only two aunts. And they had to stay in Germany. I have to pray for them every night, but I never do that aloud because I have to say those things in German." Mr. Brindley angrily felt himself getting unfair, impatient, and rather annoyed. He was a bit embarrassed, but he simply could not stand it when Little Nell turned into this damn little stranger with those really impossible problems, about which he occasionally read in the London newspapers if he mustered enough energy to study the reports and inner pages more thoroughly. The *East African Standard,* which he read more regularly and liked better since the war had started, luckily hardly ever contained matters that were beyond the reach of his imagination.

"You must know Mr. Barrett if he sends you a telegram," Mr. Brindley insisted. He no longer tried to hide his displeasure. "In any case, he can forget about taking you home five days before the end of school. You know that this is completely against the school regulations."

"Oh, sir, I do not want that at all. It is already enough for me to get a telegram. It is just like in Dickens, sir. There the poor people are lucky, too. All of a sudden. One day. At least sometimes."

"You can go now," Mr. Brindley said. He sounded as if he had had to search for his voice.

"May I keep the telegram, sir?" Regina asked shyly.

"Why not?"

Arthur Brindley sighed when Regina closed the door. When his eyes began to water, he realized that he had gotten a cold again. He felt like a sentimental and senile fool who burdened himself with thoroughly improper problems because he did not keep his mind sharp enough and left his heart unprotected. It was not good to pay more attention than necessary to a child, and he had never done that before either, but Regina's talent, her avid hunger for reading, and his own love for literature, which had been shortchanged during his monotonous years on the job, had come together to make him the addicted captive of an almost grotesque passion.

In pensive moments, he asked himself what Regina felt when he inundated her with books that she was still unable to understand. After each conversation, he made up his mind not to let the child come again. That he never adhered to his decision appeared to him upsetting and degrading for a man who had always despised weakness, but the loneliness, which he had never noticed in his younger and even his middle years, dominated his old age much more than his willpower. He himself had become as susceptible to sentiments as his bones to the humidity from the soda lake.

Regina folded the telegram so small that it could be used as a mattress for her fairy and put it into the pocket of her school uniform. She tried very hard not to think about it during the day at least, but she did not succeed. The paper crackled with every move she made and sometimes so loudly that she believed everyone would hear the treacherous sounds and stare at her. The telegram with the big black stamp seemed to her like a message from an unknown king, and she was sure that he would show himself to her if only she believed in him fervently enough.

As soon as it was time to lock her dream castle, she whipped her memory as mercilessly as any tyrant his slaves to find out if she had ever heard that name before. Regina realized very soon that it was pointless to look for Sergeant Martin Barrett in the stories her parents used to tell. There was no doubt that the foreign king had an English name, but, except for Mr. Gibson, Papa's current boss, and Mr. Morrison, the boss from Rongai, her parents did not know any Englishmen. Of course, there was Dr. Charters, who was to blame for the death of the baby because he did not want to treat Jews, but Regina reasoned that he especially was out of the question if something good had happened to her.

She hoped and feared at the same time that the headmaster would mention the sergeant to her again, but even though she stood in the corridor that led to Mr. Brindley's office during every free minute all day on Wednesday, she did not see him. Thursday was Regina's favorite day because the mail from Ol' Joro Orok arrived and her parents were among the few who wrote even during the last week before a vacation. The letters were passed out after lunch. Regina was called, too, but instead of handing her an envelope, the teacher who was on duty told her, "You are to see Mr. Brindley immediately."

Already behind the rose bed and even more when she was standing between the two round columns, the fairy told Regina that her big hour had arrived. The king who sent telegrams to unknown princesses was standing in the headmaster's office. He was very tall, wore a wrinkled khaki uniform, had hair like wheat that has gotten too much sun, and shining bright blue eyes that suddenly became light like the fur of dik-diks in the midday sun.

Regina's eyes found time to wander very quietly from his shiny black boots to his cap, which sat a bit crooked on his head. When she had finally finished looking, she agreed with the knocking in her chest that she had never seen a more handsome man. He looked as fearlessly at Mr. Brindley as if he were a man like everyone else, not split, and as if his two halves could be made to laugh as easily as Owuor when he sang "Ich hab' mein Herz in Heidelberg verloren."

There was no doubt that Mr. Brindley showed three of his teeth, which meant he was laughing. "This is Sergeant Barrett," he said, "and as I have been told, he is a very old friend of your father's."

Regina knew that she was supposed to say something, but not a single word came out of her throat. She only nodded and was glad that Mr. Brindley had already continued to speak.

"Sergeant Barrett," he said, "has come from South Africa, and will be at the front in two weeks. He wants to see your parents before he leaves and take you home for your vacation today. This puts me into a rather unusual position. This school has never made any exceptions, and we will not do so in the future either, but, after all, we are at war, and we all have to learn to make personal sacrifices."

It was easy to look bravely at Mr. Brindley when he said that and at the same time to press one's chin firmly to the chest. Whenever there was talk of sacrifice, the children had to behave that way to show patriotic enthusiasm. Despite this, Regina was as confused as if she had run into the woods without a lamp at night after dark. First, she had never heard Mr. Brindley talk so long, and second, the sacrifices that the war demanded were usually an explanation of why there were no exercise books or pencils, and marmalade for breakfast or pudding at dinner as soon as the sad news came that an English ship had been sunk. Regina wondered why a soldier from South Africa who wanted to pick her up four days before the end of school represented a sacrifice, but she was able to think only that her chin had to be tucked to her breast.

"I am not going to be able," Mr. Brindley decided, "to deny one of our soldiers the wish to take you to Ol' Joro Orok today."

"Regina, are you not going to thank your headmaster?"

Regina immediately understood that she had to be careful. Her face became rigid, even though she was almost certain that she had the feather of flamingo chick in her throat. She succeeded only at the last moment in swallowing the treacherous giggle that would have destroyed the magic. The soldier king from South Africa exhibited the same difficulties with English sounds as Oha and had pronounced only one word correctly in the entire sentence, and that of all things had been her name.

"Thank you, sir. Thank you very much, sir."

"Run along, and tell Miss Chart to help you pack, Little Nell. We cannot have Sergeant Barrett wait too long. Time is valuable during a war. We all know that."

An hour later, Regina released the air from her lungs, pulled it back in, and freed her nose from the hated scent of harsh soap, leeks, mutton, and sweat, which to her were as much among the dangers of school as the tears a child had to swallow before they turned into hard kernels of salt in her eyes. While she loosened the knot of her school tie and pulled up the tight skirt of her uniform so that her knees felt the sun, the wind endlessly invented new games for her hair. Every time she looked through the fine black net, the white school on the hill became a bit darker. When the many small buildings finally dissolved into distant shadows without contours, her body became as light as that of a young bird that uses its wings for the first time.

Regina did not dare say a word yet for fear that the king from South Africa could turn back into a wish that existed only in her heart and head, and for the same reason she also forced herself not to look at Martin. She allowed herself only to glance at his hands, which gripped the steering wheel so tightly that the knuckles turned into precious white stones.

"Why does the old bird call you Little Nell?" Martin asked when he drove the jeep out of Nakuru and onto the dusty road towards Gilgil.

Regina laughed when she heard the king speak German and with the same intonation as her father. "That is," she said, "a long story. Do you know anything about fairies?"

"Of course. One stood next to your cradle when you were born."

"What is a cradle?"

"Okay, you tell me all you know about fairies. And I'll explain to you what a cradle is."

"And you will tell me why you lied that you are a friend of father's."

"I didn't lie. Your father and I are very old friends. We were young together. And your mother was not much older than you are now when I first saw her."

"I thought you wanted to kidnap me."

"Where to?"

"Somewhere where there are no schools and no bosses. And no rich people who dislike poor people. And no letters from Germany," Regina enumerated.

"Sorry that I have disappointed you. But I did fib after all. To your headmaster. I am coming from the farm. We had a wonderful time, your parents, I, Kimani, and Owuor. And, of course, Rummler. And I did not want to leave without seeing you."

"Why?"

"I really do have to leave in three days. To go to war. You know, I knew you when you were very little."

"That was in my other life, and I cannot remember it."

"In mine, too. Unfortunately, I still can remember."

"You talk like Papa."

Martin was surprised how easy it was to talk to Regina. He had practiced the usual questions that any adult who has no experience with children would ask them. But she talked about school in a way that fascinated him because he recognized Walter's humor from their youth and, at the same time, he was confronted with a sense of irony, which stunned him in an eleven-year-old. Soon, he also found his way in the rapid alternation of fantasy and reality and was able to follow her without any effort from one world to the other. Regina put long pauses between one story and the next, and, when she noticed Martin's irritation, she gave him an explanation as if he were a child and she the teacher.

"Kimani has taught me this," she said. "It is not good for the head when the mouth is open for too long."

Between Thomson's Falls and Ol' Joro Orok, when the road became more and more narrow, steep, and stony, Regina asked, "Why don't we wait here till the sun turns red? This is my tree. When I see it, I know that I am almost home. Maybe the monkeys will come. We can make a wish then."

"Is a monkey something like a fairy?"

"There are no fairies really. I only pretend. It helps, even though Papa says that only the English are allowed to dream."

"Well, today, the two of us are dreaming. Your Papa is a fool."

"But no," Regina objected and crossed her fingers, "he is a refugee." Her voice had become low.

"You love him very much, don't you?"

"Very much," she said. "Mama, too," she added quickly. She saw how Martin, who was leaning against the thick trunk of her tree, closed his eyes, and shut hers, too. Her ears caught the first *shauris* of the drums and her skin the upcoming wind, even though the grass was not moving yet. The happiness of returning home made her body hot. She opened her blouse to let out small sighs and enjoyed the sounds of contentment that she had missed for so long.

The whistling sounds woke Martin. He looked at Regina too long and noticed his uneasiness too late. For a while, he pretended that the power of solitude, which he had never experienced this strongly, the inexplicable noises, and the forest with the dark giant trees were confusing him, but then he realized that memories that he had considered long forgotten were oppressing him.

When the figures on his watch started to form a black circle that attacked his eyes with purple sparks, he finally gave in to the intoxicating pleasure and looked back. First, his English name dissolved into syllables, which he was unable to reassemble, and immediately afterward, he was back in Breslau and saw Jettel for the first time. Martin was a little surprised that she was naked, but he found it pleasant that her black curls were dancing. His reason was still more powerful than his memory. Before the pictures could declare the ultimate war on him, he remembered those strange stories that European men tell each other about Africa. They were all afraid of the moment when the past paralyzed them and robbed them of their sense of time.

"Damn tropics," Martin cursed. He started when his voice erupted in the silence, but when only a bird answered him, he realized that he had not spoken out loud at all; for a while, which seemed interminable, it was enough for him to enjoy this soft reprieve as salvation from an emergency.

Regina did not look like her mother and was not nearly as beautiful as Jettel had been as a young girl. But she was no child. The notion that some stories start all over again made Martin feel his heartbeat. Jettel had once made him aware that he was a man. Regina awakened in him the wish for a future instead of the past.

"Come on," he said, "we are going. You want to be home soon."

"But I am already at home."

"You love the farm, don't you?"

"Yes, but that is my secret. My parents must not know that. They love Germany."

"Will you promise me something? That you will not be sad when you have to leave the farm some day."

"Why should I have to leave?"

"Maybe your father will be a soldier, too, some day."

"That would be nice," Regina imagined, "if he had a uniform like you. Mr. Brindley says you cannot make soldiers wait. The others will envy me then, just like they did today."

"You have forgotten your promise," Martin smiled, "that you will never be sad."

Regina recognized again that Martin was more than only a human being. He knew that it was good to say important words more than once. She took her time before she asked, "Why do you not want me to be sad?"

"Because I am going to come back to you after the war. You will be a woman then. But in the meantime, I have to go to the front. And the world is not as beautiful there as it is here. And I would at least like to imagine that you are as happy as you are now. Would that be very difficult?"

"No," Regina said, "I will simply imagine that you are a king, after all. My king. You don't mind, do you?"

"Not at all," Martin laughed, "this godforsaken place teaches you to dream." He bent down and pulled Regina up at her shoulders, and, when he touched her skin, time started to get confused again for him. First, he felt young and carefree, then, when he heard how heavily he was breathing, old and foolish. He reached out to overcome his melancholy, but Regina's voice was faster than his self-restraint.

"What are you doing?" she laughed. "That tickles."

12

In early December 1943, Colonel Whidett received an order that thoroughly spoiled his anticipation of a carefully planned Christmas vacation at the exclusive Mount Kenya Safari Club and in addition proved to be the most difficult challenge of his entire military career. The Ministry of War made him responsible for Operation "J," which subsequently was to bring about a restructuring of the armed forces stationed in Kenya.

The Colony was, and at that immediately, to follow the example of the mother country and the other members of the Commonwealth and accept into His Majesty's army volunteers who were not in possession of the British citizenship "inasmuch as they are friendly towards the allied cause and do not pose a risk to internal security." The phrase "for any refugees to be considered, an anti-German attitude has to be demonstrated beyond a doubt" confirmed Colonel Whidett's knowledge, acquired over a period of two world wars, that sound British common sense was not a prerequisite for employment in the English war ministry.

In addition, an extraordinarily long-winded addendum pointed out that even the community of German emigrants should definitely be considered. The colonel found precisely this part of the order as confusing and superfluous as it was schizophrenic. He remembered the guidelines from the beginning of the war only too well. Only refugees from Austria, which had involuntarily been annexed by Germany, or from brutally invaded Czechoslovakia and wretched Poland were considered friendly at that time; the ones from Germany, without exception, were considered enemy aliens. Since then, at least according to the common opinion of the leading military officials in Kenya, nothing had happened to require an overthrow of the established principles.

Colonel Whidett first sent his family on vacation to Malindi, disappointedly canceled his own holiday, and then, with some bitterness, but also with the kind of discipline that despite all the pertinent temptations he had never sacrificed to the idle colonial lifestyle, prepared himself for the required process of rethinking matters. With a clarity that he otherwise lacked in matters beyond his comprehension, he realized as quickly as at the beginning of the war that the community of refugees, which was suspect to him before as after, created problems that could not be solved by the usual military routine.

Whidett considered the order from London an almost completely unreasonable demand for the change of an until then generally satisfactory situation, to which the Colony at least owed the fact that the people from the Continent were well taken care of on farms in the highlands. They certainly posed no security risk there and besides were a real help to the British farmers who served in the army. In addition, officers like Whidett did not have to deal with their views and past lives.

To call all the persons who were now being considered into His Majesty's service in such a vast country as Kenya without a sufficient road system for wartime traffic was certainly harder for the people concerned than it might have appeared on a green table in the mother country. At the officers' club in Nairobi, where Whidett, contrary to his usual habit of not talking about official business, expressed his concerns, the phrase "Germans to the front" soon made the rounds. The colonel considered the annoying aphorism not only a challenge to his solid British sense of humor but also a kind of disloyalty that exposed his helplessness.

His memory, which in this case, unfortunately, was working only too well, made it overly clear to him that in most cases he was dealing with people with rather complex life stories that had already poisoned the outbreak of the war for him. Among his most intimate friends, he admitted openly that the beginning of the war, at least in this regard, had been a "delicate finger exercise" compared to the dilemma that he had not yet solved by February 1944, two whole months after the order had come from London.

"In 1939," Whidett declared with his admired sense of sarcasm, "the fellows were delivered to us on trucks, and we were able to put them into camps. Now, obviously, Mr. Churchill expects us to drive out to their farms and check personally if they still eat sauerkraut and say 'Heil Hitler.'"

Strangely enough, though, the nostalgic memories of the start of the war were just what it took to provide the colonel with a solution. Just in time, he remembered the Rubens family and, with that, the remarkable people who in 1939 had fought so vociferously for the release of the interned refugees. A thorough study of the records led the colonel to their names, which he now unfortunately needed once again.

Whidett established contact with the Rubens family through a letter that he wrote with some uneasiness, because he was used to giving orders and not to asking for favors. Two weeks later, a very important meeting took place in his office. The colonel was surprised to discover that four of the sons of the family Rubens, who in his eyes were still far too expressive, yet quite useful after all, were in the military. One of them was in Burma, which certainly did not have the reputation of a slacker's paradise, and one was in the air force in England. Archie and Benjamin were still stationed in Nairobi. David lived at home with his father, which meant that Whidett had an additional adviser.

"I believe," Whidett told the four men, who, he felt, just as the first time, gave a somewhat foreign air to his conference room, "that matters were not thought through to the last detail in London. I mean," he started over again, not without embarrassment, because he did not know how to put his reservations into the right words, "why should someone here join the army voluntarily if he does not have to? After all, the war is far away."

"Not for people who suffered under the Germans."

"Did they?" Whidett asked with interest. "As far as I can remember, most of them were already here when the war started."

"In Germany, you did not have to wait for the war to begin to suffer under the Germans," the older Rubens said.

"Of course not," Whidett agreed hastily, while he wondered whether that sentence might mean even more than he understood.

"Why do you think my sons joined the military, sir?"

"I rarely wrack my brain to find out why someone is in the military. I do not even ask myself why I am wearing this lousy uniform."

"Well, you should, Colonel. We do. The war against Hitler is not just any war. Few of us were given the choice whether we wanted to fight or not. Most were slaughtered without being able to defend themselves."

Colonel Whidett allowed a small disapproving sigh to escape. He remembered, even though he did not show it, that the hefty man in front of his desk had shown a tendency toward unsavory expressions when they met the first time. Experience and logic, however, told him that Jews in general were better able to solve their problems than outsiders, who were not entirely objective.

"How," he asked, "am I even supposed to reach your people in this damn country and let them know that the army all of a sudden is interested in them?"

"Just let us worry about that," said Archie and Benjamin. They laughed out loud when they realized that they had talked simultaneously and then suggested, together again as if each of them was unable to speak alone, "If you don't mind, we will drive to the farms and inform the men who should be considered."

Colonel Whidett nodded with some measure of approval. He did not try too hard to hide his relief. Even though he appreciated unconventional solutions only in moderation, he had never been a man to reject spontaneity when it appeared useful to him. Within a month, he received official permission from London to free Archie and Benjamin from their regular duties and to assign them to special orders. He wrote a friendly letter to their father and asked for his continued support. This saved him from another meeting, which in Whidett's opinion would have been too personal for both sides.

The following Friday, old Mr. Rubens delivered a small speech after the service, in which he spoke of the duty of young Jewish men to show their appreciation to their host country, and, beyond that, he took care of the necessary organization without wasting any time. David took it upon himself to establish contact with the refugees who lived between Eldoret and Kisumu, Benjamin was supposed to drive along the coast, and Archie was going to go to the highlands.

"I am going to start with the man in Sabbatia. I am not going on this trip without an interpreter," he decided.

"Do you mean to tell me that our fellow believers don't even know English yet?" his brother asked.

"There are some real strange stories. For two years, we have had a weird Polish fellow in our regiment who hardly says a word," Archie reported.

"This, of course, would not have happened to my clever sons if they had had to emigrate. They would all have learned the best Oxford English from the Kikuyu on the farms," his father said.

Since the rainy season had not yet started in Ol' Joro Orok, the Gibson farm was one of the first on Archie's tour. This way, Walter, in March 1944, just like Colonel Whidett, was reminded of the outbreak of the war. It was Süßkind again who announced the decisive turn of events in his life.

Late one afternoon, he arrived on the farm with Archie, in the uniform of a sergeant major, and shouted, before barely getting off the jeep, "This is it! If you want to, your days here will be numbered as of now. They finally want us." Then he ran up to Jettel, whirled her around, and laughed. "And you will be the most beautiful war bride in Nairobi. I bet my head on that."

"Now, what is that supposed to mean again?" Jettel asked.

"You have three guesses," Walter said.

The farm was just getting ready to say goodbye to the day. Kimani hit the water tank louder than usual with his iron rod because of a strong wind. The echo had a deep sound when it rebounded from the mountain. The vultures flew screeching out of the trees and immediately returned to the trembling branches.

Breathing heavily, Rummler climbed into Archie's jeep and, panting, started to warm his wet fur on the seats. Kamau, in a shirt that looked like a piece of young grass, carried wood for the kitchen stove. The hollow sound of the evening drums could be heard clearly from the forest. The air was still warm and soft from the sun that had just set but was already moist from the first pearls of the evening dew. In front of the huts, fires were lit, and the dogs of the *shamba* boys barked loudly when they caught the scent of the hyenas that were beginning to howl.

Walter realized that his fingers were numb and his throat dry. His eyes burned. He felt as if he were seeing these sights for the first time and as if he had never before heard the familiar sounds. The racing of his heart made him insecure. Even though he tried to fight it, he sensed the hated, cutting, inexplicable pain of a farewell that might come up to him soon.

"Like Faust," he said too loud and too suddenly, "two souls in one breast."

"Like who?" Süßkind asked.

"Oh, nothing. You don't know him. He is not a refugee."

"Don't you want to explain it to them finally?" Archie asked. His voice had the impatience of a man from the city. He realized it and smiled at the dog in the car, but Rummler jumped out and pushed growling rejection through his teeth.

"Not necessary," Süßkind calmed him down. "They already know. We have not been thinking about anything else for months out here."

"Are you in such a hurry to leave the farms? Or are you afraid that the war will be over before you can play heroes?"

"We have families in Germany."

"Sorry," Archie stammered as he followed Süßkind into the house. He had that unpleasant feeling in his knees that he used to get when his father reprimanded him for some impertinent remark, and he felt the need to sit down. But before he even reached one of the chairs, he lifted his head and looked around. He looked, at first by chance and then with a thoroughness that amused him, at a drawing of the Breslau town hall. The yellow paper was framed in black.

Archie was not used to looking at any pictures other than the portrait of his grandfather in the dining room and photos from his childhood days and of hunting safaris with his cousins from London, but the building with the many windows and the imposing entrance, in front of which several men with high hats were standing, and the roof, which seemed quite beautiful to him, fascinated and irritated him. The picture seemed to him part of a world of which he knew no more than his father's houseboys knew about the Jewish holidays.

He thought the comparison grotesque. While he pulled at the sleeve of his uniform with the crown over the three white cloth stripes, he pondered whether the air force had already thrown bombs on the town with the impressive house and whether his brother Dan had been there. He was a little surprised that he did not like his thoughts; the disapproval annoyed him. It was too late to continue on to the next farm.

Jettel asked Owuor to make coffee; Archie was surprised to hear her fluent Swahili. He asked himself why he had not expected it and felt foolish because he could not find an answer. When he smiled at her, he became conscious that she was beautiful and quite different from the women he knew in Nairobi. Just like the picture in the black frame, she seemed to come from a different world.

His own wife, Dorothy, certainly would not have worn a dress on the farm, but trousers instead, and most likely his. The red checks on the black cloth of Jettel's low-cut dress started to dissolve in front of Archie's eyes, and when he turned away and looked at the town hall again, it seemed to him as if the many small windows had become bigger. He felt that he was about to get one of his headaches and asked if he could have a whisky.

"There is no money here for something like that," Süßkind said.

"What did he say?" Walter wanted to know.

"He likes your picture," Süßkind explained.

"The town hall in Breslau," Jettel said. She noticed that Archie had said "sorry" again, and this time it was she who smiled at him, but the lamps were not lit yet and she was unable to see if he returned her glance. She became conscious that such a harmless exchange might have been the beginning of a flirtation in her youth but realized before there was any time for animation that she had forgotten how to be coquettish.

Dinner was rice with sharply fried onions and dried bananas. "Please, explain to our guest that we were not prepared for visitors," Jettel excused herself.

"Besides, we have not eaten meat since Regina was inconsiderate enough to outgrow her shoes," Walter said. He tried to make his irony cheerful by smiling.

"This is an old German national dish," Süßkind translated and decided to look up the English word for *Schlesien* in the lexicon the next time he got a chance.

It was almost a physical effort for Archie not to pick at his food. He recalled how in his third year in boarding school he had been late for dinner once and as a punishment had had to learn by heart a silly poem about a stupid girl who did not like rice pudding, but he could remember only the first line. The futile search for the second line did not keep him busy long enough.

He tried to swallow the rice and, especially, the salty bananas without chewing them, so that he would taste them less. This was easier for him than to get rid of the shame that overcame him. At first, he thought that only his aversion to the unfamiliar food and the strange atmosphere had made him overly sensitive, but very quickly he became unpleasantly burdened by the awareness that his family and the other long-established Jews in Nairobi had always helped the emigrants freely with money and good advice but had never thought about their past, their lives, their concerns and feelings.

In addition, Archie became more and more embarrassed that he had to have every word he wanted to say to his hosts translated by Süßkind. He felt an almost crazed longing for whisky and yet at the same time had the sensation of already having downed three double ones on an empty stomach. He felt again like he did as a child, when he had been caught listening at the door. It had taken a long time to break him of that habit. Finally, he gave up fighting for self-control and announced that he was tired. Relieved, he accepted the suggestion to retire to Regina's room.

Süßkind stared into the fire, Jettel scraped the last bit of rice from the bowl and pushed a bite into Rummler's jaws, Walter let his knife spin around its own axle. It was as if all three were just waiting for a sign to embrace the carefree cheerfulness of Süßkind's usual visits, but the silence loomed too large, and the release did not come. They all sensed it, even Süßkind, and he was quite surprised that they were no longer able to take change in stride. The possibility alone, that life could become different, frightened them. It had become easier to bear the chains than to throw them off. Tears, which she did not even know were already in her eyes, started running down Jettel's face.

"How can you do this to us?" she shouted. "Just to get killed in the war, after all we have been through. What is supposed to become of me and Regina?"

"Jettel, don't make one of your scenes. The army has not even accepted me yet."

"But they will. Why should I be lucky for once?"

"I am forty," Walter said. "Why should I be lucky for once? I cannot imagine that the English have just been waiting for me to finally win the war."

He got up and wanted to caress Jettel, but he felt no warmth in his hands, let his arms sink, and went to the window. The familiar smell emitted by the wet wooden walls suddenly seemed soft and sweet. His glance took in only the darkness, and yet he was able to sense the beauty that normally gave only happiness to Regina's eyes. How could he tell her? He realized too late that he had spoken out loud.

"You don't have to worry about Regina," Jettel cried. "She is praying every night that you will be able to join the army."

"Since when?"

"Since Martin was here."

"I did not know that."

"And you probably also don't know that she is in love with him."

"Nonsense."

"She has forgotten nothing that Martin ever said to her. She clings to every word. You must have asked him to prepare her to say goodbye to the farm. You two always were hand in glove."

"As far as I recall, it was you who used to hold hands with Martin. Tightly. Martin, by the way, was tight, too. Do you really believe that I do not remember what happened in Breslau at that time?"

"Nothing happened at that time. You were only unreasonably jealous. As always."

"Children, don't fight. At least, something good has happened here," Süßkind said. "Archie has told me how things are being handled. You will be called before a commission and have to tell them why you want to join the army. And don't be a fool. The English certainly do not want to hear that the two of you are perishing on the farm."

"But I don't want to leave the farm at all," Jettel sobbed. "The farm is my home." She was quite content that she had been able to combine deception, naïveté, and stubbornness in her voice and face without too much effort, but then she became aware that Walter had looked right through the beautiful old game.

"Jettel has spent the entire time of our emigration longing for the fleshpots of Egypt," Walter said. He looked only at Süßkind. "Of course, I want to get off the farm, but that is not all. For the first time in years, I have the feeling that I am being asked whether or not I want to do something and that I can do something for my conviction. My father would have wanted me to join the army. He, too, did his duty as a soldier."

"I thought you did not like the English," Jettel reproached him. "Why do you want to die for them, then?"

"Dear God, Jettel, I am not dead yet. Besides, it is the other way round; the English do not like me. But, if they want me, I will join. Maybe then I will be able to look in the mirror again one of these days without feeling like the last nebbish. If you really want to know the truth, I have always wanted to be a soldier. From the first day of the war on. Owuor, what are you doing there? Why are you throwing such a big piece of wood into the fire? We are almost ready to go to bed."

Owuor had put on his attorney's robe. Quietly whistling, he put several more branches into the fireplace, retrieved warm air from his lungs, and gently fed the flames. Then he rose as slowly as if he had to wake each individual limb to life again. He waited patiently until the time had finally come for him to speak.

"*Bwana,*" he said and enjoyed the big surprise in advance for which he had lain in wait ever since the arrival of the *bwana askari*. "*Bwana,*" he repeated and laughed like a hyena that has found its prey, "when you are leaving the farm, I will come along. I do not want to search for you again as on the day when you went on safari from Rongai. The *memsahib* needs her cook when you join the *askari*."

"What are you saying? How do you know?"

"*Bwana,* I can smell words. And the days that have not yet come. Have you forgotten that?"

13

ON THE MORNING of June 6, 1944, two hours before the wake-up call, Walter was sitting in the empty mess hall. The invigorating cool of the yellow moonlit night crept through the narrow open windows and evaporated into the wooden walls, which for short, unexpectedly pleasant moments smelled as fresh as the cedars of Ol' Joro Orok. The time between darkness and dawn was a welcome present his sleeplessness gave to Walter, ideal for sorting out thoughts and images, writing letters, and, undisturbed by the suspicious glances of those soldiers who had the good fortune of having the right country of birth and too little imagination also to appreciate it, searching for the news in German. He tucked the big khaki shirt, which was much more suited to war during a European winter than to the hot days at the southern edge of the soda lake of Nakuru, into his trousers and enjoyed his contentment as the most exciting occurrence of his new security.

After his first four weeks in the military, he had still not sufficiently gotten used to running water, electric light, and fulfilled days not to enjoy them consciously as blessings, of which he had been deprived for so long. Like a child, he found happiness in going to the orderly room in his free time and looking at the telephone there. Sometimes, he even lifted the receiver just to get pleasure from the sound of the dial tone.

Every day anew, he enjoyed listening to the radio and not having to worry about the battery. When the army dentist, roughly and not too skillfully, pulled the two teeth that had plagued him since the first days at Ol' Joro Orok, he even considered this pain as proof that he had come far—he did not have to worry about the bill. Whenever his physical exhaustion and, during the last few days, his heavy sweats allowed it, he granted himself the luxury of pedantically preparing a balance sheet for his once again abruptly changed life.

In one month, Walter had heard, talked, and even laughed more than during the five years on the farms in Rongai and Ol' Joro Orok. He ate four meals a day, two of them with meat, which did not cost him anything, had underwear, shoes, and more trousers than he needed; was able to buy his cigarettes at a soldiers' discount; and was entitled to a weekly ration of alcohol, which a Scotsman with a moustache had already twice traded him for two friendly slaps on the back. His pay as a private in the British army enabled him to afford Regina's school and even send a pound to Jettel in Nairobi. In addition, she received a monthly allowance from the army. Above all, Walter lived without the constant fear that each letter could bring the dismissal from an unloved position and destroy him.

His locker contained paper and envelopes; between empty bottles and full ashtrays stood an inkwell, and next to it lay a pen. The thought that he had only to take what he wanted and that the army would even pay the postage and transport his mail made him feel like the hungry beggar in front of the mountain of sweet pudding in the land of milk and honey. There was a faded picture of George VI on the wall. Walter smiled at the serious-looking king. Before he added water to the dried-out ink, he counted the drops of water that fell from the rusty faucet into the sink and whistled the melody of "God Save the King."

"My darling Jettel," he wrote and was a little startled, as if he had provoked fate and now had to face the envy of the gods, he put down the pen. He realized that he had not said anything like that to his wife for years and had also not felt this way about her. For a moment, he pondered if the tenderness, which had come so naturally to him, should make him happy or ashamed but could not find an answer.

Still, he was not dissatisfied with himself when he continued writing. "You are quite right," he scratched onto the yellow paper, "we are writing letters to each other again just as during the time when you were still in Breslau waiting to emigrate. Only now, the three of us are safe and can await quietly what life has in store for us. And, in contrast to you, I think that we have to be especially grateful and should not complain just because we have to get used to new surroundings. After all, we have had some experience with that in the meantime.

"Now about me. I am on the go all day long and am having a hard time imagining how the English did get this far without me. They are training us as thoroughly as if they had only waited for the bloody refugees to finally mount an attack. I think they are trying to turn me into a mixture of close combat fighter and mole. At night I feel as if I have malaria again, but I hope I will get better soon. At any rate, I crawl all day long through mud and sludge and sometimes do not know at night if I am still alive. But don't worry. Your old man is holding up well, and yesterday it looked as if the sergeant even winked at me. Admittedly, he is cross-eyed like old Wanja in Sohrau. Maybe he was even going to give me a medal because I had to go through all of this with blisters on my feet.

"In case you are wondering about the blisters, they have given me boots that are much too narrow, and I do not know enough English to tell them that. I have decided, however, not to ask any of the other refugees in my unit to translate for me. Maybe I will learn some English this way. Moreover, the trainers do not like it when we speak German. At least they noticed on their own that the cap was too big and constantly slid off my head. For the last two days now, I have been able to see again, even in uniform. You see, we have our worries as soldiers. Only they are quite different from before.

"That reminds me, we have to notify Regina of the most important change in her life. She no longer has to pray every night that I will not lose my job and can concentrate on asking God for victory in the allied cause. She has no idea, of course, that I am stationed in Nakuru. You may have noticed already that military correspondence is sent without a return address. Also, I would not like to put her in the same position as during your pregnancy.

"At any rate, I am sure that we have made the right decision. Some day you will agree with me. Just as you have admitted in the meantime that it was better for us to emigrate to Kenya than to Holland. By the way, I met a rather nice chap here who had a radio store in Görlitz. Of course, he is able to manipulate a radio much better than I and is well informed. He told me that there is no longer any hope for the Dutch Jews. But do not mention this to your hosts. As far as I remember, Bruno Gordon had a brother who went to Amsterdam in 1933.

"I hope that you will soon find a place to live on your own in Nairobi and maybe even some kind of work that you might like and that would help us all. Who knows if we will not be able to put aside some money for the time after the war? (They will not need soldiers anymore then, and we, on the other hand, will need a new future.) When you no longer have to stay with the Gordons and can live the way you want to again, you will surely start to like Nairobi. You always loved to be among people so much. I am enjoying just that part immensely despite all the drudgery.

"The Englishmen in our unit are all very young fellows and really quite nice. They do not fully understand why a man with their skin color does not know their language, but some of them give me a friendly pat on the back—probably because I am ancient in their eyes. In any case, it is the first time for me since we left Leobschütz that I do not feel completely like a second-class human being, even though I suspect that the sergeant is not really a philo-Semite. Sometimes, it is actually not too bad if one does not understand the language of a country.

"I miss Kimani very much. I know it sounds ridiculous, but I simply cannot forget that I was unable to find him when we were leaving the farm and could not tell him anymore what a good friend he had been to me. Be glad that Owuor and Rummler are with you, even if Owuor fights with the Gordons' boys. After all, he was not able to get along with anyone but us in Ol' Joro Orok, either. For us, he is a piece of home. Regina, especially, will see it that way when she spends her vacation in Nairobi for the first time. You see, I am getting sentimental in my old age. But the English military has been so successful of late that it can even put up with a sentimental soldier. This one has already learned some English profanities and is also longing to hear from you. Write soon to your old Walter."

Only when he thought of Regina did Walter's new confidence get its old scratches again. The fear of having failed plagued him as mercilessly then as during the days of their deepest despair. He was unable to imagine his daughter, for whom Ol' Joro Orok was home, in Nairobi. The knowledge that he had cut her roots and was asking her to make a sacrifice that she could not understand was unbearable to him.

Hopelessness and despair had never broken his pride as agonizingly as the fact that his draft into the army had degraded him to a coward in his daughter's eyes. He had had to inform her of their departure from the farm in writing. It was the first sorrow that he had consciously inflicted on Regina. In the letter, which he wrote to her at school, he had tried to paint a picture of life in Nairobi as a series of cheerful, carefree days full of diversity and new friends, but, while doing so, he had been able to think only of his parting from Sohrau, Leobschütz, and Breslau and had not found the right words. Regina had answered immediately but had not mentioned the farm, which she was never going to see again, at all. "England," she had written in capital letters, underlined in red, "expects every man to do his duty. Admiral Nelson."

When Walter had finally translated the sentence with the help of a small dictionary, which since the first day in the army had been his only reading material, he discovered that he had encountered it already during his last year in high school, but he could not quite make up his mind if he was being ridiculed by fate or by his daughter. He disliked both possibilities.

He was tortured by the fact that he did not know if Regina was really already so grown-up, patriotic, and, above all, English that she did not show her feelings or if she was, after all, a hurt child who was angry with her father. Such thoughts usually made only one thing clear to him: He knew too little about his daughter to interpret her reaction. Even though he did not doubt that she loved him, he had no illusions. He and his child did not have a common mother tongue anymore.

For a moment, while he still remained deaf to the noises of the coming day, Walter imagined how he would never talk German to Regina again after he had finally learned English. He had heard that many emigrants did this to give their children the security of being firmly rooted in their new surroundings. The picture of how he, ashamed and embarrassed, tripped over words that he could not pronounce and had to talk with his hands to make himself understood stood out in grotesquely sharp lines in the early dawn of the morning.

Walter heard Regina laugh, first quietly and then provokingly loud. Her laughter sounded like the hated howling of the hyenas. The thought that she was ridiculing him and that he was unable to defend himself threw him into a panic. How would he ever be able to explain to his daughter in a foreign language what had happened to turn all of them forever into outsiders? How could he talk in English about a homeland that tortured his soul?

It took a big effort for him to quiet down sufficiently to face the day. Hungrily, he turned the knobs on the radio to get rid of the ghosts he had conjured. When he felt cold sweat running down from the back of his neck into his shirt, he realized with a shudder that the past had caught up with him. It was the first time since joining the army that he had acknowledged the suppressed reality. He wore the stigma of homelessness on his forehead and would remain a stranger among foreigners all his life.

Snatches of conversations reached Walter's ears. Even though the radio had not been turned up fully, they were loud and excited, at times almost hysterical, and yet at first they comforted his confused senses. Soon he realized that the voices of the news reporters sounded different. Walter tried to piece the individual syllables together into words but did not succeed. He took a fresh piece of paper from his locker and forced himself to translate all the sounds he caught into letters. They did not make sense, and yet he grasped that two words were being repeated several times over a short period of time and most likely were "Ajax" and "Argonaut." Walter was surprised that he had recognized the two familiar names despite the nasal English pronunciation. The picture of his teacher Gladisch at the high school in Pless and how he had distributed the exercise books after a history exam with an unmoved face appeared in front of Walter's eyes, but he did not have enough time to hold on to his memory. The soft wooden floor emitted new sounds into the room.

Sergeant Pierce appeared simultaneously with the rising sun. His steps already had the force that enfolded him in pride, but the rest of his body was still struggling against the night, which was indifferent to his talent for forcing his subordinates into the clear, secure world of his profanities and uncompromising attitude. Without energy and concentration, the sergeant ran his hand through his thick hair, yawned several times like a dog that has been lying in the sun too long, closed his belt very slowly and looked around, searching. It seemed as if he were waiting for a special sign to begin the day.

As he stared at Walter silently and out of still half-closed eyes, he resembled a statue that has long been made obsolete by history, but then life shot into his limbs with unexpected suddenness. He took a few grotesque jumps and ran to the radio with his heavy boots hardly touching the floor. His breath came in short and very abrupt gasps while he turned the volume up loud. His pale face turned unusually red and showed an amazement that was also very unusual for him. With an effort, Sergeant Pierce straightened himself up to his full height, put both hands on his trouser seams, and shrieked, "They have landed."

Walter realized immediately that something extraordinary had happened and that the sergeant expected some kind of reaction from him, but he did not even dare look at him; instead, he stared fixedly on the paper with his writing.

"Ajax," he finally said, even though it was clear to him that Pierce must consider him an idiot.

"They have landed," the sergeant screamed again, "you bloody fool, they've landed." He gave Walter a sharp whack on the shoulder, which despite his impatience was not without friendliness, pulled him up from his chair, and pushed him in front of the badly printed map that hung between a picture of the king and the admonition not to betray military secrets carelessly. "Here," he shouted.

"Here," Walter repeated, happy that for once, at least, he had captured the same sounds as Pierce. Perplexed, he looked at the sergeant's meaty index finger, which swept across the map and finally stopped in Norway.

"Norway," Walter eagerly read out loud and tried to think hard whether Norway in English actually rhymed with fly and what on earth might have happened there.

"Normandy, you damned fool," Pierce corrected him, irritated. He moved his index finger first to the east to Finland and then south toward Sicily, and then, because Walter remained silent, he drummed with his whole tattooed hand on the map of Europe. Finally, a far-fetched idea for a man with his vocal powers struck him, and he got a pen. With unskilled movements, he wrote the word "Normandy" and like a timid child held his hand out to Walter.

Walter grasped it silently, and he gently put Sergeant Pierce's trembling index finger on the coast of Normandy. However, he found out only at breakfast, from the radio dealer from Görlitz, that the Allied forces had landed there. Instead of the pending cross-country march in full gear with the recruits, Sergeant Pierce ordered Walter to service in the orderly room, and, even though his face did not look any different than usual, Walter imagined that he had wanted to do him a favor this way.

Dinner that night consisted of mutton with mint sauce, slightly undercooked beans, and, appropriate to the miracle in France, a very heavy and firm Yorkshire pudding—a feast the like of which they had not had since the Allies landed in Sicily. In the mess hall, which had been decorated with small Union Jacks, they first sang "God Save the King" and then "Rule Britannia" before the meal and, after the fruit salad with warm vanilla sauce, "Keep the Home-fires Burning." The happiness reached its first climax with "It's a Long Way to Tipperary."

The first brandy, which they drank from water glasses, was mixed with melancholy tears. Sergeant Pierce was in high spirits and, in the pauses between songs, enjoyed the admiration of his happy men and praise because he had been the first to find out about the lucky break in the war, but his acknowledged sense of fair play functioned as well as his memory. The sergeant nipped every suspicion in the bud that he could forget himself far enough to take unearned credit.

During dinner and before a summary of the day's happy events, he insisted on some applause for Walter, because he had known instantly where "bloody Normandy" was. Pierce personally saw to it that Walter's glass did not remain empty.

Again and again, he poured in turn brandy and whisky into Walter's glass and became even more spirited than he already was when the strange silent fellow from Europe finally learned to say "cheers," and, at that, with the beautiful Cockney accent that was one of the sergeant's trademarks.

Walter considered the brandy a blessing for his stomach, which had been upset for days, and the whisky the ideal drink to distribute the cold, bad-tasting mutton fat evenly in his mouth, even though it became harder with every gulp to concentrate on the conversation, which he did not understand anyway. He felt the dizziness in his head, but also a pleasant murmur in his ears, which reminded him in an enjoyable way of his student days and which he interpreted as contentment, until he started feeling cold. At first, the sensation was not an unpleasant one, since it cooled his head in the thick haze of alcohol, tobacco, and sweat and alleviated the pounding pain in his temples.

But then, first, the furniture started to move in front of his eyes and, soon, the people, too. Sergeant Pierce became larger and larger with downright astonishing speed. His face looked like one of those impudent red balloons that Walter had seen last during a shipboard party on board the *Ussukuma*. He thought it very childish and also enormously imprudent that the Allied forces had deployed such cheap balloons when they landed in Normandy, especially because they burst in short intervals and dissolved into tiny swastikas, which brazenly and loudly started singing "Gaudeamus igitur."

As soon as the song stopped and there was a pause in the rush of pictures, Walter realized that he was the only one who could not take the alcohol. He was embarrassed and, despite his sweats, tried to stay as upright as possible by pressing his back against the chair and clenching his teeth. When he discovered that the cold mutton fat had turned to hot blood in his mouth, he would have liked to get up but told himself that as a refugee he should not attract unnecessary attention. So he stayed seated and dug his fingernails into the edge of the table.

The new sounds attacked him more painfully than before; they were so violent that they paralyzed him. Walter heard Owuor laughing and, soon afterward, his father calling, but he was not able to distinguish their voices long enough before they turned into a frightened whimpering. Despite that, Walter was tremendously relieved to know that his father was safe in Normandy, only a little worried that he could not remember his sister's name. He could not hurt her under any circumstances if she should also call out to him, but the effort to remember in time and to justify himself after such a long interval to his father, because he had left him and his sister alone in Sohrau, caused his body to melt in the heat. Walter knew that this was now the very last opportunity to thank old Mr. Rubens because he had sponsored Regina and Jettel and gotten them out of hell. It was good that he no longer felt cold. All of a sudden, it was easy for him to get up and walk over to his rescuer.

Walter woke up three days later, and then only for a short while, not in the military barracks but in the General Army Hospital in Nakuru. When this happened, Corporal Prudence Dickinson, who was admired very much by most of the patients because of the enviable mobility of her hips and whom they called Prue, was fortuitously present. She was, however, not in the mood for a conversation with a man who, during his disturbing attacks of febrile delirium, without a doubt had spoken German and thus injured her patriotic ear even more than the enemy himself could ever have done.

Prue, however, did wipe the sweat of the sick man's forehead, smoothed his pillow and the olive green hospital gown with the same absentminded movements, pushed the thermometer between his teeth, and uttered, in complete contrast to her usual behavior with patients whom she disliked, a complete sentence. With a kind of self-irony that did not correspond to her intellect and sense of humor, which she considered the only weapon for making the disgusting service in this lousy Colony bearable, Prue told herself that she could have saved herself the trouble. Walter had already fallen asleep again and, for the time being, had missed the only opportunity to learn that neither whisky nor brandy and mutton were responsible for his condition. He had black water fever.

He owed his life to the fast reaction of Sergeant Pierce, who as a soldier had had too much experience with alcohol and as a child in the slums of London had seen too many in a delirium to misinterpret Walter's condition during the great victory celebration. When Pierce saw the strange bird from the continent collapse in the mess hall, he was not for a moment misled by the suggestions of his jubilant comrades, who wanted to dunk Walter into a tub of cold water. Pierce had Walter transported to the hospital immediately. The news of his action even got around to Nairobi, because it showed the exceptional organizational talent of a capable soldier who had succeeded in finding a sober driver on the day of the invasion of Normandy.

Even though the sergeant had sufficient reason to concentrate on himself since the first rumors of his promotion to sergeant major had reached him, he had received a daily report on Walter's progress. He talked as little as possible about this behavior, which struck him as strange; Pierce considered any interest in one of his people as not quite appropriate and, above all, as favoritism, which was beneath him. He found it disturbing. He could explain this unusual excursion into the private sphere only by the fact that it had been the funny refugee with whom he had first learned about the "thing in Normandy." Occasionally, he was teased because he repeatedly said "funny" and only rarely "bloody" anymore, but Pierce did not have a tendency to examine linguistic subtleties and thus did not see any need to correct himself.

After a week, he visited Walter in the hospital and was shocked when he saw him lying in bed listlessly with blue lips and yellow skin. Walter's happiness to see him and the fact that he actually said "cheers" with a beautiful Cockney accent touched Pierce. After this promising greeting, though, the two men could only look at each other silently, but when the pauses got too long, Pierce said "Normandy" and Walter laughed, whereupon Pierce almost always clapped his hands without feeling ridiculous about it. On his visit at the beginning of the second week, he brought along Kurt Katschinsky, the radio dealer from Görlitz, and understood for the first time in his life how important it is for people to be able to communicate with each other.

The well-nourished, tight-lipped messenger from heaven in short khaki pants whose name was Katschinsky and who was actually in the process of losing his mother tongue told Walter about the black water fever and finally absolved him of the torturous self-reproach that had made him believe that he had acted like a dunce and had poisoned himself with alcohol. Katschinsky told his sergeant, whose duty it was in case of severe illness to arrange for a visit by a spouse but who did not have Jettel's address, that Walter had a twelve-year-old daughter in school only a few miles away. The next morning, Pierce appeared with Regina.

When Walter saw his daughter coming into the hospital room on tiptoes, he was certain that he was having a relapse and high fever again. He quickly closed his eyes to hold onto the wonderful picture before he would find out that it was an illusion. During the first days of his illness, he had experienced over and over again how his father and Liesel sat at his bedside but dissolved into ethereal substances the moment he addressed them; he could not repeat this irreparable mistake with Regina.

Walter realized that his daughter was still too young to understand what happened to refugees who did not want to forget. It was more merciful for both of them not to establish contact so that they would not have to separate again. Regina would be grateful to him some day. When it became clear to him that she was not willing to learn from his experiences, he raised his hands in front of his face defensively.

"Papa, Papa, don't you recognize me?" he heard her say.

Her voice came from so far away that Walter could not decide whether his daughter had called out to him from Leobschütz or from Sohrau, but he felt that he could not lose any time if he wanted to bring her to safety. Just standing around in the homeland as if she were a child like all the other children, too, posed a mortal danger. Regina was too old for dreams, which outlaws could not afford to have. Her resistance made Walter furious, but his anger also gave him strength, and he realized that he had to force himself to slap her in the face in order to save her. He succeeded in straightening himself up in bed by pushing both hands to the back. Then, the warmth of her body pushed onto his, and Regina's voice was so close to his ear that he felt the tremor of the individual sounds.

"At last, Papa, at last. I thought you would never wake up again."

Walter was so stunned by the reality that revealed itself very slowly to him that he dared not say a word. He was also oblivious to the fact that Sergeant Pierce stood at the head of his bed.

"Were you wounded?" Regina asked in faulty German.

"My God, I had forgotten that you can't speak German properly anymore."

"Were you?" Regina insisted.

"No, your father is just a very stupid soldier who got black water fever."

"But he is a soldier," Regina insisted proudly.

"Cheers," Pierce said.

"Three cheers for my daddy," Regina shouted. She held her arms above her head, and then she noticed that this funny soldier, who spoke such strange English that she had to make every effort not to laugh, lifted his right arm and cheered "hip, hip, hooray" together with her.

Much later, Walter suggested to his daughter, "Tell him he should find out for me why this battle-ax of a nurse cannot stand me."

Sergeant Pierce listened attentively while Regina excitedly reported what she had found out and, after that, called for Corporal Prudence Dickinson. First he asked a few polite questions, but all of a sudden he stood erect, placed his hands on his hips, and, to Regina's amazement, called Nurse Prue "a nasty bitch," upon which she left the room wordless, without swinging her hips and with a face redder than a bushfire that does not have to be afraid of the rain.

"Tell your father the woman is a stupid ass," Pierce explained. "She was annoyed that he spoke German in his fever. But I think you should only tell him that after he has gotten well again."

"He wants to know something else," Regina said quietly.

"Just ask."

"He wants to know if he can no longer be a soldier now."

"But why?"

"Because he immediately fell ill."

Pierce felt a pebble in his throat and had to emit a little cough. He smiled, even though the occasion did not seem quite fitting to him. He somehow liked the little girl. Although she had no braids, red hair, or freckles, she somehow reminded him of his sisters, but he could not remember which one. Possibly, of all five. Some time. It was almost certainly too long ago since he had last seen the girls. At any rate, the child with the damn arrogant Oxford accent of the rich had courage. He sensed it, and he liked it.

"Explain to your father," Pierce said, "that the army still needs him."

"He says you can keep your job," Regina whispered. She quickly kissed her father on both eyes so that the sergeant would not notice that he was crying.

14

THE HOVE COURT HOTEL, with its sand-encrusted palms on both sides of the exquisitely shaped black wrought iron gate, its lemon trees with their hard green and bright yellow fruit, its profuse mulberry bushes, giant cactus plants, long-stemmed roses in the big garden, and bougainvillea blooming in deep purple in front of flat little white houses clustered around a well-trimmed lawn, was almost as old as the town of Nairobi itself. When the extensive establishment was built by an architect from Sussex in 1905, it served as the first quarters for the newly arriving government employees until they brought their families to the Colony and moved into their own houses.

The expansive elegance, which in the wild founding years of the young town had provided a very English enclave, did not exist anymore since Mr. Malan had become the hotel's owner. He saw to it, quickly and scrupulously, when he ordered new signs and, sharply calculating, dispensed with the word "hotel," that the Hove Court was no longer the right address for people who knew how to live in style. The experienced merchant from Bombay recognized the requirements of the new times with a practiced eye. It was no longer government officials with nostalgic dreams of the old homeland or even safari guests with their pronounced desire for elegance and comfort before their departure into great adventure who needed lodgings, but refugees from Europe. Malan, who owed his fortune to a marked instinct for the low points in life, thought that they could be handled easily. They all needed to start over again, and in their industry and eagerness they were as parsimonious and modest as his own compatriots who dared to start life over in Kenya.

Refugees, who could not afford sentimentality, were served much better by low prices than by the tradition of old English country houses. As early as the thirties, when the first immigrants came from the Continent, Malan had the big rooms converted into small flats. He changed the parlors, small kitchens, and bathrooms into single rooms with washstands behind a curtain, installed shared toilets, and left only the small dingy huts with the corrugated tin roofs for the black personnel in the free area behind the large garden in their original condition. This one concession to the customs of the country would soon prove to be an especially clever move.

Even though Malan's tenants exhibited a poverty and a modesty that were unusual for whites and lived almost as primitively and as crowded as his relatives in Bombay, they were, thanks to his cleverly thought-out psychological coup, still able to afford the help that an unwritten law required for the white upper classes, and with that the illusion that they were on their way to integration and had the same standard of living as the English in the houses at the edge of town. Whoever, after a long waiting period and, often also, after paying a high sum in addition to the first month's rent, succeeded in getting into the Hove Court settled there for a long time. Some families had lived there for years.

Mr. Malan knew very little about European geography and the prejudices to which a man of his wealth was entitled. It just so happened that he preferred refugees from Germany when choosing his tenants. They were much more subdued than the self-assured Austrians, cleaner than the Poles, and above all punctual in their payments, and they did not make a pained face like the local whites when they heard an accent; naturally, because of their difficulties with the language, they tended not to give him arguments, which he despised.

He had discovered that the Germans, against whom he had nothing even after the outbreak of the war because he himself hated the English, were afraid of change and, even more than other people, wanted to live among their own people. This was to his advantage. Quick turnovers at the Hove Court and the necessary renovations that were connected with them would have strained his finances. This way, however, his bank account and his standing grew with every year, even outside the small group of Indian businessmen, and it did not trouble him in the least that his prosperous property had to be measured by standards completely different from those applied to the elegant hotels in town.

Malan appeared three times a week in the Hove Court, mainly to demonstrate to people with complaints that they were now living in a free country and had the right to move out at any time and to settle down somewhere else. He did not pay any attention to the hierarchy in the Hove Court. The most beautiful flat with a eucalyptus tree in front of its window and a tiny garden with blood-red, vanilla-yellow, and pink carnations was occupied by old Mrs. Clavy and her aging dog, Tiger, a brown boxer with an aversion to harsh German sounds. Mrs. Clavy herself, whose bridegroom had died six weeks after his arrival in Nairobi and long before the First World War, however, was considered friendly. She did not judge children by their mother tongue and smiled at them without reservations.

Lydia Taylor, once a waitress at the London Savoy, was the second Englishwoman who tolerated life in a community of foreign-language individuals with a composure that was not considered at all natural by the refugees. Her third husband was a captain in the army who was not willing to pay more than the monthly rent for two rooms at the Hove Court for her and her three children, of whom only one was his.

Her expensive and low-cut silk dresses from the short period of her second marriage to a textile merchant from Manchester and her three houseboys and aged *aya,* who shortly after sunrise pushed the pram through the garden, singing loudly, provided topics of conversation. Mrs. Taylor's terrace was a subject of envy. Here, she nursed her baby during the day and received her many vocal young friends in uniform at night. They ensured her social status, since her husband, to her relief, had been transferred to Burma.

Also not too badly off, almost always on the shady side of the garden and often with a tiny porch in front of the windows, just big enough for flowerpots with thriving chives, were the earliest emigrants. They attracted the jealousy of the refugees who had arrived after them and, for their part, treated the newcomers with the kind of good-natured condescension that in the old country had been deemed appropriate for poor relations.

The elite immigrants, favored by fate, included the old Schlachters, from Stuttgart, who could not be persuaded to share their recipes for puff pastries and spaetzle, which was what they lived on; the surly cabinetmaker Keller, from Erfurt, who had become a manager in a sawmill, with his wife and his impertinent adolescent son; and Leo Slapak, from

Krakau, with his wife, mother-in-law, and three children. Slapak earned good money with his secondhand shop but was not willing to spend it, of all things, on better living quarters.

Elsa Conrad was counted among the longtime residents of the Hove Court, not justifiably so but because she had quickly attained status through the sovereign way in which she handled Mr. Malan. Even though she had moved in only after the beginning of the war, she had two large rooms and a terrace that was almost as big as Mrs. Taylor's. Eighty-year-old Professor Siegfried Gottschalk actually was one of Mr. Malan's early tenants. Even the unlucky ones in the small sheds found him likable; he was the only one who did not boast of his status as a farsighted early immigrant who had recognized the signs of the impending doom in time.

He had sacrificed the mobility of his right arm to the Kaiser in the First World War and, after that, with the same enthusiasm served his hometown as a professor of philosophy. On a spring day in 1933, which first because of its mild air and later because of a tempest in his heart remained forever etched in his memory, he had been chased into the street by yelling students from Frankfurt University. Until that fateful hour, they had carried him, with articulately expressed love for his extraordinary mentoring, on a soft pillow of illusions.

In contrast to the general custom in the Hove Court, Gottschalk rarely spoke of the glamour of his good days. Every morning, he got up at seven o'clock and walked to the small hill behind the huts of the houseboys, whom he steadfastly called "Adlati," wearing his sun helmet, which he had bought for the emigration, and a dark suit with a gray tie, which also hailed from his hometown; he did not even permit himself to wear lighter clothing or to take the customary rest in the midday heat.

"Our professor," as even those people in the Hove Court who had never had any connection to academic life in the home country and who considered him absent-minded and strange called him, was Lilly Hahn's father. Invariably, he rejected her repeated pleas to move in with her and Oha on the farm with the argument "I need people around me, not cattle."

For almost ten years now, he had asked himself and his books why he, of all people, had had to witness the apocalyptic riders and keep on living, but he never complained. Then he received a letter from his daughter, which for a few days at least simultaneously invigorated and excited him. Lilly asked her father to look up Jettel at the Gordons' and to put in a good word to Malan so that she and her daughter could live at the Hove Court.

Even though the task confronted him with the most difficult problem since landing in the harbor of Kilindini, the old man was happy about the prospect of spending part of his time in the company of people other than Seneca, Descartes, Kant, and Leibniz. Sunday morning at eight o'clock, he went cheerfully and with a small bottle of drinking water in his suit pocket through the wrought iron gate of the Hove Court. He did not dare use the bus, because he was unable to give the driver his destination in English or Swahili, so he walked the two miles to the Gordons' house.

To his great delight, the hospitable couple came from Königsberg, where he had often as a boy spent his vacations with his uncle. He was touched by Jettel's pale complexion, her dark eyes, childlike expression, and black curls, which reminded him of the charming picture that had hung in his office, and he was all the more embarrassed that he was unable to help her.

"I can only offer to accompany you," he said after the third cup of coffee, "but not to speak for you. I have not learned English."

"Oh, Mr. Gottschalk. Lilly told me so many good things about you. If you could only come along to Malan, it would make me feel better. I don't even know him."

"I understand, he is not a philanthropist."

"You will bring me luck," Jettel said.

"No woman has said that to me for a long time," Gottschalk smiled, "and such a beautiful one, at that, never. Tomorrow I will first show you the Hove Court, and maybe we can think of something we can do there."

"This was," he wrote to his daughter two days later, "the best idea I have ever had in this crazy country." Actually, though, it was not he but a coincidence and Elsa Conrad who got things moving. Gottschalk was just in the process of pointing out the fragile hibiscus flowers that, surrounded by yellow butterflies, grew against a wall when Elsa Conrad poured the rest of the water in her watering can on Mrs. Clavy's boxer and called him a "stupid cur." Jettel immediately recognized her vivacious companion from the first days of the war by her long flowery robe and by the red turban on her head.

"My God, Elsa from the Norfolk," she cried excitedly, "do you still remember me? We were interned there together in 1939!"

"Do you think," Elsa asked exasperated, "that you can spend a lifetime in a bar without remembering faces? Just come on in, you too, Mr. Gottschalk. I can recall every detail. Your husband was a lawyer. And you had a cute, scared child. You lived on a farm. What are you doing in Nairobi? You did not run away from your husband, did you?"

"No. My husband is in the army," Jettel said proudly. "And I," she continued, "do not know what to do. I have no place to live, and Regina's vacation is about to start."

"I remember that helpless tone, too. Are you still the delicate lawyer's wife? You don't seem to have to grown up, at any rate. Well, it doesn't matter. Elsa has always helped when she could. Especially war heroes. You need someone who will go with you to Malan. No offense, professor, but you are not the right man for that. We will go to him tomorrow. And just don't start bawling. The Indian terror is not impressed by tears."

Malan suppressed his anger and sighs when Elsa stormed into his office and introduced Jettel as a courageous soldier's wife who needed lodging immediately and, of course, at a price that even his favorite brother would not have expected from him. He knew from too many sad experiences that it was pointless to contradict her. So, he limited himself to looks that would have brought anybody else instantly in line and to the comforting thought that this noisy person with the strength of an enraged ox more and more resembled the battleships that since the landing in Normandy were shown even in the unflaggingly anti-English Indian newspapers.

Mrs. Conrad could not be silenced by his usual tricks. Her voice was much more penetrating than his, and the woman herself had a tendency toward arguments to which he could not find any answers, especially since the tirades were interspersed with some heated violence that was thrown at him in a language that he did not understand. In addition, Malan unfortunately had to consider his large family and could not endanger his relationship with this diabolic volcano.

This giant woman with the provocative turban and the ridiculous carnation on top, which tantalizingly even came from his own garden, not only knew that he kept a room in the Hove Court empty most of the time for special circumstances, but she also was the manager of the Horse Shoe. The small bar, which because of its intimacy, its vanilla ice cream, and its curry dishes was a favorite meeting place of the soldiers from England, employed in its kitchen exclusively Indian personnel, among them many members of Mr. Malan's industrious family.

The negotiations with the soldier's wife, who made Malan feel uncharacteristically sentimental because her eyes reminded him of the beautiful cows of his childhood and who, to his satisfaction, was at least a refugee from Germany, were, therefore, shorter than usual. Jettel got the empty room and permission to bring along her dog and her houseboy. His wife's youngest brother, who had two fingers missing on his right hand and who, for that reason, was particularly hard to place, could for the time being take over the maintenance of the men's toilet in the Horse Shoe.

Everyone who mattered in the Hove Court knew that the new tenant was under Elsa Conrad's protection. This way Jettel did not have to deal with the many small harassments that newcomers otherwise had to tolerate without objections unless they wanted to be labeled as troublemakers whom decent people strenuously avoided forever. Jettel's complaints were now limited only to the humidity of Nairobi, which was unfamiliar to her, to the crowded conditions after "life in the wonderful freedom of our farm," and to the fact that Owuor had to prepare meals on a tiny electric hot plate. Elsa Conrad, however, stifled these in time with the remark "Every dachshund was an Alsatian before the emigration. You'd be better off finding some work."

When Regina came to the Hove Court on her first vacation, Jettel had gotten used to the new life and, above all, to the many people with whom she could talk and lament sufficiently that she could promise Regina daily, "You will forget the farm very quickly here."

"I do not want to forget the farm," Regina replied.

"Not even for your beloved father's sake?"

"Papa understands me. After all, he does not want to forget his Germany, either."

"You will never be bored here, and you can take the bus to the library every day and borrow as many books as you like. It is free for army families. Mrs. Conrad is already looking forward to your getting books for her."

"Whom can I tell what I have read when Papa is not here?"

"There are many children here."

"You want me to talk about books to children?"

"Well, then, to your stupid fairy," Jettel answered impatiently.

Regina crossed her fingers behind her back so that she would not arouse her mother's suspicions. On the first day of vacation, she had installed her fairy in a guava tree with an intoxicating scent and heavy branches. She herself could easily climb onto the tree with the green fruit. The foliage provided her with protection and the possibility of dreaming the day away as she had done at home in Ol' Joro Orok. It was hard for her to get used to the new environment. Above all, the women frightened her when they walked around in the garden in the late afternoons with brightly colored lips and in long garments, which they called housecoats, and talked to Regina as soon as she left her tree.

Opposite the small dark room, in which two beds, a washbasin, two chairs, and a table with an electric hotplate stood and which Jettel, Regina, and Rummler shared, lived Mrs. Clavy. Regina liked her because she smiled at her without saying a word, petted Rummler, and fed him the leftovers that her dog, Tiger, did not eat. The regularity with which a smile and finely ground white meat were exchanged very soon developed into a habit, which Regina in her dreams magnified into the great adventure of her vacation.

In those days that she wanted never to end, she imagined that Rummler and Tiger had turned into horses and that she was riding back to Ol' Joro Orok on them. Diana Wilkins, however, who lived next to Jettel in a flat that consisted of two large rooms, tore down the walls of Regina's lonely fortress in a single attack.

When Regina, on a day that was hot and dry like an overfed bushfire, came back to her tree after lunch, Diana was crouching on one of the branches. The graceful woman, with her blue eyes, long blond hair, and skin that shone like moonlight in the thick foliage, wore a transparent white lace dress that went down to her feet. Her lips were painted a light pink, and on her head she wore a golden crown with small colored stones on each point.

For a heartbeat, Regina was amazed that she had succeeded in bringing her fairy, in whom she had not believed for a long time now, to life. She did not dare take a breath, but when Diana said, "If you do not come to me, I will come to you," such violent laughter shook her body that shame scalded her skin. The English the refugees spoke, which raged in Regina's ears like a wind fighting against a forest full of giants, was a soft murmur compared to Diana's hard pronunciation.

"I have never seen you laugh," Diana stated with satisfaction.

"I have not yet laughed in Nairobi."

"Sadness will make you ugly. You are laughing again."

"Are you a princess?"

"Yes. But the people here do not believe it."

"I do," Regina said.

"The Bolsheviks have stolen my homeland from me."

"My father's homeland was also stolen."

"But not by the Bolsheviks!"

"No, by the Nazis."

Diana Wilkins came originally from Latvia. As a young girl, she had fled via Germany, Greece, and Morocco and had stayed in Kenya in the early thirties only because someone had told her that a theater was to be opened in Nairobi. She had been a dancer and was convinced that her best days were yet to come. She owed her English surname and widow's pension, both of which, even more than her beauty, were the envy of the inhabitants of the Hove Court, to a very short marriage to a young officer. A jealous rival had shot him.

When she showed Regina her flat for the first time, she proudly pointed to the dried bloodstains on the wall. Those were actually from dead mosquitoes, but Diana thirsted even more for romanticism than for whisky and found the thought that the late Lieutenant Wilkins had left no traces in her life other than his name distressing.

"And were you there when he was shot?" Regina asked.

"Oh, yes. He said to me, 'Your tears are like dew' before he died."

"I have never heard anything more beautiful."

"Just wait. One day you will experience something like this, too. Do you already have a boyfriend?"

"Yes. His name is Martin, and he is a soldier."

"Here in Nairobi?"

"No, in South Africa."

"And it is your greatest desire to marry him?"

"I don't know," Regina said doubtfully. "I have not thought about that yet. At the moment, I would prefer having a brother."

She was alarmed when she heard herself talk. Since her farewell from Martin on the farm, Regina had mentioned his name only in her diary. That she now was talking about him and the dead baby at the same time puzzled her. The wild dance in her head seemed to her like some special magic that makes sorrow dry out like rivers do during the dry season.

After Regina had shared her two secrets with Diana, the days raced by her as fast as oxen that whirl around in a feverish delirium. Her ears grew deaf to her mother's tearful entreaties and even more so to Elsa Conrad's orders to look for a girlfriend her own age.

"Don't you like Diana?"

"Yes," Jettel said, hesitating, "but you know that Papa is a bit funny."

"Why?"

"Because he is a man."

"All men love Diana."

"That's just it. Your father does not like women who sleep with every man."

"Diana," Regina stated the next day, "says she does not sleep with all men. She only sits on the sofa with them."

"Go and explain that to your papa."

The only male beings Diana really loved were her tiny dog, Reppi, which she carried on her arm when she walked in the garden and which, as only Regina knew, was in reality an enchanted prince from Riga, and her houseboy. Chepoi was a tall, gray-haired Nandi with pockmarks in his face and delicate hands that were full of strength and even more gentleness. With the look of a concerned father, he took care of Diana, whom he considered a binding legacy from his dead *bwana*, who had once saved him from a mad water buffalo.

At night, after the last suitor had gone, Chepoi returned from his tiny hut behind the personnel quarters, snuck into Diana's smoky den, which smelled of liquor, took the bottle out of his *memsahib*'s hand, and put her to bed. Rumors in the Hove Court had it that he often even had to undress her and soothe her jittery nerves with songs, but Chepoi was not a man of words. It was enough for him to be the protector of his beautiful *memsahib,* and he could be that only if he did not talk to people who had tongues that were as evil as their ears.

Regina became the exception. Despite Jettel's initial concerns and Owuor's jealous clamoring, Chepoi often took her to the market, where he bought meat and, after lively quarrels and bitter bargaining, decided on huge heads of cabbage to cook the only meal that gave his *memsahib* her strength back after the exertions of the night.

For Regina, the market in the center of Nairobi opened a new world. Bright orange mangoes next to green papayas, bunches of bananas in red, yellow, and green, plump pineapples with crowns of shiny, dark green spikes, and open passion fruit with seeds like shimmering gray glass beads intoxicated her eyes; the scent of flowers and dark roasted coffee and the stench of rotting fish and bloody meat assailed her nose; the abundance of beauty, originality, and disgust was finally able to extinguish her longing for the days that were past.

There were mountains of baskets of woven sisal, which were called *kikapu* and had more colors than the rainbow, delicate carvings made of ivory and smoothly polished warriors with long spears of black wood, belts embroidered with colorful beads, and fabrics with patterns that told stories of enchanted people and the very rare kind of wild animals that only the imagination can tame. Scaly snakeskins, pelts of leopards and zebras, stuffed birds with yellow beaks, buffalo horn, giant shells from Mombasa, delicate bracelets made of elephant hair, and gold-colored necklaces with colorful stones were offered by Indians with black eyes and quickly grasping hands.

The air was heavy and the concert of voices as overpowering as the clamoring waters of Thomson's Falls. Chickens clucked and dogs barked. Older Englishwomen with paper-thin, pale skin, faded straw hats, and white gloves walked among the stands with the grace of old days. Behind them ran their houseboys with the heavy *kikapu* like well-trained dogs. Excited Goans talked as fast as chattering monkeys, and Indians with colorful turbans walked slowly and very attentively past the wares.

There were many Kikuyu in gray trousers and multicolored shirts, who emphasized their city look with heavy shoes, and there were silent Somalis, many of whom appeared as if they were about to go to a war of the old kind. Feeble beggars who smelt of pus, with dead eyes, many of them plagued by leprosy, asked for alms, and mothers with stony faces crouched on the ground and nursed their babies.

The market made Regina fall in love with Nairobi and Chepoi. First, she became his business partner and, later, his confidante. Since she knew Kikuyu, she was even better at bargaining with the men at the market stands than he, a Nandi, who had to use Swahili as a common language. Chepoi often bought her a mango from the money they had saved or a roasted ear of maize, which tasted wonderfully of burnt wood, and on the most beautiful day of her vacation, he presented her, after first consulting with his *memsahib*, with a belt embroidered with tiny colorful beads.

"There is magic in each of the small stones," he promised and made his eyes big.

"How do you know that?"

"I know. That is enough."

"I would like to have a brother."

"Do you have a father?"

"Yes. He is an *askari* in Nakuru."

"Then you have to wish first that he will come to Nairobi," suggested Chepoi. His yellow teeth became light when he laughed. The hoarseness in his throat was a sound that warmed Regina's heart.

"I like smelling you," she said and rubbed her nose.

"What do I smell like?"

"Good. You smell like a clever man."

"You are not stupid, either," Chepoi said. "You are young. But that is going to change."

"The first stone," Regina rejoiced, "has already helped. You have never said anything like that to me before."

"I have said it often. Only you did not hear me. I don't always speak with my mouth."

"I know. You talk with your eyes."

When they returned to the Hove Court, past the giant cactus plants that were covered with red dust, the thirstiest hour of the day had scorching power, but the heat had not yet driven the inhabitants back into their black dens as usual. Old Mr. Schlachter looked out of the window, sucking on ice cubes. He had a weak heart and was not allowed to drink much. Everybody knew this, and yet, they all envied the Schlachters their refrigerator.

Regina watched for a while as the tired man with the gloomy eyes and the round stomach took one cube after another from a small silver-colored bowl and slowly put it into his mouth. She wondered intensely whether she should use one of the little beads to wish for a sick heart and many ice cubes, but the way old Mr. Schlachter looked at her and said "I would like to be able to jump like that once more" confused her.

The pink baby in its light blue outfit at Mrs. Taylor's breast chased envy, which could devour tranquility quicker than safari ants a piece of wood, into Regina's mind. To empty her head, which had become too full, she watched Mrs. Friedlander shake out the black curly fur coat that she had bought for the emigration and never worn.

Mrs. Clavy stood in her garden telling her red carnations that she was allowed to bring them water only after sundown. Regina licked her lips so that she could smile at her, but before she was able to get moisture into her mouth, she saw Owuor with Rummler behind a parched lemon tree. She called the dog, who only lazily moved his ears, and realized with regret that she had not paid attention to him all day. She considered how she could show Owuor the belt without exciting his jealousy of Chepoi. Then, she saw that his lips were moving and that there was fire in his eyes. When she ran toward Owuor, his voice raced up to her.

"'Ich hab' mein Herz in Heidelberg verloren,'" he sang loudly, as if he had forgotten that there was no echo in Nairobi.

Regina felt the stabbing pain of expectation, which she had yearned for in vain for such a long time.

"Owuor, Owuor, is he here?"

"Yes, the *bwana* is here," Owuor laughed. "The *bwana askari* is here," he reported proudly and lifted Regina up as on the day when the magic had begun and pressed her close to his body. For a short happy moment, she was so near to his face that she could see the salt that stuck to his eyelids.

"Owuor, you are so clever," she said softly. "Do you still remember the day the locusts came?"

Filled with happiness and recollections, she waited until the clicking of his tongue left her ears; then she flung her shoes from her feet so that she could fly faster across the lawn, ran impatiently to the flat, and tore the door open violently.

Her parents were sitting close together on the small bed and separated with such a sudden movement that the small table in front of them shook for a moment. Their faces were the color of Mrs. Clavy's healthiest carnations. Regina heard Jettel breathe loudly and quickly, and she also saw that her mother was wearing neither blouse nor skirt. So she had not forgotten her promise after all to have a baby in better times. Had the good times already gone on safari?

It made Regina insecure that her parents did not say anything and appeared as stiff, silent, and serious as the wooden figures at the market. She felt her skin turning red, too. It was difficult to get her teeth apart.

"Papa," she finally said, and then the words, which she had wanted to hold back, tumbled out of her mouth like heavy stones: "Did they fire you?"

"No," Walter said and pulled Regina on to his naked knee and extinguished the fire in his eyes with a smile. "No," he repeated. "King George is very happy with me. He asked me especially to tell you that." He lightly tapped the sleeve of his starched khaki shirt. On it were two stripes of white linen.

"You have been promoted to corporal," Regina marveled. She touched the small beads of her new belt and licked her father's face with the new strength of just vanquished fear, the way Rummler did at every greeting while happiness shook his body.

"Corporal is bloody good for a fucking refugee," Walter said.

"You are speaking English, Daddy," Regina giggled.

The sentence caught some prey in her head that made her feel dismayed and oppressed by guilt. Did her father ever suspect that, for a long time, she had wished for a daddy who looked like other fathers, who spoke English and had not lost his homeland? She was very much ashamed that she had been a child.

"Do you still remember Sergeant Major Pierce?"

"Sergeant," Regina corrected and was glad that she had swallowed her sadness without choking.

"Sergeant Major. Englishmen get promoted, too. Just guess what I taught him! He is able to sing 'Lilli Marleen' in German now."

"I want to be able to do that, too," Regina said. She needed only a split second to change the lie in her mouth into the kind of sweetness that Diana maintained was the true taste of great love.

15

THAT ON MAY 8, 1945, all radio broadcasts of the day started with the sentence "No special events in the forecast" was a result of the weather, which from Mombasa to Lake Rudolf was unusually stable and dry for the season. In deference to the farmers who, particularly during the first weeks of the harvest after the long rains, could not be expected to listen to faraway world events every hour before receiving information of great interest to them, the Nairobi broadcast had always given priority to the meteorological news.

Neither the death of George V, nor the resignation of Edward VIII, the coronation of George VI, nor the outbreak of World War II had been judged sufficient reasons to break with this tradition. The unconditional surrender of the Germans, therefore, was not considered grounds for an exception either. Nevertheless, the Colony gave way to a flush of victory that in every way rivaled the celebrations in the suffering mother country.

In Nakuru, Mr. Brindley ordered the entire school to be decorated with flags, which challenged the improvisational talents of teachers and students alike as never before. The school owned only one, rather faded Union Jack, which fluttered from the main building every day. They solved the problem by hurriedly pasting together and quickly sewing flags out of old bed sheets and the costumes of the red monkeys from the last school theater production.

For the missing blue of the little flags, some of the school and guide uniforms of the rich students who had big enough wardrobes were cut up, and they afterward went to a lot of trouble not to show their pride in the gladly made sacrifice too blatantly.

Regina was not sad that she had only one school skirt and a Girl Guide uniform that was too faded and thus could be only a quiet spectator in this patriotic scissor fight. Fate had allotted her something bigger. Mr. Brindley not only freed all children of army personnel from their homework for the next day but also suggested in an unusually friendly tone of command that they write their fathers in uniform letters worthy of the occasion to congratulate them, in the far-off theaters of war, on their victory in a suddenly so miraculously peaceful world.

Regina, at first, had some difficulties with this task. She thought hard about whether Ngong, only a few miles from Nairobi where her father had been stationed for three months, could qualify as a far-off theatre of war in Mr. Brindley's sense. In addition, she was ashamed because she had not really been willing to sacrifice her father for the British Empire. In view of the victory, it no longer seemed right to her that she had been so relieved and had even thanked God that his application to be sent to Burma had been denied.

Despite this, she started her letter with the words "My hero, my father" and concluded with the line "Theirs but to do and die" from her favorite poem. She suspected that her father would be unable to appreciate the beauty of the language and would also not know enough about the fateful battle of Balaclava and the Crimean War, but she felt compelled to give praise to English courage at such an important moment in world history.

However, in order to please her father, especially in England's greatest hour, she gave him a present in his own language and added in very small letters in faulty German, "Soon we will go to Leobschütz," which Mr. Brindley, despite his suspicion of things he did not understand, generously overlooked. The famous quotation, though, he read with approval, nodded even twice, and asked Regina to help some of the other girls who were unable to express themselves that well.

Unfortunately, he embarrassed the weaker students in a rather un-English manner this way, but Regina still felt as if an old dream had come true for her and she had been awarded the Victoria Cross. When the director afterward invited the children of army personnel to take tea in his room, she asked for her letter back one more time so that she could report the honor that had just been bestowed upon her. Luckily, Mr. Brindley did not notice that her hero's appreciation, which he had praised and read in public, now ended with "Bloody good for a fucking refugee." Regina knew very well how much he disliked vulgarity.

In Nairobi, too, the news of the end of the war in Europe was celebrated with enthusiasm, as if the Colony exclusively had contributed to the victory. Delamare Avenue turned into a sea of flowers and flags, and even the cheap stores with the tiny windows in which whites almost never shopped displayed hastily obtained photos of Montgomery, Eisenhower, and Churchill next to the picture of King George VI. Just as moviegoers had seen in the weekly newsreels showing the liberation of Paris, strangers jubilantly fell into each other's arms and kissed men in uniform, and it even happened in the euphoria that sometimes especially light-skinned Indians were embraced.

Quickly established men's choirs began to sing "Rule Britannia" and "Hang Out Your Washing on the Siegfried Line"; older ladies decorated their hats and little dogs with red, white, and blue ribbons; screeching Kikuyu children put on paper hats that they had folded from the extra edition of the *East African Standard*. By noon, the reception desks at the New Stanley Hotel, Thor's, and the Norfolk were unable to accept any more reservations for their festive victory dinners. Big fireworks were planned for the evening, and a victory parade for the next few days.

At the Hove Court, Mr. Malan, in a surge of patriotism that confused him even more than his tenants, had the sand-encrusted cactus plants at the gate hosed off, the paths around the rosebeds raked, and the Union Jack hoisted on the old flagpole, which had to be repaired for the occasion. It had not been used since Malan had taken over the hotel. In the afternoon, Mrs. Malan, in a festive sari of red and gold, had a mahogany table and silk-covered chairs placed under the eucalyptus tree with the low-hanging heavy branches and took her tea with her four adolescent daughters, who all looked like tropical flowers and during their frequent bouts of giggling moved their heads like full-blown roses in the wind.

Despite Chepoi's angry protests, Diana could not be prevented from running through the garden barefoot, in a transparent nightgown and with a half-full bottle of whisky, while she alternately called "To hell with Stalin" and "Damned Bolsheviks." She was reminded in a stern tone by a major who was visiting Mrs. Taylor that the Russians had contributed substantially and with admirable sacrifice to the victory. When Diana realized that not even her dog believed that she was the youngest daughter of the czar, even though she swore it to him by his life, she became so inconsolable that she threw herself crying on the ground under a lemon tree. Chepoi came running to calm her down and was finally able to take her back to her flat. He carried her in his arms and hummed the sad song of the lion that has lost his strength.

Professor Gottschalk had become thin and very quiet over the past few months. He walked as if each step caused him pain, no longer talked to the babies in their prams, and only rarely petted a dog, and it also hardly ever happened anymore that he complimented young women. People in the know were convinced that his decline had started just at the time when the Allied forces began bombing German cities daily, but the beloved professor had not been willing to talk about this topic. Now, on the day of the glorious triumph, he sat on an old kitchen chair in front of his flat with a pale face and, instead of reading as usual, stared gloomily into the trees and murmured repeatedly, "My beautiful Frankfurt" to himself.

Like Professor Gottschalk, many refugees found it unexpectedly difficult to show their relief about the end of the war, which had been expected for days, in a suitable way. There were some who had not wanted to speak German for a long time and really believed that they had forgotten their mother tongue. Strangely enough, they were the ones who found at precisely such a happy moment that their English was quite insufficient to express their liberated feelings. With a bitterness that they could not explain to themselves, they envied people who cried unabashedly. Such tears of release, on the other hand, led their English neighbors to suspect that the refugees had, after all, secretly been on the German side and now mourned the well-deserved English victory.

Jettel felt only a fleeting regret that she could not spend this extraordinary evening with Walter, as was appropriate for the wife of a serviceman. She had gotten too used to the biweekly rhythm of his visits and found the togetherness so pleasantly spread out that even on a day that was very promising indeed, she wanted no change. In addition, she was in too good a mood to be bothered unnecessarily by her conscience. It was three months to the day since she had started working at the Horse

Shoe, and since then, every night she had received the long-missed confirmation that she was still a young and attractive woman.

The Horse Shoe, with its eponymous bar, was the only pub in Nairobi in which white women provided the service. Even though it did not offer alcohol, the friendly establishment with the red walls and white furniture was considered a bar. The mainly male clientele favored it just because women were serving here and not native waiters. The young officers from England who frequented the Horse Shoe on a regular basis were constantly homesick and had an insatiable appetite for contact and flirt. They were not alienated by Elsa Conrad's hard, excessively loud English with its Berlin accent or by Jettel's pitiful vocabulary. As a matter of fact, the guests found them pleasant; they were able to exhibit their charm without having to speak too many words. It was a mutual gift. Jettel gave them a feeling of an importance that they did not have, and the friendliness and happy mood that she elicted seemed to her like a kind of medicine that after a severe illness brings recovery to someone who had not expected it anymore.

When Jettel put on her makeup in the late afternoon, tried out new hairdos, or simply attempted to remember a particularly thrilling compliment from one of the young soldiers, who strangely enough were all called John, Jim, Jack, or Peter, she fell in love with her reflection in the mirror over and over again. On some days she was even inclined to believe in one of Regina's fairies. Her light skin, which had always been gray or yellow on the farm, now showed the old beautiful contrast to her dark hair, her eyes shone like those of a child pampered with praise, and a beginning roundness lent an attractive femininity to the seeming carelessness of her being.

In the Horse Shoe, Jettel was able to forget for a few hours that she and Walter continued to be refugees with scant income and remained expelled from their homeland, leaving them full of apprehension about the future. She suppressed the reality with enthralling joy. She felt again like the popular teenager who during the student dances in Breslau, could not pass up a single dance. She was happy, even if it was only Owuor who clicked his tongue and called her his "beautiful *memsahib*."

If it had not been for Elsa Conrad, who told her every night, "If you cheat even once on your husband, I will break every bone in your body,"

Jettel would have given in to her intoxicating vanity as freely as she did to her occasional dreams of the future in which Walter was an army captain and built a house in the best neighborhood in Nairobi, where Jettel would host members of the high society, who would, of course, be enchanted by her slight accent and think her to be Swiss.

Jettel was aware that the victory would be celebrated joyously in the Horse Shoe, too, and that it was absolutely her patriotic duty to prepare for the fighters who were so far away from home. When the first news of German capitulation started to circulate, she immediately had her name put on the bath list, and, after a very violent fight with Mrs. Keller, who just on this day, which was so important for Jettel, insisted on her husband having a bath completely out of turn, she succeeded in getting the washroom at midday. After a lengthy deliberation, she decided, not without putting a little damper on her good mood, on the long evening gown that she had never worn yet and which since her arrival in Rongai had been the cause of a continuous conflict with Walter, because he was not willing to forget about the icebox.

She needed more time than expected to push the dress, of heavy blue taffeta with a yellow and white striped bodice, puffed sleeves, and tiny buttons on the back, over her breasts and hips. It took even longer till she found the woman she was looking for in the small mirror on the wall, but she smiled long enough at herself to gain courage and illusions so that she was finally satisfied.

"I always knew that I would need the dress," she said and pushed her chin toward the mirror, but the obstinacy that she had wanted to enjoy for a short time melted like the vanilla ice cream that was a specialty in the Horse Shoe and turned into a knife. With a sharp cut it destroyed the wonderful portrait of the beautiful young woman intoxicated with victory.

With a suddenness that made her breath grow heavy, she saw the farmhouse in Rongai with the roof that protected them neither from rain nor heat, saw Walter standing disappointed over the boxes from Breslau, and heard him scold, "You will never wear that thing here. You don't know what you have done to us." She tried to suppress the two sentences immediately and with giggles, but her memory blocked the flight path, and the words now seemed symbolic of the years that had followed.

The broad white and yellow stripes that encircled her breast turned into thin, tight iron rings. As if they had a whip, they drove Jettel into painfully suppressed memories. With unusual, agonizing detail, she relived the day on which Walter's letter had arrived in Breslau with the news that the papers sponsoring her and Regina's emigration were ready. Intoxicated with relief, she had bought the evening gown with her mother. How both of them had laughed when they imagined Walter's surprised face upon seeing the dress instead of the icebox.

The thought that her mother had never laughed as much and as happily as she had with her warmed Jettel's heart only shortly. Without mercy, the final picture took over. Her mother had said to her, "Be kind to Walter, he loves you so much," when she was standing at the harbor in Hamburg crying and waving and already becoming smaller and smaller. Jettel felt that she had hardly enough time to return to the present. She knew that she could not think of her mother, her tenderness, courage, and selflessness, and especially not of her last letter, if she wanted to save her dream of happiness. It was too late.

First, her throat became dry, and then the pain attacked her body so violently that she was no longer able to take off the dress before she threw herself on the bed with small, sobbing sounds. She tried to call for her mother, then for Walter, and finally, in her greatest despair, for Regina, but she could not open her teeth anymore. When Owuor returned with Rummler from the festivities on Delamare Avenue, he found his *memsahib*'s body lying on the bed like a skin that is left to dry in the sun.

"Don't cry," he said softly and stroked the dog.

Owuor swallowed his satisfaction. For a long time, he had wanted a *memsahib* who was like a child so he that could be like Chepoi when he snatched Diana from the claws of fear and then had pride turn his face smooth and big. Owuor found living in Nairobi exciting, but he often had full eyes and an empty head. The *bwana*'s jokes tickled his throat only too rarely, and the little *memsahib* talked and laughed too much with Chepoi during her vacations. Owuor felt like a warrior who has been sent to war but whose weapons have been stolen.

A yellow fever with a bright streak of lightning scorched him whenever he saw Chepoi carrying his *memsahib* through the garden. His envy confused him. He certainly did not want to see Jettel drunk or half-dressed under a tree, and for his *bwana,* too, that would have been like a blow that fells a tree. But a man like Owuor had to feel his strength over and over again if he did not want to be like everyone else.

Jettel was lying on the bed in the dress that had gotten its colors from the sky and the sun, and she even looked like the child Owuor had wished for, yet uneasiness scratched at his head with sharp claws. The painted red mouth of the *memsahib* looked like the bloody foam on the mouth of a young gazelle that, after a deadly bite on the back of its neck, suddenly rears up one more time. The fear that flowed from the lifeless body on the bed smelled like the last milk of a poisoned cow. Jettel moaned when Owuor opened the window.

"Owuor. I never wanted to cry again in all my life."

"Only animals don't cry."

"Why am I not an animal?"

"Mungu does not ask us what we want to be, *memsahib.*"

Owuor's voice was calm and so full of compassion and protection that Jettel sat up and, without his saying anything, drank the glass of water that he offered her. He pushed a pillow behind her back and touched her skin while doing so. In this short moment of mercy, Jettel felt as if his cool fingers with a single grip had extinguished all her shame and despair, but the release did not last. The pictures that she did not want to see, the words that she did not want to hear, oppressed her more vehemently than before.

"Owuor," she murmured, "it is the dress. The *bwana* was right. It is not good. Do you know what he said when he saw it the first time?"

"He looked like a lion that has lost track of its prey," Owuor laughed.

"You still remember that?"

"It was a long time before the day that the locusts came to Rongai," Owuor remembered. "It was during the days when the *bwana* did not know yet that I was clever."

"You are a clever man, Owuor."

Owuor took only the time a man needs to lock the beautiful words in his head. Then he closed the window, pulled the curtain shut, stroked the sleeping dog again, and said, "Take the dress off, *memsahib.*"

"Why?"

"You just said it. It is not a good dress."

Jettel let Owuor open the many small buttons at the back, and she also let herself experience his touch as pleasant again and his strength as something that brought her salvation. She sensed his glance and knew that the intimacy of the never-before-encountered situation should have made her uncertain, but she felt nothing but the pleasurable warmth that her calmed nerves emitted. Owuor's eyes had the same gentleness as on the day, many years ago, when he had lifted Regina out of the car, pressed her against his body, and enchanted her forever.

"Have you heard, Owuor?" Jettel asked and wondered why she was whispering. "The war is over."

"Everyone says so in town. But it is not our war, *memsahib.*"

"No, Owuor, it was my war. Where are you going?"

"To the *memsahib monenu mingi,*" Owour giggled because he knew that Jettel always laughed when he called Elsa Conrad this because she talked more than the biggest ear could hold. "I am going to tell her that you are not coming to work today."

"But you cannot do that. I have to go to work."

"The war in your head has to end first," Owuor recognized. "The *bwana* always says, 'The war has to end first.' Is he coming here today?"

"No. Next week."

"Wasn't it his war?" Owuor asked and gave the door a small kick. The days without the *bwana* were to him like nights without women.

"It was his war, Owuor. Hurry back. I do not want to be alone."

"I will take good care of you, *memsahib,* until he comes."

The war in Walter's head started in the peaceful landscape of Ngong when he least expected any uproar. He stood at the window of his bedroom at four o'clock in the afternoon and looked on without sadness as most of the members of the Tenth Unit of the Royal East Africa Corps climbed into jeeps to celebrate the victory in nearby Nairobi. He had voluntarily taken on the night shift and had been celebrated shortly and enthusiastically as "a jolly good chap" by the elated soldiers of his unit and even by Lieutenant McCall, a reserved Scotsman.

Walter did not feel like celebrating. The news of the capitulation had not caused any jubilation or feeling of liberation in him. He was plagued by the contradiction in his feelings, which he considered as a particularly nasty irony of history, and he became as depressed in the course of the day as if his fate had been sealed with the end of the war. It struck him as typical of his situation that giving up a night outside of the barracks did not seem like a sacrifice to him. The need to be alone on a day that meant so much to others and not enough to him was too great to exchange it for the inconvenience of an unannounced visit with Jettel.

Shortly after he had been transferred to Ngong and she had started to work at the Horse Shoe, Walter had realized that his marriage was beginning to change. Jettel, who had written him affectionate and sometimes even yearning letters to Nakuru, was no longer interested in his unexpected visits. He understood her. A husband with a corporal's stripes on his sleeve who sat at the bar gloomily and in silence had no place in the life of a woman surrounded by a crowd of cheerful admirers in officers' uniforms.

Paradoxically, his jealousy had at first invigorated rather than tortured him. In a gentle, romantic way, it had reminded him of his student days. During this period of mercy that was only too short, Jettel was again the fifteen-year-old in a ballgown with purple and green checks, a beautiful butterfly in search of admiration; he was not quite nineteen, in his first semester and optimistic enough to believe that life at some point would be generous to those who were patient. In the monotony of the military routine, and even more through his experiences in his free time, however, the nostalgic jealousy, with its transfigured and pleasing images of Breslau, had turned into the tedium of Africa. He had thought that the years of emigration had destroyed his hypersensitivity in the same way that they had taken his dreams of better days, but now it had flared up again.

When Walter had to wait at the Horse Shoe until Jettel had finished work, he felt her nervousness and sensed her rejection of him. Even more hurtful were the haughty and suspicious looks from Mrs. Lyons, who disapproved of private visits to her employees and with twitching eyebrows seemed to count every ice cream that Jettel put in front of her husband to keep him in good spirits and quiet until they could go home.

The thought of Mrs. Lyons and her Horse Shoe and the mood there on the night of the end of the war aroused in Walter just the kind of desire for fight and flight that delivered sharp blows to his pride. He stared through the window with the dead flies for a little longer and deliberated disgustedly how he could kill simultaneously time, his distrust, and the first signs of pessimism. He was satisfied when he remembered that he had not heard any German news for days and that this was a good opportunity for a new attempt. The mess hall, with its excellent radio, would be empty; therefore, there would not be a riot when the broadcast emitted foreign sounds, and those on the night of the great victory.

The few refugees in Walter's unit were the ones who protested the loudest during German programs, while the Englishmen only rarely lost their calm. Most of the time, they were not even aware of what language they were hearing if it was not their own. Walter had experienced this over and over and in most cases without any emotion, but all of a sudden the need of the refugees not to attract attention seemed to him not ridiculous but an enviable confirmation of their talent to separate themselves from the past. He, however, had remained an outsider.

On his way from the barrack to the mess hall in the main building, he continued to try to escape the kind of melancholy that invariably ended in depression. Like a child who is learning his homework by heart without looking for any meaning, he told himself over and over again, and at times even aloud, that this was a happy day for mankind. Still, he felt only emptiness and exhaustion. Wistfully, and blaming himself for this especially foolish form of sadness, Walter remembered the beginning of the war and how Süßkind had informed him from the truck of the internment and the farewell to Rongai.

The memory escalated, with a speed that was insulting to his self-esteem, into the wish finally to be able to talk to Süßkind again. He had not seen the protector of his first days in Africa for a long time, but they had stayed in contact. In contrast to Walter, who had been rejected for deployment to the front because of his age, Süßkind had been sent to the Far East and had been wounded there. Now, he was stationed in Eldoret. His most recent letter was less than five days old.

"We will probably lose our wonderful positions with King George soon now," Süßkind had written, "but out of gratitude he might give us jobs that make us neighbors again. A great king owes that much to his soldiers." What Süßkind had meant as a joke and Walter originally also had taken as such appeared to him, on this lonely afternoon of May 8, as a merciless and significant hint of a future that he had not been willing to face since his first day in uniform. He straightened his shoulders and shook his head, but he also noticed that he had started to drag his steps.

It was less than two hours before sunset. Walter experienced the pressure of his helplessness like bodily pain. He knew that his brooding was about to turn into ghosts that he could not escape and that their attacks were going to be merciless. Worn out, he sat down on a big stone with a wind-polished top under a large thorn-acacia with a heavy crown. His heart was racing. He winced when he heard himself saying out loud, "Walter von der Vogelweide." Confused, he started thinking who might have spoken. The situation seemed so grotesque to Walter that he laughed out loud. He wanted to get up, and yet he remained seated. He did not know yet that this was the moment in which his eyes were opened to the serenity of a landscape against which he had fought for so long.

The shining blue Ngong Hills rose out of the dark grass and stretched toward a band of fine clouds, which started to fly in the upcoming wind. Cows with large heads and the hunched backs that gave them the look of ancient animals made their way through red clouds of dust to the narrow river. The shrill calls of the herdsmen were clearly audible. Far away, bars of black-and-white light opened the view on a big herd of zebras with many young.

Nearby, giraffes that hardly moved their long bodies were stripping the trees of their leaves. Walter caught himself thinking that he envied the giraffes, which he had never seen before his time in Ngong, because they could not exist in any other way but with their heads held high. It made him insecure that he all of sudden saw the landscape as a paradise from which he was about to be expelled. The realization that he had not felt like this since leaving Sohrau shook him deeply.

The coolness of the night beat sharply against his arms and whipped his nerves. The darkness, which fell like a stone from the sky that had just been light, obstructed his view of the hills and robbed him of his orientation. Walter wanted to imagine Sohrau once again, but this time in more detail, yet he saw not the marketplace and the house with the trees in front of it but only his father and his sister on a large empty plain. Walter was sixteen again and Liesel fourteen years old; his father looked like a medieval knight. He came back from the war, showed his medals, and wanted to know why his son had abandoned his homeland.

"I am a jolly good chap," Walter said; he was embarrassed when he realized that he had spoken English to his father.

It took him some time to return to the present, and he saw himself counting the hours until daybreak on some farm. Rage burned his skin.

"I did not survive to plant flax or to crawl into a cow's ass," he said. His voice was calm and low, but the white dog with the black spot over its right eye that came daily to the barracks and was in the process of snooping through a rusty bucket full of smelly refuse heard him and shook its ears. First, it barked to chase away the unexpected sound; then it listened for a moment with its nose held high, ran up to Walter, and pushed itself against his knee.

"You can understand me," Walter said. "I can tell that. A dog does not forget either and always finds its way home."

Surprised by the unaccustomed tenderness, the animal licked Walter's hand. The thin hairs around its nose became moist, its eyes large. The head made a small upward movement and ended up between Walter's legs.

"Did you notice that? I just said 'home.' I will explain it to you, my friend. In detail. Today is not only the end of the war. My homeland has been set free. I can say home again. You don't have to look so dumb. I did not realize it right away either. It is over for the murderers, but Germany is still there."

Walter's voice had been reduced to a tremor, but the realization was invigorating. Pedantically, he tried to explain his mood swing to himself, but he could not organize his thoughts. His feeling of liberation was too overwhelming. He sensed that he had to challenge himself once more with the truth that he had suppressed for so long.

"I will not tell anyone but you," he told the sleeping dog, "but I am going back. I just cannot do anything else. I do not want to be a stranger among strangers anymore. At my age a man has to belong somewhere. And guess where I belong?"

The dog woke up and whimpered like a young animal that has for the first time dared to go into grass that is too high. The light brown of its eyes shone in the dusk.

"Come on, you son of a bitch. The Pole in the kitchen is cooking cabbage soup. He is homesick, too. Maybe he will have a bone for you. You deserve it."

In the mess hall, Walter turned all the knobs on the radio, but he could find only music. Later, he drank half a bottle of whisky with the Pole, whose English was even worse than his own. His stomach burned as much as his head. The Pole scooped the steaming cabbage soup into two bowls and started crying when Walter said "Dziekuje." Walter decided to teach the dog, which had not left his side since the early evening, the text and melody of "Ich weiß nicht, was soll es bedeuten."

All three of them went to sleep, the Pole and Walter on a bench, the dog under it. At ten o'clock that night, Walter woke up. The radio was still on. It was tuned to the German-speaking station of the BBC. The summary of the news of the unconditional surrender of the Third Reich was followed by a special report on the liberation of the concentration camp Bergen-Belsen.

16

REGINA PLACED the hat, which in the earliest days of fear and homesickness had been dark blue, carefully on the luggage rack above the seat of light-brown velvet and with a long practiced move smoothed out the rough felt. When she let herself fall into the seat, she had to press her mouth and nose tightly against the small window so that she would not giggle aloud. The habit of first taking care of her hat and only after that of herself seemed funny to her in view of the changes that were in store for her. The hat, which had been too tight for years now and was bleached out by the sun and the salty air of the soda lake, would be only a hat like any other at the end of her trip.

The slim blue-and-white-striped hatband with the emblem "Quisque pro omnibus" was almost new. The writing, embroidered with thick golden thread, glinted provocatively in the small spot of sun that entered the train compartment. It seemed to Regina as if the emblem were laughing at her. She tried to warm herself with expectations of her vacation but realized quickly that her thoughts were running away and became insecure.

For years, she had wished in vain for the hatband of the Nakuru School so that she finally would no longer be an outsider in a community that judged people by their uniforms and children by their parents' income; then she had gotten the band for her thirteenth birthday, almost too late. As soon as the locomotive entered Nairobi, Regina would not need the hat or the band anymore. The Nakuru School, which had swallowed her father's pay as the voracious monsters of the Greek myths had their defenseless victims, was her school for only a few more hours.

After the vacation, Regina would attend the Kenya Girls' High

School in Nairobi, and she knew for certain that she would hate the new school just as much as the old one. The small torments that accumulated every night of every day into a great agony would start all over again—teachers and fellow students who could not pronounce her name and who, while trying to do so, made a face as if every short syllable were causing them pain; the futile effort to play hockey well or at least to remember the rules, and to act as if it were important to a loser in sports in which goal the ball had landed; the mortification of being among the best students in class or, even worse, being at the top of the class again; and, most distressing of all, to have and to love parents whose accent gave a child no chance to be an unobtrusive, recognized part of the school community.

It was good, Regina brooded, while staring fixedly at the scratched leather of her suitcase, that Inge, the only friend whom she had met and wanted in her five years in Nakuru, would also be going to school in Nairobi. Inge no longer wore dirndl dresses, and maintained without blushing that she knew only one language, English, and was quite embarrassed to have a German name. Yet, Inge still liked the homemade cooked cheese that her mother sent her for tea better than the spicy ginger cookies that the English children favored, and she still kissed her parents when she had not seen them for a while instead of indicating with a slight wave of the hand that she had learned to control her feelings. Above all, Inge never asked dumb questions. She knew why Regina had no family other than her father and mother and why she never closed her eyes or opened her mouth during evening prayer in the school auditorium.

Thinking of Inge made Regina exhale with relief into the brown curtain in front of the train window. Startled, she looked around to see if anyone had noticed. The other girls who were traveling with her to Nairobi on their vacation were preoccupied with their futures; their thin voices were excited and filled with the kind of self-assurance that they owed to their home and to their mother tongue. Regina no longer envied her fellow students. Anyway, she would not see them again. Pam and Jennifer had been accepted at a private school in Johannesburg, Helen and Daphne were going to London, and for Janet, who had not passed the final exam at the Nakuru School, waited a wealthy aunt with a horse breeding farm in Sussex. Regina permitted herself to sigh again, this time with pleasure.

Only the blinding light in the compartment made her aware that the train had already moved out of the shade of the flat station building. She was glad that she was sitting at the window and could see her old school, undisturbed, one more time. Even though she felt like an exhausted ox that has been unyoked too late, she still felt the need for a long goodbye—not like at Ol' Joro Orok, where she had left the farm unsuspectingly and had not been able to use her eyes at that time for all the days that followed.

The train was noisy and slow. The individual white buildings of the school, which had frightened Regina so much as a seven-year-old that for a long time she had had only one wish—to fall down a big hole like Alice in Wonderland—looked very light on the red sandy hill in the haze of the beginning heat of the day. The small houses with the gray corrugated tin roofs and even the main building with its thick columns seemed smaller to Regina and in their familiarity even friendlier than the day before.

Even though she knew that she was only feeding her head with illusions, Regina imagined she could see the window of Mr. Brindley's room and Mr. Brindley himself waving a flag of white handkerchiefs. She had already known for many disquieting months that she was going to miss him, but she had not anticipated that her longing would take as little time to grow as flax after the first night of the long rains. The headmaster had had her come to him once more on the last day before the break. He had not said much and had looked at Regina as if he were searching for a certain word that he had lost. It had been her mouth that had been unable to hold anything. Regina felt hot again when she thought about it, how she had killed the beautiful silence and had stuttered: "Thank you, sir. Thank you for everything."

"Do not forget anything," Mr. Brindley had said and looked as if he and not she had to go on a safari without return. Then he had murmured "Little Nell." And because she already had difficulties swallowing, she had answered quickly, "I will not forget anything." Without really wanting to, she had added, "No, Mr. Dickens." They both had to laugh and also to clear their throats at the same time. Luckily, Mr.

Brindley, who did not like crying children, had not noticed that Regina had tears in her eyes.

The certainty that from now on there would be neither Mr. Brindley nor anyone else who knew Nicholas Nickleby, little Dorrit, or Bob Cratchitt and surely not Little Nell scratched in her throat like an accidentally swallowed chicken bone. It was the same feeling that drummed in her head when Regina thought about Martin. His name suddenly occurred to her. It had hardly reached her ears when the fog before her eyes showed holes from which small, well-sharpened arrows were shot.

Regina remembered only too clearly how Martin in his uniform had picked her up from school and how the two of them had driven to the farm in his jeep and shortly before reaching their destination had lain under her tree. Did she decide then or later to marry the enchanted blond prince? Was Martin still thinking of his promise to wait for her? She had kept hers and never cried when she thought of Ol' Joro Orok. At least, no tears.

The experience that a big sorrow could eat the sadness in store for her was new to Regina, but not unpleasant. The train rocked her senses into a state in which she still heard individual words but could not put them together into a sentence. When she was just about to explain to Martin that her name was not Regina but Little Nell, causing Martin to break into this wonderful laugh that after all this time still made her ears burn like fire, the first wagon of the train puffed into Naivasha. The steam of the locomotive enveloped the small light yellow house of the station master with a moist, white veil. Even the hibiscus on the walls lost its color.

Old, emaciated Kikuyu women with distended stomachs under white shawls, dull eyes, and heavy banana bunches on their bent backs knocked at the windows. Their nails made the same thrashing sound as hail on an empty water tank. If the women wanted to have any business, they had to sell their bananas before the train moved on. They whispered as beseechingly as if they had to charm a snake away from its prey. Regina made an extensive movement with her right hand to indicate that she had no money, but the women did not understand her. So she pulled down the window and called out loud in Kikuyu, "I am as poor as a monkey."

The women slapped their hands in front of their breasts laughing and howled like the men when they sat alone in front of their huts at night. The oldest, a small figure, defeated by climate and life, in a bright blue kerchief and without a single tooth, loosened the leather strap on her shoulders, put the heavy bunch on the ground, tore off a big green banana, and held it out to Regina.

"For the monkey," she said, and all who heard it laughed like neighing horses. The five girls in the compartment looked curiously at Regina and smiled at one another, because they understood one another without words and felt too grown-up to show their disapproval in any way other than through glances.

When the woman pushed the banana through the window, her stiff fingers touched Regina's hand for a brief moment. The old woman's skin smelled of sun, sweat, and salt. Regina tried to keep the familiar, long-lost scent as long as possible in her nose, but when the train stopped in Nyeri, there was nothing left of the memory but the kind of salt with sharp grains that pinched the eyes like the tiny bloodsucking mdudu under one's toenails.

On the station platform in Limuru were many people with heavy loads wrapped in colorful blankets and wide sisal baskets filled with brown paper bags full of maize meal, bloody pieces of meat, and untanned animal skins. They were only an hour away from Nairobi now.

The voices no longer had the melodious softness of the highlands. They were loud and yet hard to understand. Even men, who like their fathers and grandfathers before them were still holding chickens in their hands and drove their wives in front of them like the cows at home, had shoes on their feet and colorful shirts as if they had cut up a rainbow immediately after a thunderstorm. Some of the young men had silver-colored watches on their wrists, many, instead of the customary stick, an umbrella in their hand. Their eyes resembled those of hunted animals, but their gait was even and strong.

Indian women with red dots on their foreheads and bracelets that even in the shade glittered like dancing stars had their luggage lifted into the railroad carriage by silent blacks, even though they were allowed to travel only second class. Light-skinned soldiers in khaki who despite their years in Africa still believed in punctual departure times rushed toward the first-class compartments. While they were marching, they sang the postwar hit "Don't Fence Me In." The young Indian conductor held the door open without looking at them. A shrill whistle from the locomotive announced the departure.

In the yellow afternoon sun, which lengthened the shadows, the mountains looked like giants at rest. Herds of gazelles skipped to shimmering light-gray water holes. Baboons climbed over earth-colored rocks. The rears of the loudly shrieking male leaders shone in red. Young monkeys clung to the fur on their mother's bellies. Regina watched them enviously and tried to imagine that she, too, was a young monkey with a big family, but the beautiful game of her childhood days had lost its magic.

As always, when she saw the first Ngong Hills, her usual worries started: Would her mother have time to pick her up at the station, or did she have to go to work at the Horse Shoe and therefore send Owuor? It was a special gift if her mother had time, but after the three-month separation, Regina also loved to exchange those glances, jokes, and word plays with Owuor of which only he and she were capable. Still, she had been a bit embarrassed at the end of her last vacation when only the houseboy had been there to greet her. She swallowed a mouthful of content when she realized that this time everything was going to be different and that after the train arrived in Nairobi, she would never have to see her fellow students again.

Regina knew for a fact that her mother was going to spoil her with Königsberger Klopse, meatballs in a special white sauce, and would once again say, "There are no capers in this stupid country." Her favorite meal was never served without this complaint, and Regina also never missed asking, "What are capers?" She considered these habits an invariable part of home and, at every return, her hungry eyes and ears drank in the assurance that nothing had changed in her life. The thought of her parents, who always tried to make her homecoming into a special day, excited her more than usual. It was as if the tenderness that she expected was already stroking her. She remembered that her mother had written in her last letter, "You will be amazed, we have a big surprise for you."

To prolong the anticipation, Regina had not allowed herself to think of the surprise until she saw the first palm tree, but the train was going faster on the last stretch of the way than all the time before and arrived with unexpected suddenness in Nairobi. Regina did not have time to stand up at the window as she normally did. She was the last one to get her suitcase and had to wait till the girls in her compartment had left before she could even look to see who was coming to meet her. For a short moment, which seemed an eternity to her, she stood in front of the train and saw only a wall of white skin. She heard excited calls, but not the voice for which her ears lay in wait. Without allowing any time to pass between apprehension and terror, Regina was instantly shaken by the old anxiety that her mother might have forgotten the day of her homecoming, that Owuor had started out too late to come to the station on time.

In a panic that made her feel ashamed because it seemed exaggerated and undignified, but that threatened to fling her heart out of her body, Regina remembered that she did not have any money for the bus to the Hove Court. Disappointed, she sat down on her suitcase and smoothed out the skirt of her school uniform with hasty movements. Without hope, she forced her eyes to look into the distance again. There, she saw Owuor. He stood calmly at the other end of the platform, almost in front of the locomotive—big, familiar, and laughing, in the black attorney's robe. Even though Regina knew that Owuor would come toward her, she rushed up to him.

She had almost reached him and even put the joke he expected between tongue and teeth when she realized that he was not alone. Walter and Jettel, who had hidden behind a pile of boards, slowly straightened themselves up and waved with ever more hasty gestures. Regina stumbled and almost fell over her suitcase, ran on, opened her arms, and, running, could not decide whom to embrace first. She decided to push Walter and Jettel so forcefully together that all three of them would be one. She was only a few yards away now from this old dream, which had seemed lost for a long time, when she realized that her feet had turned into strong roots. Her father was a sergeant, and her mother was pregnant.

The enormousness of her happiness paralyzed Regina's legs for only a short while but her senses for so long that every breath had its own melody. It seemed to her as if she could not keep her eyes open for another moment without destroying the blissful picture. It turned dark when she ran up to Owuor. She pressed her head on the now coarse material of the worn robe, saw his skin with the many tiny holes, and smelled the memory that made her into a child again, listened to his heart, and started to cry.

"I will never forget this," she said when her lips were able to move again.

"I did promise you," Jettel laughed. She wore the same dress in which she had waited for the baby in Nakuru, who was not allowed to live. The dress, now as then, was tight over her breast.

"But I thought you had forgotten," Regina admitted and shook her head.

"How could I? You would not let me."

"I played a part in it, too."

"I know, Sergeant Redlich," Regina giggled. She slowly put on the hat that was lying on the ground, extended three fingers of her right hand into the air, and gave him the Girl Guide salute.

"When did it happen?"

"Three weeks ago."

"You are trying to tease me. Mama has already gotten round."

"Your father became a sergeant three weeks ago. Your mother is in her fourth month."

"And you did not write to me! I could already have prayed."

"It was supposed to be a surprise," Jettel said.

"We wanted to be sure first. And we have already started praying," Walter added.

While Owuor clapped his hands and sent his eyes to the *memsahib*'s belly as if he had learned about the beautiful *shauri* just now, all four of them looked silently at one another and each one knew what the others were thinking. After that, six arms made a unity of gratefulness and love for Walter, Jettel, and Regina. It was not a child's dream, after all.

The palms at the iron gate of the Hove Court were still filled with the juice of the last long rains. Owuor pulled a red cloth out of his pants pocket and blindfolded Regina. She had to sit on his back and put her arms around his neck. It was still as strong as in those days at Rongai, which had long been swallowed by time, even though his hair had become much softer. Owuor clicked his tongue temptingly, softly said *"memsahib kidogo,"* and carried her like a very heavy sack through the garden and past the rosebed that surrendered the heat of the day to the first coolness of the late afternoon.

Behind the cloth, which simultaneously filled her with expectation and made her blind, Regina was able to smell the tree with the fragrant guavas; she heard her fairy softly play the children's song about the star that twinkled like a diamond in the night. Even though she could not see anything but the sparkles in her fantasy sky, she knew that the fairy was wearing a dress of red hibiscus flowers and held a silver flute to her lips. "Thank you," Regina cried as she rode past, but she spoke Jaluo, and only Owuor laughed.

When he, finally, with the groan of a donkey that has not found any water for days, shook Regina from his back and tore the cloth from her forehead, she stood in front of a small oven in a strange kitchen that smelled of fresh paint and moist wood. Regina recognized only the blue enamel pot, in which her special meatballs were swimming in a thick sauce, which was as white as the sweet pudding in German fairy tales. Rummler came howling from another room and jumped up on her, panting.

"This is our flat now. Two rooms with a kitchen and a private wash-basin," Walter and Jettel said, and their voices turned into one.

Regina crossed her fingers to show Lady Luck that she knew what was proper. "How did this happen?" she asked and took a tentative step in the direction from which Rummler had just come.

"Empty flats have to be given to soldiers first," Walter explained. He spoke the sentence, which he had read in the newspaper and learned by heart, so quickly in his hard English that his tongue got caught in his teeth, but Regina remembered just in time that she was not permitted to laugh.

"Hurray," she called after the lump in her throat had slid back to her knees. "Now we are no longer refugees."

"Yes, we are," Walter qualified, but he was laughing. "We are going to stay refugees. But not bloody ones."

"But our baby will not be a refugee, Papa."

"Some day none of us will be refugees anymore. I promise."

"Not now," Jettel said annoyed. "Not today."

"Don't you have to go to the Horse Shoe today?"

"I am not working anymore. The doctor does not permit it."

The sentence drilled into Regina's head and stirred the recollections, which she had buried, into a thick loam of fear and helplessness. Small dots danced in front of her eyes, which had grown hot, when she asked, "Is he a good doctor this time? Does he treat Jews?"

"Oh, yes," Jettel said.

"He is Jewish," Walter explained, emphasizing every word.

"And such an attractive man," Diana said enthusiastically. She was standing at the door in a light yellow dress that made her skin as pale as if the moon were already in the sky. Regina at first only saw the hibiscus flowers shine in her blond hair and for an intoxicating second she actually thought that her fairy had come down from its tree. Then she realized that Diana's kiss tasted like whisky and not like guavas.

"I am always so confused nowadays," Diana giggled when she wanted to stroke Regina's hair but forgot to take the dog off her arm in the process. "We are going to have a baby. Have you heard? We are going to have a baby. I can't sleep anymore at night."

Owuor served dinner in the long white *kanzu* with the red sash and gold embroidery. He did not speak a word—as he had been taught by his first *bwana* in Kisumu—but his eyes could not be set back to the intense calm of an English farm house. His pupils were as big as on the night when he had chased the locusts away.

"There are no capers in this stupid country," Jettel complained and stabbed the meatball with her fork.

"What are capers?" Regina chewed contentedly, enjoying the pleasant magic of fulfilled longings, but for the first time she did not give herself enough time to forward the answer to her heart.

"What are we going to call the baby?" she asked.

"We have written to the Red Cross."

"I don't understand."

"We are trying," Walter explained and stuck his head under the table, even though Rummler was standing behind him and he did not have anything in his hand to give to him, either, "to find out something about your grandparents, Regina. As long as we do not know what happened to them, we cannot name the baby Ina or Max in their memory. You know that with us, children do not get the names of living relatives."

Regina for only a moment allowed herself to wish that she did not understand the words with poisoned arrows anymore than Diana did, who whispered endearments in her dog's ear and pushed small balls of rice into its mouth. But she saw how the seriousness in her father's face turned into an expression of dark burning pain. Her mother's eyes were moist. Fear and anger fought for victory in Regina's head, and she envied Inge, who was allowed to say, "I hate the Germans" at home.

With the slowness of a mule, she gathered the strength to concentrate on the question why the meatball had changed into a small mountain of salt and sharpness in her throat. Finally, Regina succeeded in looking at her father as if she, and not he, were the child who needed help.

17

AFTER THE WAR, tolerance and cosmopolitism were, even in the conservative circles of the Colony, considered unavoidable concessions to the new times, for which the Empire had had to make so many sacrifices. However, people with a sense of tradition were in absolute agreement that in this matter, only the sound British sense for proportion was able to protect them from precipitous and also, unfortunately, rather tasteless exaggerations. Janet Scott, the headmistress of the Kenya Girls' High School in Nairobi, therefore, in her conversations with worried parents, did not expressly point to the fact that the boarding part of her school accepted a significantly smaller number of refugee children than its annex, the institute for day students, which was of a much lower social standing. The high standards of the boarding school, which was unconditionally committed to the old ideals, quickly became known during these times of social upheaval anyway.

Only in a trusted circle of likeminded people did Mrs. Scott with a small blush that betrayed her pride, indicate that she had solved the awkward problem in a rather elegant manner. Students who lived less than twenty miles from the school could attend the renowned boarding school only by application and under special circumstances. Other girls were just accepted as day scholars and, as such, not treated as equal members of the school community by their fellow students or teachers.

Exceptions to the normal procedures for admission to the boarding school were made only if mothers had already been students there or if fathers had shown themselves to be particularly generous sponsors. This offered sufficient guarantees that things would be kept in balance, which was appreciated by the self-confident traditionalists. The initiated regarded the solution of accommodating oneself to the new conditions and yet not losing sight of the essence of the conservative element as both diplomatic and practical.

"It is strange," Mrs. Scott used to wonder in her fearlessly loud tone of voice, "that it is just the refugees who have a tendency to congregate in town and who, for the most part, are also out of the question for the boarding school. Most likely, the poor devils in their oversensitivity will still feel somewhat discriminated against, but how can that be helped?" Only when the headmistress felt really secure among her equals and safe from annoying modern misinterpretations did she delight them with her objective opinion, agreeably stated without any cheap sarcasm, that some people luckily were more practiced in dealing with discrimination than others.

During her two months as a day scholar, without the kind of social status that carried more weight in the school life of the Colony than anywhere else, Regina had seen Janet Scott only once and then from afar. That was during the celebration in the school auditorium in which they gave thanks for the capitulation of Japan. Given the correspondingly inconspicuous behavior that was expected of day students, there was hardly any need to meet the headmistress personally.

The enforced distance, however, did not lessen Regina's appreciation of Mrs. Scott. On the contrary. She was infinitely grateful to the school's headmistress, who did not ask anything from her but the limited self-assurance to which she was used anyway, for a regulation that saved her from being sentenced again to life in a boarding school.

Owuor, too, owed his now permanently high spirits to the unknown Mrs. Scott. Once again, every day, he enjoyed going to the market with two *vikapu* instead of one tiny bag and no longer having to be despised by houseboys with rich *memsahib*s. He was able to cook in big pots again and, above all, to keep his ears open for the events in three people's lives, just as during the best days on the farm. At night, when he carried the food from the tiny kitchen into the room with the round table and hammock in which the little *memsahib* slept, he said, with the satisfied delight of a successful hunter, "We are no longer tired people on a safari."

As soon as Regina felt the first bite of food in her mouth, she gave Owuor's head and her own heart the ever-again intoxicating joy of repeating the beautiful sentence in just the right intonation with a voice full of contentment. At night, in her narrow swinging bed, seven days a week she extended the magic into a long-winded thank-you to the generous God Mungu, who after all the years of longing and despair had finally answered her prayers. The two-hour bus trip before and after school seemed to her like a feather-light price to pay for the certainty that she never again would have to be separated from her parents for three long months.

Even before sunset and before the first lamps were lit in the small huts of the personnel, she boarded the overcrowded bus to Delamere Avenue with her father, and from there another, even more crowded one, which left the town and was used only by natives. Walter had, finally—in the sixth month of Jettel's pregnancy, after many written applications to Captain McDowell, who had four children in Brighton, many nostalgic recollections of a family life, and never enough room in the barracks in Ngong for his men—received permission to live at home.

He commuted daily to his job in the mail and information division of his unit and returned only late in the evening to the Hove Court; on Fridays, though, nearly always early enough to go to the synagogue with Regina. When he took up the tradition of his childhood matter-of-factly, as if he had never in the despair of the emigration rejected it forever, Regina first thought that it was only important for her father to pray for the baby in the right place.

"It is for you," he had told her, though. "You have to know where you belong. It is high time." She had not dared to ask him for the explanation that she needed, but in any case, stopped her nightly conversations with Mungu on Fridays.

One Friday in December, Regina heard her father talking excitedly before she had reached the lemon trees behind the palms. She had not even been able to smell the chicken soup and the sweet fish in those flats in which the inhabitants did not yet speak English exclusively to each other and had started to sacrifice the Sabbath to their strenuous assimilation efforts. The untimely return was unusual but basically did not contradict earlier experiences. She, therefore, initially did not have any reason to be disturbed.

Still, she ran faster than at other times through the garden and very suddenly decided on a shortcut between the ant hills to the flat. Fear was faster than her legs. It fell too quickly from her head into her stomach and admitted pictures that she did not want to see into her eyes. When Regina crawled out of the small hole in the thorn-hedge, the door to the kitchen was open. She found her parents in a state that she had not experienced for herself but about which she knew everything. Even though the afternoon was still boiling from the heat of the day and her mother found every movement in the humid air even more strenuous than ever, it looked to Regina as if her parents had just been dancing.

For a moment full of longing, Regina believed that the great miracle of Ol' Joro Orok had repeated itself and that Martin had come as surprisingly on a visit, as in the days when he was still a prince. Her heart was already racing in her body, and her imagination galloped into a future that was woven like a blanket of golden stars with points of ruby-red shining stones. At that moment, she saw a slim yellow envelope with many stamps on the round table. Regina tried to read the writing between the wavy lines of the stamp, but even though every word was in English, none of them made sense. At the same time she noticed that her father's voice was as high as that of a bird that feels the first raindrops on its wings.

"The first letter from Germany has arrived," Walter shouted. His face was red, but without fear; his eyes were clear and lit with small sparks.

The letter had been sent as military correspondence from the occupation forces of the British Zone, was addressed to "Walter Redlich, Farmer in the Surrounding of Nairobi," and came from Greschek. Owuor, who had gotten it from the administration office of the Hove Court and had unsuspectingly caused the jubilation that even hours later still blazed like a bushfire, was already able to pronounce the name so well that his tongue hardly stuck to his teeth anymore.

"Greschek," he laughed, put the envelope into the hammock, and watched how the thin envelope rocked as if it were one of those small boats that he had seen in Kisumu once as a young man. "Greschek," he repeated and let his voice waver.

"Josef, he made it," Walter rejoiced, and Regina noticed only then that his tears had already fallen down to his chin. "He survived. He has not forgotten me. Do you even know who Greschek is?"

"*Greschek v. Krause*," Regina said happily. As a child she had thought that sentence to be the greatest magic in the world. She had only to say it and her father would laugh. It had been a wonderful game, but then one day she realized that her father looked like a dog that has been kicked while he laughed. After that, she had buried the three words, which she did not understand anyway, in her head.

"I have forgotten," she continued, embarrassed, "what that means. But you always said it in Rongai. *Greschek against Krause.*"

"Maybe your teachers are not that stupid after all. You really seem to be a smart child."

The praise tickled Regina's ear softly and reassuringly. She pondered with pleasure how she could turn the freshly sown approval into a big harvest without appearing vain. "He went with you," she finally remembered, "to Rome when you had to leave home."

"To Genoa. Rome does not have a harbor. Don't you learn anything in school?"

Walter held the letter out to Regina. She noticed that his hand shook, and she understood that he expected the same kind of excitement that was burning in his body from her. But when she saw the thin letters with curves and points that looked like the writing of the Maya to her, which she had seen in a book a little while ago, she was unable to swallow her laugh in time.

"Did you write like that, too, when you were a German?" she giggled.

"I am a German."

"How is she supposed to read the old script?" Jettel scolded and stroked the embarrassment from Regina's forehead. Her hand was hot, her face glowing, and the sphere in her belly moved from side to side.

"The baby is all excited, too, Regina," she laughed. "It has been kicking like mad since the letter arrived. My God, who would have thought that I could get this excited about a letter from Greschek? You can't imagine what a strange fellow he was. But one of the few decent ones in Leobschütz. I will not have anything said against him. He sent his Grete to help me pack when I did not know whether I was coming or going. I will never forget that."

Immersed in the past, which through a single letter had become the present again, Jettel and Walter retreated into a world in which there was only room for the two of them. They sat close to each other on the sofa and held hands while they called out names, sighed, and drank in sadness. Together, they had only eight fingers and two thumbs. Then they started fighting about whether Greschek had had his store on Jägerndorfer Street and had lived on Troppauer Street or the other way around. Walter could not convince Jettel nor she him, but their voices remained soft and happy.

Finally, they agreed at least that Doctor Müller had had his office on Troppauer Street. For a few dangerous seconds, the friendly flames of their good mood threatened to turn into the usual fire of never-forgotten insults because of Doctor Müller. Jettel maintained that he was to blame for her chest infection after Regina's birth, and Walter retorted angrily, "You did not give him a chance and immediately sent for the doctor from Ratibor. I am still embarrassed about that today. After all, Müller was one of my fraternity brothers."

Regina almost stopped breathing. She knew that Doctor Müller could as quickly incite a war between her parents as a stolen cow among the Masai. She noticed, however, with relief that the fight this time was carried out with nonpoisonous arrows. She did not find it as unpleasant as expected, and it even became absorbing when Walter and Jettel debated whether the day was good enough to open the last bottle of wine from Sohrau, which was still waiting for a special occasion. Jettel was for, Walter against it, but then Jettel changed her mind and Walter, too. Before they had a chance to chase their anger into the room, both of them said simultaneously, "Let's wait a little longer; maybe there will still be an even better day."

Owuor was sent to the kitchen to make coffee. He served it in the slim white pot with the pink roses on the lid and pinched his left eye shut while doing so, which always meant with him that even he knew about things that he could not talk about. Already, when the *bwana* and the *memsahib* had acted like happy children as soon as they saw the letter, Owuor had started the yeast for the small rolls, which only his hands could turn into the perfect round shapes of the sons of a fat moon.

The *memsahib* did not forget to be surprised when he carried in the plate with the hot tiny loaves, and the *bwana*, instead of *"assante sana,"* said to Owuor, "Come, Owuor, we are going to read the letter to the *memsahib kidogo.*" Satiated by the honor, which warmed his stomach without his having to eat, and even more his head, Owuor sat in the hammock. He hugged his knees, said, singing, "Greschek," and, with the last rays of the sun, fed his ears with the laugh of the *bwana,* who had a face that was as soft as the skin of a young gazelle.

"Dear Dr. Redlich," Walter read out loud, "I do not even know if you are still alive. I was told in Leobschütz that a lion had eaten you. I never really believed it, though. God would not save a man like you just so a lion could eat him up. I have survived the war. Grete, too. But we had to get out of Leobschütz. The Poles gave us only one day to clear out. We are living in Marke now. It is an ugly village in the Harz Mountains. Even smaller than Hennerwitz. They call us Polacks and Eastern rabble here and act as if we alone have lost the war. We do not have enough to eat, yet more than others, because we also work harder. After all, we have lost everything and want to get ahead again. That annoys the people here especially. You know your Greschek. Grete collects scrap iron, and I sell it. Do you still remember how you always used to say, Greschek it is not decent what you are doing with Grete. So, I married her during our flight, and now I am quite happy about it.

"Until the damned war started, I often went to Sohrau and brought groceries to your father and sister. They were not doing very well. Grete prayed for them every Sunday in church. I was unable to. If God saw all that and did nothing, he did not listen to prayers anymore. Mr. Bacharach was beaten by the SA in the street and taken away. Shortly after you left Breslau. We never heard from him again.

"I hope this letter will arrive in Africa. I found a steel helmet for an English soldier. They are all after these things. The man knew a little German and promised me that he would send this letter to you. Who knows if he will keep his word? We are not allowed to send out any mail yet.

"Are you going to come back to Germany? When we were in Genoa you said, Greschek, I am going to come back once the swine are gone from Germany. Why do you still want to stay among the Negroes? You are a lawyer. People who were not Nazis are getting good jobs here and also a place to live much more quickly than others. If you come, Grete will help the Missus again. People in the West cannot work as well as we do. They are all lazy brutes. And stupid, too. Please write to me if you have time. And give my regards to the Missus and the child. Is she still afraid of dogs? Your old friend Josef Greschek."

After Walter had finished reading the letter, only Rummler's even, snoring sounds scratched at a silence that was as thick as the fog in a forest heavy with rain. Owuor was still holding the envelope in his hand and was about to ask the *bwana* why a man sent words on such a big safari instead of saying things to his friend for which his ears had waited for so long. But he saw that the *bwana* was in the room only with his body, not with his head. Owuor's sighs, as he got up slowly to prepare dinner, woke the sleeping dog.

Much later, Walter said, "The spell is broken now. Maybe we will hear more from home soon," but his voice was tired when he added, "We are not ever going to see our Leobschütz again."

They all went to bed, as if it were the custom on Fridays and not the other way around, before the voices of the women in the garden faded away. For a while, Regina heard her parents talk on the other side of the wall, but she did not understand enough to follow them into the world of foreign names and streets. The image of Greschek's strange handwriting tore her out of her first sleep, and after that it seemed as if the snatches of conversation from the next room also had points and curves that attacked her. She was annoyed that she was unable to defend herself and talked, even though it was Friday and her conscience had to swallow stones while doing so, for a long time to Mungu.

The following day, the extraordinary humidity in Nairobi was the first thing mentioned in the news. The heat raged like a wounded lion. It burned the grass, flowers, and even cactus plants, left trees lifeless, birds silent, dogs vicious, and people discouraged. They were not able to stand the heat even in the spacious flats with the expensive curtains but gathered in the small shades of the big trees and, half ashamed, yet with a sadness that put them at a loss and proved addictive, took pictures of winter landscapes out of their long-buried photo albums and memories.

The last day of the year 1947 was so hot that many hotels first pointed out the number of fans in the dining room and only then the courses of their festive menus. In Ngong, the biggest bushfire in years was aflame; in the Hove Court, water was rationed and flowers could no longer be watered, and even Owuor, who had been a child in the heat of Kisumu, had to wipe the sweat from his forehead while cooking. There was no doubt that the short rains had not come and that no relief could be expected before July.

Jettel was too exhausted to complain. From the eighth month of her pregnancy on, she had sentenced herself to a complete retreat from life and was deaf to all consolations and good advice. She could not be dissuaded that the air outside was more tolerable than that in closed rooms and escaped at eight o'clock in the morning to Regina's guava tree. Even though Doctor Gregory told her after each checkup that she had gained too much weight and needed exercise, she did not move for hours from the chair, which Owuor carried into the garden for her and covered as carefully with a white sheet as if he were setting up a throne.

The women in the Hove Court admired Owuor's idea so much that they visited Jettel under the tree as regularly as if she were indeed a queen who grants an audience to her people only at certain hours. Very few of them, though, had the patience to listen to her raving about the healthy winters in Breslau, and they very quickly took flight into their own past, which Jettel in her irritable state of mind considered a simply unbearable habit. She found the burdens of other people's lives even harder to tolerate than the constant fear that the heat might harm the baby and it would also be stillborn.

"I can no longer concentrate when somebody tells me something," she whined to Elsa Conrad.

"Nonsense, you are only too lazy to listen. Just wake up, finally. Other people have children, too."

"I cannot even fight anymore," Jettel complained at night.

"Don't worry," Walter consoled her. "It will come back. You never forgot how, under any circumstances."

Only when Regina came home from school and sat under the tree with her did Jettel emerge from her state of semiconscious despair and deep sleep. Regina's world of fairies and fulfilled wishes, which she did not want to give up even though her father immediately made fun of her if he caught even a word, along with the enthusiasm with which she imagined life with the new baby, relieved Jettel of the discomfort of her heavy body and provided again, as during the hapless pregnancy in Nakuru, a strong bond with her daughter.

It was the last Sunday in February that drove Jettel back to reality with a force that she would not be able to forget all her life. In the morning, the day was no different from all the preceding ones. After breakfast, Jettel sat down, groaning, under the tree, and Walter stayed in the flat to listen to the radio. At noon, Owuor, who was never far from the *memsahib,* did not respond to her calls. Angrily, Jettel sent Regina to the kitchen to get her a glass of water, but Regina did not come back. The thirst turned very suddenly into such a violent burning sensation that Jettel finally did get up herself. She noticed how reluctance made her limbs stiff, but she fought in vain against the lethargy, even though it seemed to her undignified and ridiculous.

Only very slowly did she put one foot in front of the other and hope with every step that Owuor or Regina would show up to save her the rest of the way. But she saw neither of them and assumed, exhausted by an anger that took even more out of her than the short, shadeless walk along the dried out thorn-hedge, that she would find Owuor and Regina in one of their many conversations about the farm, which always appeared to her like a betrayal of her helpless state.

When she opened the door, she saw Owuor. He stood in the kitchen with his head bent far down, did not seem to notice Jettel at all, and only said several times *"bwana"* softly, as if he were talking to himself. The curtains were drawn in the room. In the heavy air and the pale light, the few pieces of furniture in the room looked like tree stumps in a barren landscape. Walter and Regina, both strangely pale and with red eyes, sat on the sofa and held onto each other like two confused children.

Jettel was so shocked that she did not dare talk to either of them. Her glance became fixed. She felt that she was getting cold, and, at the same time, she became aware that the cold, for which she had longed so much, hurt her skin like needle pricks.

"Papa has known all the time," Regina sobbed, but her loud crying immediately turned into a low whimper.

"Be quiet. You promised not to say anything. We cannot upset Mama. All of this can wait until the baby is born."

"What is the matter?" Jettel asked. Her voice was firm, and even though some shame overcame her that she was unable to explain to herself, she felt stronger than she had for weeks. She even bent down to the dog without feeling her back, and she put her hand on her heart but did not feel it beat. She was just about to repeat her question when she saw Walter hastily and clumsily try to hide a piece of paper in his pants pocket.

"Greschek's letter?" she asked without hope.

"Yes," Walter lied.

"No," Regina shouted, "no."

It was Owuor who forced his tongue to the truth. He was leaning against the wall and said, "The *bwana*'s father is dead. His sister, too."

"What is going on? What does all of this mean?"

"Owuor has told you everything. I only told him."

"How long have you known?"

"The letter came a few days after Greschek's. They handed it to me at the camp. I was so happy that it had to go through military censorship because it came from Russia and I did not have to tell you about it. I did not cry. Not until today. And just then, Regina had to catch me. I read it to her. I did not want to, but she kept insisting. My God, I am so ashamed of myself crying in front of the child."

"Give it to me," Jettel said quietly. "I have to know."

She went to the window, unfolded the yellowed paper, saw the capital letters, and tried at first to read only the name and address of the sender.

"Where is Tarnopol?" she asked but did not wait for the answer. She felt as if she would be able to escape from the horror that was facing her only if she did not give herself time to grasp what had happened.

Jettel read the words "Dear Doctor Redlich" out loud, but then her voice retreated into the loneliness of silence, and she realized with a helplessness that made her shudder that she could no longer expect any mercy from her eyes.

"Before the war in Tarnopol, I was a teacher of German," Jettel read, "and today, I have the sad task of informing you about the death of your father and sister. I knew Mr. Max Redlich well. He trusted me because he was able to speak German with me. I tried to help him as far as I could. A week before his death, he gave me your address. I knew then that he wanted me to write to you if anything happened to him.

"Your father and your sister made their way to Tarnopol after many dangers and terrible deprivations. During the first time of the German occupation, there was still some hope for him and Miss Liesel. They were able to hide here in the basement of the schoolhouse and planned to go on to the Soviet Union at the first opportunity. Then, two SS men beat your father to death in the street. He died quickly and did not have to suffer anymore.

"Miss Liesel was deported a month later from the schoolhouse and brought to Belsec. We were unable to do anything for her and have not heard from her again. It was the third transport to Belsec. Nobody returned from that one. I am not sure if you know that Miss Liesel married a Czech during the flight. Erwin Schweiger was a truck driver and was forced to join the military by the Russian army. So he had to leave your father and Miss Liesel behind.

"Your father was very proud of you and talked often about you. The last letter you wrote to him was always in his breast pocket. How often did we read it, and how often did we imagine how well and safe you and your family were on the farm. Mr. Redlich was a courageous man and trusted in God to the end, believing that he would see you again. God bless his soul. I am ashamed for all humanity that I have to write a letter like this, but I know that in your religion the son gives a prayer for his father on the day of his death. Most of your brethren will not be able to do so. If I only knew whether it will be a consolation to you that you can, it would make my task easier.

"Your father always said you had a kind heart. May God preserve it for you. Do not write back to me in Tarnopol. Letters from abroad cause difficulties here. I include you and your family in my prayers."

While she waited for the tears that would relieve her, Jettel carefully folded the letter, but her eyes remained dry. It confused her that she could not scream and not even talk, and she felt like an animal that can feel only physical pain. Embarrassed, she sat down between Walter and Regina and smoothed out her sweaty frock. She made a small movement as if she wanted to pat both of them but could not lift her arms high enough and, instead, she stroked her belly over and over again.

Jettel asked herself whether it was a sin to give life to a child who would be asking for its grandparents a few years from now. When she looked at Walter, she knew that he sensed the revolt within her, because he shook his head. Yet, his helpless obstinacy consoled her, for she said, without letting her voice get weakened by despair, "It will have to be a boy; we now have a name for him."

18

DURING THE LONG NIGHT preceding March 6, 1946, many exhausted people in the Hove Court did not find rest, which in times of great heat waves they defended even more strenuously than their possessions. In the majority of rooms and flats, the lamps were lit until sunrise; babies were still crying at midnight for their *ayas* and bottles; houseboys lost their sense of right, duty, and order and heated the water for the morning tea before the first birds had started to twitter; dogs barked at the moon, shadows, parched trees, and angry people. With hoarse growling, they got into the kind of fights that invariably lead to merciless quarrels between their owners; radios played hit songs at the volume heard last at the end of the war in Europe; even the almost completely deaf Miss Jones appeared in her nightgown in front of the closed administration building to make it known that she was bothered by the noise.

Owuor, who was alone with the *memsahib kidogo,* did not go to his quarters to eat or be with the young woman whom a week ago he had asked to come from Kisumu. In the third hour after sundown, he shook out all the blankets and mattresses, swept the wooden floors, and brushed the dog; finally, he took care of his fingernails with the *memsahib*'s nail file, which she would never have allowed if she had been home.

With a heavy burden in his breast and stomach, he rocked his exhaustion to rest in Regina's hammock, without having enough sleep come to him to burn off the images in his head. From time to time, he tried to sing the sad song of the woman who is searching for her child in the forest and keeps hearing only her own voice, but the melody got stuck in his throat too often, and he finally had to cough his impatience away.

Regina lay in her school blouse and delicate gray skirt, which needed even more care than a newly hatched chick, on her parents' bed. She had intended to read *David Copperfield* from the first to the last page without even getting up for a glass of water, but after the first two paragraphs of the book the letters ran into one another and raced past her eyes like fiery red circles. Her hands were moist from the exertion of stroking the colored beads on her magic belt; her tongue recoiled from the effort of formulating the only wish that Regina would ever ask of fate again exactly right so that she could convince the taciturn God Mungu that He had to be on her side this time and not on that of Death, as in the days of swallowed tears.

Ever since Walter and Jettel, with a small suitcase and emitting the scent of dogs running amok, had left in the middle of dinner in Mr. Slapak's car, Regina had been fighting a fear that had more evil strength than a starving snake. The uncertainty raged in her entrails like a fuming waterfall after a storm. Only when the stony mountain in her throat threatened to slide between her teeth did she run to Owuor, feel the familiar roundness of his shoulders with her fingertips, and ask, "Do you think it is going to be a good day?"

Owuor immediately opened his eyes wide and said, as if all his life he had learned to speak only this one sentence, "I know it is going to be a good day." As soon as the words had come out of his mouth, he and the *memsahib kidogo* always looked on the ground, because both had heads that could not forget. And both knew that a good memory on significant days is more painful than the vengeful stick of a man who has been robbed on the naked skin of a thief who has been caught.

At three o'clock in the morning, Elsa Conrad watered the camellias in front of her window and so loudly called herself a senile fool that Mrs. Taylor angrily rushed out on her balcony and shouted for quiet. Despite this, no fight started, because at precisely the moment when Elsa could finally think of the appropriate English swearwords and also became sure of their pronunciation, Professor Gottschalk appeared. He walked through the dark garden with his hat on and the tiny porcelain bowl from which he ate in his porridge in the morning in his hand. Both called out to each other, "It is time" and simultaneously tapped their index fingers against their foreheads to indicate to each other that they both doubted their sanity.

Much earlier, Chepoi had had to send two disappointed officers away without giving the hungry young men a chance to judge the charms of the famous Mrs. Wilkins with as much as a glance. Diana herself was still standing at the window at daybreak. She wore the golden crown with the multicolored stones that during her one Moscow appearance had given her the illusion of a future that never had become reality. During the short breaks that she permitted herself in her easy chair, she sprayed her dog so often with her favorite perfume that he bit her finger with unusual boldness to protect his nose.

For her part, Diana insulted the exhausted dog by calling him "dirty Stalin." Crying from pain and fury and plagued by a vague aversion against everything that she would have labeled "Bolshevik" when sober, she finally gave in to Chepoi's efforts to calm her. She let him take the whisky bottle away after an unusually short struggle and let herself be put to bed with the promise that he would wake her immediately if there was any news.

Without the smallest sign marking the significance of the moment in the Hove Court, Max Ronald Paul Redlich was born one minute after five in the Eskotone Nursing Home, five miles away. His first cry and a sudden muffled rumble in the sky that sounded like the stampede of a herd of threatened gnus came at the same time. When Nurse Amy Patrick put the baby on the scale and noted his weight of five pounds and four ounces, as well as the long, hard-to-pronounce name, on a piece of paper, her dull eyes turned a fine shade lighter, and she talked of a miracle.

The smile, exaggerated for the occasion, of the midwife, who was worn out from her third sleepless night, as well as the euphoric invocation of a higher power, was intended not for the child and even less for the contented mother, whose accent, so painful to sensitive ears, Nurse Amy had considered as extremely troublesome during this difficult birth. Amy Patrick's spontaneous joy was only the expression of an understandable surprise that the short rains had, after all, and without corresponding notice in the previous day's weather forecast, released Nairobi from the trauma of a never-before-experienced heat wave. The midwife felt so relieved that, despite the regrettable circumstance that there was no appreciative audience, she gave voice to her British humor. When she applied the umbilical bandage to the newborn, she said, with a hint of satisfaction, "My goodness, that chap cries just like a little Englishman."

The blessing from the skies was unusually sparse for a late rainy season. At most, it would give people something to talk about for a week, and at best, it would be sufficient to free the wings of the smallest birds, the corrugated tin roofs, and the upper branches of the thorn-acacias from dust. That the rain had started at all, though, confirmed for all well-meaning people who had voluntarily sacrificed their night's rest the belief that the Max Redlich's birth was an extraordinary event and that the child might even be a symbol of hope for the second generation of refugees.

Regina and Owuor, at first, did not notice that Walter had returned. They did not hear the strong push that he gave to the door, which was stuck, or the curse when he stumbled over the sleeping dog. They were startled from their twilight state, but then like two soldiers under sudden combat order, only when they heard loud retching sounds from the kitchen. Owuor gave the open door a kick that even as a young man he would not have used to drive a stubborn mule to work. His *bwana* was kneeling in front of a rusty pail, which he clutched with both hands, groaning.

Regina ran to her father and tried to embrace him from the back before disappointment and terror paralyzed her. When Walter felt her arms on his breast, he raised himself up like a tree that has experienced the thirst of its roots and just in time feels the saving drops on its leaves.

"Max has arrived," he gasped. "This time God blessed us."

The silence persisted until Walter's gray skin had changed back into the light brown that matched his uniform. Regina had left her father's words too long in her ear to be able to do anything but force her head into small regular movements. It took a difficult half minute before she felt the refreshing flow of her tears.

When she was finally able to open her eyes, she saw that her father was crying, too; she pressed her face to his for a long time, to share the hot salty mush of joy with him.

"Max," Owuor said. His teeth shone like new candles in the dark room. "Now," he laughed, "we have a *bwana kidogo*."

Again, nobody said a word. But then Owuor repeated the name again, which he pronounced as clearly as if he had always known it, and then the *bwana* slapped him on the shoulder. Doing so, he laughed just like on the day when the locusts had flown away and he had called him his *rafiki*.

The smooth, soft word for friend, which Owuor could enjoy with pride only when the *bwana* said it quietly and a little hoarsely, flew to his ears like a butterfly on a hot day. The sounds drove warmth into his breast and extinguished the fear of the long night, which had been carved with too sharp a knife.

"Have you seen the child already?" he asked. "Does it have two healthy eyes and ten fingers? A child has to look like a little monkey."

"My son is more beautiful than any monkey. I have already held him in my hands. This afternoon the *memsahib kidogo* is going to see him. Owuor, I asked if I could bring you along, but the nurses and doctors in the hospital said no. I wanted you to be there."

"I can wait, *bwana*. Have you forgotten? I have waited for four rainy seasons."

"You know exactly when the other child died?"

"You know, too, *bwana*."

"Sometimes I have the feeling that Owuor is my only friend in this damn town," Walter said on the way to the hospital.

"One friend is enough for an entire life."

"Where did you get that from again? From your stupid fairy?"

"From my stupid English friend Dickens, but Mr. Slapak is a little bit of a friend, too. After all, he lent you his car. Otherwise, we would have to take the bus now."

Regina pulled a small piece of filling out of the torn car seat and tickled Walter's arm with the tips of the horsehair. She became aware that she had never before seen her father at the wheel of an automobile and that she had not even known that he could drive a car. She was just about to tell him that, but she sensed, without being able to explain the reason why quickly enough to herself, that the remark might hurt him and said instead, "You drive well."

"I already drove a car when nobody even thought of you."

"In Sohrau?" she asked obediently.

"In Leobschütz. Greschek's Adler. Dear God, if Greschek knew what a day it is today."

The rattling Ford groaned up the hill, leaving thick clouds of fine red sand behind. The car did not have any glass on the left side or in front, and there were big holes in the rusty roof, through which the sun burned. The heat, with its fast wings, and the humid headwind scratched their skin red. Regina felt as if she were riding in the jeep in which Martin had picked her up on her vacation. She saw the dark woods of Ol' Joro Orok more distinctly than she had for a long time, and then a head with blond hair and light eyes from which small stars flew into the distance.

For a while, she enjoyed the past as happily as the present, but a sudden burning sensation in the back of her neck brought back the painful longing that she had thought had been swallowed forever by the days of waiting. She chewed air to free her eyes from the pictures that she was no longer allowed to see and her heart from a sadness that did not belong with her intoxicating joy.

"I love you very much," she whispered.

The Eskotene Nursing Home, a sturdily constructed white building with windows of light-blue glass and slim portal columns with climbing roses the color of the sky at sunset, was situated in a park with a pond in which goldfish darted out under water lilies and a short-cropped carpet of green grass. Superb starlings that formed fans out of their blue shining feathers sat on the branches of high cedars, which still steamed after the morning rain. In front of the iron gate stood an *askari* with broad shoulders in a navy blue uniform and a broad club in both hands. A coffee-colored Irish wolfhound with a gray beard was asleep at his feet.

The expensive private clinic only reluctantly assisted babies of refugees with their start into life, but Doctor Gregory, who otherwise was quite willing to compromise, could not be talked into giving in this time. On principle, he did not treat patients in the government hospital, where physicians had to walk through the corridors with sickrooms for black patients before they reached the wards for Europeans. His fees during her pregnancy had already exhausted all the reserves from Jettel's work at the Horse Shoe, and the stay in the Eskotene would certainly consume any additional pay to which a sergeant was entitled for the birth of a child.

Despite this, Doctor Gregory was a sympathetic and meticulous physician, even for patients who could not afford him and who fell short of his high standards. He had, as he mentioned with a smile in his own circles, mildly surprised about his unexpectedly tolerant manner, even gotten used to Jettel's pronunciation. Every time, after he had examined her, he caught himself rolling his R's in an almost absurd way.

Above all, he did not make the rather strange bird in his distinguished office aware that he had, very discreetly and with reference to Jettel's age and the complications that were to be expected during pregnancy and birth, called on the Jewish community in Nairobi for the remaining enormous amount of money that was due to him. After all, he had been a member of the board with old Mr. Rubens for years and had never hesitated to continue professing his Judaism openly, even after he changed his originally Polish name to a pleasant, easy-to-pronounce English version.

Doctor Gregory, who visited his patients twice a day for the simple reason that the Eskotene was on the way to the golf course and that he had from youth on exhibited a special talent for combining duty with pleasure, was with Jettel when Walter arrived with Regina. The two of them remained standing at the door when they saw him. Their awkwardness, the father's embarrassment, which turned immediately into dejected servility, and the daughter with the body of a child and a face that had been stamped by premature experiences in life, touched the physician.

He asked himself, a little dismayed by a shame that was more irritating to him than he liked, whether he should not have gotten more involved in the fate of this small family that in its obvious closeness, which appeared laughably old-fashioned to him, reminded him of his grandfather's stories. It had been years since he last thought of the old man who, in a small, damp flat in the London East End, in an annoying way, used to appeal to just those roots from which the ambitious young medical student actively wanted to liberate himself. The impulse, however, was too fleeting for him to give in to it.

"Come on in," he called, therefore, in the somewhat exaggerated volume that he adopted particularly for the people from the Continent, with their longing for cordiality, and then, with a feeling of connection that he could explain to himself only as sentimentality, he added, a lot more quietly and even a little shyly, "Mazel tov." He patted Walter on the back, stroked Regina's head a bit absentmindedly, his hand sliding to her cheek, and hurried out of the room.

Only after the physician had pulled the door shut behind him did Regina notice the tiny head with a crown of dark fuzz in the crook of Jettel's arm. She heard her father's breath as if it were coming out of a fog that swallows sounds and, immediately afterward, the low whimpering of the newborn and how Jettel calmed the child with cooing sounds. Regina wanted to laugh out loud or, at least, scream as happily as her fellow students had when winning a hockey game, but she was able to make only a gurgling sound in her throat, which seemed very pitiful to her.

"Come," Jettel said, "the two of us have been waiting for you."

"Hold on to him; we cannot afford another one," Walter cautioned as he put the baby into Regina's arms. "This is your brother Max," he said in a strangely solemn voice. "I heard him cry this morning. He knows exactly what he wants. When he is a man, he will take good care of you. Not like I did for my sister."

Max had opened his eyes. They shone blue out of a face that had the color of young ears of maize at Rongai, and his skin smelled sweet like freshly cooked *posho*. Regina touched her brother's forehead with her nose to take possession of his scent. She was absolutely certain that she could never again be this overcome by happiness in all her life. At this moment, she said a last goodbye to her fairy, whom she would never have to trouble again. It was a short farewell without pain and hesitation.

"Don't you want to say something to him?"

"I don't know in which language I should talk to him."

"He is not a real refugee yet and is not embarrassed when he hears his mother tongue."

"Jambo," Regina whispered, *"jambo, bwana kidogo."* She startled when she realized that her happiness had lulled to sleep her watchfulness for words, which frightened her father. Regret made her heart beat too fast. "Does he really," she asked timidly, "belong to me?"

"To all of us."

"And to Owuor, too," Regina said and thought about the conversation during the night.

"Of course, as long as Owuor can stay with us."

"Not today," Jettel, said, annoyed. "Just not today."

With determination, Regina swallowed the question that curiosity tried to put into her mouth. "Just not today," she explained to her new brother, but she said the magic words only in her imagination and changed the laughter that chafed her throat into a few high notes of joy so that her father and mother would not find out that their son was already learning Owuor's language.

Owuor sat until sundown with his head between his knees and sleep under his eyelids in front of the kitchen, before he heard the car, which screeched more than a tractor that has been mistreated by mud and stones. Because the *bwana* first had to return the car to the scoundrel Slapak, it would still be some time until Owuor's wait was over, but Owuor had never counted the hours, only the good days. He slowly moved his arm and then his head a bit in the direction of the person who leaned against the wall behind him and contentedly dozed on.

Slapak, too, liked the taste of joy. After the birth of his fourth child, who was now just starting to crawl, he looked at the birth of a son in his own family and at the warehouse in his secondhand shop, which had been flourishing ever since the end of the war, with the same soberness; yet he longed for other people's happiness. When they returned his car key, he pulled Walter and Regina into his cramped living room, which smelled of damp diapers and cabbage soup.

Most people in the Hove Court saw in Leon Slapak only a shrewd businessman who would sell his own mother down the river if it would be of the slightest advantage to him, but at heart he was a pious man who took the mercy that befell others as confirmation that God took care of good people. And he had always liked this modest and friendly soldier in the foreign uniform, whose eyes showed that he had gotten his wounds not on the battlefield but in the fight against life. Slapak greeted Walter whenever he saw him and was always happy about the gratitude with which his greetings were acknowledged and that reminded him of the men in his homeland.

So, Slapak, who was despised by his neighbors, poured a glass of vodka, which he carefully wiped with his handkerchief, and pushed it into Walter's hand, took a swig from the bottle himself, and said a whole lot of words, of which Walter understood almost nothing. It was the usual mixture spoken by refugees from the East and included Polish, Yiddish, and English expressions, which reminded Walter, the more Slapak provided him with a warm heart and cool alcohol, more and more of Sohrau, because Slapak soon gave up any effort to speak English and, after that, also Yiddish and spoke only Polish. Slapak for his part enjoyed the few words of Polish that Walter knew from his childhood as much as if he had made an unexpectedly good business deal.

It became an evening of agreement between two men who pursued their memories, who came from two very different worlds, and yet had the common root of suffering. Two fathers thought not about their children but about their duty as sons that they had not been allowed to fulfill. Even though his guest was his own age, Slapak said goodbye to him shortly before midnight with the blessing of the fathers. After that, he gave Walter a pram, which he would need back in a year at the earliest, a package of torn diapers, and a red velvet dress for Regina, for which she would need to gain at least another ten pounds and grow almost as many inches.

"I celebrated my son's birth with a man with whom I cannot talk," Walter sighed on the short way to the flat. He gave the pram a push. The wheels with the worn rubber made a crushing noise on the stones. "Maybe I will be able to laugh about this one day." He felt the need to explain to Regina why, despite the agreeable warmth, he regarded his visit to Slapak as symbolic of his life as an outsider, but he searched in vain for the right words.

Regina, too, was in the process of telling her head to hold on to those confusing thoughts that were not supposed to come out, but then she did say, "I am not at all sad that you now love Max more than me. After all, I am no longer a child."

"How did you come up with that kind of nonsense? Without you, I would not have been able to survive all these years. Do you think I have forgotten that? I am a great father. I could never give you anything but love."

"It was enough." Regina noticed too late that she had been unable to find the right German words in time. She ran after the pram as if it were important to catch it before it reached the eucalyptus trees, stopped it, ran back, and embraced her father. The smell of alcohol and tobacco that came from his body and the feeling of safety that churned in her own combined into such giddiness that she became dizzy.

"I love you more than anyone else in the world," she said.

"And I love you, too. But we must not tell anyone that. Never."

"Never," Regina promised.

Owour stood as upright in front of the door as the *askari* with the club in front of the hospital. *"Bwana,"* he said, his voice saturated with pride, "I have already found an *aya*."

"An *aya*? You are a fool, Owuor. What are we going to do with an *aya*? Nairobi is not Rongai. There, *Bwana* Morrison paid for the *aya*. She lived on his farm. In Nairobi, I have to pay for an *aya*. I cannot do that. I have only enough money for you. I am not a rich man. You know that."

"Our child," Owuor answered angrily, "is just as good as other children. No child can be without an *aya*. The *memsahib* cannot push such an old baby carriage in the garden. And I cannot work for a man who does not have an *aya* for his child."

"You are the great Owuor," mocked Walter.

"This is Chebeti, *bwana*," Owuor explained and fed each of the four words with patience. "You do not have to give her much money. I have told her everything."

"What have you told her?"

"Everything, *bwana*."

"But I don't even know her."

"I know her, *bwana*. That is enough."

Chebeti, who had been sitting at the kitchen door, got up. She was tall and slim and wore a blue dress that covered her bare feet and hung from her shoulders as a loosely tied wrap. She had a white cloth wrapped around her head like a turban. She had the slow, graceful movements of the young women of the Jaluo tribe and their self-assured bearing. When she held her hand out to Walter, she opened her mouth but did not speak.

Regina was not even standing close enough to see the white in the stranger's eyes in the darkness, but she instantly noticed that Chebeti's skin and Owuor's had the same scent. Like dik-diks at midday in the high grass.

"Chebeti is going to be a good *aya*, Papa," Regina said. "Owuor sleeps only with good women."

19

CAPTAIN BRUCE CARRUTHERS ROSE briskly, stepped on a bug on the floor to kill it, then squashed a fly, which he thought to be a mosquito, on the window pane and sat down listlessly. His annoyance was heightened by the fact that he had to dig for a certain letter in a pile of papers on his desk before talking to the sergeant whom, despite some hard-to-explain reservations, he had found not too disagreeable, who always saluted as if he stood before the king and who spoke English like a lousy Indian. Carruthers had an aversion to any lack of discipline and an almost pathological disgust for the disorder that he himself had caused. He brooded—too extensively, as he thought moodily—about the fact that he, of all people, who despised discussions even more than all the nonsense of the military, always had to get stuck with the task of telling people what they did not want to hear.

He, who wanted nothing else but to stroll along Princes Street on a foggy autumn morning and feel the first promise of winter on his skin, had to be the only one not to be told that his application for leave from the army had been "deferred until further notice." He had had to fish this disappointment out of the mail two days ago himself. Since then, the captain had become even more aware that Africa was no good for a man who five long years ago, in addition to his heart, had left a very young wife in Edinburgh who took increasingly more time to answer his letters, and who for a long while now had not been able to explain why that was so.

Captain Carruthers considered it a double irony of fate that he now had to explain to this strange sergeant with the eyes of a devoted collie that His Majesty's army was not interested in extending his service.

"Why in the world does that bloke even want to go to Germany?" he grumbled.

"Because I am at home there, sir."

The captain looked at Walter with surprise. He had not heard him knocking at the door and also had not noticed that he had been talking to himself, which, regrettably, happened quite often lately.

"You want to join the British occupation army?"

"Yes, sir."

"Not a bad idea. I assume you speak German. Somehow you seem to be from there."

"Yes, sir."

"You would be just the man to straighten out the fucking Jerries."

"I think so, sir."

"Those in London think differently," Carruthers said, "if they think at all," he laughed with that touch of mockery that had earned him the reputation of being an officer with whom it was easy to talk at any time. When it dawned on him that he had wasted his wit, he silently held out the letter to Walter. He observed for some time and with an impatience that was out of proportion for the event how Walter struggled with the convoluted formulations of the arrogant London bureaucrats.

"Those at home," he said with a gruffness he regretted a little as soon as he noticed it, "don't want any soldiers in the occupation forces who do not have an English passport. Why do you actually want to go there?

"I wanted to stay in Germany after I was dismissed from the army."

"Why?"

"Germany is my homeland, sir," Walter stuttered. "Sorry, sir, that I am saying that."

"Never mind," the captain answered distractedly.

He knew that he did not have to carry on the conversation any further. It was his duty only to inform his people of events that concerned them and to make sure that they understood the decision. With the many foreigners and the damned coloreds, that truly was no longer a given as in the good old times. The captain shook a fly off his forehead. He realized that he would only get unnecessarily involved in a case that was none of his business if he did not end the exchange immediately.

Some compulsion, however, that he later could explain only as a trick of fate and melancholy, made him delay the short nod that would dismiss the sergeant in the usual way and thereby free himself for the next battle against those idiotic mosquitoes. The man in front of him had spoken of his homeland, and precisely this foolish, misused, sentimental word had for months now pierced Bruce Carruthers's rest.

"My home is Scotland," he said, and for a moment he actually thought that he was talking to himself again, "but some fool in London has gotten it into his stubborn head that I am supposed to rot here in stupid Ngong."

"Yes, sir."

"Do you know Scotland?"

"No, sir."

"A really beautiful country. With decent weather, decent whisky, and decent people whom you can still trust. The English do not have the faintest idea about Scotland and what they did to us when they took our king and stole our independence," the captain said. He was aware that it was somewhat ridiculous to discuss Scotland and the year 1603 with a man who evidently could not say much more than yes and no.

"What do you do in your civilian life?" he, therefore, asked.

"I was a lawyer in Germany, sir."

"Really?"

"Yes, sir."

"I am a lawyer, too," the captain said. He remembered that he had last said this sentence when he joined the damn army. "How in God's name," he asked despite a sudden uneasiness about his unexpected curiosity, "did you ever end up in this strange country? A lawyer needs his mother tongue. Why didn't you stay in Germany?"

"Hitler did not want me."

"Why not?"

"I am Jewish, sir."

"Right. It says so here. And you want to return to Germany? Didn't you read the terrible reports about the concentration camps? Hitler seems to have treated your people damned badly."

"Hitlers come and go, but the German people remain."

"All of a sudden you seem to know English. The way you said that!"

"Stalin said that, sir."

Years in the army had taught Captain Carruthers never to do more than was asked of him and, above all, not to burden himself with other people's concerns, but the situation, as grotesque as it was, fascinated him. He had just had his first rational conversation in months and, at that, with a man with whom he could communicate no better than with the Indian mechanic of the company, who took every piece of paper with writing on it as a personal affront.

"I am sure you wanted the army to pay for your passage. A free trip home. We all want that."

"Yes, sir. That is my only chance."

"The army is required to dismiss every soldier and his family to his homeland," the captain declared. "You know that, don't you?"

"Pardon, sir, I did not understand you."

"The army has to bring you to Germany if that is your homeland."

"Who says that?"

"The regulations."

The captain dug in the papers of his desk but did not find what he was looking for. Finally, he pulled a yellowed sheet with closely spaced writing out of his desk drawer. He did not expect Walter to be able to read the text but held the ordinance out to him anyway and realized, a little surprised and also a little moved, that Walter at least seemed to understand instantly what applied to him. "A man of the word," Carruthers laughed.

"Pardon, sir, I do not understand you again."

"It doesn't matter. Tomorrow, we will apply for you to be dismissed to Germany. Did you by any chance understand me now?"

"Oh, yes, sir."

"Do you have a family?"

"A wife and two children. My daughter is going to be fourteen, and my son is eight weeks old today. I thank you very much, sir. You do not know what you are doing for me."

"I think I do," Carruthers said pensively, "but don't get your hopes up too high yet," he added with an irony that did not come as easily as usual. "Everything is very slow in the army. How do the damned blacks say that here?"

"Pole, pole," Walter was pleased to inform Carruthers. He felt like Owuor when he repeated the two words very slowly. When he saw the captain nod, he hurried to leave the room.

At first, he was unable to explain his wavering emotions. What he had interpreted as the foresight of a man who had courage enough to admit failure to himself now all of a sudden seemed to him like irresponsible recklessness. And yet, he sensed that a flicker of hope had been sparked that neither doubts nor fear of the future would be able to extinguish.

When Walter returned to the Hove Court, he was still numb from the unsettling mixture of euphoria and uncertainty. He stopped at the gate and stood there between the cactus plants for a time that seemed like an eternity to him, counted the flowers, and tried in vain to add them up. He needed even more time to resist the temptation to stop at Diana's first, to refresh himself with her good mood and especially her whisky. His steps were slow and too light when he went on, but then he saw Chebeti with the baby sitting under the same tree that had provided Jettel with consolation, protection, and shade during her pregnancy. He allowed his nerves to relax.

His son was lying sheltered in the folds of Chebeti's light blue dress. Only the child's tiny white linen cap was visible. It touched the woman's chin and appeared in the light wind like a ship in a quiet ocean. Regina crouched with crossed legs in the grass, a wreath of leaves from the lemon tree in her hair. Since she could not sing, she read a children's song with many repeating sounds in a solemn deep voice to her brother and the *aya*.

Owuor was sitting under a cedar with dark leaves and watching the smallest move of the baby with close attention. Next to him lay the stick with the carved lion's head on the handle that he had acquired on the first day of Chebeti's employment. He worked on his teeth with a small piece of young sugar cane at which he gnawed with forceful bites, and in regular intervals spat at the long blades of grass till they shone in the late sun in the same multiple colors as the dew in the early morning. He was running his left hand through Rummler's fur; even while dozing, the dog was breathing loud enough to chase away any flies before they could bother him.

In its harmony and abundance, the scene reminded Walter of pictures in the books of his childhood. He smiled a little when he realized that people in the European midsummer are not black and do not sit under cedars and lemon trees. Since the conversation with the captain was still churning in him, he wanted to prevent his eyes from drinking in the idyll that floated over to him, but his senses allowed themselves to be restrained only for a short time.

Even though the air was heavy with steaming humidity, he enjoyed every breath. He felt an uncertain longing to capture the picture that fascinated him with its innocence and was glad when Regina noticed him and released him from his dreams. She waved to him, and he waved back.

"Papa, Max already has a real name. Owuor calls him *askari ya usiku*."

"A little exaggerated for such a small child."

"Don't you know what *askari ya usiku* means? Night soldier."

"You mean night watchman."

"But yes," Regina said impatiently, "because he sleeps all day and is always awake at night."

"He is not the only one. Where is your mother?"

"Inside."

"What is she doing in the hot flat at this hour?"

"She is getting excited," Regina giggled. She remembered too late that her father was unable to interpret voices or eyes and that she was about to steal his calm. "Max," she said quickly and full of regret, "is in the newspaper. I have already read it."

"Why didn't you tell me right away?"

"But you did not ask me where Mama is. Chebeti says a woman has to close her mouth when a man sends his eyes on safari."

"You are worse than all the Negroes together," Walter scolded, but it was an energizing impatience that made his voice loud.

He ran so quickly to the flat that Owuor rose, worried. Hurriedly, he threw the sugar cane to the ground, picked up his stick, and hardly took the necessary time to shake out his limbs. Rummler woke up, too, and ran after Walter, his tongue hanging out, as fast as his heavy legs permitted.

"Let me see, Jettel," Walter called still running. "I did not think it would happen this fast."

"Here. Why didn't you tell me about it?"

"It was supposed to be a surprise. When Regina was born, I was able to give you a ring. With Max, I could afford only a notice in the paper."

"And what a beautiful one. I was really happy when old Professor Gottschalk came with the paper earlier. He was quite impressed. Just think of all the people who are going to read it."

"I hope so; that was the purpose of the matter. Have you already found someone you know?"

"Not yet. I wanted to leave the pleasure for you. You always used to be the first."

"But you always found the good news."

The newspaper lay open on a small stool next to the window. The thin paper crackled with every gust of wind and hinted at the familiar and yet always new melody of hope and disappointment.

"Our drums," Walter said.

"I am starting to be like Regina," Jettel recognized and put her head to the side with a trace of her old coquettishness. "I hear stories before they are being told."

"Jettel, you are becoming poetic in your old age."

They stood at the open window and stared happily at the full, purple bougainvillea against the chalk-white wall without noticing how close their bodies and heads were; it was one of those rare moments in their marriage when each approved of the other's thoughts.

Der Aufbau was a paper unlike any other. Published in America and written in German, the paper was, during the war and especially afterward, more than a voice for emigrants the world over. Each edition, whether the persons concerned wanted it or not, nourished the roots of the past and drove the carousel of memories into a tempest of mourning.

A few lines could seal one's fate. It was not the reports and the lead articles that people read first. Everyone always started with the advertisements for missing persons and families. Through them, people who had not heard from each other since emigrating found each other. References to the old homeland could bring persons reputed to be dead back to life and give information about who had escaped from hell and who had perished in it, long before any of the official humanitarian organizations had the information. Even eleven months after the end of the war in Europe, the *Aufbau* was often still the only way for survivors to find the truth.

"The advertisement really is huge," Walter was amazed. "It is even on top of the page. You know what I think? The letter must have fallen into the hands of somebody who still knows us from former times and wanted to do us a favor. Just think, there is someone sitting in New York and, all of a sudden, he reads our name and that we are from Leobschütz. And finds out that I have not been eaten by a lion after all."

Walter cleared his throat. He remembered that he had always done that before addressing the court, but he repressed the thought with an embarrassment that felt almost like an admission of guilt. Even though he realized that Jettel already knew the text by heart, he read the few lines out loud: "Dr. Walter Redlich and his wife Henriette née Perls (formerly Leobschütz) announce the birth of their son Max Ronald Paul. P.O.B. 1312, Nairobi, Kenya Colony. March 6, 1946. What do you say, Jettel? Your old man is Doctor again. For the first time in eight years."

Even while he was speaking, Walter became aware that fate had just given him the opening for talking to Jettel about the great opportunity to return to Germany at the expense of the army. He had only to find the right words and, above all, the courage to tell her as carefully as possible that he had finally decided on the path without return. For a moment full of longing, and against his better judgment, he gave in to the illusion that Jettel would surely understand and, perhaps, even admire his foresight, but his experiences allowed him to deceive himself for only a short moment.

Walter knew from the day that he had mentioned returning to Germany for the first time that he could not count on Jettel's understanding. Since then, insignificant discussions had turned with increasing frequency into battles without rationale and logic and full of bitterness. He considered it ironic that he envied his wife's uncompromising attitude in this. He himself had often doubted that he would be strong enough to overcome the sorrow that would leave open wounds forever, but whenever he checked his motives, he had never found any way other than the one to which his longing for his language, roots, and profession sentenced him. He had only to imagine life on a farm and he instantly knew that he wanted and had to go back to Germany, no matter how painful the way would be.

Jettel felt differently. She was content among people for whom the hatred of Germany was enough to experience the present as the only happiness to which those who had escaped were entitled. She wanted nothing more than the certainty that others thought the way she did; she had always resisted change. How she had fought the emigration to Africa at a time when each day of hesitation had been a lethal threat!

The memory of the time before the emigration in Breslau gave Walter his ultimate certainty. He heard Jettel cry, "Rather dead than away from my mother"; he saw her childishly stubborn face behind the big curtain of tears as clearly as if he were still sitting on his mother-in-law's plush sofa. Disappointed and disillusioned, Walter understood that, since then, nothing had changed in his marriage.

Jettel was not a woman who was ashamed of her faults. She insisted on repeating them in every situation of life. Only, this time, Walter no longer could use the arguments of a man who wanted to save his family to persuade his wife to follow him. He was still lost and hunted, and everyone could denounce him as a man without character and pride. He waited for the anger that he could not show but felt only pity for himself, which made him tired.

Walter's heart raced when he cleared his throat to give his voice the firmness that he did not feel anymore. He noticed his strength deteriorating. He was too powerless against his hesitant timidity to talk about returning home and his homeland. The words that had come easily in a foreign language with the captain were mocking him, but he did not admit defeat yet. It only seemed to make more sense and, in any case, to be more diplomatic to use the English expression that he had heard for the first time a few hours ago.

"Repatriation," he said.

"What does that mean?" Jettel asked reluctantly. At the same time, she tried to fathom whether she should know the word, and whether she should call the *aya* with the child in or whether she should wait until Owuor had heated the water to boil the diapers. She sighed, because decisions in the late afternoon tired her more than at the time before the baby was born.

"Oh, nothing. I was only thinking about something the captain said today. I had to look for hours for him to find an ordinance, which the old donkey had lying in front of him on the desk all that time."

"Oh, you went to see him? I hope you used the opportunity to tell him that he could promote you once in a while. Elsa says, too, that you are not aggressive enough in such matters."

"Jettel, just face the fact that refugees do not get promoted any further than to sergeant in the army. Believe me, I am a master at using opportunities."

The chance to talk to Jettel quietly about Germany did not come back. The *Aufbau* did not permit it. Six weeks after the announcement appeared, the first of many letters arrived that conjured so much of the past that Walter did not find the courage to paint a picture of a future for Jettel that he himself, even in an optimistic mood, could only vaguely imagine.

The first letter came from an old woman in Shanghai. "I ended up here from beautiful Mainz," she wrote, "and feel that there is a very slim chance that I might find out something about my only brother's fate through you, Doctor Redlich. I heard last from him in January 1939. At that time, he wrote to me from Paris that he was going to try to emigrate to his son in South Africa. Unfortunately, I do not have my nephew's address, and he does not know that I got to Shanghai with the last transport. Of course, it would be a coincidence if you had met my brother, but we, who are alive, all owe that to coincidence. I wish you the best of luck for your son. May he grow up in a better world than was granted to us."

Many letters followed from unknown senders who clung to a spark of hope that they might get some news about missing family members because they either came from Upper Silesia or had written from there last. "My brother-in-law was murdered in Buchenwald in 1934," one man wrote from Australia, "and my sister with her two small children moved to Ratibor afterwards, where she found work in a weaving mill. Despite all inquiries to the Red Cross, her and the children's names have not been found on any of the deportation lists. I write to you because my sister mentioned Leobschütz to me once. Maybe you have heard her name at some point or still have contact with Jews in Ratibor who have survived. I know that my request is foolish, but I am not ready yet to bury all hope."

"And I always thought that nobody knew Leobschütz," Jettel said, surprised, when the next day a similar letter arrived. "If we would only get some good news once."

"And I am only now becoming aware," Walter said, depressed, "how short a distance it was from Upper Silesia to Auschwitz. It troubles me."

The extent of suffering and futile hope from strangers that flooded into Nairobi not only made their own wounds bleed again; its force made them apathetic.

"You started something there," Walter said to his son.

On a Friday in May, Regina took the mail out of Owuor's basket. "A letter from America," she announced. "Somebody who is called Ilse."

She pronounced the name the English way, and Jettel had to laugh. "Nobody is called that in Germany. Give it to me."

Regina just had time to say, "Do not tear the envelope; the ones from America are so beautiful," when she saw her mother turn pale and her hands tremble.

"I am not really crying," Jettel sobbed. "I am just so happy, Regina. The letter is from my childhood friend Ilse Schottländer. My God, that she is still alive!"

They sat down next to each other at the window, and Jettel started reading the letter aloud very slowly. It was as if her voice wanted to hold on to every syllable before pronouncing the next one. Regina did not understand some of the words, and the foreign names whirled in her ears like locusts over a field of young maize. She had to make a big effort to laugh and cry whenever her mother did so, but she drove her senses hard to keep up with the storm of sadness and joy. Owuor was making tea, even though it was not time for that, got the handkerchiefs, which he had ready for days with foreign stamps, out of the closet, and sat down in the hammock.

When Jettel had read the letter for the fourth time, she and Regina were so exhausted that both did not say another word. Only after lunch, which to Owuor's chagrin went back the way it had been carried in, were they able to talk again without first retrieving their breath from their chests.

They deliberated how they should tell Walter about the letter and finally decided not to mention it at all and to put it on the round table like any other mail. In the early afternoon, though, excitement and impatience drove Jettel out of the house. Despite the heat and the shadeless road, she went with Regina, Max in the pram, the *aya*, and the dog to the bus stop.

The bus was still moving when Walter jumped off the step. "Has anything happened to Owuor?" he asked, startled.

"He is baking the smallest rolls of his life," Jettel whispered.

Walter understood instantly. He felt like a child who wants to enjoy the anticipation to the fullest and does not open an unexpected gift. He kissed first Jettel and then Regina, petted his son, and whistled the melody of "Don't Fence Me In," which Chebeti loved so much. Only then did he ask, "Who has written?"

"You will never guess."

"Someone from Leobschütz?"

"No."

"From Sohrau?"

"No."

"Just tell me, I am bursting."

"Ilse Schottländer. From New York. I mean from Breslau."

"The rich Schottländers? From Tauentzienplatz?"

"Yes, Ilse was in my class at school."

"Good God, I haven't thought of her for years."

"Neither have I," Jettel said, "but she has not forgotten me."

She insisted that Walter read the letter while they were still at the bus stop. There were two pitiful thorn-acacias on the side of the road. Chebeti pointed to them and, after the *memsahib*'s last words, still humming the *bwana*'s beautiful melody, got a blanket out of the pram and spread it under the bigger of the two trees. Laughing, she lifted Max out of the pram, let his shadow dance on her face for a moment, and put him down between her legs. Green sparks were burning in her dark eyes.

"A letter," she said, "a letter that has swum through the big water. Owuor brought it."

"Aloud, Papa, read it out loud," Regina said with the imploring voice of a small girl.

"Didn't Mama read the letter to you for the nth time already?"

"Yes, but she cried so much doing it that I still haven't understood it."

"My dear Jettel," Walter read, "when my mother came home with the *Aufbau* yesterday, I almost went crazy. I am still excited now and can hardly believe that I am writing to you. I congratulate both of you with all my heart on the birth of your son. May he never live through what we had to live through. I still remember vividly how you came to visit us in Breslau with your daughter. She was three at the time and a very timid child. She probably is a young lady now and does not speak German anymore. The refugee children here are all ashamed of their so-called mother tongue. And rightly so.

"I did hear that you had emigrated to Africa but lost track of you then. So, I don't even know where to start. Our story, in any case, is quickly told. On November 9, 1938, the brutes demolished our apartment and dragged my dear father, who was in bed with pneumonia, out onto the street and deported him. That was the last time we saw him. He died four weeks later in jail. I still cannot think about that time without feeling the powerlessness and despair that will never leave me. I did not want to go on living at the time, but Mother did not permit it.

"This small, delicate woman, whose every wish Father had fulfilled for a lifetime and who never had to make even the smallest decision, turned everything we owned into money. She found a remote cousin in America who was decent enough to get affidavits for us. To this day, I do not know who took us under his wing in Breslau and how we acquired the ship passage. We did not dare talk to anyone about it. Above all, we did not dare say goodbye to anyone (I saw your sister, Käthe, once in front of Wertheim's, but we did not meet), because once it was known that someone wanted to emigrate, the difficulties became ever greater. We arrived on the last boat to America and literally had nothing but a few worthless mementos. One of them, the cookbook of our old maid Anna, who even after the Kristallnacht was not to be prevented from her clandestine visits, proved to be an unexpected treasure.

"In a room with two hotplates, Mother and I, who all our lives had been cared for by cooks and maids, started a lunch place for refugees. We started out not knowing how long an egg had to be in water until it was soft, and yet, somehow we began to cook all the meals that had been served on the Schottländers' nicely set table during better days. What a blessing that Father loved home cooking. But it was not our cooking that kept us above water; it was Mother's indomitable optimism and her imagination.

"With dessert, she always served gossip about the fine Jewish society in Breslau. You cannot believe how people who have lost everything long for stories that are quite foolish and meaningless at a time when everyone has to fight much harder for their bare existence than the farmhands and maids ever had to at home. We are still selling homemade jams, cakes, pickles with mustard seeds, and pickled herring, even though I have been very successful in the meantime. I am a clerk in a bookstore, and, while I still do not know English too well, I can at least read and write it, which is valued here. I have long forgotten that I wanted to become a writer once and already had my first modest success.

I am thinking of the dream of my youth only today, because I am writing to you and always had to help you with your essays.

"We are in touch with some people from Breslau. We meet the two Grünfeld brothers regularly. The family owned a textile wholesale business at the railroad station and supplied half of Silesia. Wilhelm and Siegfried came with their wives to New York in 1936. Their parents did not want to emigrate and were deported. The Silbermanns (he was a dermatologist but was never able to pass the required language exam here and now is a doorman in a small hotel) and the Olschewkis (he was an apothecary and did not save anything but his sister's child) live in our area, which is generally referred to as the Fourth Reich. Mother needs the past; I do not.

"Jettel, I cannot imagine you in Africa. You were always afraid of everything. Even of spiders and bees. And, if I remember correctly, you did not like any activity for which you could not wear the most elegant clothes. I remember your handsome husband well. I must admit, I always envied you because of him. Just as I always envied you your beauty. And your success with men. I have, just as you predicted when we had a fight at age twelve, really become an old maid, and even if someone had been blind enough to propose to me, I would have said no.

"After all that Mother did for me, I could never have left her. There is something else I have to tell you. Do you remember our school janitor Barnowsky? He occasionally helped our gardener in the spring and our Gretel on washdays. Father paid the tuition for his eldest son, who was very talented, and thought Mother and I did not know. I do not know how the good man Barnowsky found out about our emigration, but on the last evening in our house, he stood all of a sudden at the door and brought us sausages as travel provisions. He had tears in his eyes and continually shook his head and ensured for all times that I cannot hate all Germans.

"I really have to finish now. I know that you never liked to write, and yet I hope that you will answer this letter. There is so much I would like to know. And Mother cannot wait to find out if anyone else from Breslau is in Kenya. The old stories only make me sad. When Father died, a part of me died with him, but complaining would be sin. None of us who have survived have been able to save our souls. Write soon to your old friend Ilse."

The shadows were long and black when Walter put the letter into his shirt pocket. He got up, pulled Jettel up from the ground, and for a moment it seemed as if both were going to say something, but they only lightly shook their heads together. On the short way from the bus stop to the Hove Court, only Chebeti could be heard. With snatches of a soft melody, she calmed the baby, who was starting to turn hunger into vexation, and laughed happily when she noticed that her song was good enough even to dry the eyes of the *memsahib* and the *bwana*. "Tomorrow," she said with satisfaction, "another letter will come. Tomorrow will be a good day."

20

When Max was exactly six months old to the day, he put, with unexpected resolve, an end to the rumor that Chebeti's gentleness had mollycoddled and made him lethargic like the children of her own people, who still nursed at their mother's breast when they were already able to walk. Chebeti's little *askari* overcame the pessimism of experienced German mothers and sat up, on his own accord, in his pram. This happened on a Sunday morning. At that time, the garden at the Hove Court did not present a suitable backdrop for the heavy baby to attract attention.

Most of the women, though bashfully—the word *brunch* had become more and more popular—because it was in conflict with the custom of the country, still held on to the European tradition of a lavish midday Sunday meal. They were busy supervising their personnel while cooking and complaining about the insufficient quality of the meat. The men struggled with the Sunday *Post*, which, with its linguistic subtleties, literary ambitions, and complicated reports about the life of the high society in London, challenged most refugees so much that they could measure up to the stress of reading it only by stopping for long breaks and not admitting to themselves that their determination was stronger than their ability.

Had Owuor, as usual, looked out of the window at regular intervals, he would have seen his pride, whom despite quieter nights he still stubbornly called *askari*, sit upright in his pram. But, at the decisive moment, Owuor was storming about the kitchen like a young Masai on his first hunt, because the potatoes had gotten too much rain before the harvest and were falling apart in the water. Potatoes that after boiling looked like the clouds above the big mountain at home at Ol' Joro Orok left Owuor with a feeling of failure and the *bwana*'s face with a ditch of anger between his nose and mouth.

Chebeti ironed the diapers, which Owuor considered a jealous attack on his manhood: washing the laundry, and not handling the heavy charcoal iron, which obeyed only him, was the work of an *aya*. Jettel and Walter had adjourned their fight of the previous evening with the kind of exhaustion that prematurely ended all conversations since the day on which Jettel had understood the ominous meaning of the word *repatriation*.

She and Walter went to visit Professor Gottschalk. He had sprained his ankle and for the last three weeks had been dependent on his friends for food and news of the world, with which he could stay in contact not through the radio or newspaper but only through personal conversations.

So, only Regina was there when her brother, with a forceful move and loud crowing, which, however, attracted only Diana's dog, attained his new position in life. In less time than a bird needs to spread its wings in danger, Max changed from a baby who saw nothing but the sky at all times and needed to be picked up if it wanted to extend its horizon into a curious being that could at all times look into other people's eyes and, when it suited him, could observe life from a higher point of view.

The pram stood in the shade of the guava tree, in which the English fairy had lived previously. Since the class-conscious lady no longer was in charge of the wishes and worries of a lonely refugee child, Regina retreated into the shelter of her imagination only when the sun, with its merciless strength, chased her into the shade and, with that, into the past.

When Max left the comfort of his pillows with a surprise that made his eyes round like the moon that in the nights of its full brilliance provides daylight, his sister had just made an irritating discovery. She realized for the first time that a familiar smell alone was able to awaken those well-buried memories that caused one's head pain. The sweet smell of days that were now past, tickled her nose with sadness. Above all, Regina could not satisfactorily make up her mind whether she wanted her fairy back. The choice between the possibilities made her insecure.

"No," she finally decided, "I do not need her anymore. I now have you. You smile, at least, if I tell you something. And I can speak English to you just as well as to the fairy before. At any rate, when we are alone. Or do you like Swahili better?"

Regina opened her mouth as wide as a bird when feeding its brood, pushed coolness into her throat, and laughed without disturbing the silence. She still loved the fact that she was able to conjure joy on her brother's face just by laughing with the same happiness as on the first day on which that miracle had been granted to her. Max gurgled with contentment and joined the sounds that were in him together into a gush of jubilation, which Regina interpreted as *Aya*.

"Just don't let Papa hear that," she giggled. "He is going to be mad if his son's first word is in Swahili. He wants to talk to you only in his language and about his homeland. Say Leobschütz. Or at least Sohrau."

Regina noticed too late that she had behaved like an inexperienced young vulture that through rash calls attracts the members of its species and then has to share the prey with them. She had allowed her imagination to rush her into a battle from which she could not escape without wounds. The beautiful old game with the listener who never gave an answer and, therefore, always responded the way she wished had turned into the present with a smirking grimace and thus reminded her of her parent's fights, which now recurred as predictably as the howling of the hyenas at night in Ol' Joro Orok.

Even earlier, Regina had known how much the word *Germany*, as soon as her father only formed the first two syllables, spelled sorrow and unhappiness. For a while now, though, Germany had become a threat to all of them that was stronger than the concentrated power of all the incomprehensible words that Regina had learned to fear since childhood. If her ears did not succeed in shutting themselves in time against her parents' merciless battles, they heard over and over again about the farewell, which Regina imagined to have been even more painful than the parting from the farm that she was unable to forget despite all efforts and her promise to Martin.

It was not only the malice with which her parents tortured each other that frightened Regina but even more so the feeling that she would have to make the terrible decision whether to follow her head or her heart. Her head was on her mother's side; her heart beat for her father.

"You know, *askari*," Regina said and spoke to her brother in beautiful, soft Jaluo, the way Owuor and Chebeti did as soon as they were alone with the child, "you will feel the same way. We are not like other children. Other children are not being told anything; us, they tell everything. We have parents who cannot keep their mouths shut."

She got up, enjoyed the sting of the hard bunches of grass under her naked feet for a while like an invigorating bath, then ran quickly to the flowering hibiscus and picked a purple blossom from the lavish plant. She carried the fragile flower carefully to the pram and stroked the baby with it till he started shrieking and released monosyllabic sounds from his throat again that sounded like a mixture of Jaluo and Swahili.

"If you do not tell anybody," she whispered, taking Max on her lap, and continuing, a little louder, in English, "I will explain it to you. Yesterday, Mama shouted 'Nobody is going to get me into that country of murderers,' and I just had to cry with her. I knew that she was thinking of her mother and sister. You know, they were our grandmother and aunt. But then Papa yelled back, 'Not everyone was a murderer,' and he was so pale and trembled so much that I felt terribly sorry for him. And then, I cried for him. That is the way it always goes. I do not know whose side I am on. Do you understand now that I like to talk to you best? You don't even know that Germany exists."

"Well, Regina, are you stuffing your brother with English poems, or are you drumming some other nonsense into him?" Walter called from afar and appeared behind the mulberry bush.

Regina lifted her brother up and hid her face behind his body. She waited till her embarrassment no longer colored her skin and felt like a hunter who had stepped into his own trap. This time Owuor had not been right. He maintained that she had eyes like a leopard, but she had not seen her father come.

"I thought you were at Professor Gottschalk's," she stuttered.

"We went to see him. He says hello and you should come by some time. You'll have to do that, Regina. The old man is getting ever lonelier. We have to give him every little bit of help we can. We cannot do anything for him but give of ourselves. Mama already went back to the flat. And I thought my children would be happy to see me. But my daughter looks like a thief who has been caught redhanded."

Regina was shaken by the strength of her regret when she saw

Walter's disappointment. Awkwardly, like an old woman without teeth and without strength in her limbs, she got up, put Max back into his pillows, went slowly and very hesitatingly up to her father, and embraced him as closely as if she could take back the thoughts he was not supposed to know about with her arms alone. The tremor in his body, more than his face, betrayed the distress of the previous night. Even though she fought against it, Regina was oppressed by a sadness that burdened her conscience; she was searching for words to hide her compassion from him, but he was faster.

"You have not been very careful in the choice of your parents," Walter said and sat down under the tree. "Now they want to go to a foreign country with you for a second time."

"You want to; Mama doesn't."

"Yes, Regina, I want to and have to. And you have to help me."

"But I am still a child."

"You are not, and you know it. Could you at least make it easy for me? I would never forgive myself if I made you unhappy."

"Why do we have to go to Germany? Others don't have to, either. Inge says her father will become English next year. You could do that, too. You are at least in the army, and he is not."

"Did you tell Inge that we want to return to Germany?"

"Yes."

"And what did she say?"

"I don't know. She does not speak to me anymore."

"I did not know that children could be that cruel. I did not want to do that to you," Walter murmured. "Please try to understand. Inge's father may be getting an English passport, but that does not mean that he is going to be an Englishman. Just tell me, can you imagine that any English families will invite him? Let's say, your esteemed headmistress?"

"She? Never."

"And nobody else, either. Don't you see? I do not want to be a man with a name that does not belong to me. I finally need to know again where I belong. I can no longer be a bloody refugee who is not respected by anyone and looked down upon by most. Here, I'll always only be tolerated and will always be an outsider. Can you even imagine what that means?"

Regina bit her lower lip, but she answered immediately. "Yes," she said, "I can." She asked herself whether her father had any idea what she had experienced and learned in her years at school, first in Nakuru and now in Nairobi. "Here," she explained to him, "it is even worse. In Nakuru I was only German and Jewish; now I am German, Jewish, and a bloody day scholar. That is worse than just a bloody refugee. Believe me, Papa."

"You never told us about that."

"I was not able to. First, I did not have enough words in my head, and later, I did not want to make you sad. And, besides," she added after a long pause, "I don't care. Not anymore."

"Max will feel the same way when he gets into school. I hope he has a big heart like you and does not blame his father for being a failure."

When the love of a child turned into the admiration of a woman, Regina became silent, but she knew that her eyes betrayed her. Her father was not stupid, full of dreams, and weak as her mother thought. He was not a coward and did not run away from problems as she maintained during every fight. The *bwana* was a fighter full of strength and as clever as only a man could be who did not open his mouth when the time to do so had not come yet. Only a winner knew when to take out his best arrows and took measure very carefully to find the most vulnerable spot in the person he wanted to hit. The fearless *bwana* had struck her heart, as deeply as Cupid and as cunningly as Ulysses. Regina asked herself whether she should laugh or cry.

"You are fighting with words," she recognized.

"That is the only thing I ever learned. I want to do it again. For all of you. You will have to help me. I have only you."

Being aware of the burden with which her father was saddling her weighed heavily, and Regina tried once again to resist, but at the same time she felt as if she had gotten lost in the forest and just discovered a clearing that would save her. The tug-of-war for her heart was over. Her father once and for all had the longer part of the rope in his hand.

"Promise me," Walter said, "that you will not be sad when we go home. Promise that you will trust me."

While her father was still talking, memories hit Regina as piercingly as a sharpened axe a sick tree. She smelt the forest at Ol' Joro Orok, saw herself lying in the garden, felt the fire of an unexpected touch and immediately afterward again the penetrating pain.

"Martin said the very same thing. When he was still a prince and picked me up from school. You must not be sad when you will have to leave the farm, he said. I had to promise him that. Did you know that?"

"Yes. One day you will forget the farm. I promise you. And another thing, Regina; forget Martin. You are too young for him, and he is not good enough for you. Martin always loved only himself. He already turned your mother's head. She was hardly older than you are today when that happened. Has he ever written to you?"

"He will," Regina said eagerly.

"You are like your father. A stupid fool who believes everything. Who knows if we will ever hear from Martin again? He is going to stay in South Africa. You have to forget him. First love never works out in life, and it is good that way."

"But Mama was your first love. She told me herself."

"And what has become of it?"

"Max and me," Regina answered. She looked for such a long time at her father that she finally succeeded in attracting a smile from his mouth.

"If we have to go back to Germany," she asked on the way back to the flat, "what is going to happen to Owuor? Can he come with us again?"

"Not this time. It will break a piece of our hearts, and the wound will never heal. I am sorry, Regina, that you are no longer a child. One can lie to children."

It was easy to mask the tears during lunch as physical discomfort. Owuor had firmly mashed the dissolved potatoes with much pepper and even more salt.

On Thursday, Regina went to the market with Chepoi to go shopping for Diana's birthday. Afterward, she had to spend a lot of time and use many words, which she got from a poem by Shakespeare and translated rather freely, to extinguish Owuor's jealousy and was finally able to visit Professor Gottschalk. He sat again, for the first time after his fall, in his heavy black velvet jacket on the unsteady folding chair in front of his door. The familiar book also lay on the blanket over his knees, but the red leather cover with the gold script, which always fascinated Regina so much that she could not concentrate on the letters, was dusty.

She realized with an uneasiness that pushed its sour taste of fear between her teeth and which she learned to interpret as pain only the day after, that the old man did not want to read anymore. He had sent his eyes on safari into a world where the lemon trees, under which he had so often walked in healthy days, did not bear any more fruit. Since her last visit, the black hat had become bigger and the face under it smaller, but his voice was strong when the professor said, "It is nice that you are still coming; time is getting short."

"But, no," Regina objected fast and with the obliging politeness that she had often had to practice as the Girl Guide law, "I am on vacation."

"I had those, too, in earlier times."

"But you are always on vacation now."

"No, at home I had vacations. Here, one day is like the other. Year in, year out. Forgive me, Lilly, that I am so ungrateful and talk such nonsense. You cannot imagine what I mean. You are still young enough to embrace the wonder of life."

When Regina realized that the professor was taking her for his daughter, she wanted to tell him so immediately, because nothing good could come of it if a person borrowed another's name, but she did not know how she could explain such a complicated matter without using Owuor's words and language.

"My father says such things, too," she whispered.

"Not much longer; his heart is ready for a farewell and a new beginning," the professor said. He blinked a bit, but his eyes did not find any joy. For a short moment his face became as big as his hat again. "Your father is an intelligent man. He may hope again. The inner voice never deceives hope."

Regina brooded, irritated, about why her skin had gotten cold, even though the shadow of the wall could not reach her. Then she knew. The howling of hyenas that were too old to get their prey during the night sounded like the professor's laugh during the brightest time of the day. At the same time, she pondered how old he might be, and why people often said things that were even harder to decipher than the inexplicable riddles in ancient myths.

"Are you looking forward to Germany?" the professor asked.

"Yes," Regina said and quickly crossed her fingers, the way she had learned as a child from Owuor, to protect her body from the poison of a lie that the mouth had not been able to hold back. She was quite certain now that the professor was not talking to her, but it did not bewilder her anymore. Had she not learned from her father that a man needs someone to listen to him, even if that friend has the wrong ears?

"How I would love to change places with you. Just imagine, you are at home, go into the street, and all the people speak German. Even the children. You have only to ask them a question, and they immediately understand and answer you."

Regina opened her mouth slowly and closed it even more slowly. She needed time to find out whether the professor still knew that she was sitting on the ground next to his chair. He smiled a little, as if all his life he had talked to yawning monkeys that do not have to utter loud sounds in order to attract attention to themselves.

"Frankfurt," he said and scratched the good silence with his soft voice, "was so beautiful. Do you remember? 'How can a person not come from Frankfurt?' You were able to recite that even as a really small girl, Lilly. Everyone used to laugh. Dear God, how happy we were then. And foolish. Give my regards to the homeland when you see it. Tell it that I was not able to forget it. I have tried over and over again."

"I will do that," Regina said. She swallowed her confusion too hastily and started to cough.

"And thank you that you made it in time. Tell Mother not to scold if you are late for your singing lesson."

Regina closed her eyes while she waited until the salt under her lids turned into small dry granules. It took longer than she had thought before she could see clearly again, and then she realized that the professor had fallen asleep. His breath was so loud that it hushed the low whistling of the wind; the brim of his black hat rested on his nose.

Even though Regina ran without shoes and her steps did not make much more noise on the crusty earth than a butterfly that comes to rest on a withered rose, she made sure that only her toes touched the ground. After about half the way, she turned around, because all of a sudden it seemed right and important to her that the professor should not wake up before he found the strength to put the shapes and colors in his head in order.

She became content and even, in a way she could not explain to herself, happy to see him sleeping quietly. Since she knew he would not hear her, she gave way to a sudden urge to call out *"kwaheri"* instead of "Auf Wiedersehen."

It was evening before the inhabitants of the Hove Court began to wonder that Professor Gottschalk, who had an aversion to the sudden coolness of African nights, was still sitting quietly in his chair. But then the news spread, as fast as if drums had reported it from the forests with enchanted echoes, that he was dead.

The funeral took place the next day. Since it was Friday and the deceased had to be buried before the Sabbath, the rabbi refused, despite all mention of the extraordinary fury of the rainy season in Gilgil, to postpone the funeral any longer than to noontime. With the hint of a smile and many conciliatory gestures, he tried to demonstrate his understanding of the excitement that his obedience to the religious law caused among the mourners but closed himself to all objections, even to arguments that were presented in absolutely comprehensible English, that the professor had a right to be accompanied by his daughter and his son-in-law on his last journey.

"If he listened to the radio instead of praying, he would know that the road from Gilgil to Nairobi is nothing but mud," Elsa Conrad said bitterly. "You don't bury a man like the professor without his family."

"Without such pious men as the rabbi here, there would be no more Jews left," Walter tried to mediate. "The professor would have understood that."

"Damn it, do you always have to be so understanding of other people?"

"I have been bearing that cross all my life."

Lilly and Oscar Hahn arrived at the cemetery when the sun barely cast a shadow anymore and the small circle of helpless people were standing sadly at the grave. After the prayers, the rabbi had given a short speech in English full of knowledge and wisdom, but the anger and above all the poor language skills of most of the people present had only increased the unrest.

Oscar, in khaki pants and a dark jacket that was too tight, came without a tie, had traces of dried mud on his pants and forehead, and was breathing heavily. He was unable to say a word and smiled, embarrassed, when he stepped up to the grave. Lilly was wearing the pants in which she fed the chickens at night and a red turban on her head. She was so nervous that she forgot to close the car door at the gate of the cemetery. Her poodle, who, just like Oscar, had become much older, grayer, and heavier during the past two years, hurried after her, panting. On the other side of the high trees, Manjala, whom Regina recognized immediately because of his hoarse voice, called the dog. He insulted it as the son of the greedy snake of Rumuruti and threatened it alternately with the fury of the snake and the revenge of the irreconcilable God Mungu.

Regina had to choke down the laugh that came into her throat with the force of a raging waterfall, like overripe and thoughtlessly chewed pepper-berries; thinking of the professor, she also tried to keep her face free of joy when she saw Lilly and Oha. She stood between Walter and Jettel under a cedar on which a superb starling, despite the noontime heat, sought attention with light, high sounds. When Regina saw how Lilly ran and that the effort drilled wrinkles into her face, she remembered that the professor had been worried that his daughter might be late for her singing lesson. First Regina thought that she had to laugh after all, and she bit her lips; then she felt tears, even though her eyes were still dry.

At the moment when Lilly reached the grave and sighed with relief, the poodle followed Regina's scent and jumped up at her with a shrill howl of joy before hiding between her legs. She petted the animal to calm it and herself and him down and, with that, caught the rabbi's attention, who stared at her and the whimpering dog with tightened lips.

Oha, very softly and still out of breath, said Kaddish for the dead, but his parents had died such a long time ago that he was not able to remember the text of the prayer quickly enough and for each syllable had to conjure a past, which in his excitement fed him the wrong words. Everyone noticed how painful it was for him that he had to accept the help of an eager, small man whom nobody knew and who had just at the right moment appeared behind a gravestone.

The stranger, with his beard and his high black hat, showed up at every funeral among the refugees for the simple reason that he knew from experience that very few of them were orthodox enough to recite the prayer for the dead fluently and that they almost always showed their gratitude with the generosity of people who cannot afford to give.

After Oha had finally stuttered the last word of the mourning prayer, the grave was quickly covered. Even the rabbi seemed to be in a hurry. He had already taken several steps away when Lilly released herself from the arms of those consoling her and, with a childlike shyness that made her into a stranger, softly said, "I know the song is not proper for a funeral, but my father loved it. I would like to sing it here for him one last time."

Lilly's face was pale, but her voice clear and strong enough for several echoes from the blue shimmering Ngong Hills when she sang, "Ich weiß nicht, was soll es bedeuten." Some hummed the melody with her, and the stillness after the last note was so solemn that even the poodle seemed moved, because he broke—for the first time in years—with the habit of accompanying Lilly's song with his howling. Regina tried at first to hum with the grown-ups and then to cry with them, but she did not succeed in one or the other. She was upset that she had forgotten what she was supposed to say to Lilly and Oha, even though her father had practiced the three German words, which she had thought very beautiful and fitting, with her only this morning.

Jettel asked Lilly and Oha to dinner. Owuor proudly showed them little Max and explained to them at length why he called him *askari*. He was even more proud that he remembered how the beautiful *memsahib* from Gilgil liked her fried eggs. Hard with a brown crust, not soft with a skin of glass like the *bwana*. It was also Owuor who told Lilly that her father had spoken to Regina shortly before his death.

"She went," he said, "with him on the big safari."

Regina was distressed because she had thought that her last meeting with the professor had to stay a secret, but then she recognized once again how clever Owuor was, for Lilly said first, "I am glad that you went to see him," and later she suggested, "Maybe you would like to tell me what you talked about."

When Jettel put Max to bed and the two men went for a walk through the garden, Regina took out the words that she had held locked in her head since the professor's death. Even the sentence "How can a person not come from Frankfurt?"

Regina at first felt awkward talking about his confusion, but that just pushed itself into her mouth as if it had only waited to be released. The story seemed to console Lilly; she laughed for the first time since she had rushed out of the car at the cemetery, and then once again and much louder when she heard about the singing lesson.

"Typical," she remembered. "My father was always afraid that I might be late."

"You are now something like the little sister I never had," she said when she and Oha said goodbye to spend the night in the professor's room.

The next morning at breakfast she asked, and left Regina even more speechless than the night before, "How would you like to drive to Arcadia with us? I have already asked your parents. They have agreed."

"I cannot," Regina refused. While speaking, she already knew from the burning of her skin that she had mastered only her mouth, not her body, and she was ashamed because she knew how much longing her eyes showed.

"Why not? You are on vacation."

"I would really like to see a farm again, but I also want to stay with Max. I have just got him."

"Max already told me quite clearly last night that he would like to see Gilgil," Oha said with a smile.

21

IN GILGIL, the days could fly faster than the wild ducks on their long safari to Lake Naivasha. Regina tried to fight the flight of time only during her first days there. When she realized how unsettling the attempt to hold onto happiness was to her, she started to observe the travelers with the shiny green and blue feathers more closely. The birds gliding under the swirling clouds became for her part of the inimitable magic of Arcadia, the farm with the three mysteries, none of which could be solved.

Between the hills, with their domes eroded by storm and heat, and the huge *shamba*s with maize, pyrethrum, and flax, the eyes never encountered a fence or ditch. In this endless plane, the God Mungu ruled the people of Gilgil with an even firmer hand than at Ol' Joro Orok. They were satisfied when they and their cattle had enough to eat. They had not been tamed by the orders or the money of the whites, they knew everything about life on the farm. The farm knew about them only that they existed. Mungu alone was permitted to determine life and death for these proud people who wanted to take care of themselves and let only the familiar smells get into their nose.

Behind the first herds of grazing sheep, the goats that jumped nimbly between small covered rocks, the cows lying down in their content complacency hardly even moving their heads, and the huts that were built close together with tiny white stones in their mud walls, Mungu raised His voice only in the thunder of the early morning rain, but even there His power could still be felt everywhere. In this realm of familiar pictures and sounds lay the small *shamba*s that belonged to the boys in the huts.

Here grew high tobacco plants, sweet-smelling bushes of healing herbs with powers that only the wise old people knew, and low maize plants with strong leaves that talked quietly in each breeze of the wind. In the mornings and afternoons, women with shaved heads, naked breasts, and infants in colorful cloths on their backs worked here. When they put their hoes down and their babies to their breasts, the chickens picked little shiny beetles from their dirt-encrusted feet. The women only seldom sang the way the men did while working; when they drilled holes into their long silences with laughter like that of children, they often talked, among giggles, about the *memsahib* and her *bwana* who loved words that scratched both the throat and the tongue.

Lilly, with her voice that flew over the trees and effortlessly reached the hills, became for Regina the beautiful queen of a white castle who received messages from foreign worlds. The castle had big windows that stored the heat of the day far into the night and turned the smallest raindrops into big spheres. The sun painted more colors than anywhere else in any African paradise into the glass, which was polished daily under Manjala's supervision by two Kikuyu boys until they could spit into their own faces.

In the living room with the wide stone fireplace, which turned a pale pink as soon as the wood began to crackle, a kindly king climbed out of Oha's pipe. He had a round belly and bones that were already heavy from a burden that Regina could not interpret, but he ascended easily and slyly up on the gray tobacco hills and from there, smiling, blessed the house with loud laughter, low music, and the friendliness of beautiful, strange, foreign sounds.

There were evenings when only the high flames illuminated the room and submerged it in a fiery red glow. The scent, a finely tuned mixture of cedars in which the forest still lived and *tembo* freshly distilled from sugar cane, which Oha drank after dinner out of small cups of colored glass, delayed its departure again and again. In such nights, silent magic spirits were about. They were deaf to the men's voices but had the forceful desire to send their eyes on a safari that had no beginning or end.

Then, well-nourished men with wide orange-colored sashes, high black hats, and white collars folded into small stiff pleats stepped out of the dark wooden frames of the pictures. They were followed by serious-looking women in white lace bonnets, with pearls that were as white as the young moon around their necks and heavy blue velvet dresses. The children were dressed in light silk, which clung to their bodies like a second skin, and tight caps with tiny pearls at the seams. They laughed with their mouths, but never with their eyes.

These people from mysteriously colored places sat down for a short moment in the depths of the soft dark green easy chairs. Before they returned to their places on the stone walls with a laugh that was no louder than the first cooing of a child, they whispered hoarsely in a language that had the same throaty sounds as that of the Boers.

When Regina watched the high society escape from its narrow picture frames at night, she felt like the little mermaid in the fairy tale, who has been swept ashore by a storm and is unable to walk but is afraid to return to the sea. Yet, when she sat during the day in the big chair with the carved lion heads on the armrests in the shadow of the house wall, which was covered with pink and white vetches, and watched the foaming dance of the clouds immediately after the rain abated, she felt as strong as Atlas with the heavy globe on his back.

The idea of being exactly at the intersection of three worlds excited her. They could not have been more different from one another if Mungu Himself had tried to give each one an unmistakably different shape. The three worlds got along together as well as people who do not speak the same language and therefore cannot agree on a common word for strife.

The grass, which extended from the reddish glowing hills into the valley, had stored too much sun to turn as green during the rainy season as in the rest of the highlands. Big yellow bushes colored the light as if the dried-up plants were trying to protect themselves from view. The landscape was, this way, imbued with a softness that it did not have and became clearly visible. The broad stripes of the zebras shone on their well-rounded bodies till the sun suddenly fell from the sky, and the fur of the baboons appeared like thick blankets woven out of brown earth.

There were very bright days that turned the monkeys into immobile spheres, and, in the white light that tolerated no shade, her eyes could distinguish them only after many difficult attempts from the rounded backs of the cows that chewed not too far from her. But there were also the short hours that belonged neither to the day nor to the night. During those, the half-grown baboons, which had not yet been scratched in the face by experience or caution, came so close to the house that each of their sounds developed its own tone.

The forest with the cedars, so tall that their crowns could not see their roots anymore, and the low thorn-acacias with their thin branches lay behind the last field of maize. When the drums were beaten, they left an echo that imposed a short, tense silence on a furious wind. These noises, which she had missed so long in Nairobi, caressed Regina's ears most. They turned the memories that she had never learned to swallow into a present that intoxicated her on joyous days as much as the *tembo*, the alcoholic drink made from sugar cane, delighted the men in the huts. Each individual drum took away the fear that she was only a traveler without destination who was allowed to nourish herself shortly with borrowed happiness and confirmed to her that she was in reality Ulysses who had returned home forever.

When her skin was permitted to feel the wind, sun, and rain and her eyes held the horizon like a jackal its first prey of the night, Regina was drunk from the never-before-experienced intoxication of oblivion. It combined the familiar and the unfamiliar, imagination and reality, and took away the strength to think of the future that her father had already captured. A thick net of confusing stories of a foreign place in which Lilly turned into Scheherazade filled her head.

Every time Chebeti carried the warmed milk bottle on a small silver tray into the room and Regina put it into her brother's mouth, a door was pushed open to a paradise to which the queen of the castle alone held the key. Chebeti sat down on the floor and placed her slim hands on the big yellow-cloth flowers of her dress. Regina waited for the first smacking sounds from the sucking baby, and then she told Max and Chebeti in the same solemn voice in which she had recited Kipling's patriotic poems in school about the things with which Lilly had filled her ears.

In Gilgil, even the milk was magical. In the morning, it was given by the brown Antonia, who was not permitted to sing and let herself be lured to death by a violin. The midday meal for the little *askari* came from the white Cho-Cho-San, who, with her father's dagger in her hand and the song "Honorably Die" on her lips, sang her life away. At night, Max fell asleep with Konstanze's story while Lilly sang "Traurigkeit ward mir zum Lose," the poodle howled, and Oha wiped tears from his eyes with the rough fabric of his jacket.

After the first few days in Gilgil, Regina understood that Lilly's darlings only camouflaged themselves as ordinary milk cows. Nothing about them was the same as other cows. Each syllable of their names, which nobody but Lilly and Oha could pronounce, held meaning. These beautiful-sounding names, which made Lilly's voice melodious even when she only spoke, were a burden for everyone else's head and tongue on the farm. Not one of the cows understood Swahili, Kikuyu, or Jaluo. When only Chebeti and Max in his pram were with her, Regina often tried to talk with Aida, Donna Anna, Gilda, and Melisande about the mystery of their origins. But the enchanted cows just let the sun burn on the back of their heads as if they did not have any ears. They could reveal their secrets only through Lilly's mouth. Arabella was the last one. But she was also the first to make Regina sense that the happiness in Lilly's paradise was as fragile as the delicate hibiscus flowers.

"Why," asked Regina, "do you speak to Arabella as if she were a baby?"

"Oh, my dear, how can I explain that to you? *Arabella* was the last opera I was allowed to see. Oha and I drove to Dresden just for that. It will never happen again in this life. The opera house in Dresden is as much in ruins as my dreams."

Since Lilly had only an hour before, at breakfast, said, "I never dream," Regina had a hard time understanding the meaning of her complaint, but from the day of Arabella's story, she knew that not only Lilly's cows had their secrets. The lady of the castle, with her magic voice, could laugh so loud with her mouth that her laughter echoed in the small pantry, but her eyes often had a hard time holding back the tears. Little wrinkles left traces on Lilly's face then. They looked like trickles of water on parched ground and let her mouth appear too red and her skin thin like fur that is stretched over stones.

Oha seemed to be plagued by similar troubles. He laughed from his throat and his breast shook when he called the animals, but after Arabella had betrayed Lilly, Regina quickly found out that Oha, too, was not always the friendly, gentle giant whom she had loved from childhood on. In reality, he was Archimedes reborn, who does not like to see his circles disturbed.

He had given names to the chickens and oxen. There were the cocks Cicero, Catalina, and Caesar; hens were male for Oha, too, and Romans.

The most beautiful ones were named Antonius, Brutus, and Pompejus. When Lilly called the chickens to be fed, Oha often sat down in his easy chair, always took the same book from the shelf over the fireplace, and read without making any sound when turning the pages. For a while, he always laughed loudly back into his chest as if he had swallowed wrong on his cheerfulness. When Regina, however, looked at him closely, she thought more and more of Owuor, who had been the first to reveal to her that sleep with open eyes can make the head sick.

The oxen were named after composers. Chopin and Bach were the best draft animals; the bull was called Beethoven, his youngest son of four hours Mozart. At the happy end of the long night in which he was born, when Manjala had to get his brother to help because of Desdemona's weak contractions and sudden breathing difficulties, Lilly suggested in a solemn voice that Regina name the calf that had just been saved from an emergency.

"Why Regina?" Oha objected. "She does not know her way around here. Such a name becomes a bond for a whole life."

"Don't be silly," Lilly said. "Just let the child have some fun."

Regina was too filled with Desdemona's good fortune to realize that Lilly had just thrown a part of Oha's prey to her. She put her hand on the cow's head and let the scent of contentment into her nose and memories into her head, which too quickly became ready for a fight. Since she had to think simultaneously of her mother's dead baby and her brother's birth, she forgot at the decisive moment that the cattle in Gilgil had to be enchanted by music. The calf's salvation, which had almost come too late, entered her mind. "David Copperfield," she said happily.

Oha shook his head, knocked over the paraffin lamp in Manjala's hand with an unusually violent movement, and said, a little angrily, "Nonsense." The flickering light made his eyes small; his lips seemed like two white bolts in front of his teeth, and for the first time Regina found out that Oha and Lilly, too, fought—even though much more quietly and not for such a long time as her parents.

"We will call the little one Jago," Lilly suggested.

"Since when," Oha asked and cut his own voice with a knife, "are you naming the bulls? I had been looking forward to Mozart. And you cannot take that away from me."

The next morning, Oha was the big-bellied giant again who smelled not of confrontation or of the impatience of sudden irritation but only of sweet tobacco and the mild aroma of sympathetic calm. He made an effort to send his eyes past Lilly, looked at Regina, and said, "I meant no harm yesterday." He carefully counted the black seeds of his papaya and then continued as if he had not needed a long time to catch his breath, "But, you know, it would be strange if we were to use an English name here. You know," he smiled, "we are not too familiar with that one."

"It does not matter," Regina smiled back at him. Her instant politeness confused her, and she believed that she had from habit, as with any excuse without regret, spoken English. "David Copperfield," she explained, embarrassed, and noticed too late that she had not really wanted to open her mouth, "is an old friend of mine. Little Nell, too," she added.

She wondered with a start whether she now had to keep on talking and explain the story of Little Nell to Oha, but she realized that he was far away in his thoughts. When he did not answer, Regina swallowed her relief without attracting his attention. It was not good to talk about things that made the heart race when there was no other mouth that could come to its rescue.

Manjala, who had been standing all this time next to the cabinet with the polished glasses, gold-rimmed white bowls, and delicate white porcelain dancers, brought movement into his body and took his hands out of the long sleeves of his *kanzu*. He collected first slowly, and then ever faster, the plates and made the silverware dance. Max sat up in his pram and accompanied every sound by clapping, which warmed Regina's heart.

Chebeti pushed the poodle off her bare feet, got up, looked at Manjala out of half-closed eyes, for he had stolen her rest, and said, "The little *askari* wants to drink," and went to get the bottle. Her steps made the wooden floor vibrate lightly like a wind that is suddenly caught between trees.

Lilly took the golden mirror that was decorated with tiny stones out of her trouser pocket, painted the contours of her lips until they looked as if they had been cut out from her red blouse, and blew a kiss into the air. "I have to go to Desdemona," she said.

"And to Mozart," Regina laughed. She laughed again when she realized that she had finally succeeded in pronouncing the name without an English accent. She blew, as she had just seen Lilly do, a kiss toward her brother's head and felt the heaviness flee from her limbs and the frenzied thoughts of the night from her head.

It was a good feeling that made her full like the *posho* in the huts at night. She heard the first drums of the day in the forest. Behind the big windows, the sun gave many colors to the sand. Regina squeezed her eyes together until they became slits that could change the pictures. The outlines of the zebras consisted of stripes. The blue of the sky was a small colored spot, the thorn-acacias lost their green, and the cedars became black.

Regina took Max out of his pram, put his head on her shoulder, and fed his ears. She listened intently for the high notes that indicated to her that her brother was already smart enough to enjoy intimacy. When Chebeti came with the bottle and put the nipple into the child's mouth, silence made the large room small.

The bottle was almost empty when Oha made circles with his head and said, "I envy you your David Copperfield."

He had swallowed too much air with the last two words, and Regina retched too long at her giggle to change it to the proper cough in time. "I am sorry," she said. This time, she knew instantly that she had spoken English.

"It is all right," Oha assured her, "I would laugh, too, if I were you and heard me speak mangled English. That is why I would like to have David Copperfield as a friend."

"Why?"

"To feel at home here a little."

Regina first separated the words into syllables and then assembled them again. She even translated them into her language, but she did not succeed in finding out why Oha had let them out of his throat.

"But you are at home here."

"You can call it that."

"This is your farm," Regina insisted. She felt that Oha wanted to tell her something, but he put his tongue between his lips without getting out a sound, and so she repeated, "You are at home here. This is your farm. Everything here is so beautiful."

"*Pro transeuntibus,* Regina. Do you understand that?"

"No, Papa says the Latin I am learning in school is for the dogs."

"For the birds. Ask your father what *pro transeuntibus* means when you are back in Nairobi. He is a smart man. The smartest of us all, but nobody dares to admit that."

It was Oha's voice and also his eyes that convinced Regina that Oha, just like her father, wanted to talk about roots, Germany, and home. She prepared her ears for the familiar, unloved sounds.

At that moment, Lilly came in. "The calf," she laughed and pressed her mouth into a small red ball, "already is a credit to its name."

Oha laughed back when he asked, "Can it already moo 'A Little Night Music'?"

Lilly giggled musically and made her eyes big, but she still did not realize that her husband's cheerfulness had come only from his mouth. She rubbed her hands together as if she wanted to clap and said, "I have to get dressed in honor of the day."

"Absolutely," Oha agreed.

Without wanting to, Regina looked at him and knew that he had not yet returned from the safari, about which Lilly had no idea. Her skin turned cold, and she felt as if she had pressed her ear to a hole in a strange wall and learned things that were not intended for her. Regina needed strength to fight the need to get up and console Oha, as she did with her father when wounds from his earlier life tormented him. For a while she succeeded in suppressing every movement in her body, but her legs did not let her rest and finally overcame her willpower.

"I am going outside with Max," she said. Even though she usually needed both hands to hold her brother, one of them got free and was gliding over Oha's head.

The carved lions on the chair were warmed by the sun, which had only a short shadow left. The stems and roots of the cedars held the rain of the night. Whenever a branch moved, Regina looked for a monkey, but she only heard the noises that told her that the mother monkeys were calling for their young.

For a while, she was thinking of Owuor and the beautiful arguments of her childhood days about whether monkeys were smarter than zebras, but when her heart started to pound, she realized that her father was in the process of displacing Owuor. For the first time since her arrival in

Gilgil, she felt a longing to go home. She said the word a few times to herself, first happily in English, then reluctantly in German. In both languages, the syllables hummed like a bee filled with anger.

Mozart was called out to the grass by the two herdboys, who heard the language of the cows but not that of the people. Desdemona pushed her son softly forward with her big head, stood in a spot of sun, and licked his soft fur into small, light-brown curls. A starling flew onto Desdemona's back. The brilliant blue of its feathers blinded the eye to all other colors.

Lilly stepped out from behind a bush of yellow roses, wearing a long white dress that enclosed her neck with a mountain of ruffles. She looked as if she had already received Mungu's order to fly to heaven, but she did not move till the calf started to suck. Then she released air from her lungs, lifted her head, and sang, "Dies Bildnis ist bezaubernd schön."

The birds fell silent, and even the wind was unable to resist Lilly's song and moved along with individual high notes. They flew faster than usual up to the mountains. Before the last echo reached Regina, she realized that she had been wrong. She was not Ulysses happily returned. She had only heard the sirens in Gilgil.

22

Dr. Walter Redlich
Hove Court
P.O.B. 1312
Nairobi
Kenya

Wiesbaden, October 23, 1946

Re.: Your Application for Employment in the Hessian Department of Justice, Dated May 9, 1946

Dear Dr. Redlich,
We are very happy to inform you that your application of May 9 of the current year for employment in the Hessian Department of Justice has been approved by a decision of the 14th of this month. You will first be employed as a judge at the District Court of the city of Frankfurt and are asked to report as soon as possible after your return to the president of the court Dr. Karl Maaß, who already has been notified by us. Please advise him once the date of your move to Frankfurt has been set. In the determination of your salary, the years since your cancellation as attorney

in 1937 in Leobschütz (Upper Silesia) have been taken into account as years of service.

The undersigned has been instructed to tell you that you are known personally in the Hessian Department of Justice. Your wish to contribute to the rebuilding of a free justice system is being regarded as a special sign of hope for the young democracy in our country.

We are sending our best wishes for the future to you and your family, and remain,

Yours faithfully,
signed Dr. Erwin Pollitzer,
by order of the Minister of Justice in the Hessian Ministry of State.

Owuor had caught the significance of the hour with the eyes, nose, ears, and head of a man whom experience has made smart and whose instincts are supple like those of a young warrior. He was a hunter who stays awake all night and catches the long expected prey only by constantly sharpening his senses. On this day, which had started out like any other, he had brought a letter that was more important than any letter ever before.

The trembling hands of the *bwana* and the suddenness with which his skin changed color when he tore open the thick yellow envelope would have been enough for Owuor. Even more revealing, though, were the sour smell of fear that emanated from two bodies and the impatience that made four eyes flicker like a fire that has been started too fast. In the same room in which Owuor, without excitement and haste, had counted the bubbles in the hot coffee before he had gone to the office of the Hove Court to get the mail, the silence now made each breath as loud as if the *bwana* and the *memsahib* had drums sewn into their breasts.

While he calmed the pounding in his own body by touching over and over again objects that he would have recognized with his eyes shut, Owuor watched the *bwana* and the *memsahib* read. If he opened only his eyes and not the box overstuffed with experiences from the days that were long past, the people with the pale skin of great fear did not look much different now than in those other hours when the letters from far away had burned as sharply as too much fat in too small a pot. And yet, his *bwana* and *memsahib* had become strange to Owuor.

First, the two of them just sat on a sofa and, like sick people dying of thirst, opened their lips over and over again, without showing their teeth. Then two heads became one and, finally, the two bodies a motionless mountain that swallowed all life. It reminded him of dik-diks, which at the height of the burning sun looked for shelter together but did not let go of each other even when the shade became too small for both of them. The image of the inseparable dik-diks disturbed Owuor. It burnt his eyes and parched his mouth.

He remembered the clever story Regina had told in Rongai many rainy seasons ago. It had been a long time before the beautiful day with the locusts. A boy had been changed into a deer, and his sister was powerless against the magic. She was unable to talk with her brother in the language of men and was afraid of the hunters for his sake, but the deer did not sense her fear and jumped out of the shelter of the high grass.

Since then, Owuor knew that too much silence could be even more dangerous to men than great noise that made the ears thick like sacks that have been stuffed too tightly. Owuor cleared his throat, coughing, even though the inside of his neck was as slippery as the freshly oiled body of a thief.

At that moment, he realized that the *bwana* had not lost his voice for all time. It was just that each sound had difficulty finding its way between teeth and tongue.

"Good God, Jettel, that I have lived to see this. It cannot be true. I don't know what to say. Tell me that I am not dreaming and have to wake up any moment now. I don't care what you say; just open your mouth."

"My parents went to Wiesbaden on their honeymoon," Jettel whispered back. "Mother often talked about the 'Schwarze Bock' and that my father got horribly drunk there. He was not able to take his wine, and she was terribly angry."

"Jettel, pull yourself together. Don't you understand what has happened? Do you know what this letter means to all of us?"

"Not quite. We don't know anybody in Wiesbaden."

"Don't you get it? They want us. We can go back. We can go back without having to worry about anything. Mr. Nebbish is a thing of the past."

"Walter, I am afraid, so terribly afraid."

"Just read it, Mrs. Redlich. They have appointed me a judge. Me, the disbarred attorney and notary from Leobschütz. I am sitting here like the last asshole in Kenya, and at home they made me a judge."

"Asshole," Owuor laughed, "I have not forgotten the word, *bwana*. You said it in Rongai."

When the *bwana* began to shout without anger in his voice and even stamped the ground like a dancer who has filled his belly with *tembo* before the others, Owuor laughed again; his throat had more spikes than the tongue of a mad cat. The *bwana* with his eyes without reflection and shoulders that were too small and cowered under every burden had turned into a bull that for the first time in its life feels the power of its loins.

"Jettel, just remember. A German official has no financial worries. And a judge even less. He carries his head high. Nobody fires him. And if he is sick, he can stay in bed and keeps on getting his salary. People greet a judge in the street. Even if they do not know him personally. Good morning, councilor. Goodbye, councilor, best regards to your wife. You cannot have forgotten all that. Good God, just say something."

"You did not say anything about being a judge. I always thought you wanted to be an attorney again."

"I still can do that later. After I have become judge, we will have a completely different start. Germany has always taken care of its officials. They even get apartments from the state. That will make things a lot easier for us."

"I thought the German cities had all been bombed out. Where do they get apartments for their judges then?"

Jettel liked this sentence so well that she started to repeat it, but when she realized that she had delayed her triumph for too long, she pulled, embarrassed, at a strand of hair. However, her excitement subsided only for a moment, and the invigorating self-assurance of her youth warmed her forehead with pleasure. How right her mother had been when she had said, "My Jettel may not have the best grades, but in practical life no one can fool her."

Jettel smiled a little at the thought that she still had the intonation of her mother's voice in her ear. She first allowed herself the soft sadness of remembering and then the certainty that she had made it clear to her husband with a single sentence that he was a dreamer who had no eye for things that were important in life. When Jettel, however, looked at Walter, she saw in his face nothing but a determination that made her first apprehensive and then angry.

"If we really have to go back," she reproached him, emphasizing every word, "why now?"

"Because I can amount to anything only if I am there from the start. One has a chance only when a country goes down or when it rises from its decline."

"Who says that? You are talking like a book."

"I read it in *Gone with the Wind*. Don't you remember the chapter? We talked about it when we read the book. The sentence impressed me very much."

"Oh, Walter, you with your dreams of home. We are happy here. We have everything we need."

"Only if we don't need any more than life itself. We are at the mercy of strangers. Without the Jewish community, we would not even have been able to pay the doctor or the hospital when Max was born. I hope Mr. Rubens will be as generous if one of us gets sick."

"At least we have people who will help us here. We know nobody in Frankfurt."

"Whom did you know when we had to leave for Africa? And when were we ever happy here? Exactly twice. With my first money from the army. And when Max was born. You will never change. My Jettel always longed only for the fleshpots of Egypt. But, in the end, I have always been right."

"I cannot leave here. I am not young enough to start over again."

"That is exactly what you said when we had to emigrate. You were thirty then, and if I had listened to you at the time, we would all be dead today. If I give in to you now, we will always remain unwanted have-nots in a foreign country. And King George is not going to keep me on forever as the company's fool."

"You say all that only because you want to return to your damn Germany. Have you forgotten what happened to your father? I have not. I owe it to my mother that I do not step on the ground that is saturated with her blood."

"Don't, Jettel. That is a sin. God does not forgive us when we misuse the dead. You have to trust me. We will make it. I promise you. Stop crying. One day you will tell me that I was right, and it will not take as long by far as you think now."

"How can we live among murderers?" Jettel sobbed. "Everyone here says that you are a fool and that one cannot forget. Do you think a woman likes to hear her husband called a traitor? You can find employment here like everyone else. They help people who have been in the army. Everyone says so."

"I have been offered work. On a farm in Djibouti. Do you want to go there?"

"I don't even know where Djibouti is."

"Neither do I. At least, not in Kenya and, in any case, in Africa."

Walter was confused by the long-forgotten yearning to take his wife into his arms and to take away the fear from her. He was even more tormented by the knowledge that Jettel and he were bleeding from identical wounds. He, too, was defenseless against the past. It would always be stronger than the hope for a future.

"We will never forget," he said and looked at the ground. "If you really want to know, Jettel, it has become our destiny to be a little unhappy wherever we are. Hitler has made sure of that for all times. We who have survived will never be able to live normally again. But I would rather be unhappy where I am respected. Germany was not Hitler. You will understand that, too, one day. The decent ones will be in charge again."

Even though she tried to resist, Jettel was touched by Walter's low voice and his helplessness. She saw how he buried his hands in his trouser pockets and searched for words, but she could not decide whether she wanted to hurt him again or console him this one time, so she remained silent.

For a while she watched Owuor ironing. He spat on the laundry with puffed cheeks and, with widely swinging movements, let the heavy iron fall from a great height onto two spread-out diapers.

"I have lived here for too long," Jettel sighed and stared into the small clouds of rising steam, and they seemed to her a symbol of all the contentment she would ever ask for again. "How am I supposed to deal with a small child and no help? Regina has never had a broom in her hand in all her life."

"Thank God, you are all right again. This is my old Jettel, as I remember her. Whenever we had to make a decision in life, you were afraid that you would not find a maid. This time you do not have to worry, Mrs. Redlich. All of Germany is full of people who will be happy to find work. I cannot tell you today what our life is going to be like, but on whatever is holy to me, I promise you a maid."

"*Bwana*," asked Owuor and stacked the ironed laundry into the beautifully fragrant mountain that only he knew how to build so smoothly and high, "shall I wash out the suitcases with hot water?"

"Why are you asking?"

"You will need your suitcases for the safari. The *memsahib*, too."

"What do you know, Owuor?"

"Everything, *bwana*."

"Since when?"

"For a long time."

"But you do not understand us when we talk."

"When you came to Rongai, *bwana*, I listened only with my ears. Those days are gone."

"Thank you, my friend."

"*Bwana*, I have not given you anything and you say 'thank you.'"

"Oh, yes, Owuor, you alone have given to me," Walter said.

He felt the pain, which hurt him only a short time and yet long enough to understand that a new wound just had been added to the old ones. His Germany did not exist anymore. He would enter his rediscovered home inebriated not with joy but with sadness and sorrow.

The separation from Owuor would not be any less painful than the farewells that lay behind him. The urge to go up to Owuor and embrace him was big, but it was Jettel whom he caressed when he said, "Everything will be all right."

"Oh, Walter, who is going to tell Regina that it is getting serious now? She is still only a child and is so attached to everything here."

"I have known for a long time," Regina said.

"Where are you coming from? For how long have you been standing there?"

"I was in the garden with Max the whole time, but I hear with my eyes," Regina explained. It occurred to her that her father would never know what it meant for one person to imitate the voice of another.

"And your parents," Walter replied, "cannot even trust their eyes. Or can you imagine, Jettel, who in the Hessian Ministry of Justice is supposed to know this old dope personally? I cannot get that out of my head."

He brooded, obsessed, about the incomprehensible coincidence that was about to turn his life around, but as much as he searched the past and examined the future for a possibility that might have escaped him, he was unable to shed any light on this important point.

Eight days later, Walter appeared before Captain Carruthers. He had translated the letter from the Department of Justice in Hessia with much effort and Regina's help. He felt like a well-prepared candidate at his first state examination; the comparison, which two weeks ago never would have occurred to him, amused him.

Before the captain had finished listlessly leafing through his mail, carefully filling his pipe, and fighting the sticking window with many annoyed movements, Walter even caught himself thinking with satisfaction that he seemed to be better off than the captain.

Captain Bruce Carruthers had similar thoughts. He said with a trace of irritation, which at some time for him had been more a successful prelude to a well-thought-out ironic remark than the expression of a sudden impulse, "You look somehow different than the last time. Are you really the right man? The one who doesn't get it?"

Even though Walter had understood him, he became unsure of himself.

"Sergeant Redlich, sir," he confirmed tensely.

"Why do all of you fellows from the Continent have no sense of humor? No wonder Hitler lost the war."

"Sorry, sir."

"We had that once before, too. I remember exactly. You say sorry, and I start all over again with all the nonsense," the captain reminded him and closed his eyes for a moment. "When did I see you the last time, anyway?"

"Almost six months ago, sir."

The captain looked older and even more careworn than during the first conversation; he knew it. There were not only the stomach aches when waking up and the vexation after the last whisky at night. He felt, above all, with a melancholy that seemed unpleasant to him, that he no longer had that healthy sense of proportion that a man his age needed to safeguard the fragile equilibrium of life. Even insignificant details disturbed Bruce Carruthers excessively—for instance, that he could remember the name of the sergeant who stood in front of him only with an almost degrading effort. After all, he had had to transfer this caricature of a name often enough from one idiotic form to another. The unnecessary problems with his memory consumed more of his strength than was proper for a man of his caliber.

In addition, Carruthers had to come to the conclusion every day again that fate was no longer kind to him. He had trouble concentrating when hunting and thought too much about Scotland; even golf, at times, seemed to him a nearly absurd pastime for a man who in his youth had dreamed of pursuing a career as a scientist. The long expected letter from his wife had arrived, telling him that she could no longer stand the separation and wanted a divorce; immediately before that, he had received the order from the damn army, which kept him in Ngong even longer.

The captain flinched when he realized that he had gotten lost in the labyrinth of his opposition. This, too, happened to him more frequently than in good days. "I assume," he said discouraged, "you still want to be released to Germany?"

"Oh, yes, sir," Walter replied quickly and pushed the tips of his boots together. "That is why I am here."

Carruthers felt a curiosity that went against his nature; he considered it improper, but at the same time strangely fascinating. Then he knew. The way in which the bizarre fellow in front of him answered his questions was different from the first time. Above all, his accent had changed. It was still torturous to sensitive ears, but the man somehow spoke better English. At least one could understand him. These ambitious guys from the Continent really could not be trusted. They buried themselves behind books and learned a foreign language at an age when others thought only of their private lives.

"Do you already know what you are going to do in Germany?"

"I am going to be a judge, sir," Walter said and held the translation of the letter out to him.

The captain was perplexed. He had the aversion of his compatriots toward vanity and pride, and yet his voice was calm and friendly after he had read the letter. "Not too bad," he said.

"Yes, sir."

"And now you expect the British army to deal with this problem so that the fucking Jerries get a judge cheaply."

"Pardon, sir, I did not understand you."

"The army is supposed to pay your passage, or not? That is what you thought, isn't it?"

"You said so, sir."

"I did? Interesting. Now, just don't look so concerned right away. Haven't you learned that in His Majesty's army a captain always knows what he has said? Even if he is stuck in this godforsaken country and cannot remember anything. Can you even imagine how demented one can get here?"

"Yes, sir, I know that quite well."

"Do you like the English?"

"Yes, sir. They saved my life. I will never forget that."

"Why do you want to leave, then?"

"The English do not like me."

"They do not like me either. I am a Scot."

Both were silent. Bruce Carruthers brooded about why a damn non-British sergeant should succeed in working in his old profession again, but not a captain from Edinburgh with a grandmother from Glasgow.

Walter was afraid the captain would end the conversation without even mentioning the word *repatriation*. In frightful detail, he imagined Jettel's reaction when she found out that he had not accomplished anything. The captain leafed through a pile of papers with his right hand and tried to swat a fly with the left, but then he got up, as if he had had nothing else on his mind, painstakingly scraped a dead fly from the wall, took his pipe out of his mouth for the first time, and said, "What do you think about the *Almanzora*?"

"Sir, I don't understand."

"The *Almanzora* is a boat. It regularly goes back and forth between Mombasa and Southampton and brings the troops home. You fellows are interested only in drinking and women, I assume?"

"No, sir."

"I don't think I will get a contingent on the old lady before March 9 of next year. But if you want to, I will try for March. How was that again? How many wives and children do you have?"

"One wife and two children, sir. I thank you very much, sir. You do not know what you are doing for me."

"I think I have heard that once before, too," Carruthers smiled. "There is something else I need to know. How is it that you know English all of a sudden?"

"I don't know. Sorry, sir. I didn't even notice."

23

CONSCIOUS OF THE FACT that the time had come for a new cultural beginning, the refugees in the Hove Court decided two days before New Year's Eve, in never-before-experienced accord, to greet the year 1947 together. Many of the emigrants hoped to become British citizens very soon; they practiced, undaunted, even though deplorably often without satisfactory results, pronouncing fateful words like United Kingdom, Empire, and Commonwealth at least approximately right. During the past two months, four couples and two single men had succeeded, thanks to naturalization, in officially discarding the status of bloody refugees and adopting English-sounding names that were much more important to their self-esteem than any material goods.

Wohlgemuths were now called Welleses, and Leubuschers had become Laughtons. Siegfried and Henny Schlachter had taken the opportunity to depart radically from the origin of their name. They firmly rejected the ironic suggestions of their neighbors that they call themselves Butcher and chose Baker, instead. It came as quite a surprise that Schlachters, of all people, were among the first of the new British subjects. They had considerable trouble with the new mother tongue and had certainly not done any more for their adopted fatherland than many others whose applications had been rejected without explanation by the officials. Jealous persons consoled themselves by maintaining that the Schlachters had gotten their British passports only because an official who came from Ireland had mistaken the old couples' Swabian stammer for a now seldom heard Welsh accent.

Mrs. Taylor and Miss Jones, of course, were invited to the New Year's party, as well as a major from Rhodesia, who had recently been released from the army and had allowed himself to be misled in the choice of his retirement home by the English-sounding name of the residence. All three, however, became indisposed on exactly the same day and with the same illness. The celebration committee tried to keep calm, but the disappointment that the first party of this kind was being overshadowed by ailments that appeared suddenly could not be suppressed in the admired British way within such a short time frame and without hundreds of years of practice.

The "young Englishmen," as they were called derisively, were in charge of the celebration committee. They were not especially grateful, in view of the threefold refusal, that Diana Wilkins had stayed well. It was indisputable that Diana Wilkins had obtained her British citizenship years ago through her marriage to the unhappily killed Mr. Wilkins, but she absolutely did not appreciate the privilege. After a quarter of a bottle of whisky, she started mistaking Englishmen for Russians, whom she stubbornly still hated.

With even more indignation, they noticed that Walter, of all people, who with his repatriation to Germany had already supplied them daily with grievances and ammunition, had the nerve to speak of the "English malady." Only the fact that he was still wearing the uniform of the beloved English king, along with sympathy for his poor wife, whose attitude toward Germany was generally known, protected Walter from open hostility.

Even though the party now had to take place without those guests who through their mere presence would have provided the requisite social prestige, those in charge felt an obligation to English tradition. Because the refugees were not quite sure how to combine this ambition with their lack of knowledge of life in British high society in a credible way, they paid painstaking attention to every detail that they could glean from regular visits to the movies. The reports of festivities in the English royal household, which at this time of year appeared extensively in the newsreels, were of immense assistance.

At sundown, the ladies appeared in long, low-cut, and strikingly old-fashioned evening gowns; most of them had not been worn during the emigration. To their regret, the gentlemen, because of a lack of foresight during their emigration, had to make do without the tuxedos that the old-established farmers in the highlands considered appropriate dinner attire, even without special occasions. The German gentlemen made up for this deficiency by exhibiting a dignified demeanor in their dark suits that were too tight. A wicked comment by Elsa Conrad spread only too quickly.

"That you dare to smell of German mothballs," she said, sniffing boldly, to Hermann Friedländer, of all people, who maintained that he was already dreaming in English, "is beyond me."

Party crackers, which in the old country had, at best, been part of children's birthdays and despite all attempts of mental reorientation still seemed a little ridiculous, were hung with almost Prussian precision between the unruly spikes of the cactus plants. With the eagerness, but also the helplessness of people who have not yet developed a real relationship to the object of their new infatuation, they bought records of all the currently popular hits; at no New Year's party in the entire Colony could "Don't Fence Me In" have been played as often between sundown and midnight as on the yellowing grass plot of the Hove Court. There was a slight mishap regarding the genuine Scotch whisky that the celebration committee, despite its exorbitant price, had uncompromisingly decreed to be the only suitable drink.

It was hardly touched and, despite the euphoric mood and paralyzing heat, it conjured sad memories of punch and jelly doughnuts in a way that could not be recreated later on but was still embarrassing. An almost abstruse discussion ensued about whether the New Year's doughnuts during the times that one wanted to forget now had been filled with plum jam or red currant jelly.

The small fireworks, however, were a success, and even more so the idea of singing "Auld Lang Syne" under the jacaranda tree. The song, which had been practiced specially in consideration of the now unfortunately indisposed English neighbors, sounded strangely harsh coming from German throats. Even though they formed the prescribed circle and held each other's hands with the distant look of Victorian ladies, only little of the smooth Scottish melody descended into the African night.

Walter had heard the old tune often in the mess hall of his company; he noticed the gap between aspiration and ability with amused Schadenfreude but held back his disdain for Jettel's sake. His smile, however, was registered with the same disapproval as if he had shouted his criticism out loud. He attracted even more unpleasant attention when, after the last note, he whispered to his wife, shamelessly loudly, "Next year in Frankfurt." Jettel did not understand the allusion to the old Passover prayer and answered angrily, "Not today." The embarrassment that she obviously had no idea of religious customs and Jewish tradition was viewed as just punishment for the blasphemy and, above all, as a deservedly appropriate damper on Walter's provocative tactlessness.

From the noise of the fireworks and at the height of a dispute that had broken out over the correct text of "Kein schöner Land zu dieser Zeit" and that was derided by a majority as incredibly disgraceful, Max woke up. He greeted the New Year in the traditional way of babies born in the Colony. Even though he was less than ten months old, he spoke his first intelligible word. Admittedly, he said neither "Mama" nor "Papa" but *"Aya."* Chebeti, who had been sitting in the kitchen and had rushed to his bed at the first whimper, said the word, which warmed her skin more pleasantly than any woolen blanket in the cold storms of her mother's mountainous home, again and again to him. Completely woken up by her throaty laugh and fascinated by the short melodious sounds, which tickled his ears, Max actually said *"Aya"* a second time and then over and over again.

Hoping that the miracle would repeat itself at exactly the right point, Chebeti carried her gurgling trophy to the celebrants under the tree. She was richly rewarded. The *memsahib* and the *bwana,* open-mouthed and with fire in their eyes, took the kicking *toto* out of Chebeti's arms and pronounced alternately "Mama" and "Papa," first quietly and laughing but soon loudly and with a determination that made them appear like warriors in a decisive battle. Most men took sides by loudly shouting "Papa"; whoever remembered his English passport in time tried "Daddy." The women supported Jettel with cooing calls of "Mama" and, while doing so, looked like the dolls of their childhood that talked when one pressed their tummy. Max, however, could not be persuaded to utter any other sound than *"Aya"* before falling asleep exhaustedly.

From that day on, the linguistic development of the young Max Redlich could not be stopped. He said *"kula"* when he wanted to eat, *"lala"* when he was put to bed, absolutely correct *"chai"* to the teapot, *"meno"* to his first tooth, *"toto"* to his reflection in the mirror, and *"mbua"* when it rained. He even picked up *"kesho,"* the word for "tomorrow," "future," and that indefinite unit of time that was a rational concept only for Owuor.

Walter laughed when he heard his son talk, and yet, a sensitivity that he tried to excuse with his overwrought nerves did not let him fully enjoy the childish prattle. Even though it seemed immature and even morbid to him to put that much weight on it, he was distressed by the idea that Africa had already estranged his son from him. He was even more bothered by the suspicion that Regina had taught those specific words to her brother and that she was happy about the excitement that every single word caused. He worried nervously, and with even more hurt, whether his daughter was trying to show him her love for Africa and her disapproval of the decision to return home this way.

Regina, however, denied, with an indignation that otherwise only Owuor could order into his face at the right moment, that she had anything to do with a development that Walter, in his depressive moods and without saying the word out loud, used to call a culture war. Matters were made worse by the fact that the Swahili vocabulary of the little Max was the subject of constant mockery in the Hove Court. It was considered, even by the few understanding and tolerant neighbors, as clear proof that the child was smarter than his irresponsible father and was demonstrating in his innocence that he should not be deported to Germany.

When Max finally made a three-syllable sound that with a lot of imagination could be interpreted as Owuor's name, Walter's nerves failed. With a scarlet face and clenched fists, he screamed at his daughter, "Why do you want to hurt me? Don't you realize how everyone here laughs at me because my son refuses to speak my language? And then your mother is surprised that I want to get away from here. I always thought that you, at least, were on my side."

Regina understood with a shudder how deviously her imagination had led her astray and had entranced her to betray her loyalty and love. Regret and shame burned her skin and pushed knives into her heart. She had lost herself so much in her role as a fairy who knows the magic of language that she had had no eyes or ears for her father. Anxiously, she looked for an excuse, but, as always when she was upset, the thought of her father's language alone paralyzed her tongue.

When she realized that her lips were starting to form the word *missuri,* which meant "good" and was also a sign that somebody finally had understood, she shook her head. Slowly, but with great determination, she walked up to her father and swallowed her sadness. Then she licked the salt from his eyes. The next day, Max said "Papa."

When he said "Mama" at the end of the week, however, his mother's ears were not receptive to the long-awaited happiness, even though her tears at just that moment were flowing to her chin. Max had already crowed "Mama" a second time and Chebeti was clapping her hands when Walter rushed into the kitchen. "We have," he shouted and threw his cap onto the sofa in high spirits, "tickets for the *Almanzora.* The boat leaves Mombasa on March 9."

"Puttfarken has made it," Jettel wept.

"What in devil's name makes you think of Puttfarken? Who is that supposed to be?"

"Puttfarken, Schützenstraße," Jettel said. She got up, dried her eyes with a hasty movement of her head on the sleeve of her blouse, and went to the window as if she had waited for this moment for a long time. Then she put her finger on her mouth and drew the curtains shut, even though it was only five o'clock in the afternoon.

Walter understood immediately. But he asked incredulously, "You are not talking about our Puttfarken from Leobschütz?"

"Who else, if I draw the curtains in the middle of the day? 'Anna,'" she said in a voice that she had thought was long forgotten, "'draw the curtain. It is better if nobody sees me here. After all, I am a civil servant and have to be careful.' Goodness, Walter, don't you remember how our Anna used to get angry? She always called him a coward."

"He was no coward. But what makes you think of him?"

"*Bwana,* the letter," said Owuor and pointed to the table.

"From Wiesbaden," Jettel said. "He has become a real big shot, a senior civil servant," she read and choked giggling on every syllable. "Let me read it to you. I have been looking forward to this all day."

"Dear friend Redlich," Jettel read, "because of a terrible case of the flu (in case you still know what that is in your sunny paradise), I am getting around to writing you only today. The letter from the ministry, therefore, will already have reached you. It should have been the other way round. I can imagine how you must have mulled over the coincidence that someone should know you in Wiesbaden. Here, we have known for some time now that coincidence is the only certainty one can still count on, but I hope very much that your experiences have been better on that score.

"How shall I describe my bafflement to you, when an application from a Dr. Walter Redlich for acceptance in the service of the Hessian Department of Justice, of all things, happened to land on my desk? I am most likely the first German civil servant who cried in his office since Bismarck's resignation. I read your application over and over and still could not believe that you are alive. In Leobschütz, there was a rumor shortly after your emigration that you had been attacked by a lion and had died that way. Only the reference to your studies in Breslau and your work as an attorney in Leobschütz convinced me that you are indeed the friend of those forever lost, good days.

"In addition, I also could not imagine that any man who had succeeded in escaping from Germany would want to come back to these ruins and to people who were responsible for what was done to him and his brethren. What you must have experienced, how terrible your life must have been that you have found the courage to make such a momentous decision! Of course, I am very happy about it. We have dismissed all politically tainted judges, and too few untainted ones have remained to build up a system of justice again. So, be prepared not to stay a district court judge for long before being promoted. You will like the president of the district court, Maaß. He is a very decent man who was chased out of office by the Nazis and had to try to stay barely alive with his family all those years.

"And now, to my fate. It did not do any good that your Anna (I wonder if she has forgiven me in the meantime, the faithful soul?) always had to draw the curtains when I visited you at Asternweg so that nobody would know that I still had contact with Jews. Shortly after you left Leobschütz, I was suspended as a judge because of my Jewish wife, but good old Tenscher interceded, and I, at least, found some kind of employment in the registry of deeds.

"After a few months, I was removed from that position, too, on the instigation of District Commander Rummler, whom, I hope, you will not remember the way I do. Before my dismissal, I was called to Breslau three times and promised immediate reinstatement in the civil service if

I would get a divorce from my Jewish wife. Up to the outbreak of the war, I was able to feed my family after a fashion through occasional work for Attorney Pawlik. Of course, nobody was to know about it. I have not been able to pay my debt of gratitude to Pawlik.

"He died in the first month of the war in Poland. I myself was considered 'unfit for military service' and was drafted to do forced labor. I will tell you about that time when we see each other again. My pen refuses to write down my experiences, even though I am aware that things could have been even worse.

"After the war, Käthe, my son Klaus, who was born the same year as your daughter, and I were able to get out of Upper Silesia with the first trek. Käthe had not been well all these years because of the constant fear that she might be deported, and during the flight, her leg was injured and we feared the worst. Although I have forgotten how to believe in God, we still have to be grateful to Him that all three of us finally landed here in Wiesbaden, where a remote relative took us in. Now, I owe to Hitler, of all people, a career that I would not even have dared dream about in Leobschütz.

"Käthe was very excited when I told her about your application. My son cannot wait to meet a man who made it to Africa. He is a withdrawn boy who has been marked by the events of the terrible years and cannot forget his parents' dread and the slights and cruelties he was exposed to from friends and, above all, from his teachers. He was not allowed to attend high school and now has difficulties with school. He is dreaming in an obsessive, unchildlike way of emigration, and I believe we are going to lose him early.

"I am afraid I went on for too long, but writing to you made me feel good. I am overwhelmed by the thought that this letter is going to Nairobi, to a free world without rubble. And yet, I feel all the time as if I were sitting in your living room in Leobschütz. With the curtains open! I do not dare ask about the fate of your father and sister, whom I met once at your home. Equally, I do not dare encourage you in your new beginning. The Germans have not only lost a good part of their country and their cities. They have also lost their souls and conscience. The country is full of people who did not see or know anything or were 'always against the Nazis.' And the few Jews who are still here and have escaped Hell are already being defamed again. In addition to the meager food rations of ordinary consumers, they receive a bonus for heavy work. This is sufficient for the perpetrators to mark the victims anew.

"Let me know as soon as possible when you have a date for your return. My pessimism and experiences do not permit me to talk about a homecoming. I will do whatever I can to help you, but do not expect too much from a senior civil servant who has the flaw of being from Leobschütz. We are considered 'Eastern rabble' here in the West, and nobody believes what material and sentimental values people may have lost in addition to their home. It is easier for me to have you promoted to president of the highest court than to get an apartment or a pound of butter for you.

"Do not let your admirable optimism be dampened by my complaints, which I consider quite improper at this point, and also not your sense of humor, which I remember and liked so well. Bring some coffee with you if you can. Coffee is the new German currency. You can buy everything with coffee. Even a white vest.

"My wife and I are waiting for you and your family impatiently and with open hearts. Until then, I remain sincerely yours, Hans Puttfarken

"P.S. I almost forgot: Your old friend Greschek has ended up in a village in the Harz. I received his address by coincidence and have written to him about your planned return."

While Jettel put the letter back in its envelope, she tried to visualize Puttfarken's face, but she could remember only that he was tall and blond and had very blue eyes. She wanted to tell Walter at least this much, but the silence had already been too long for them to find words as a release from the upheaval. With hesitant movements Jettel used the envelope to fan cool air into her face. Owuor took the letter out of her hand and put it on a glass plate.

He imitated the hissing sounds that he had learned from the birds as a boy, smiled in recollection of the one word the *memsahib* had taken out of the pages, and opened the curtains, again whistling. A beam of the low-lying afternoon sun was reflected in the glass and cast a veil of thin blue fog on the gray paper. The dog woke up, lifted his head drowsily, and, yawning, smacked his teeth together as loudly as in the days of his youth when he was still able to smell the hares in the grass.

"Rummler," Owuor laughed, "the letter called Rummler. I heard Rummler's name."

"Nebbish," Walter said. "If Puttfarken knew what happened to my sense of humor. Oh, Jettel, doesn't it feel at least a little bit good to get such a letter? After all those years when we were at the bottom of the barrel."

"I don't know. I don't know what to say. I did not understand all of that."

"Do you think I did? I only know that there is a human being who remembers me the way I used to be. And he wants to help us. Give us some time, Mrs. Redlich, to get used to the fact that things have changed. Don't listen to what people here are saying. We fell lower than they did, but we have more experience than others to start over in life. We are going to make it. Our son is not going to know anymore what it means to be an outcast."

For a moment it seemed to Jettel as if the gentleness and the yearning in Walter's voice had given her back the dreams, hopes, and security, the love and zest for living of her youth, but the accord with her husband was too unfamiliar to her to last.

"What did you say when you came home? I don't remember anymore."

"Yes, Jettel, you remember exactly. I said that we are leaving on the *Almanzora* on March 9. And this time, we do not each go on our own. We are together. I am glad that the uncertainty is over. I do not think I would have been able to stand waiting much longer."

24

AT FOUR O'CLOCK in the morning, Walter woke up from a noise that he did not recognize. He tried again and again to catch the slight vibrations that seemed to come from somewhere nearby and were more welcome to him than his fear of sleeplessness, but nothing other than the silence of the agonizing hour before sunrise reached his ears and immediately started chasing away his rest. He lay anxiously waiting for the chirping of the birds in the eucalyptus trees in front of the window, which usually was his signal to get up; tension sharpened his senses before it was time. Even though the day had not caught any trace of the first gray light yet, Walter believed that he could already see the contours of the four large, light-colored overseas boxes.

Since their arrival in Africa, they had been used as closets. They stood now, marked with Jettel's steep, childlike handwriting, one against each wall of the bedroom. Owuor had finished packing the night before and had nailed them shut so vigorously that Kellers from the flat next door had angrily knocked back. Walter felt relieved by the thought that finally the greatest part of his life of the last nine years had been stowed away. The two weeks before the departure of the *Almanzora* would now be able to pass without the exhausting fights that accompanied each decision about what could be taken or had to be left behind.

It appeared to Walter that fate was giving him a last bit of normality. The period of grace seemed only too short. He listened attentively to the gnashing of his teeth, as if the unpleasant sound had some special significance. After a while, to his surprise, he actually felt relief from the burden that continually tortured him during the day. Made defenseless by a feeling of guilt about which he could not speak if he did not want to lose his strength, he had been obliged to account to Jettel or Regina for each remark, for his sighs, for each trace of annoyance and uncertainty.

Only during the night could he admit to himself that disappointment was bothering him before the seeds of hope could start to sprout. Since the day the packing began, Walter had been grief-stricken because the boxes reminded him so strongly and exclusively of the start of their emigration. They did not symbolize the long-yearned-for departure into newfound happiness, as he had imagined for months with gratifying euphoria.

To force himself to quiet down, Walter pressed his lips together tightly until the physical pain was big enough to face the fight against the evil spirits that emerged from the past and threatened the future. At that moment, he heard the sound that had disturbed his sleep a second time. The low noise, which indicated the slow movement of bare feet on a rough wooden floor, came from the kitchen, and from time to time it seemed as if Rummler were rubbing his tail against the closed door.

The idea that the dog would even open an eye before water was poured into the tea kettle made Walter smile, but curiosity forced him to check, anyway. He got up silently, without waking Jettel, and tiptoed into the kitchen. The stub of a small candle stood on the lid of a can and, with its long flame, immersed the room in a pale, yellow light. In the corner, between some pots and the rusted frying pan from Leobschütz, sat Owuor, eyes closed, on the floor, rubbing his feet warm. Rummler lay next to him. The dog was actually awake and had a thick rope around his neck.

Under the kitchen table was a bulging blue-and-white checked kitchen towel that was tied into a bundle around a thick wooden stick. Out of one of the holes protruded a sleeve of the white *kanzu* that Owuor had worn when serving dinner since the days in Rongai. On the windowsill, freshly ironed and neatly folded into a black rectangle, lay Walter's robe. He recognized it only from the brittle silk on the collar and lapel. "Owuor, what are you doing here?"

"I sit and wait, *bwana*."

"Why?"

"I am waiting for the sun," Owuor explained. He took only the time he needed to put the same amazement into his eyes that the *bwana* had in his.

"And why does Rummler have a rope around his neck? Do you want to sell him in the market?"

"*Bwana*, who buys an old dog?"

"I wanted to see you laugh. Now, tell me, why are you here?"

"You know why."

"No."

"You always lied only with your mouth, *bwana*. Rummler and I are going on a long safari. He who goes first on safari keeps his eyes dry."

Without being able to open his mouth, Walter repeated every single word. When he felt that his throat hurt, he sat down on the floor and stroked the short stiff hair on Rummler's neck. The dog's warm body reminded him of the nights in front of the fireplace at Ol' Joro Orok, which he had thought long buried. He resisted the calmness that started to paralyze him by pressing his head against his knees. At first, the pressure against his eye sockets seemed pleasant, but then he was bothered by the colors that dissolved in the light just like his thoughts.

He felt as if he had experienced the scene, which seemed so unreal to him now, once before, but at first could not remember when. His memory quickly and too readily surrendered to the bewildering pictures. He saw his father standing in front of the hotel in Sohrau, but when the candle began the last fight for its life, his father turned away from his son and changed into Greschek, who stood in Genoa on the rail of the *Ussukuma*.

A flag with a swastika waved in the storm. Exhausted, Walter waited for the sound of Greschek's voice, the hard pronunciation and the stubborn anger in the syllables that would make the parting even harder than it was to begin with. But Greschek did not say anything and only shook his head so violently that the flag came lose and fell toward Walter. He did not feel anything but his own helplessness and the oppressive silence.

"Kimani," Owuor said, "does your head still know Kimani?"

"Yes," Walter said quickly. He was glad that he could hear and think again. "Kimani was a friend like you, Owuor. I have often thought of him. He ran from the farm before I left Ol' Joro Orok. I did not say *kwaheri* to him."

"He saw you drive off, *bwana*. He remained standing in front of the house for too long. The car became smaller and smaller. The next morning Kimani was dead. There was only a small piece of Kimani's shirt left in the forest."

"You never told me, Owuor. Why? What happened to Kimani?"

"Kimani wanted to die."

"But why? He was not sick. He was not old."

"Kimani always talked only to you, *bwana*. Do you remember? The *bwana* and Kimani were always under the tree. It was at the most beautiful *shamba* with the highest flax. You filled his head with the pictures from your head. Kimani loved the pictures more than his sons and the sun. He was smart, but not smart enough. Kimani let the salt enter his body and became dry like a tree without roots. A man has to go on safari when his time has come."

"Owuor, I do not understand you."

"'Owuor, I do not understand you.' You always said that when your ears did not want to hear. Even on the day when the locusts came. I said, 'The locusts are here, *bwana*,' but the *bwana* said, 'Owuor, I do not understand you.'"

"Stop stealing my voice," Walter said. He noticed how his hand moved from Rummler's fur to Owuor's knee; he wanted to hold it back, but it no longer obeyed his will. For a time that seemed very long to him and in which he felt the warmth and smoothness of Owuor's skin more and more strongly, he resisted the grasp. Then came the pain and, with it, the certainty that this parting was more merciless than all the ones that had preceded it.

"Owuor," he said and drove restraint into his voice, "what is the *memsahib* going to say if you do not come to work today? Shall I say, 'Owuor does not want to help you anymore'? Shall I say, 'Owuor wants to forget us'?"

"Chebeti will do my work, *bwana*."

"Chebeti is only an *aya*. She does not work in the house. You know that."

"Chebeti is your *aya*, but she is my wife. She does what I tell her. She will go with you and the *memsahib* to Mombasa and hold the little *askari*."

"You never told me that Chebeti is your wife," Walter said. His reproachful voice seemed childish to him, and, embarrassed, he wiped the sweat from his forehead. "Why," he asked quietly, "did I not know that?"

"The *memsahib kidogo* knew. She always knows everything. She has eyes like we have. You always slept on your eyes," Owuor laughed. "The dog," he continued and spoke as fast as if he had had each word in his mouth for a long time already, "cannot go on a ship. He is too old for a new life. I will go with Rummler. The way I left Rongai and then Ol' Joro Orok for Nairobi."

"Owuor," Walter said tired, "you have to say *kwaheri* to the *memsahib kidogo*. Shall I tell my daughter, 'Owuor is gone and does not want to see you anymore'? Shall I say to her, 'Rummler is gone forever'? The dog is part of my child. You know that. You were there when she and Rummler became friends."

The sigh was like the first whistling of the wind after the rain. The dog moved one ear. His howling was still in his muzzle when the door opened.

"Owuor has to leave, Papa. Or do you want his heart to dry up?"

"Regina, since when have you been up? You have been eavesdropping. Did you know that Owuor is going to leave us? Like a thief in the night."

"Yes," Regina said. When she repeated the word, she shook her head with the same slight movement that she used to prevent her brother from rummaging in the dog's bowl. "But not," she explained, sadness making her voice heavy, "like a thief. Owuor has to leave. He does not want to die."

"Dear God, Regina, stop that nonsense! One does not die from parting. Otherwise, I would have been dead a long time ago."

"Some people are dead and keep on breathing."

Startled, Regina pulled her lower lip between her teeth, but it was too late. She was already swallowing salt, and her tongue was no longer able to take the sentence back. She was so bewildered that she even thought she heard her father laugh and did not dare look at him.

"Who told you that, Regina?"

"Owuor. A long time ago. I do not remember anymore when," she lied.

"Owuor, you are smart."

Owuor had to strain his ears like a dog that hears the first sound after a long sleep, for the *bwana* had spoken like an old man who has too much air in his breast. Despite that, he was able to enjoy the praise as in the good days of the fresh happiness. He tried to reach for the dead time, but it trickled through his fingers like too finely ground maize. So, he moved his body awkwardly to the side, and Regina sat down between him and her father.

The silence was good and made the pain, which did not come from the body, light like the feather of a hen before it lays an egg for the first time. All three were silent till the daylight became white and clear and the sun colored the leaves with that dark green that announced a day with fire in the air.

"Owuor," Walter said when he opened the window, "here is my old black coat. You forgot it."

"I have not forgotten anything, *bwana*. The coat does not belong to me anymore."

"I gave it to you. Does the clever Owuor not know that anymore? I gave it to you in Rongai."

"You are going to wear the coat again."

"How do you know?"

"You said in Rongai, 'I do not need the coat anymore. It is from a life I lost.' Now," Owuor said and, laughing, as in the days that were dead now, "you have found your life again. The life with the coat."

"You have to take it along, Owuor. Without the coat you will forget me."

"*Bwana*, my head cannot forget you. I have learned so many words from you."

"Say them, say them once again, my friend."

"Ich hab' mein Herz in Heidelberg verloren," Owuor hummed. He noticed that his voice became stronger with each note and that the music still tasted as sweet in his throat as the first time. "You see," he said triumphantly, "even my tongue cannot forget you."

With trembling hands Walter took the robe, shook it out, and put it around Owuor's shoulders as if he were a child whom a father has to shield from the cold. "Go now, my friend," he said. "I, too, do not want to have salt in my eyes."

"It is all right, *bwana*."

"No," Regina cried and no longer fought the pressure of the swallowed tears. "No, Owuor, you have to lift me up one more time. I should not say this, but I have to."

When Owuor took her in his arms, Regina held her breath till the pain split her breast into two parts. She rubbed her forehead against the muscles on Owuor's neck and let her nose catch the scent of his skin. Then she realized that she had started to breathe again. Her lips became moist. Her hands grasped his hair, which every day now was touched by another small gray streak of lightning, but Owuor had changed.

He was no longer old and full of sadness. His back was straight again like the arrow in the taut bow of the Masai. Or was it Cupid's arrow that flew through the images?

For a moment, Regina was afraid she might have looked into Cupid's face and chased him forever into a country into which she could not follow, but when she was finally able to lift her eyelids she saw Owuor's nose and the brightness of his white teeth. He was once again the giant who had lifted her out of the car in Rongai and had thrown her into the air and put her down with such infinite gentleness on the red soil of the farm.

"Owuor, you cannot go away," she whispered. "The magic is still there. You cannot cut the magic. You do not want to go on safari. Only your feet want to go."

The giant with the strong arms gave her ears something to drink. There were wonderful soft sounds that could fly. They could not be caught, and yet they made even weak people with tears strong. Regina sent her eyes back into the darkness when Owuor put her down on the ground. She felt his lips on her skin, but she knew that she should not look at Owuor.

Like a beggar in the market, she let her body slide to the ground as if it were too feeble to fight against its paralysis. She listened attentively to the farewell melody; she heard Rummler panting, Owuor's steps that made the wood dance, then the squeaking of the door when it was pushed open forcefully, and in the distance a bird that announced that there was still a world other than the one with fresh wounds. For a short time, the kitchen still smelled of Rummler's wet fur; later, only of the burned down candle.

"Owuor will stay with us. We did not see him go," Regina said. First, she realized that she had spoken aloud, then that she was crying.

"Forgive me, Regina. I did not want this. You are still too young. At your age I knew what pain was only when I fell off a horse."

"We do not have a horse."

Walter looked at his daughter, surprised. Had he robbed her of so much of her childhood that she had to console herself with a joke, while, as in a child who does not understand anything but its own obstinacy, the tears were running down her face? Or was she merely enjoying the language of Africa and healing her soul with a balm that he had never tried? He wanted to draw Regina close but let his arms sink after he had hardly lifted them.

"You will not be able to forget, Regina."

"I do not want to forget."

"That is what I said, too. And what has it done for me? I am hurting the person who means the most to me in the world."

"No," Regina objected, "you cannot do anything else. You have to go on safari."

"Who said that?"

"Owuor. And he said something else."

"What?"

"Shall I really tell you? You will be offended."

"No, I promise I won't."

"Owuor," Regina remembered and looked out of the window so that she did not have to see her father's face, "said that I had to protect you. You are a child. Owuor said that, Papa, not I."

"He is right, but do not tell anyone, *memsahib kidogo*."

"*Hapana, bwana*. Don't forget. *Hapana* means 'no.'"

They held on to each other and believed that they had the same road ahead of them. Walter had for the first time entered the country that—too late—had become a piece of home for him. Regina cherished the precious moment. Her father had finally learned that only the God Mungu made people happy.